InvestiGATORS
Heist and Seek

written and illustrated by
John Patrick Green

with color by **Wes Dzioba**

First Second
New York

For Klaus, and art teachers everywhere

First Second

Drawn on Bienfang Smooth Bristol paper with Staedtler Mars Lumograph H pencils, inked with Sakura Pigma Micron and Staedtler Pigment Liner pens, and digitally colored in Photoshop.

Published by First Second
First Second is an imprint of Roaring Brook Press,
a division of Holtzbrinck Publishing Holdings Limited Partnership
120 Broadway, New York, NY 10271
firstsecondbooks.com
mackids.com

Don't miss your next favorite book from First Second! For the latest updates go to firstsecondnewsletter.com and sign up for our enewsletter.

Library of Congress Cataloging-in-Publication Data is available

ISBN: 978-1-250-84988-5 (Hardcover)
ISBN: 978-1-250-86834-3 (Special Edition)

Our books may be purchased in bulk for promotional, educational, or business use. Please contact your local bookseller or the Macmillan Corporate and Premium Sales Department at (800) 221-7945 ext. 5442 or by email at MacmillanSpecialSales@macmillan.com.

First edition, 2022
Edited by Calista Brill and Dave Roman
Cover design by John Patrick Green and Kirk Benshoff
Interior book design by John Patrick Green
Color by Wes Dzioba
Printed in China by Toppan Leefung Printing Ltd., Dongguan City, Guangdong Province

10 9 8 7 6 5 4 3 2 1

Chapter 1

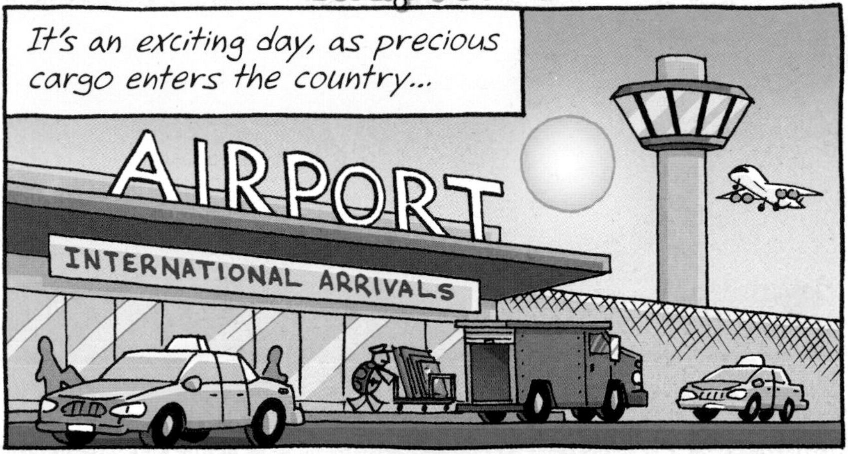
It's an exciting day, as precious cargo enters the country...
AIRPORT
INTERNATIONAL ARRIVALS

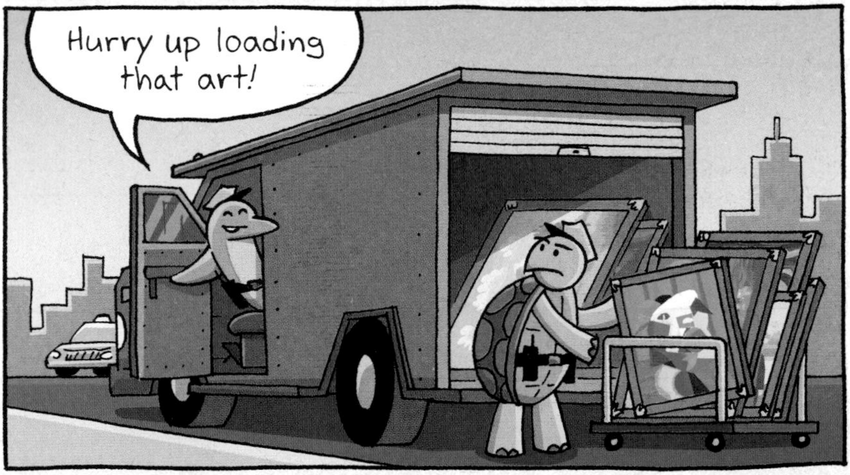
Hurry up loading that art!

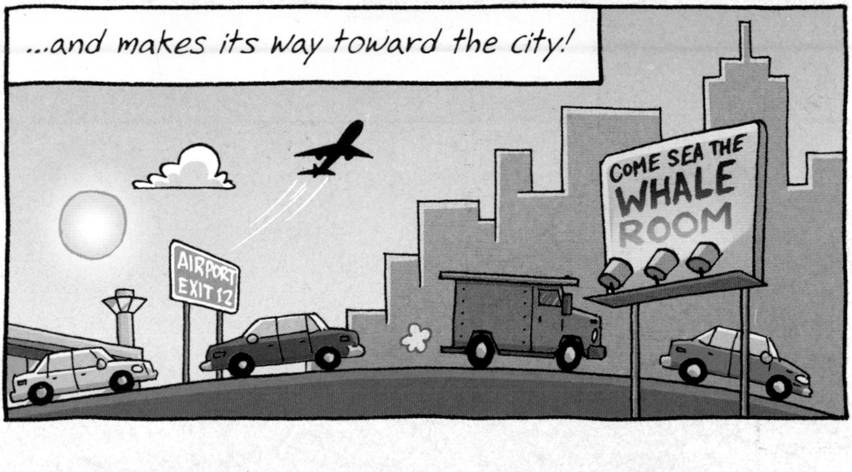
...and makes its way toward the city!
AIRPORT EXIT 12
COME SEA THE WHALE ROOM

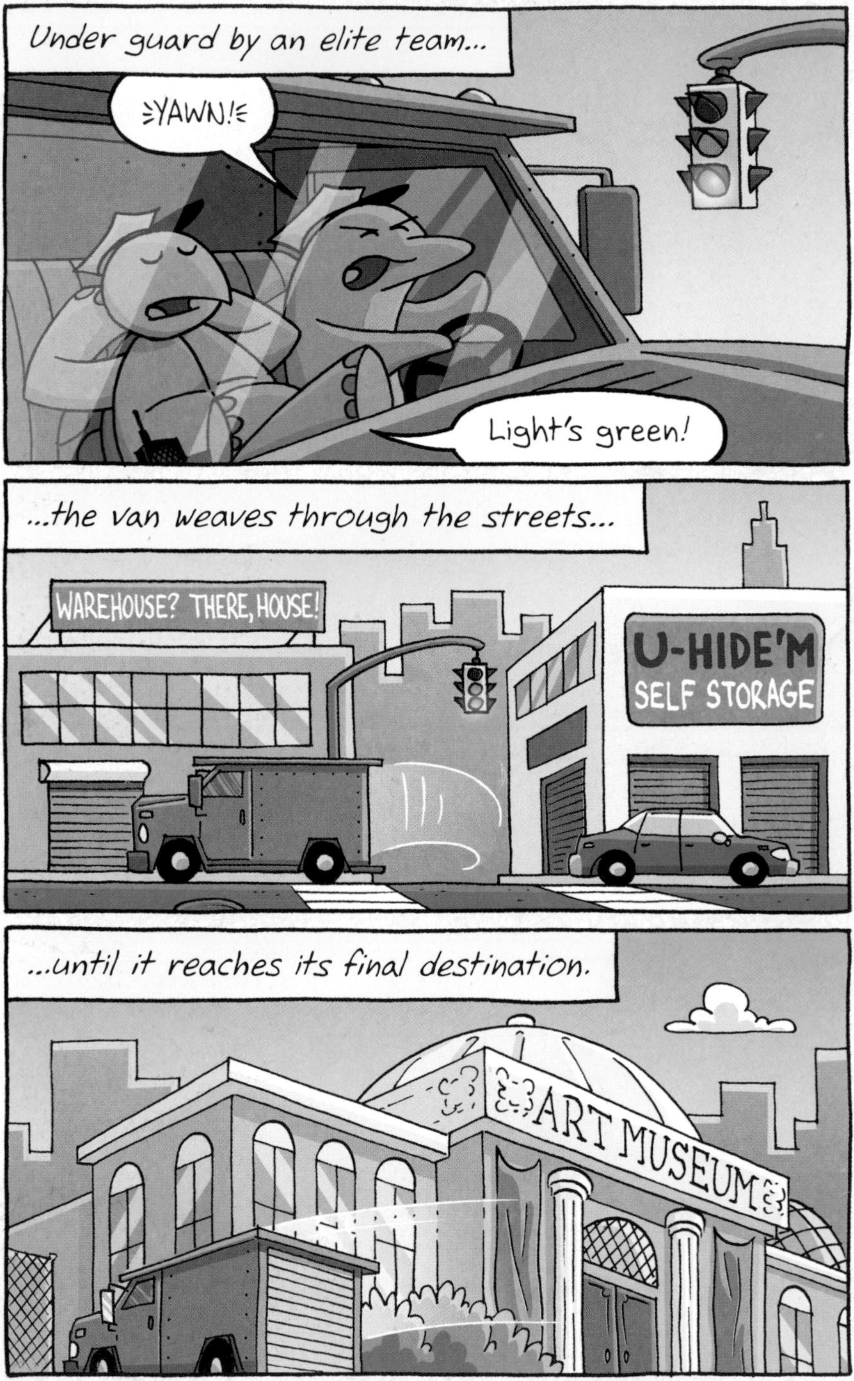
Under guard by an elite team...
YAWN!
Light's green!
...the van weaves through the streets...
WAREHOUSE? THERE, HOUSE!
U-HIDE'M
SELF STORAGE
...until it reaches its final destination.
ART MUSEUM

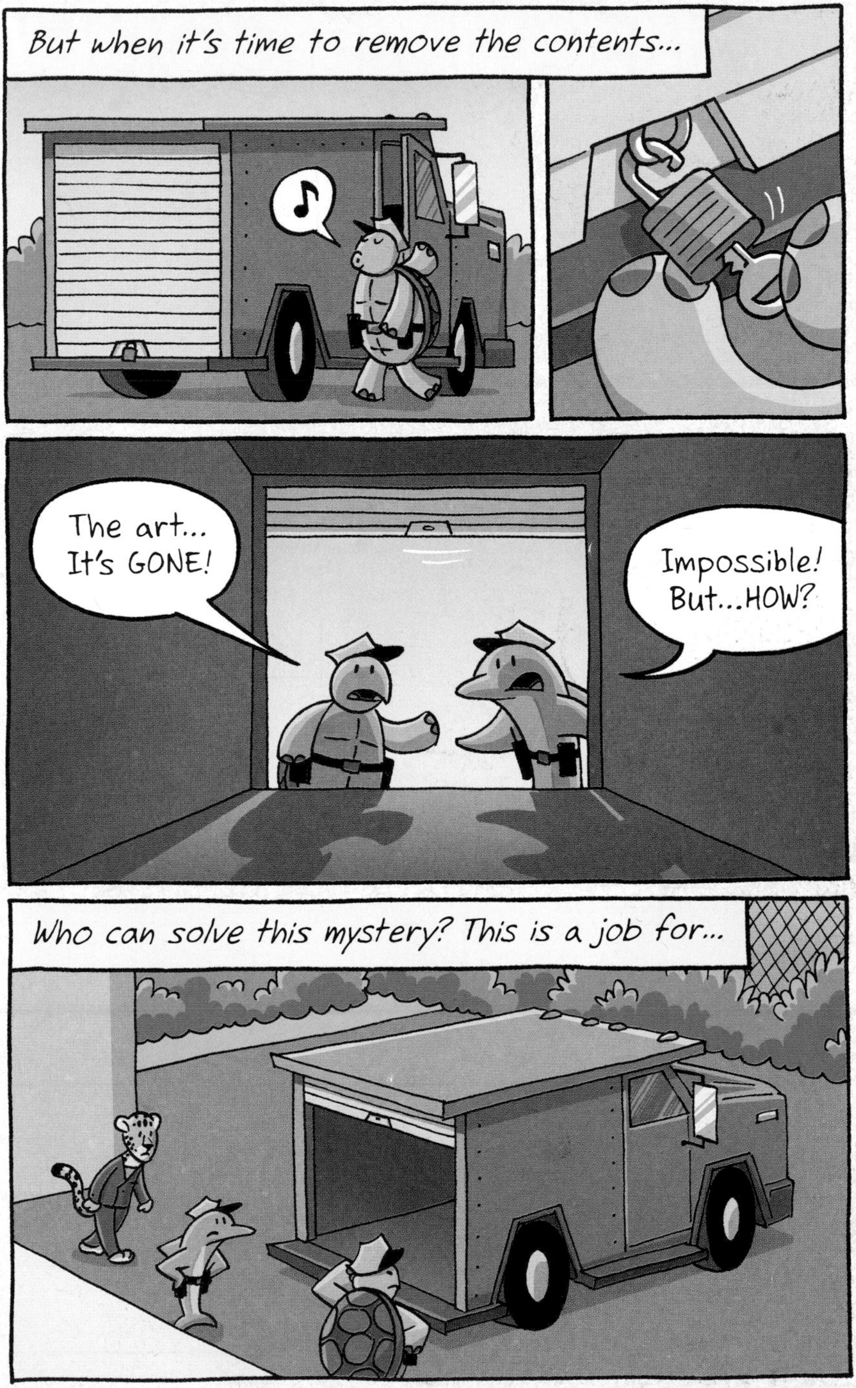
But when it's time to remove the contents...
The art... It's GONE!
Impossible! But...HOW?
Who can solve this mystery? This is a job for...

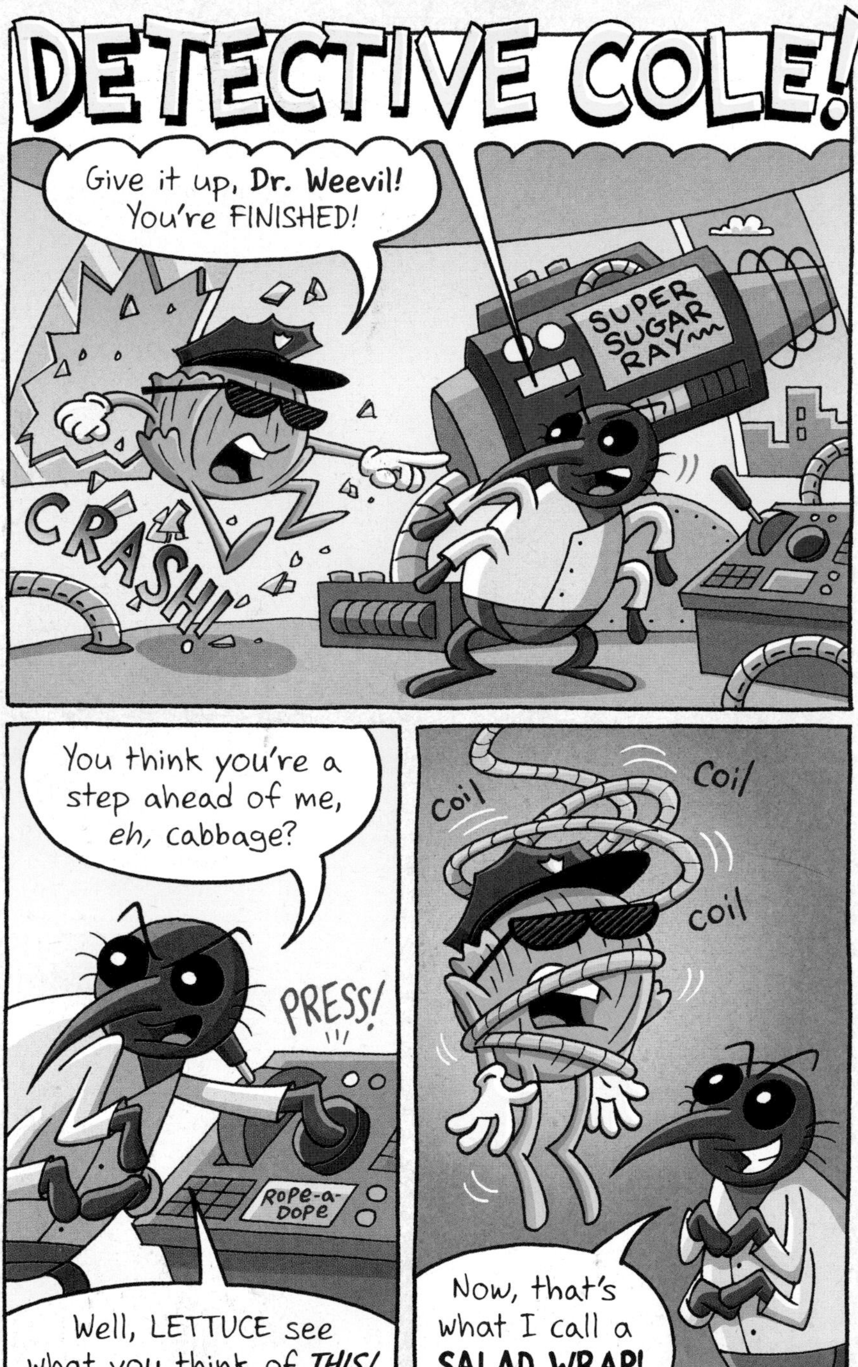
DETECTIVE COLE!
Give it up, Dr. Weevil! You're FINISHED!
CRASH!
SUPER SUGAR RAY
You think you're a step ahead of me, eh, cabbage?
PRESS!
ROPE-A-DOPE
Well, LETTUCE see what you think of THIS!
Coil
coil
coil
Now, that's what I call a SALAD WRAP!

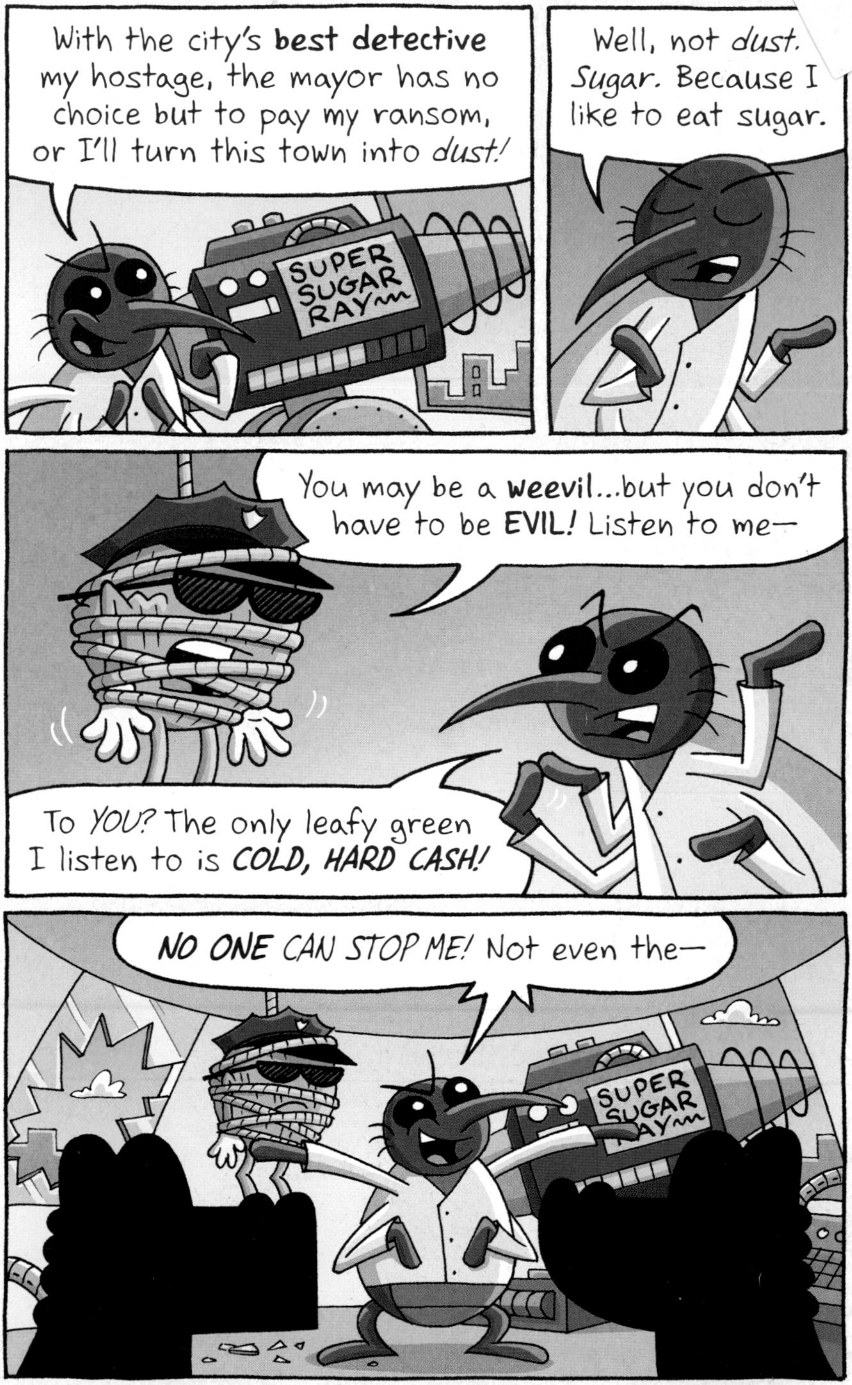
With the city's **best detective** my hostage, the mayor has no choice but to pay my ransom, or I'll turn this town into *dust!*
SUPER SUGAR RAY
Well, not *dust.* *Sugar.* Because I like to eat sugar.
You may be a **weevil**...but you don't have to be **EVIL!** Listen to me—
To *YOU?* The only leafy green I listen to is ***COLD, HARD CASH!***
NO ONE *CAN STOP ME!* Not even the—
SUPER SUGAR RAY

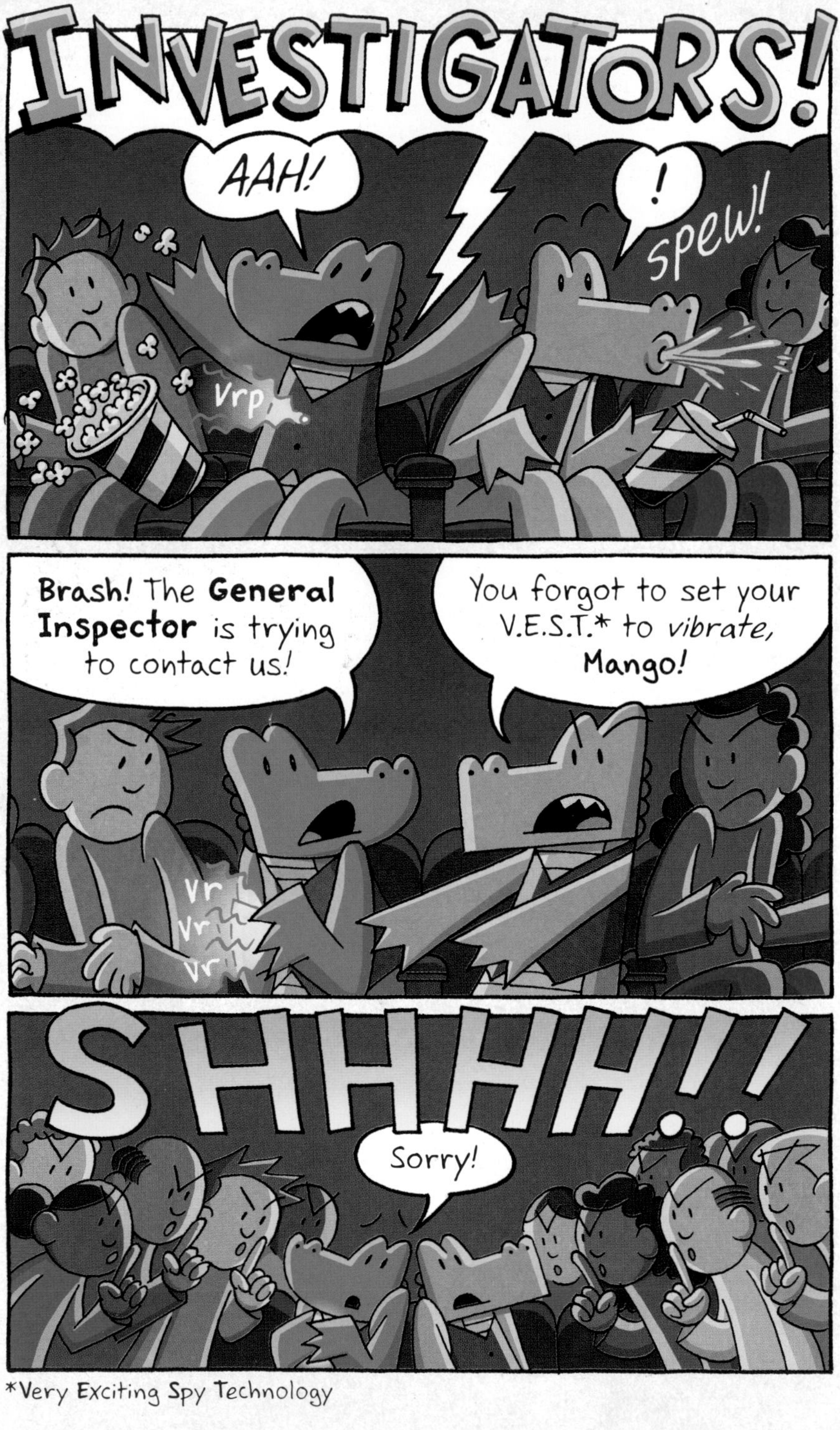
INVESTIGATORS!
AAH!
!
spew!
vrp
Brash! The General Inspector is trying to contact us!
You forgot to set your V.E.S.T.* to vibrate, Mango!
vr vr vr
SHHH!!
Sorry!

*Very Exciting Spy Technology

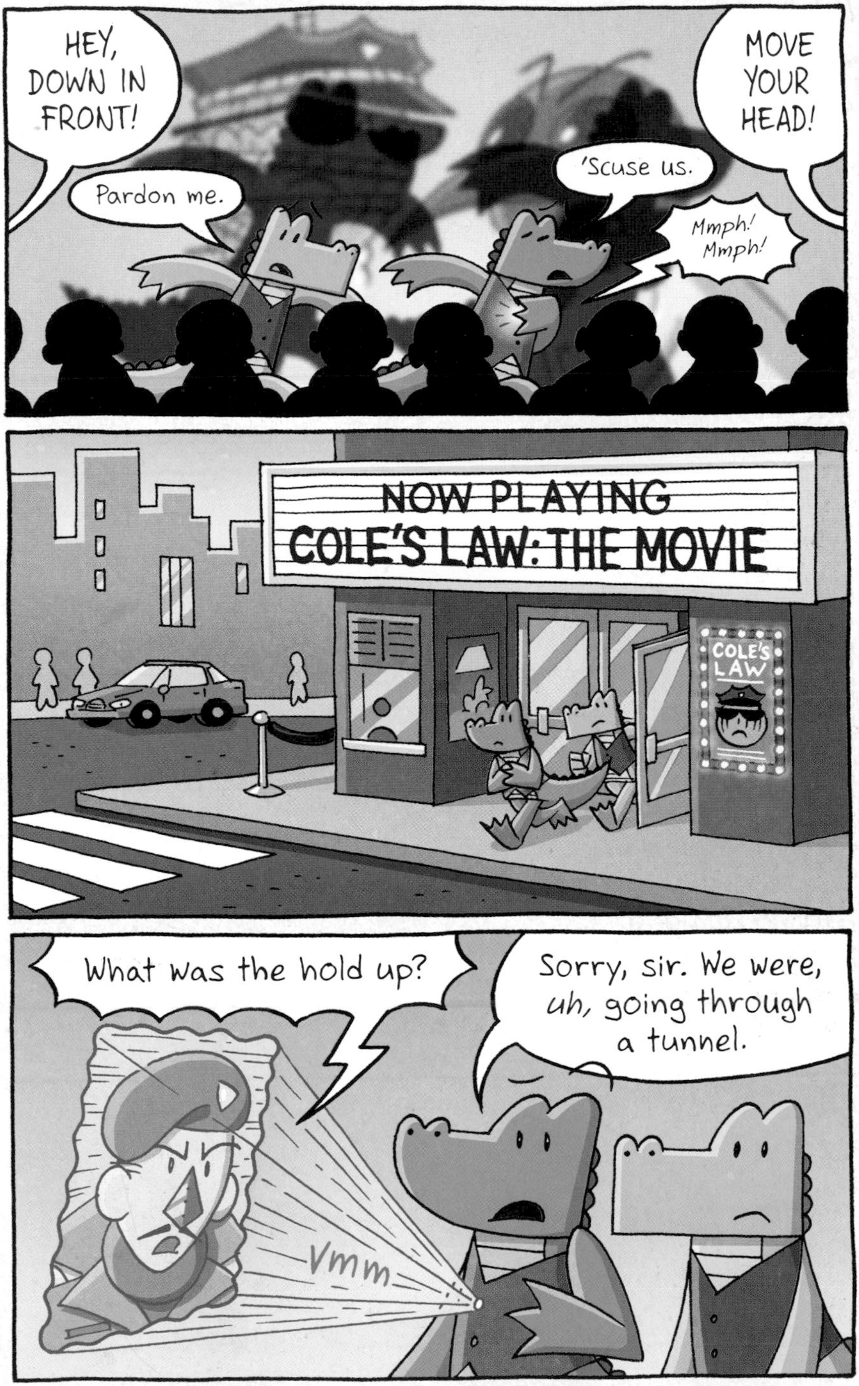
HEY, DOWN IN FRONT!
Pardon me.
'Scuse us.
MOVE YOUR HEAD!
Mmph! Mmph!
NOW PLAYING
COLE'S LAW: THE MOVIE
COLE'S LAW
What was the hold up?
Sorry, sir. We were, uh, going through a tunnel.
Vmm

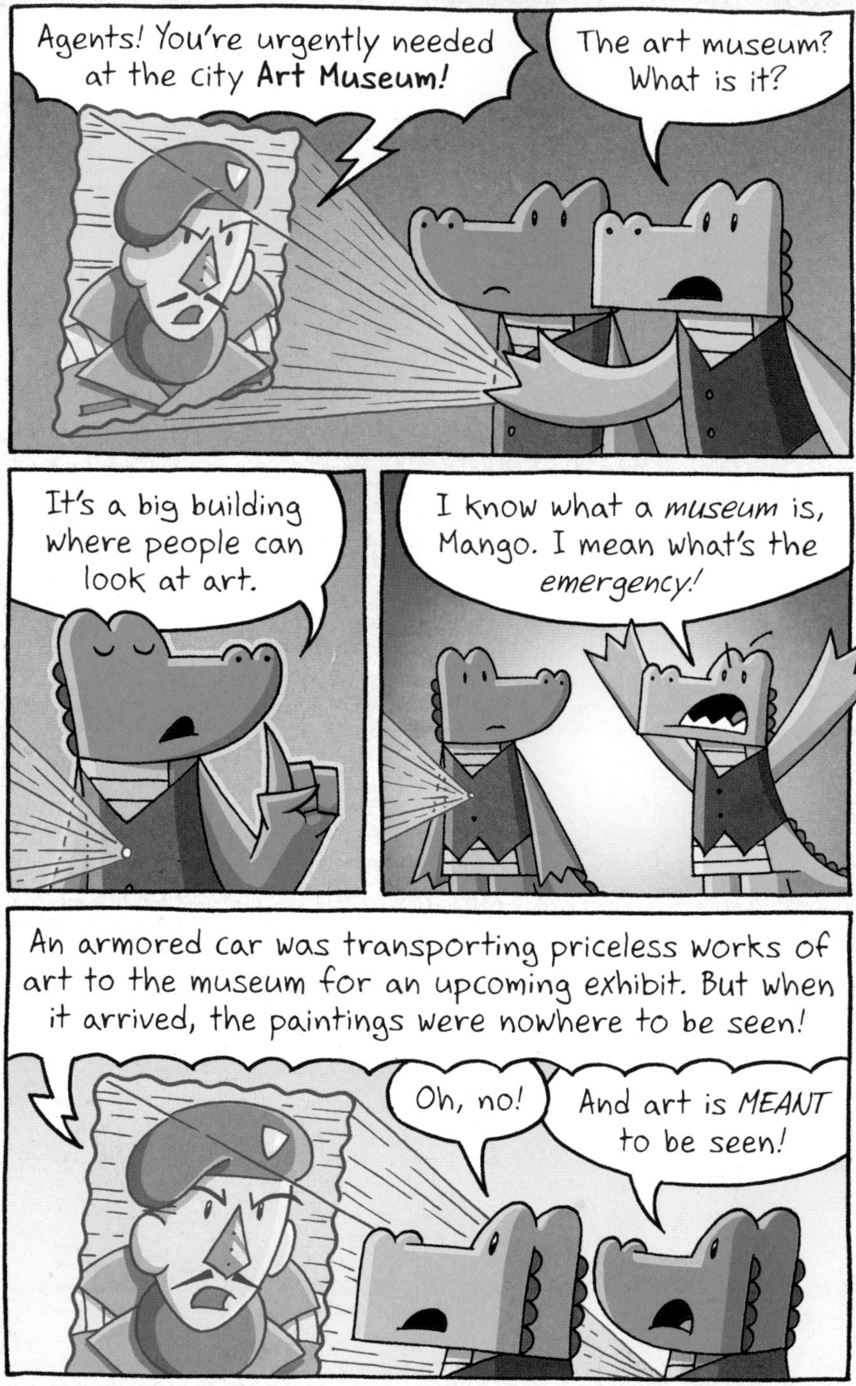

Agents! You're urgently needed at the city **Art Museum!**
The art museum? What is it?
It's a big building where people can look at art.
I know what a *museum* is, Mango. I mean what's the *emergency!*
An armored car was transporting priceless works of art to the museum for an upcoming exhibit. But when it arrived, the paintings were nowhere to be seen!
Oh, no!
And art is *MEANT* to be seen!

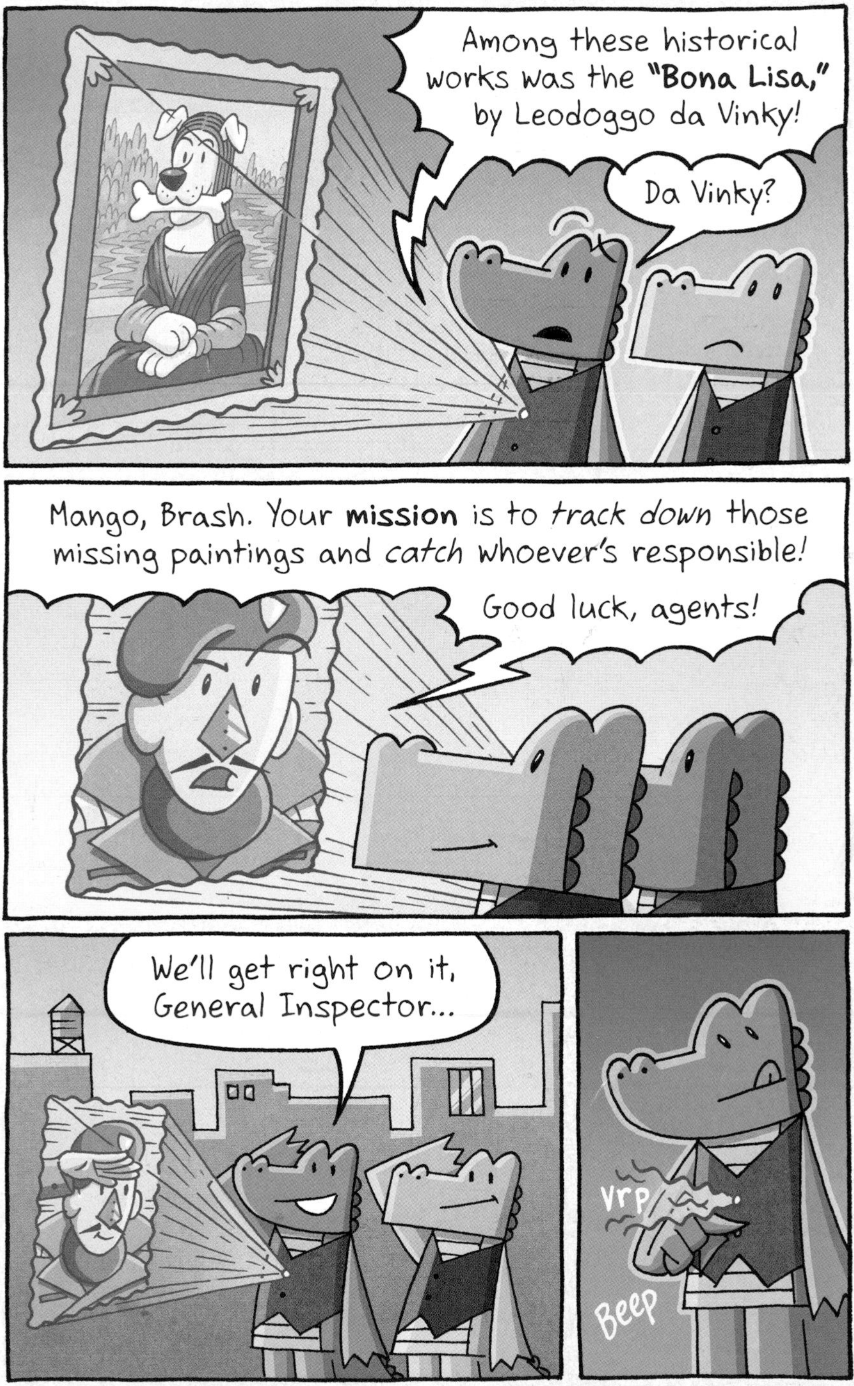
Among these historical works was the "Bona Lisa," by Leodoggo da Vinky!
Da Vinky?
Mango, Brash. Your mission is to track down those missing paintings and catch whoever's responsible!
Good luck, agents!
We'll get right on it, General Inspector...
Vrp
Beep

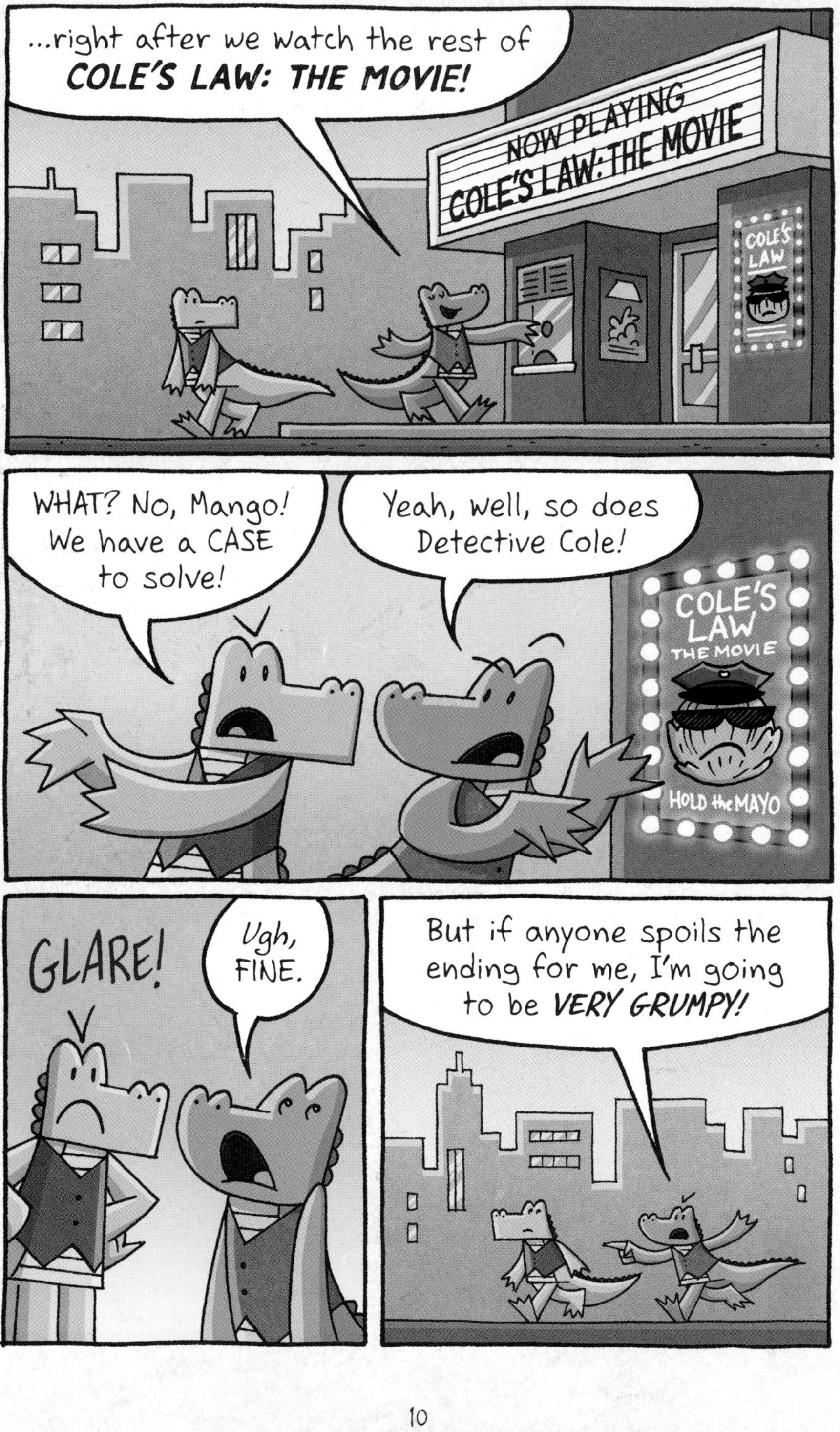

...right after we watch the rest of **COLE'S LAW: THE MOVIE!**
NOW PLAYING
COLE'S LAW: THE MOVIE
COLE'S LAW
WHAT? No, Mango! We have a CASE to solve!
Yeah, well, so does Detective Cole!
COLE'S LAW THE MOVIE
HOLD the MAYO
GLARE!
Ugh, FINE.
But if anyone spoils the ending for me, I'm going to be **VERY GRUMPY!**

Chapter 2

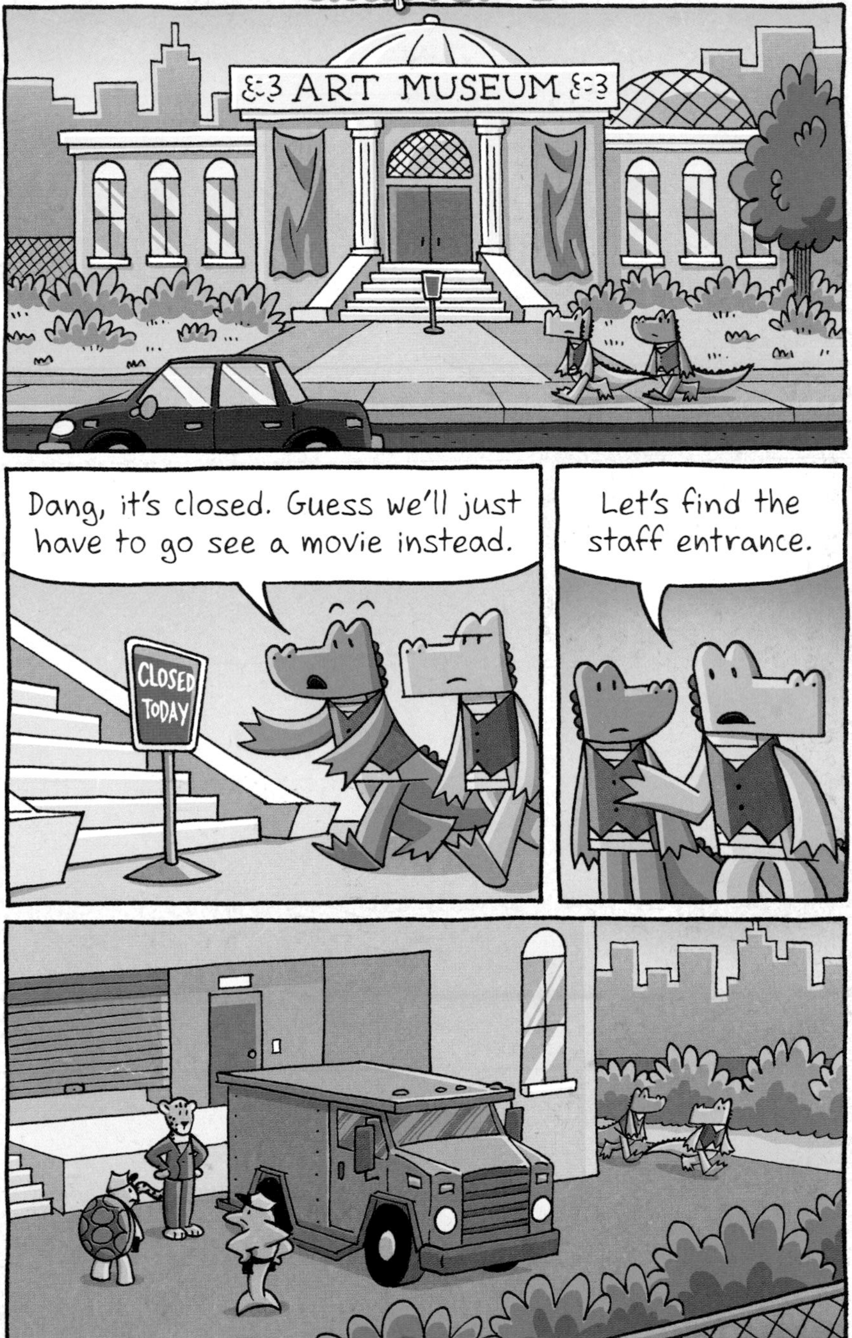
ART MUSEUM
Dang, it's closed. Guess we'll just have to go see a movie instead.
CLOSED TODAY
Let's find the staff entrance.

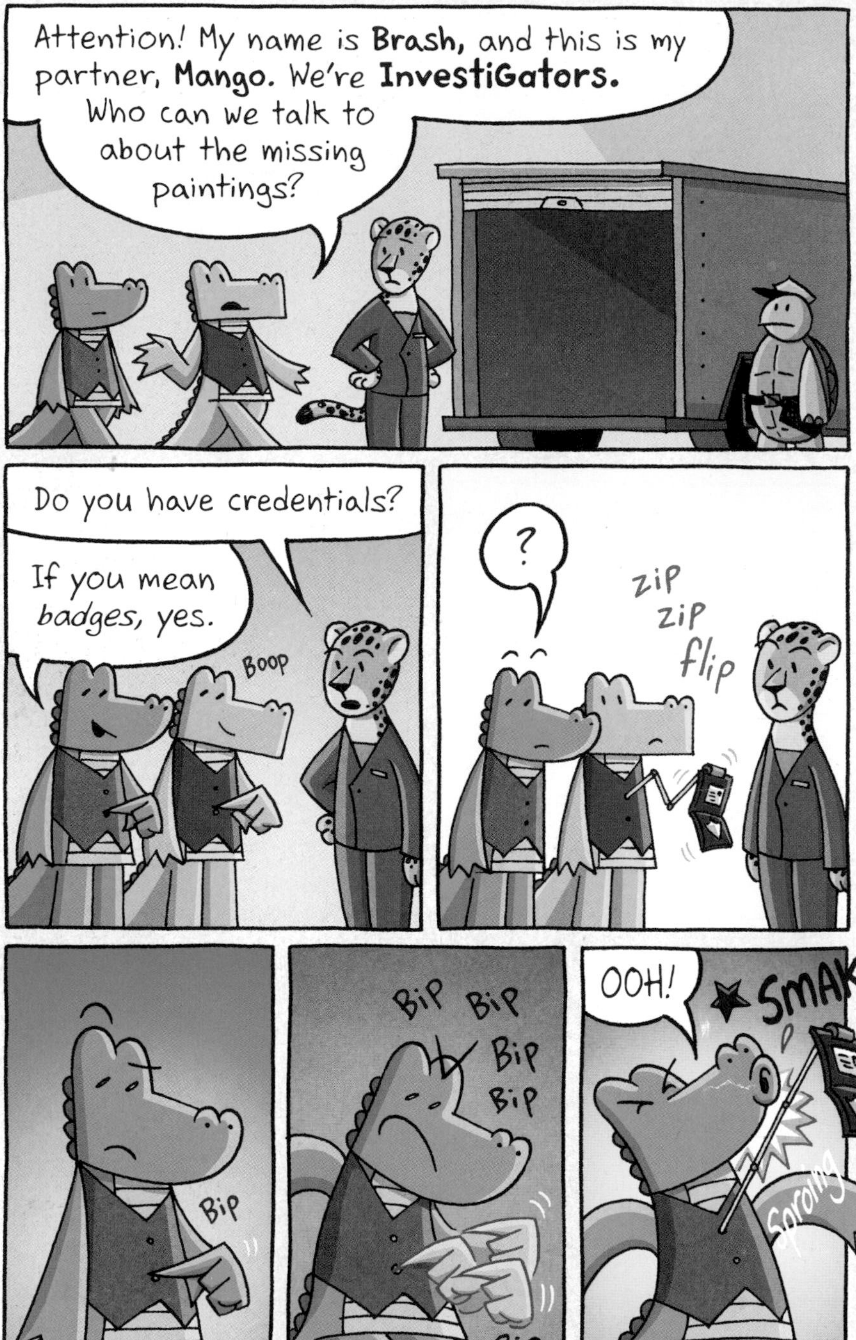
Attention! My name is Brash, and this is my partner, Mango. We're InvestiGators.
Who can we talk to about the missing paintings?
Do you have credentials?
If you mean badges, yes.
Boop
?
zip
zip
flip
Bip
Bip
Bip
Bip
Bip
Bip
OOH!
SMAK
Sproing

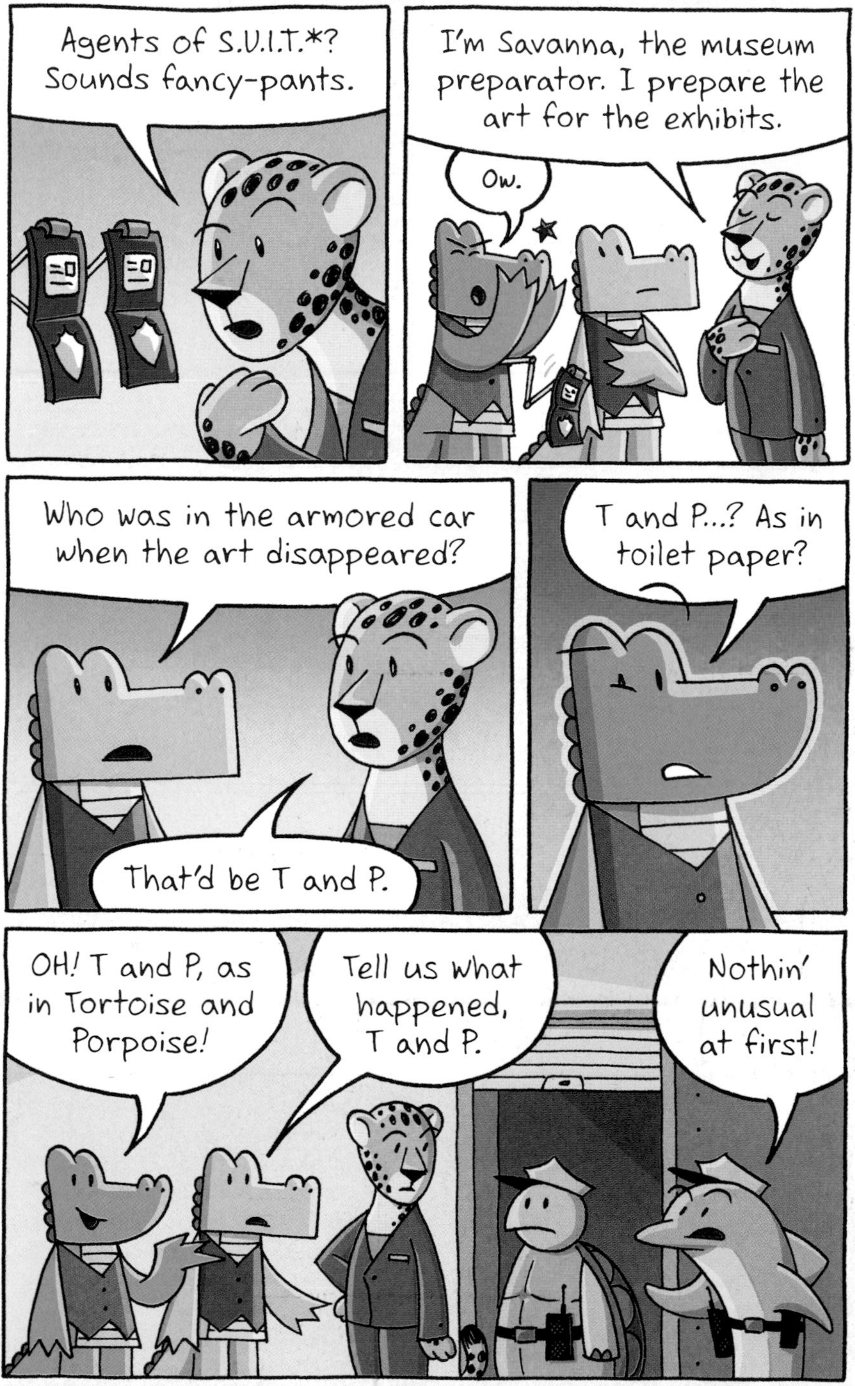
Agents of S.U.I.T.*? Sounds fancy-pants.
I'm Savanna, the museum preparator. I prepare the art for the exhibits.
Ow.
Who was in the armored car when the art disappeared?
That'd be T and P.
T and P...? As in toilet paper?
OH! T and P, as in Tortoise and Porpoise!
Tell us what happened, T and P.
Nothin' unusual at first!

*Special Undercover Investigation Teams

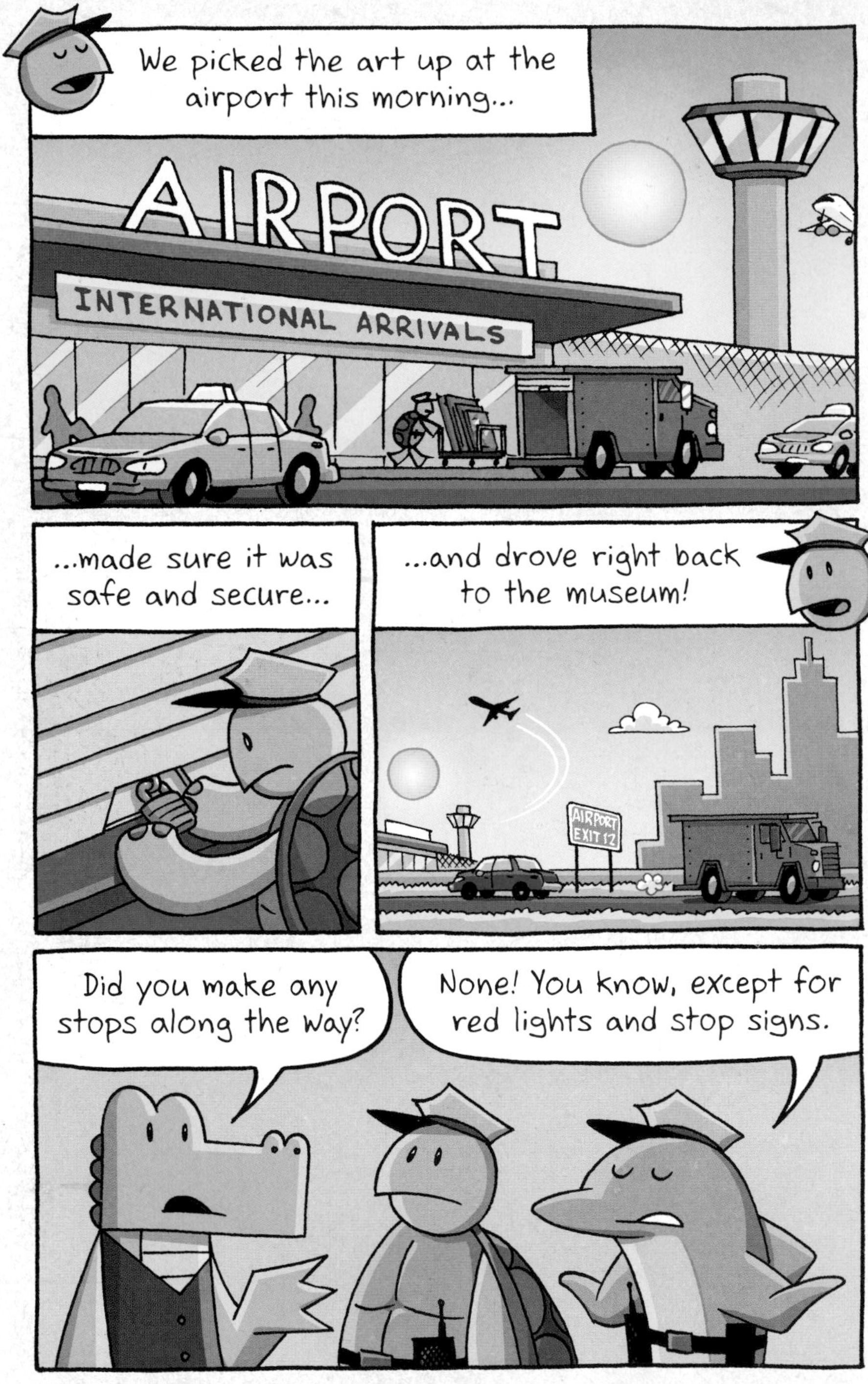
We picked the art up at the airport this morning...
AIRPORT
INTERNATIONAL ARRIVALS
...made sure it was safe and secure...
...and drove right back to the museum!
AIRPORT EXIT 12
Did you make any stops along the way?
None! You know, except for red lights and stop signs.

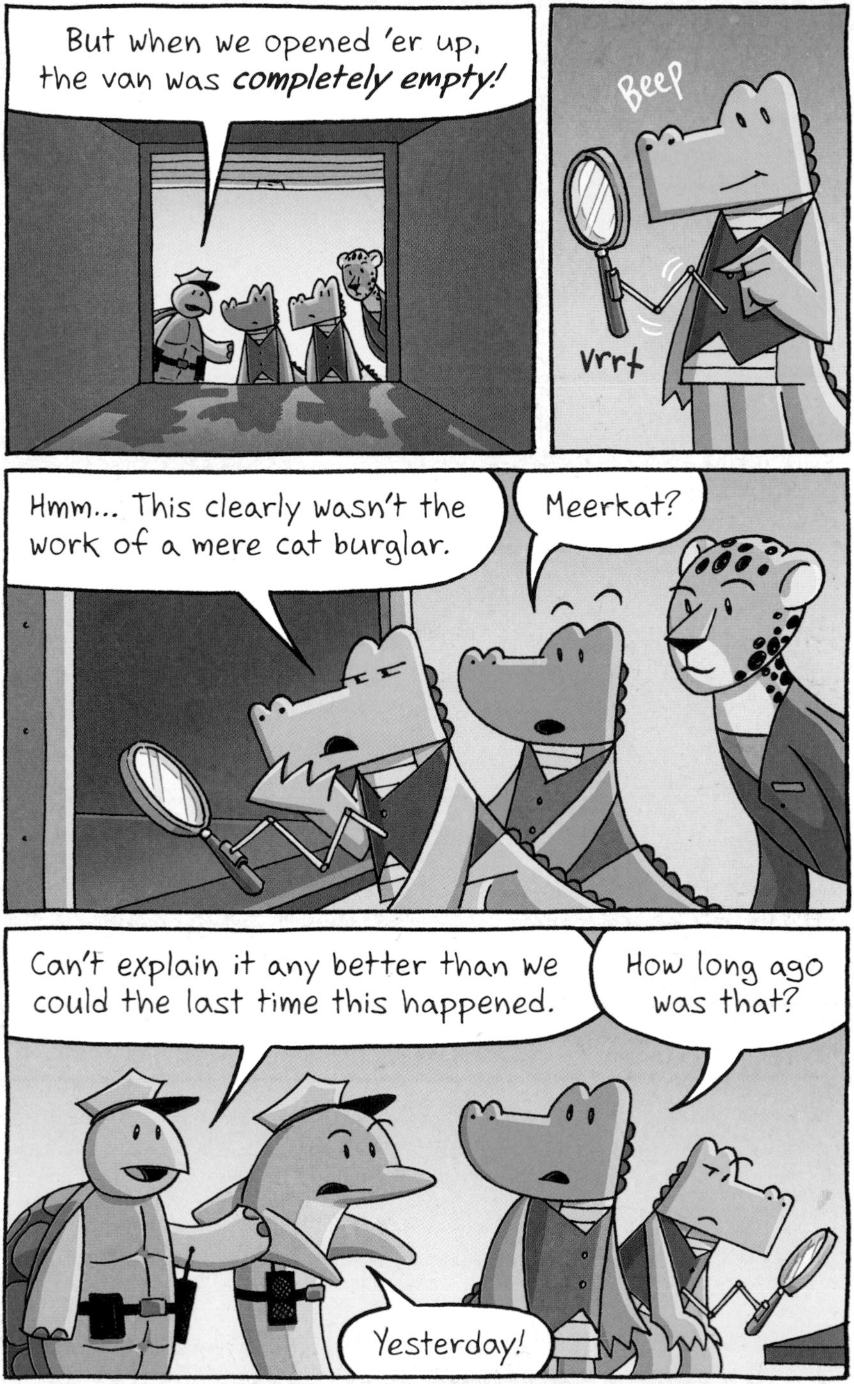
But when we opened 'er up, the van was **completely empty!**
Beep
Vrrt
Hmm... This clearly wasn't the work of a mere cat burglar.
Meerkat?
Can't explain it any better than we could the last time this happened.
How long ago was that?
Yesterday!

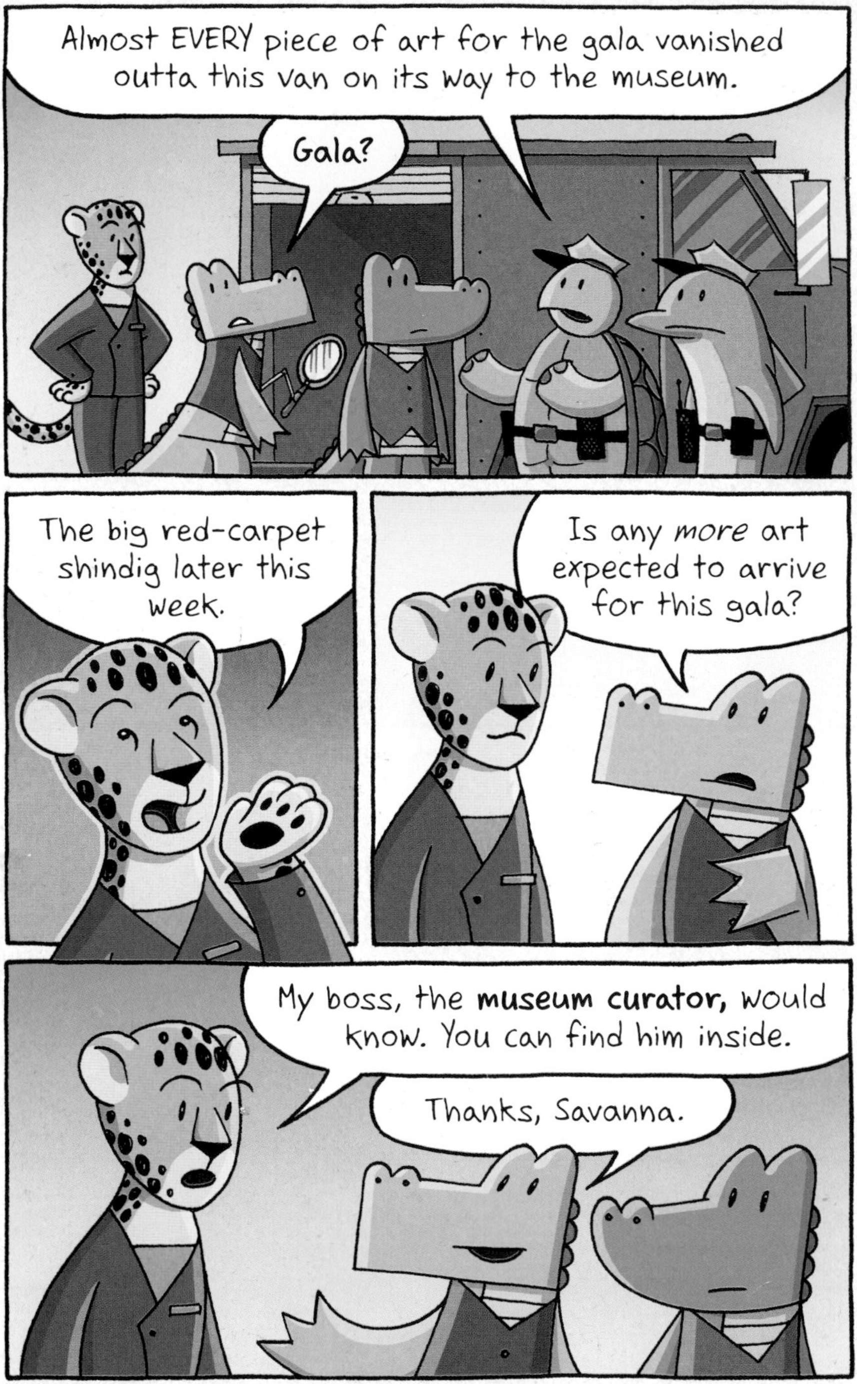
Almost EVERY piece of art for the gala vanished outta this van on its way to the museum.
Gala?
The big red-carpet shindig later this week.
Is any *more* art expected to arrive for this gala?
My boss, the **museum curator,** would know. You can find him inside.
Thanks, Savanna.

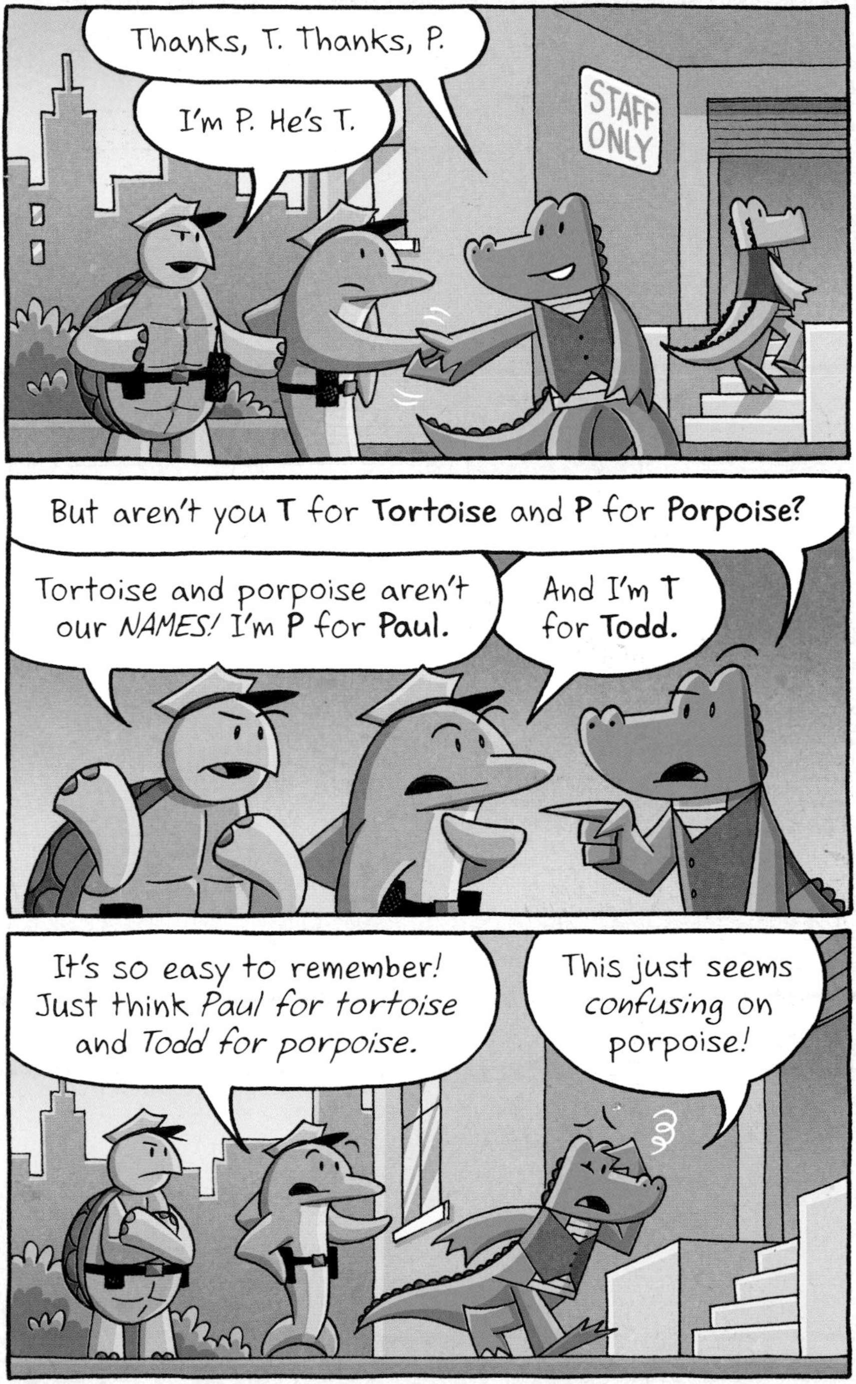
Thanks, T. Thanks, P.
I'm P. He's T.
STAFF ONLY
But aren't you **T** for **Tortoise** and **P** for **Porpoise?**
Tortoise and porpoise aren't our *NAMES!* I'm **P** for **Paul.**
And I'm **T** for **Todd.**
It's so easy to remember! Just think *Paul for tortoise* and *Todd for porpoise.*
This just seems *confusing* on porpoise!

Chapter 3

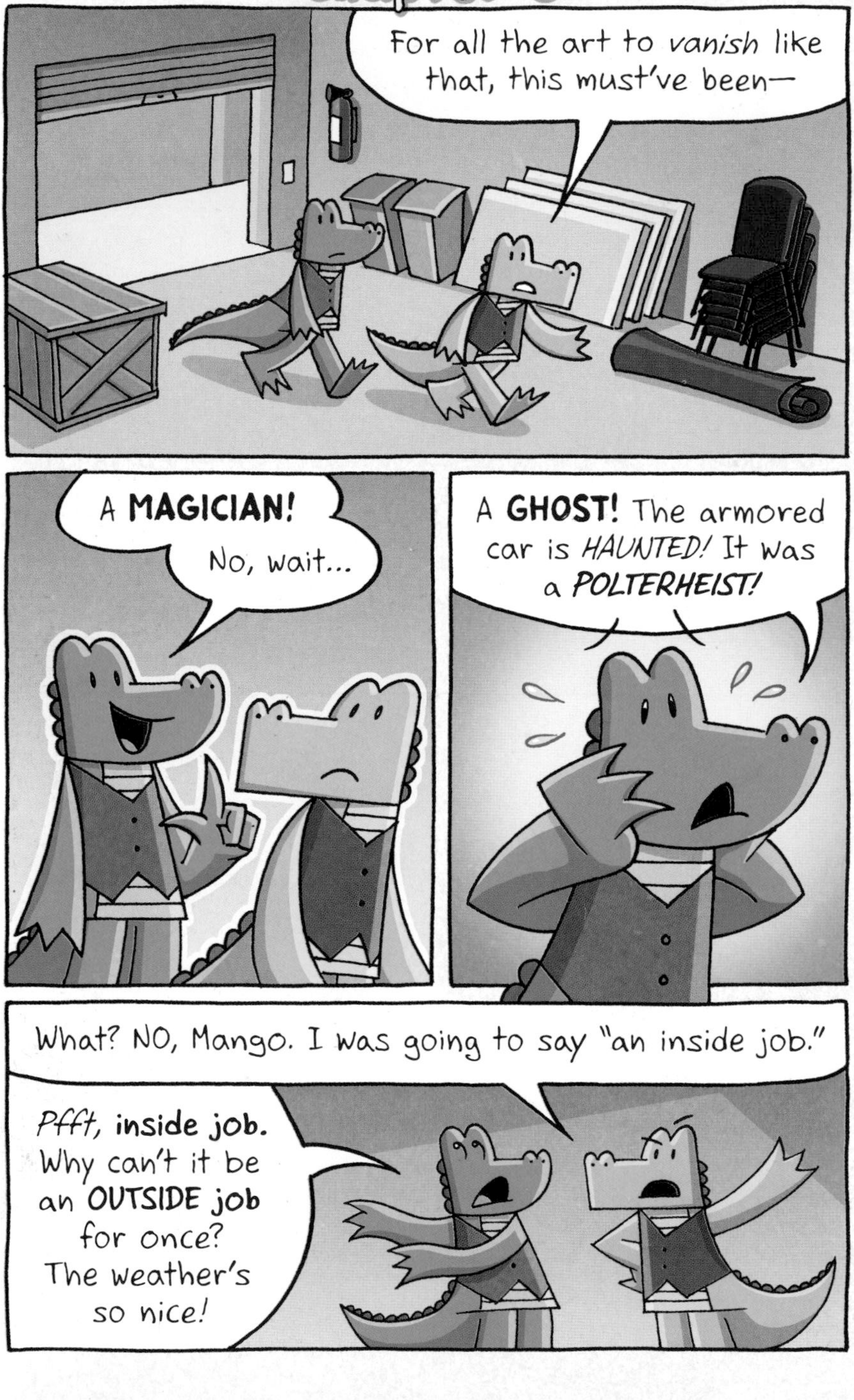
For all the art to *vanish* like that, this must've been—
A **MAGICIAN!**
No, wait...
A **GHOST!** The armored car is *HAUNTED!* It was a ***POLTERHEIST!***
What? NO, Mango. I was going to say "an inside job."
Pfft, **inside job.** Why can't it be an **OUTSIDE job** for once? The weather's so nice!

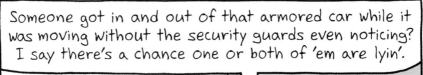

Someone got in and out of that armored car while it was moving without the security guards even noticing? I say there's a chance one or both of 'em are lyin'.

There's no **lion**. But there is a **porpoise**, a **tortoise**, and a **cheetah**, *oh my*.

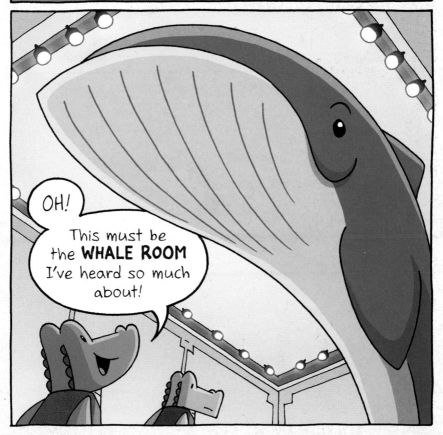

OH!

This must be the **WHALE ROOM** I've heard so much about!

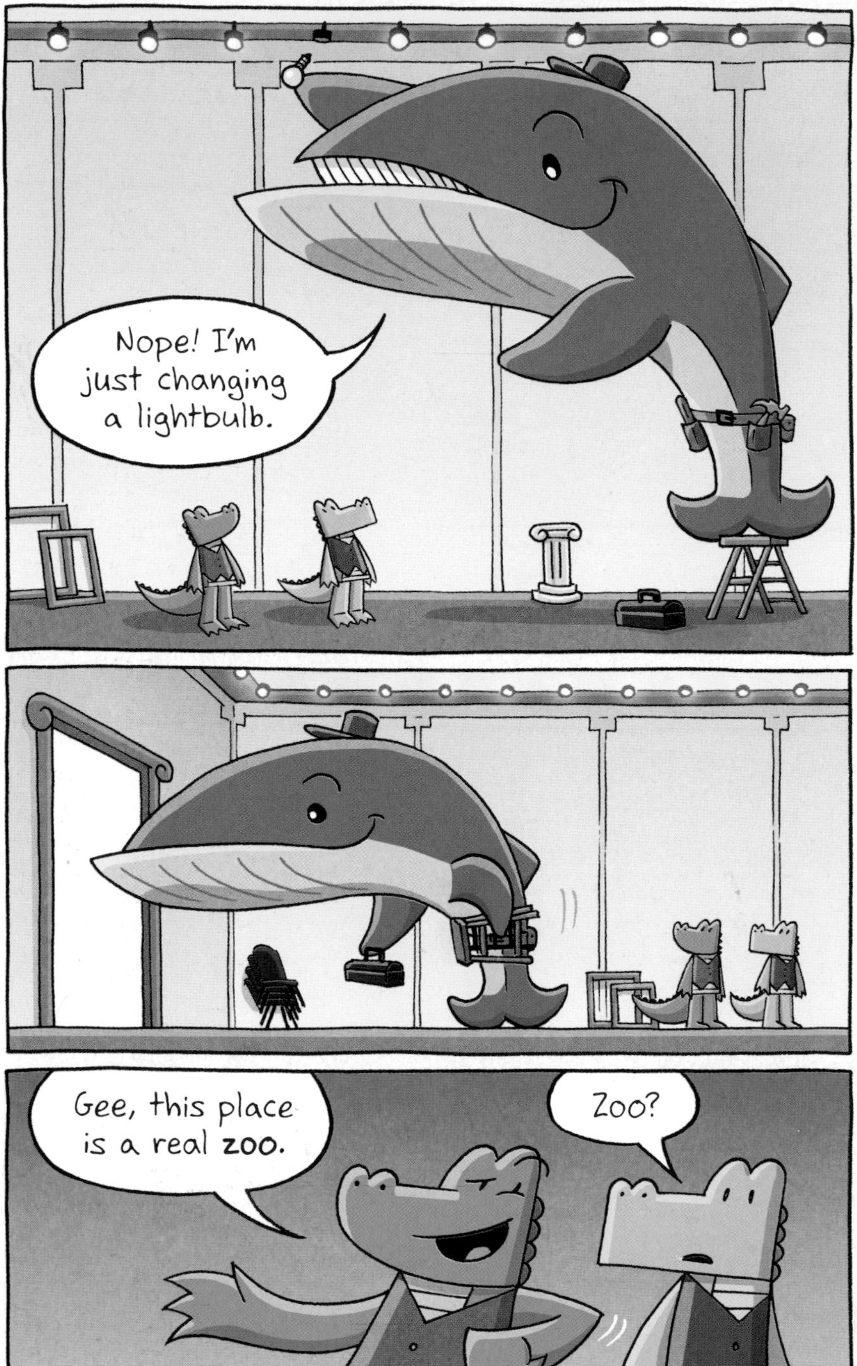
Nope! I'm just changing a lightbulb.
Gee, this place is a real **zoo**.
Zoo?

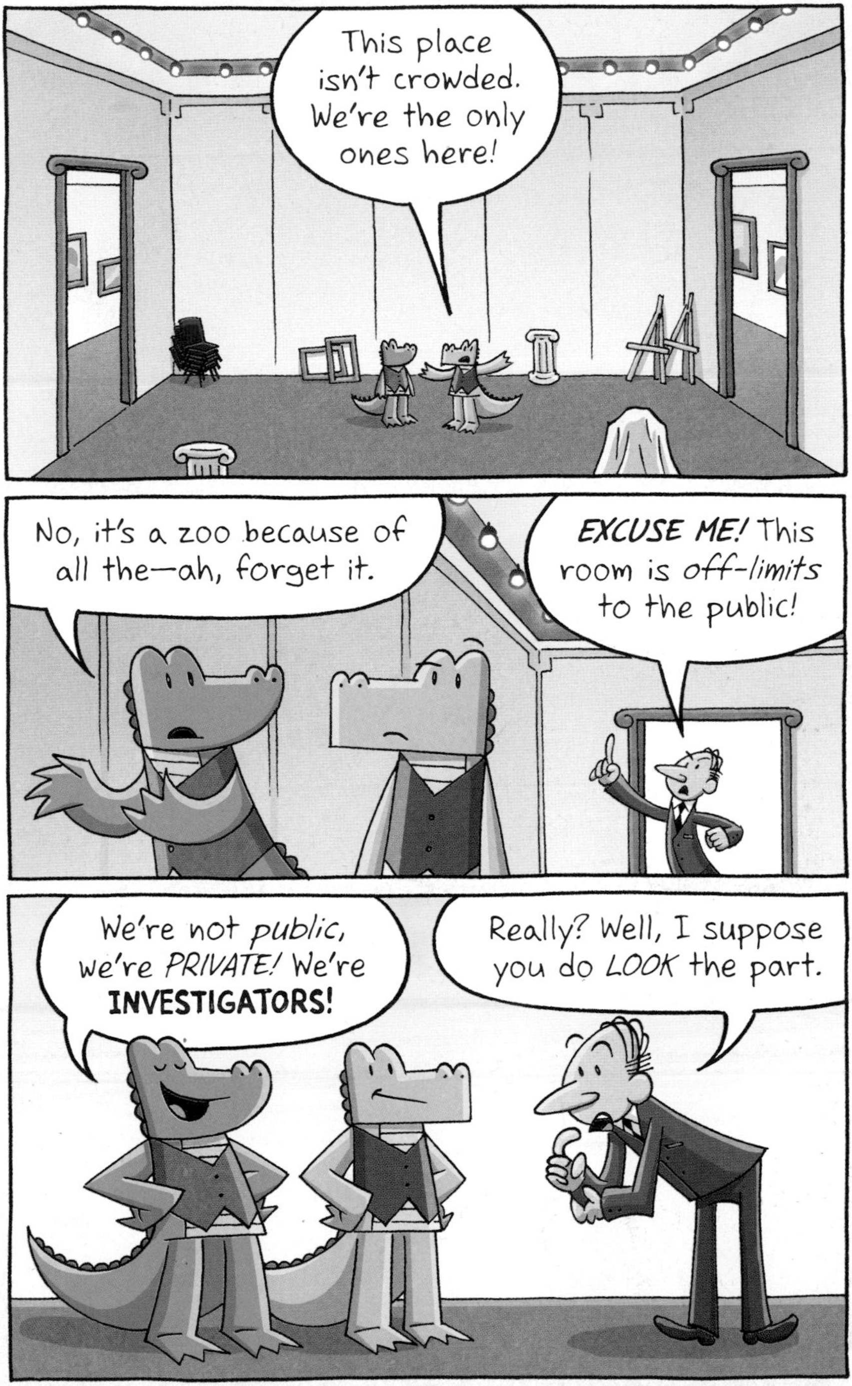
This place isn't crowded. We're the only ones here!
No, it's a zoo because of all the—ah, forget it.
EXCUSE ME! This room is *off-limits* to the public!
We're not *public*, we're *PRIVATE!* We're **INVESTIGATORS!**
Really? Well, I suppose you do *LOOK* the part.

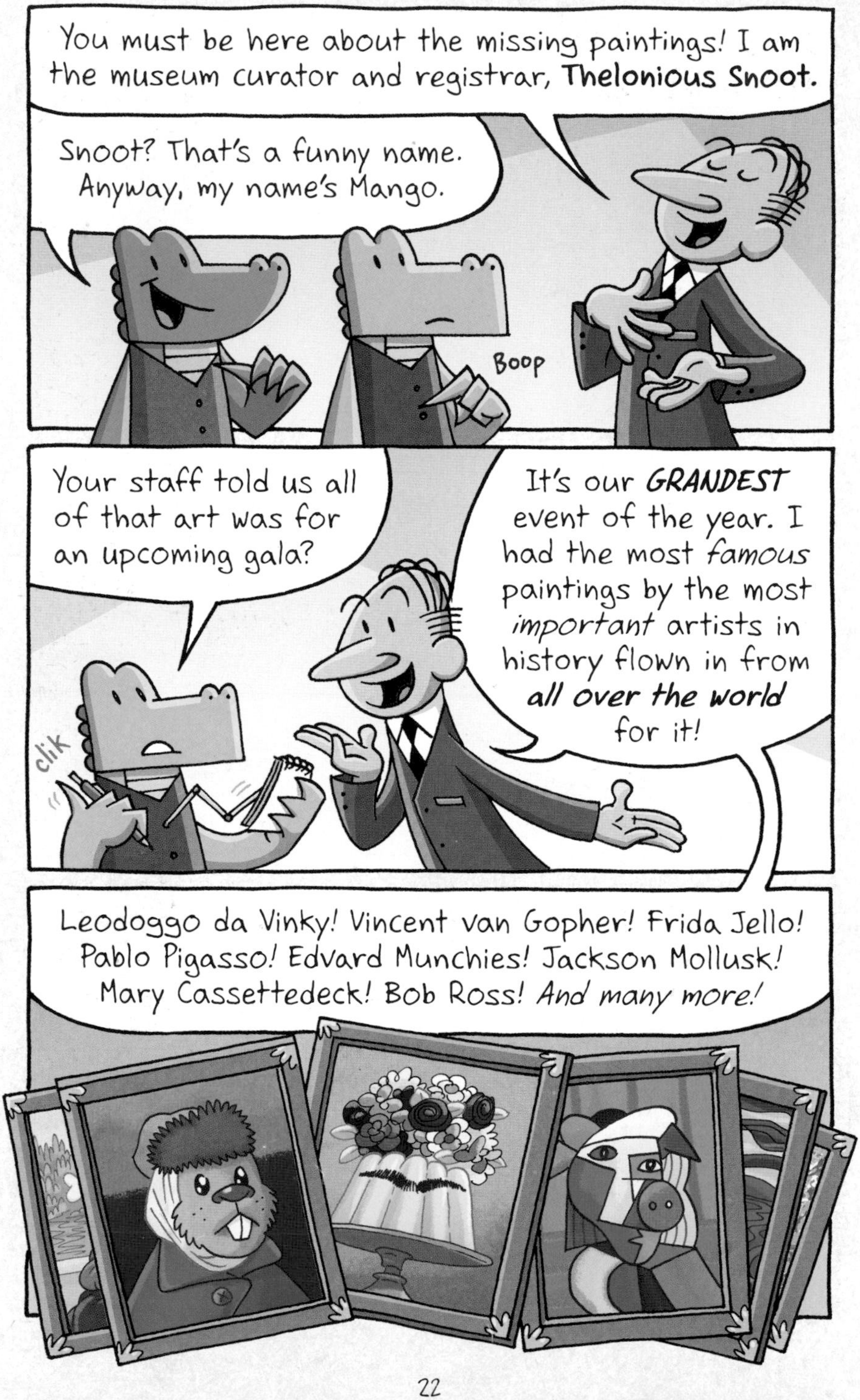
You must be here about the missing paintings! I am the museum curator and registrar, **Thelonious Snoot.**
Snoot? That's a funny name. Anyway, my name's Mango.
BOOP
Your staff told us all of that art was for an upcoming gala?
It's our ***GRANDEST*** event of the year. I had the most *famous* paintings by the most *important* artists in history flown in from ***all over the world*** for it!
clik
Leodoggo da Vinky! Vincent van Gopher! Frida Jello! Pablo Pigasso! Edvard Munchies! Jackson Mollusk! Mary Cassettedeck! Bob Ross! *And many more!*

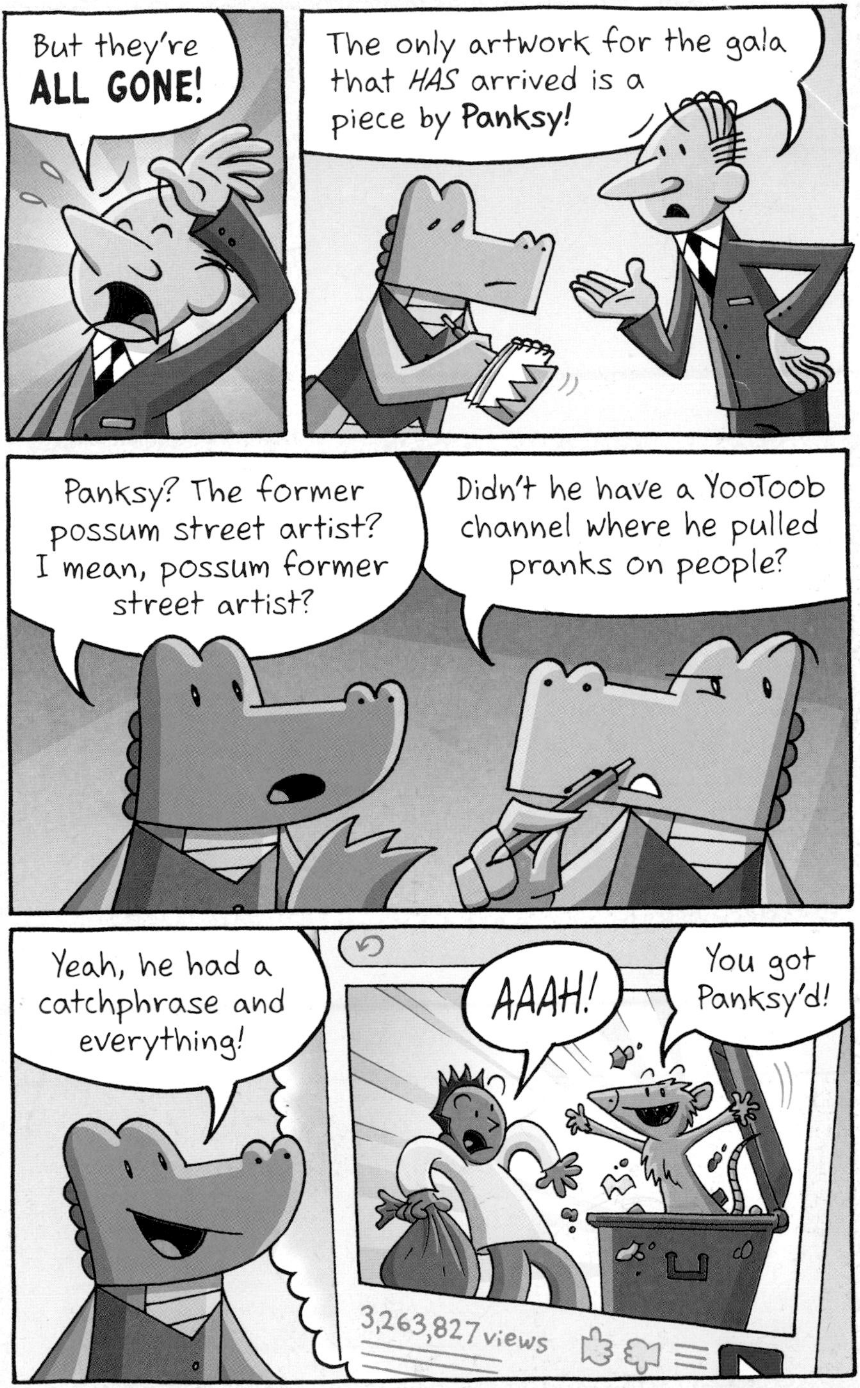
But they're **ALL GONE!**
The only artwork for the gala that *HAS* arrived is a piece by **Panksy!**
Panksy? The former possum street artist? I mean, possum former street artist?
Didn't he have a YooToob channel where he pulled pranks on people?
Yeah, he had a catchphrase and everything!
AAAH!
You got Panksy'd!
3,263,827 views

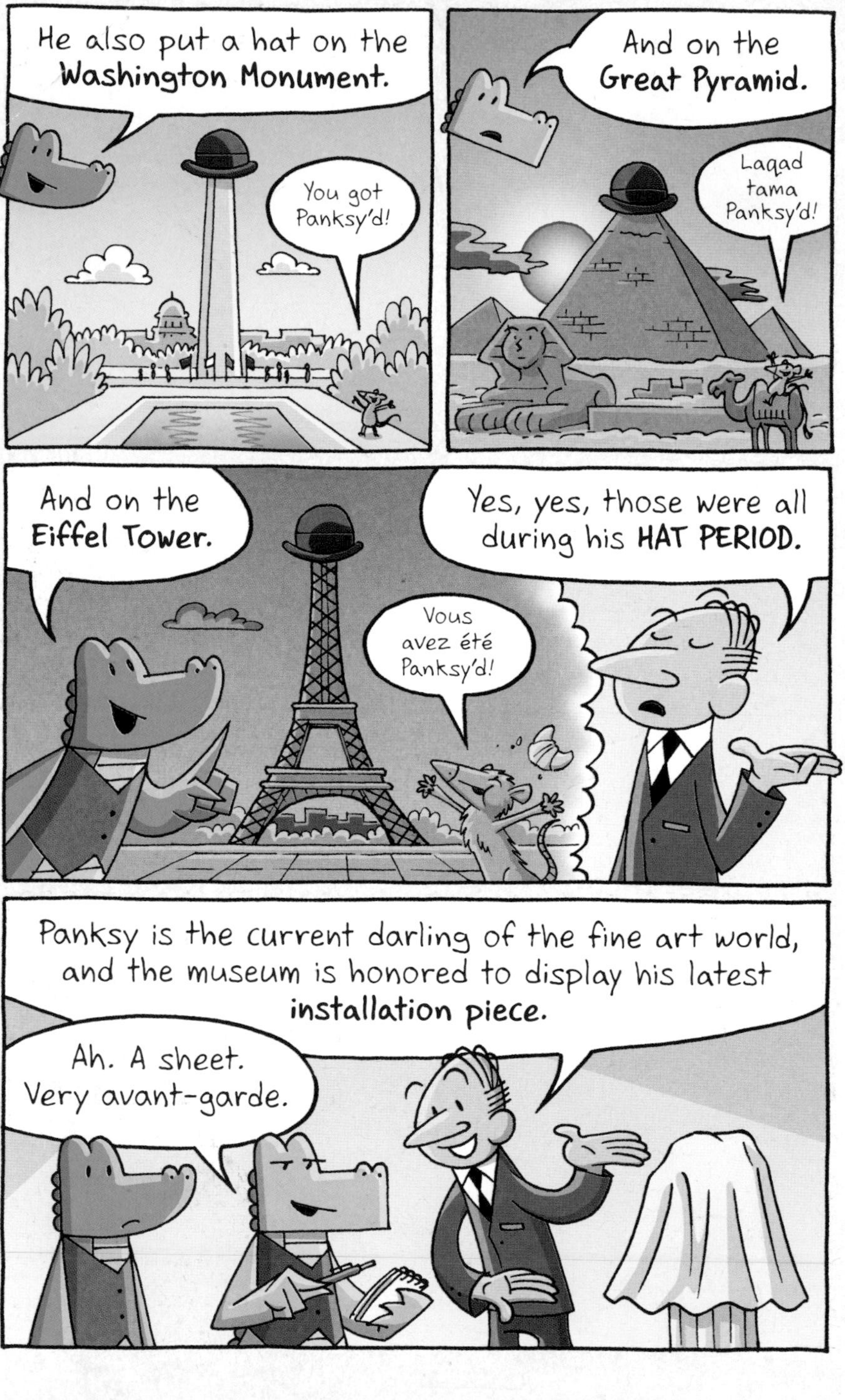
He also put a hat on the Washington Monument.
You got Panksy'd!
And on the Great Pyramid.
Laqad tama Panksy'd!
And on the Eiffel Tower.
Vous avez été Panksy'd!
Yes, yes, those were all during his HAT PERIOD.
Panksy is the current darling of the fine art world, and the museum is honored to display his latest installation piece.
Ah. A sheet. Very avant-garde.

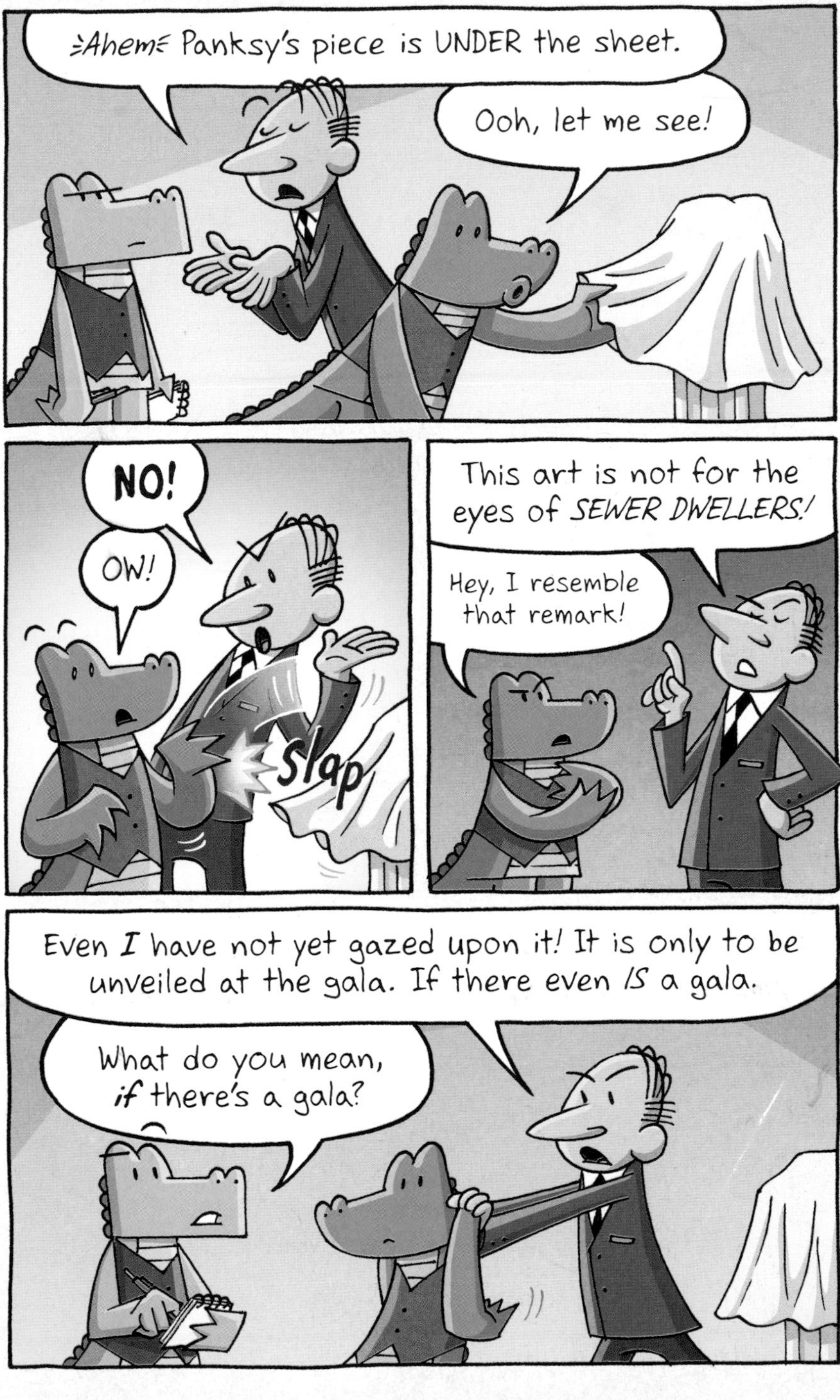

≥Ahem≤ Panksy's piece is UNDER the sheet.
Ooh, let me see!
NO!
OW!
SLAP
This art is not for the eyes of SEWER DWELLERS!
Hey, I resemble that remark!
Even I have not yet gazed upon it! It is only to be unveiled at the gala. If there even IS a gala.
What do you mean, if there's a gala?

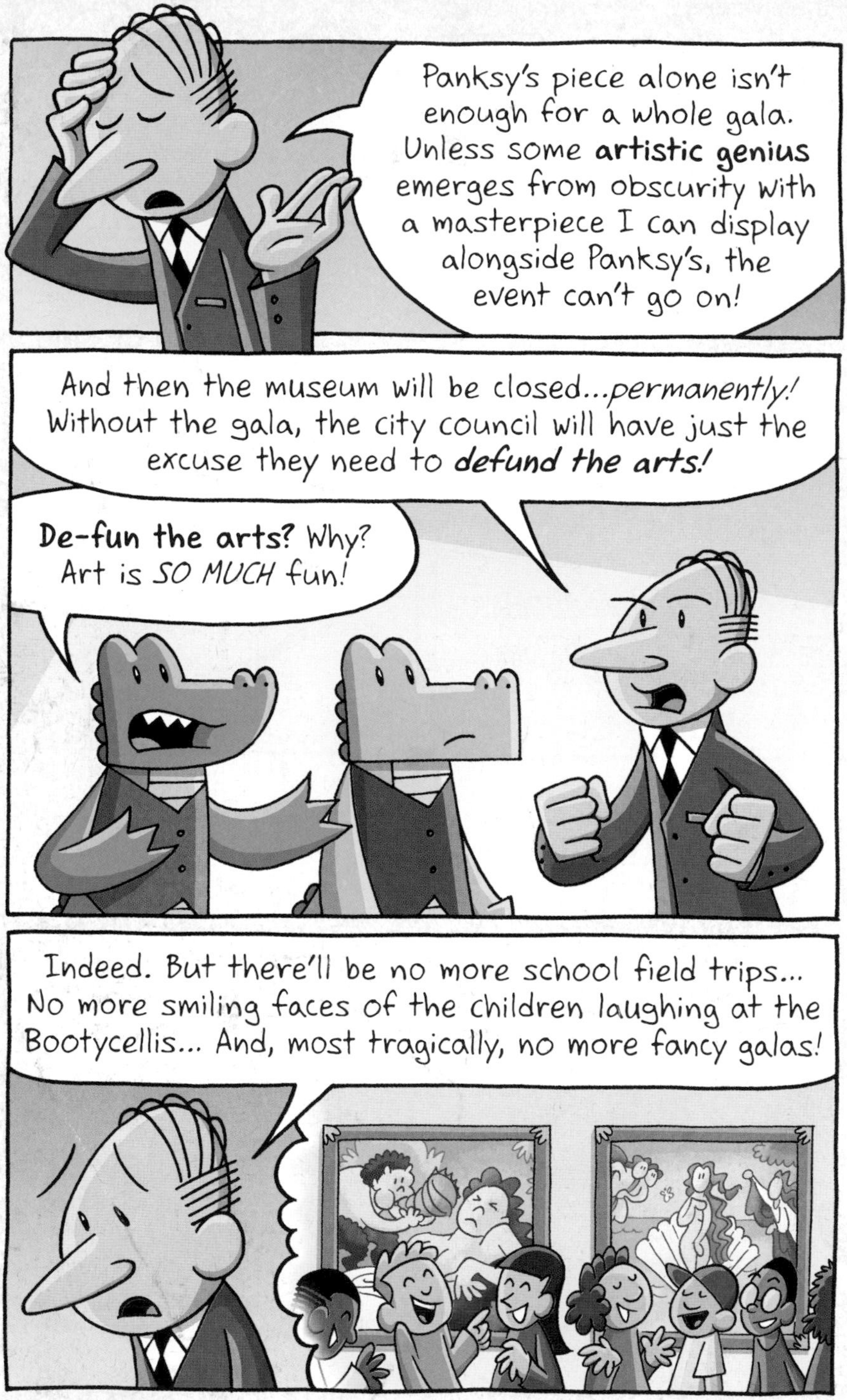

Panksy's piece alone isn't enough for a whole gala. Unless some **artistic genius** emerges from obscurity with a masterpiece I can display alongside Panksy's, the event can't go on!
And then the museum will be closed...*permanently!* Without the gala, the city council will have just the excuse they need to ***defund the arts!***
De-fun the arts? Why? Art is *SO MUCH* fun!
Indeed. But there'll be no more school field trips... No more smiling faces of the children laughing at the Bootycellis... And, most tragically, no more fancy galas!

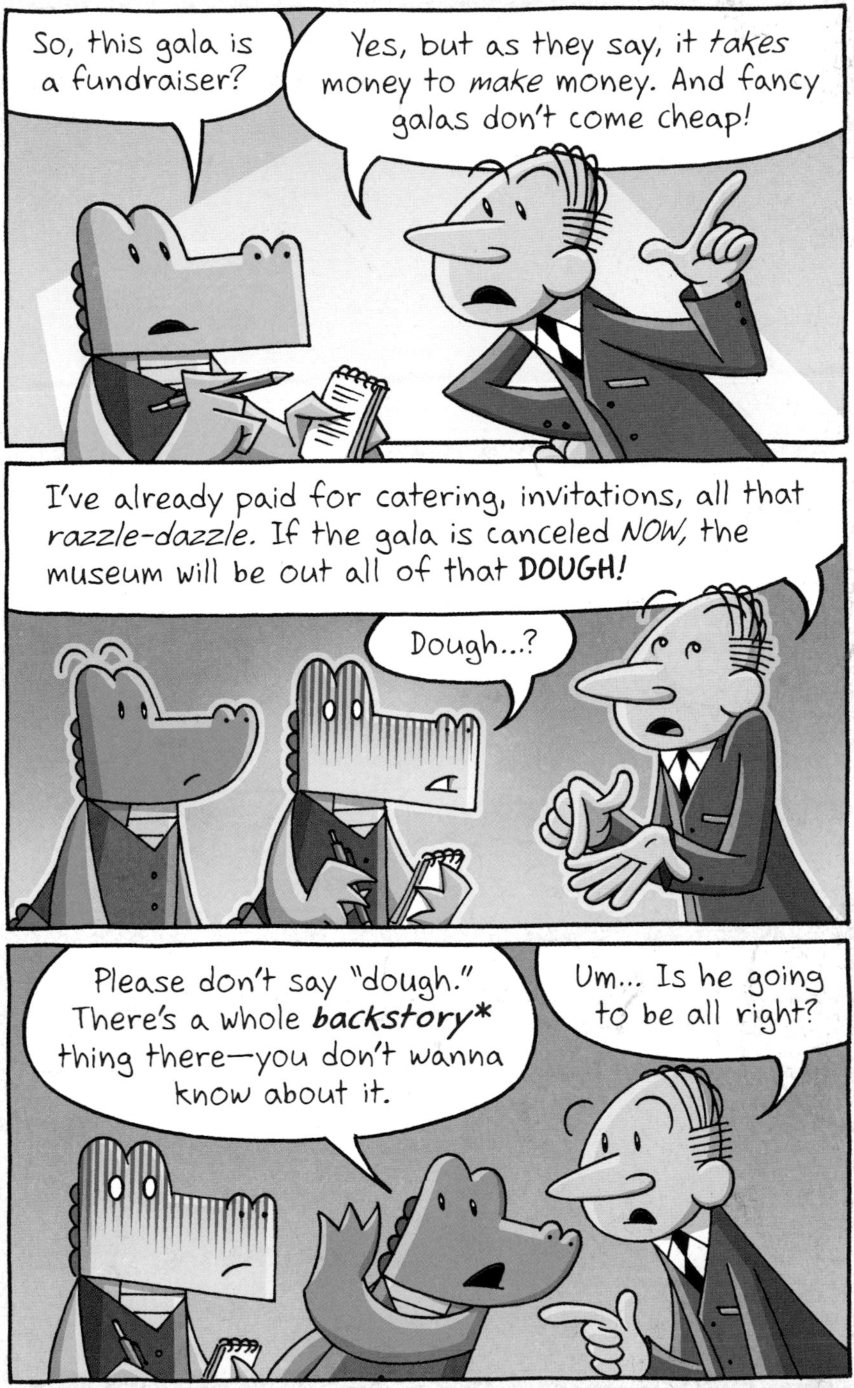
So, this gala is a fundraiser?
Yes, but as they say, it *takes* money to *make* money. And fancy galas don't come cheap!
I've already paid for catering, invitations, all that *razzle-dazzle.* If the gala is canceled *NOW,* the museum will be out all of that **DOUGH!**
Dough...?
Please don't say "dough." There's a whole ***backstory**** thing there—you don't wanna know about it.
Um... Is he going to be all right?

*See **InvestiGators** books 1–5!

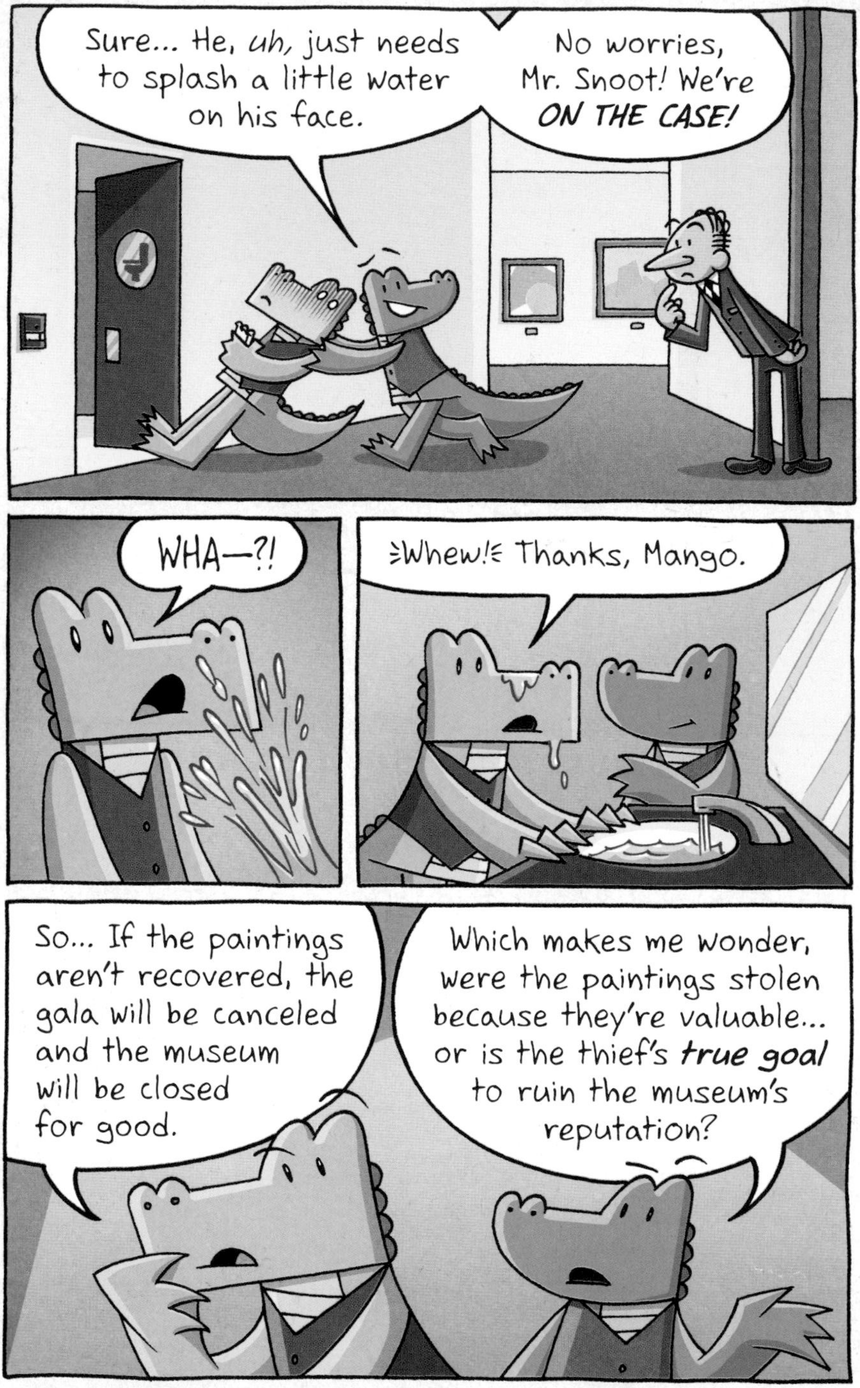
Sure... He, uh, just needs to splash a little water on his face.
No worries, Mr. Snoot! We're ON THE CASE!
WHA—?!
Whew! Thanks, Mango.
So... If the paintings aren't recovered, the gala will be canceled and the museum will be closed for good.
Which makes me wonder, were the paintings stolen because they're valuable... or is the thief's true goal to ruin the museum's reputation?

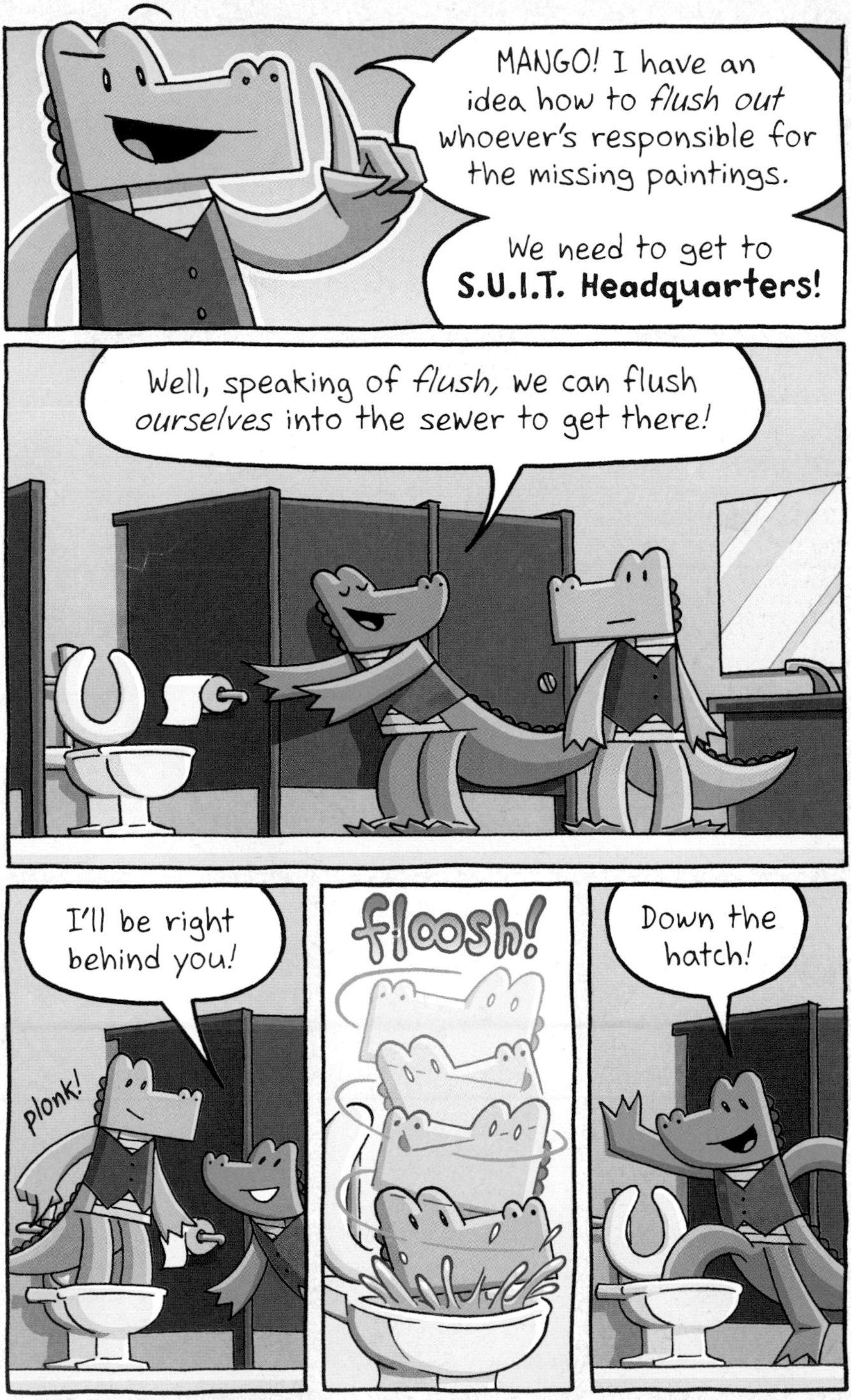
MANGO! I have an idea how to *flush out* whoever's responsible for the missing paintings.
We need to get to **S.U.I.T. Headquarters!**
Well, speaking of *flush,* we can flush *ourselves* into the sewer to get there!
I'll be right behind you!
plonk!
floosh!
Down the hatch!

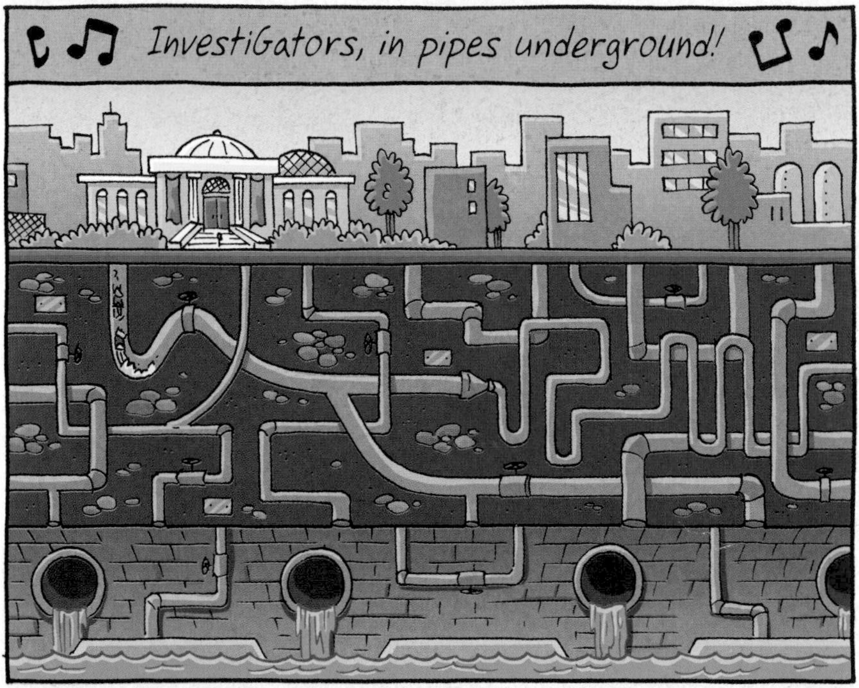
InvestiGators, in pipes underground!

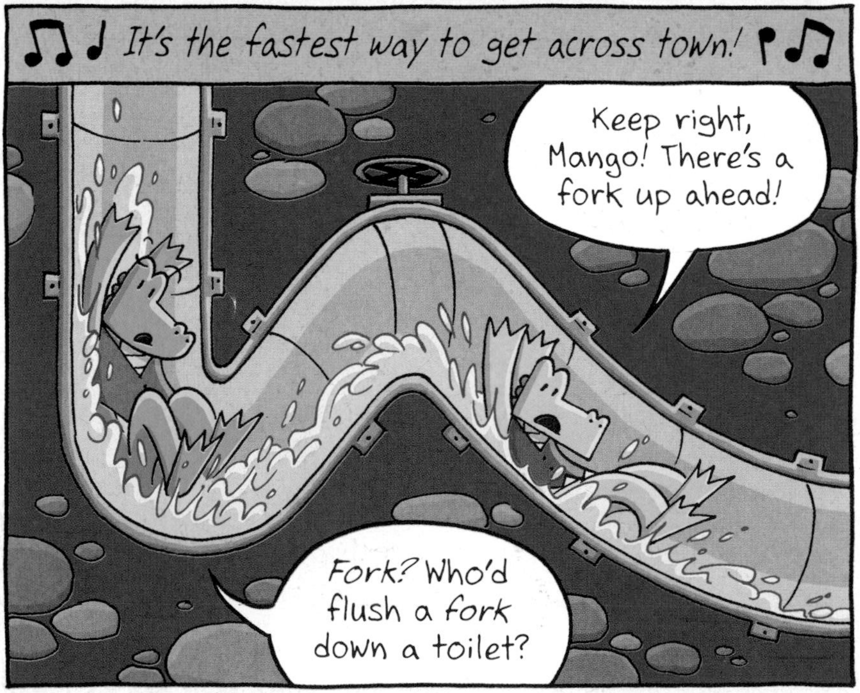
It's the fastest way to get across town!
Keep right, Mango! There's a fork up ahead!
Fork? Who'd flush a fork down a toilet?

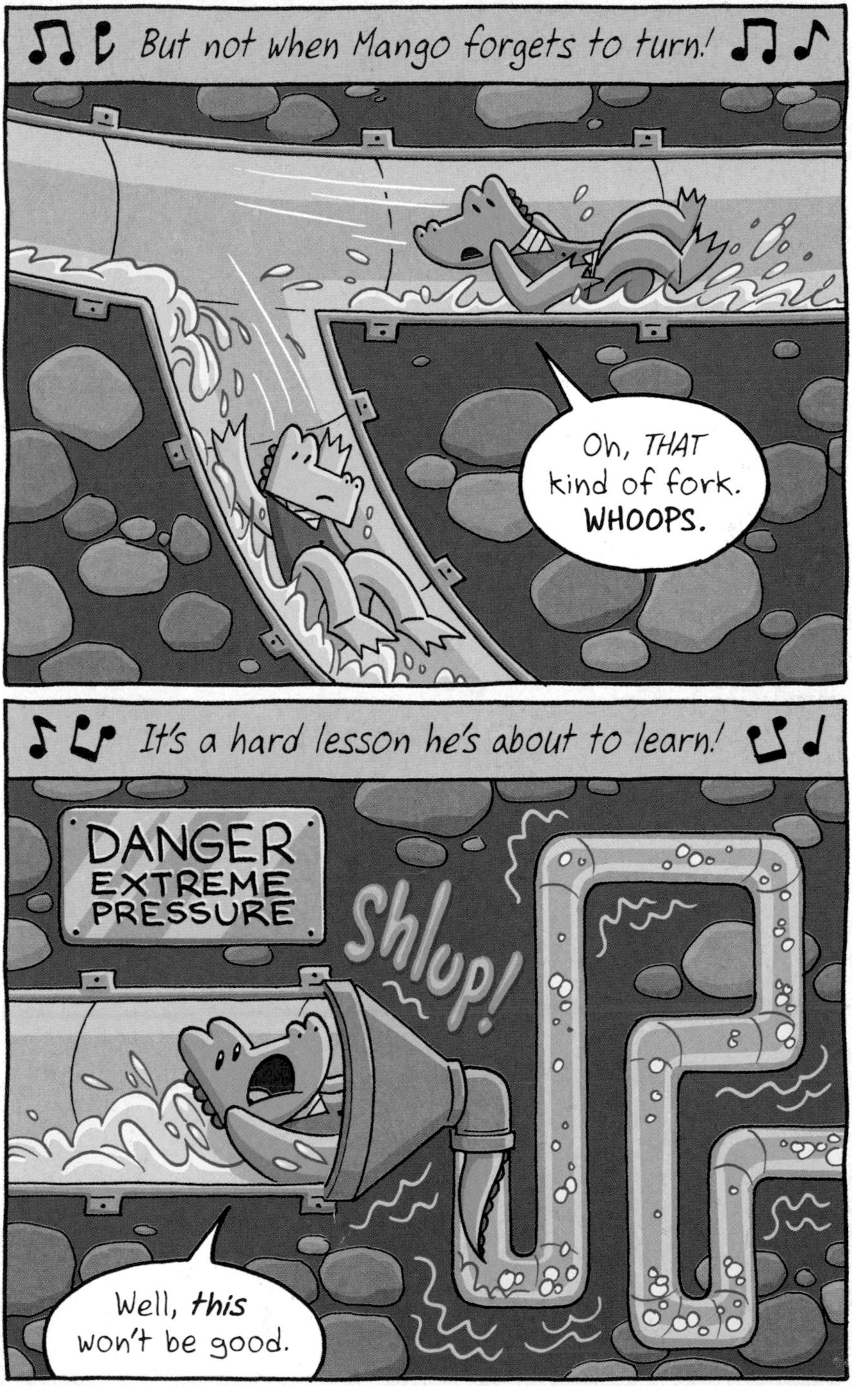
But not when Mango forgets to turn!
Oh, THAT kind of fork. WHOOPS.
It's a hard lesson he's about to learn!
DANGER EXTREME PRESSURE
Shlup!
Well, this won't be good.

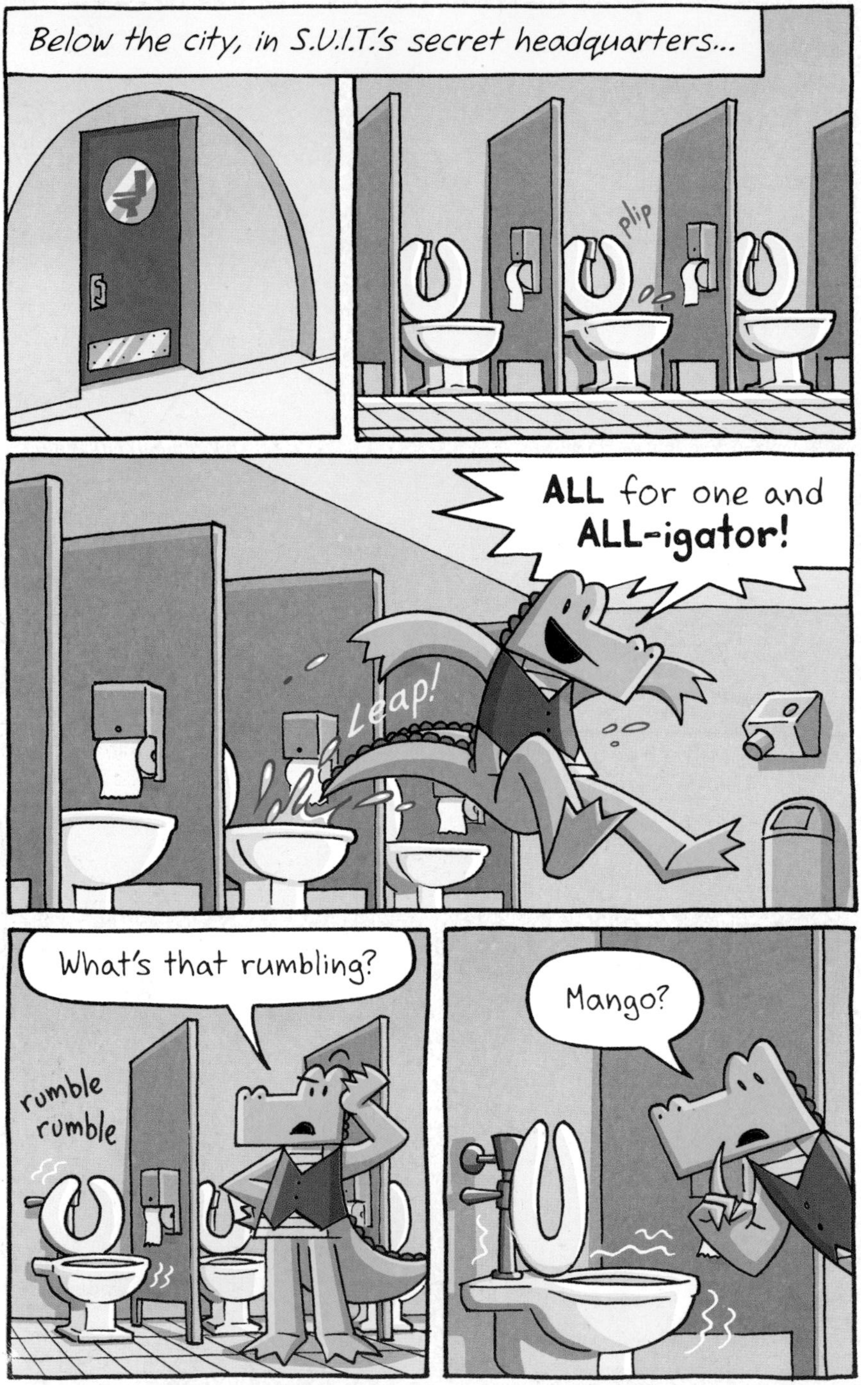
Below the city, in S.U.I.T.'s secret headquarters...
plip
ALL for one and **ALL-igator!**
Leap!
What's that rumbling?
rumble rumble
Mango?

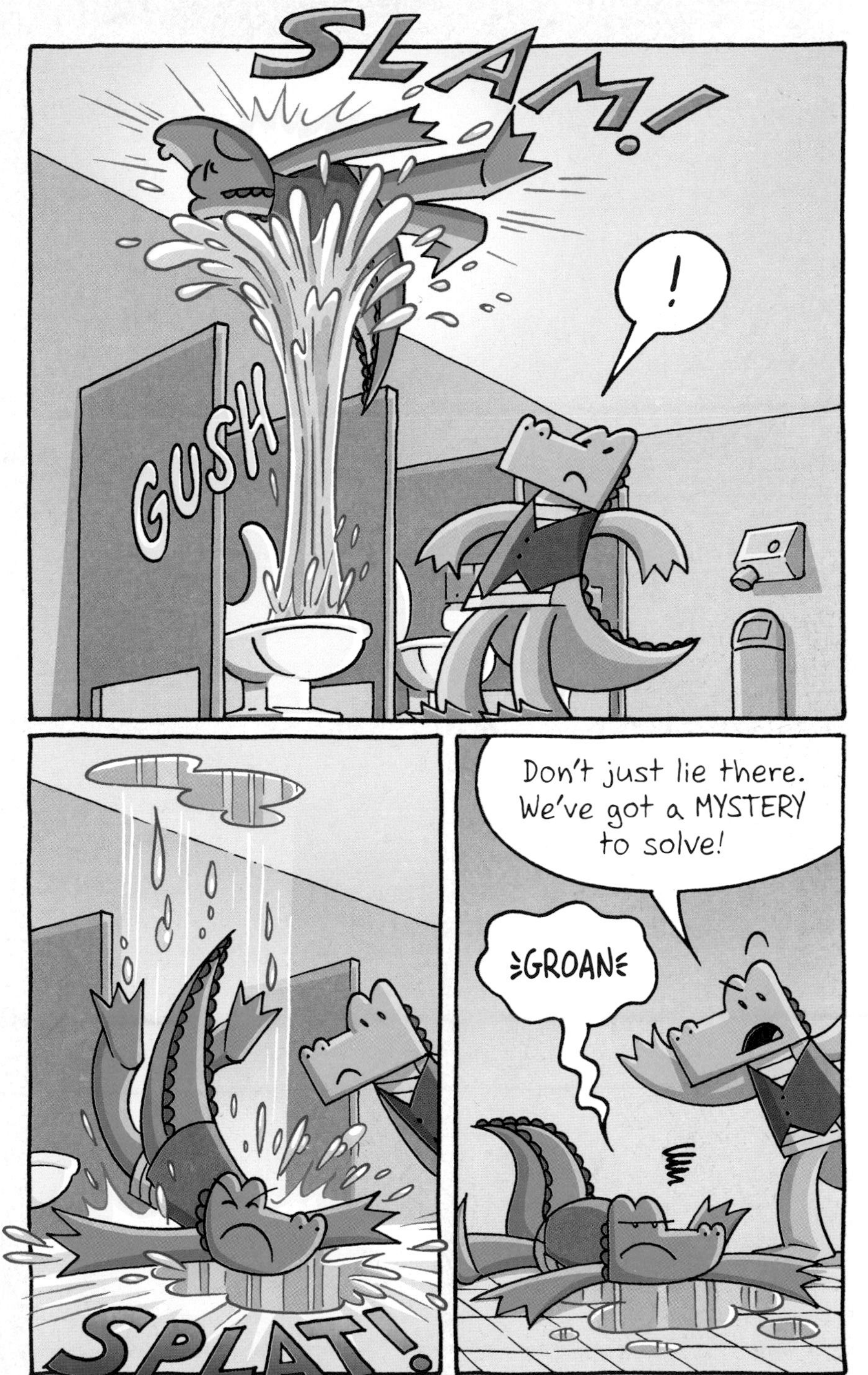
SLAM!
!
GUSH
SPLAT!
Don't just lie there. We've got a MYSTERY to solve!
GROAN

Chapter 4

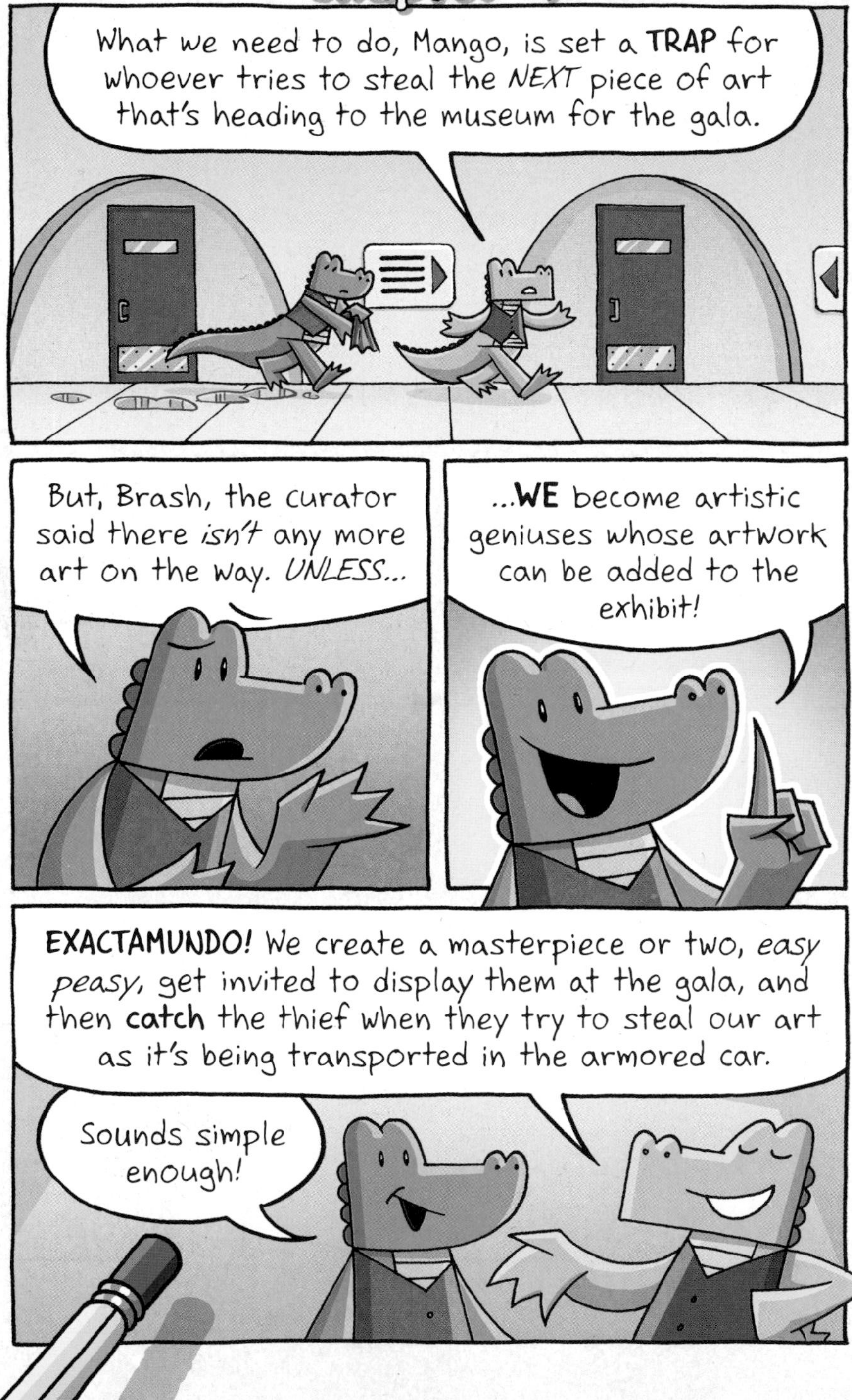

What we need to do, Mango, is set a **TRAP** for whoever tries to steal the *NEXT* piece of art that's heading to the museum for the gala.
But, Brash, the curator said there *isn't* any more art on the way. *UNLESS...*
...**WE** become artistic geniuses whose artwork can be added to the exhibit!
EXACTAMUNDO! We create a masterpiece or two, *easy peasy*, get invited to display them at the gala, and then **catch** the thief when they try to steal our art as it's being transported in the armored car.
Sounds simple enough!

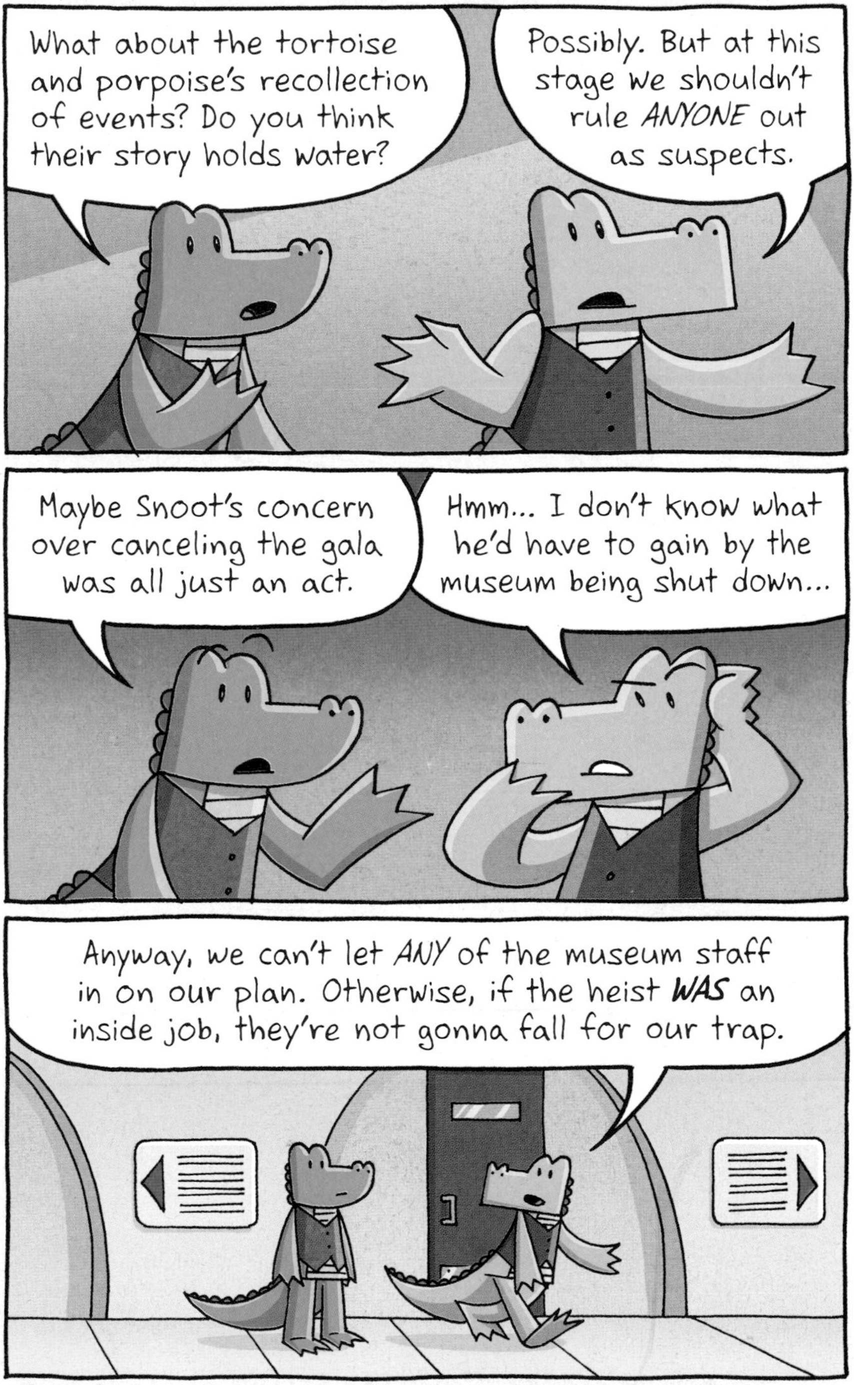
What about the tortoise and porpoise's recollection of events? Do you think their story holds water?
Possibly. But at this stage we shouldn't rule *ANYONE* out as suspects.
Maybe Snoot's concern over canceling the gala was all just an act.
Hmm... I don't know what he'd have to gain by the museum being shut down...
Anyway, we can't let *ANY* of the museum staff in on our plan. Otherwise, if the heist ***WAS*** an inside job, they're not gonna fall for our trap.

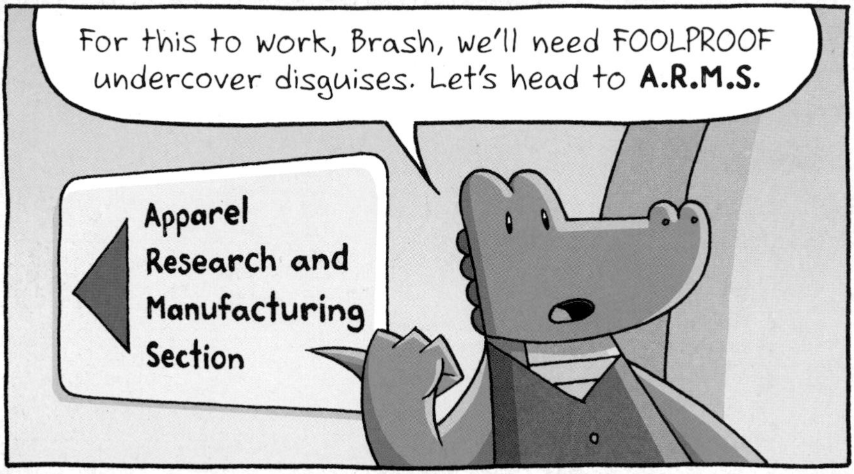
For this to work, Brash, we'll need FOOLPROOF undercover disguises. Let's head to **A.R.M.S.**
Apparel Research and Manufacturing Section

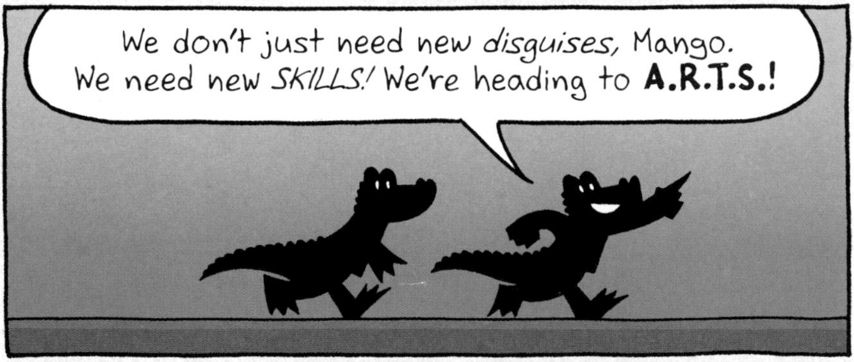
We don't just need new *disguises,* Mango. We need new *SKILLS!* We're heading to **A.R.T.S.!**

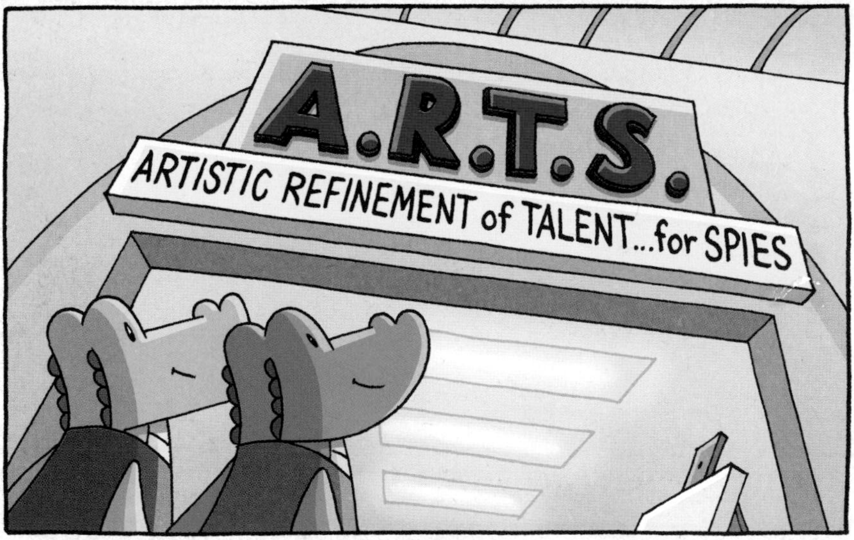
A.R.T.S.
ARTISTIC REFINEMENT of TALENT...for SPIES

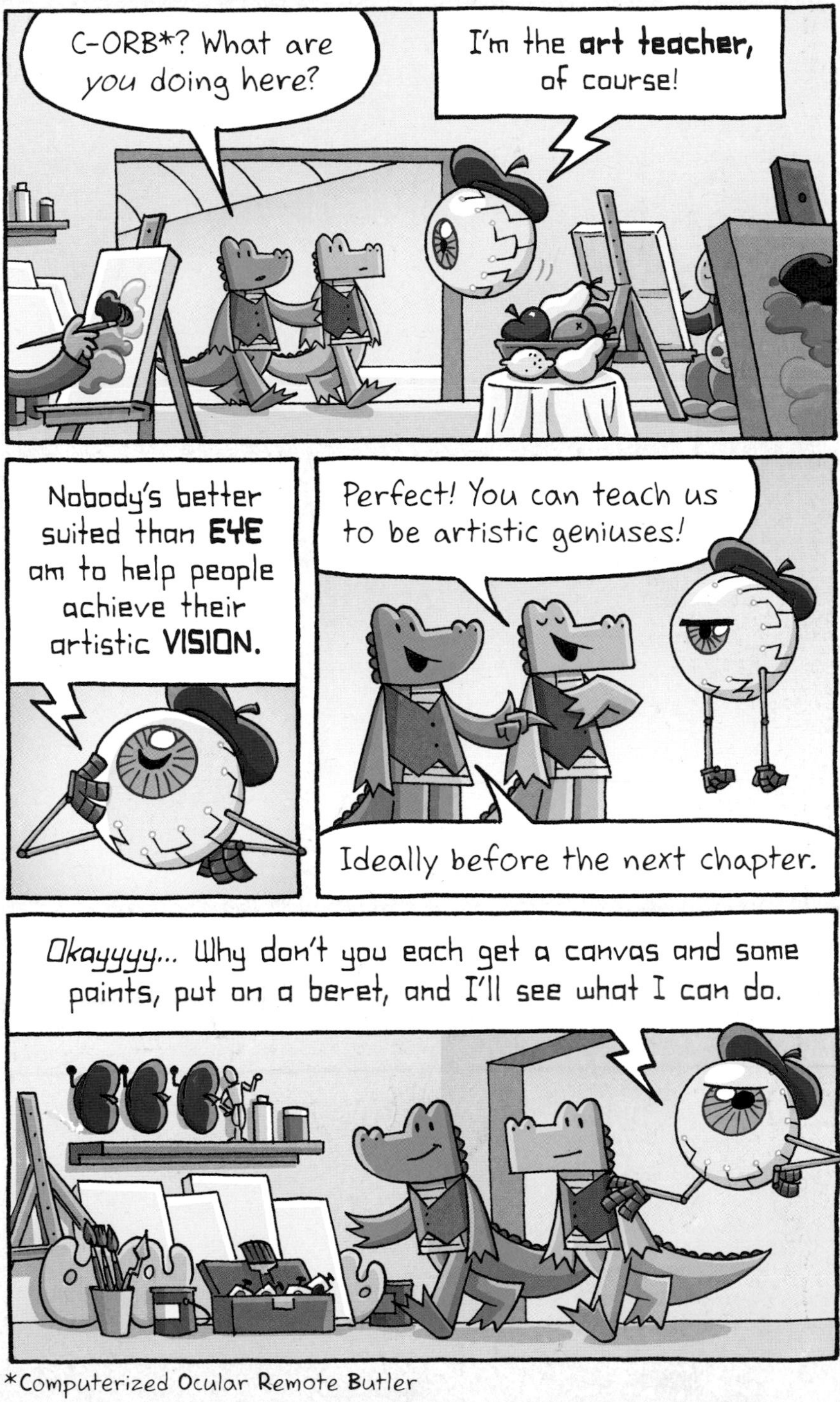
C-ORB*? What are you doing here?
I'm the **art teacher,** of course!
Nobody's better suited than **EYE** am to help people achieve their artistic **VISION.**
Perfect! You can teach us to be artistic geniuses!
Ideally before the next chapter.
Okayyyy... Why don't you each get a canvas and some paints, put on a beret, and I'll see what I can do.

*Computerized Ocular Remote Butler

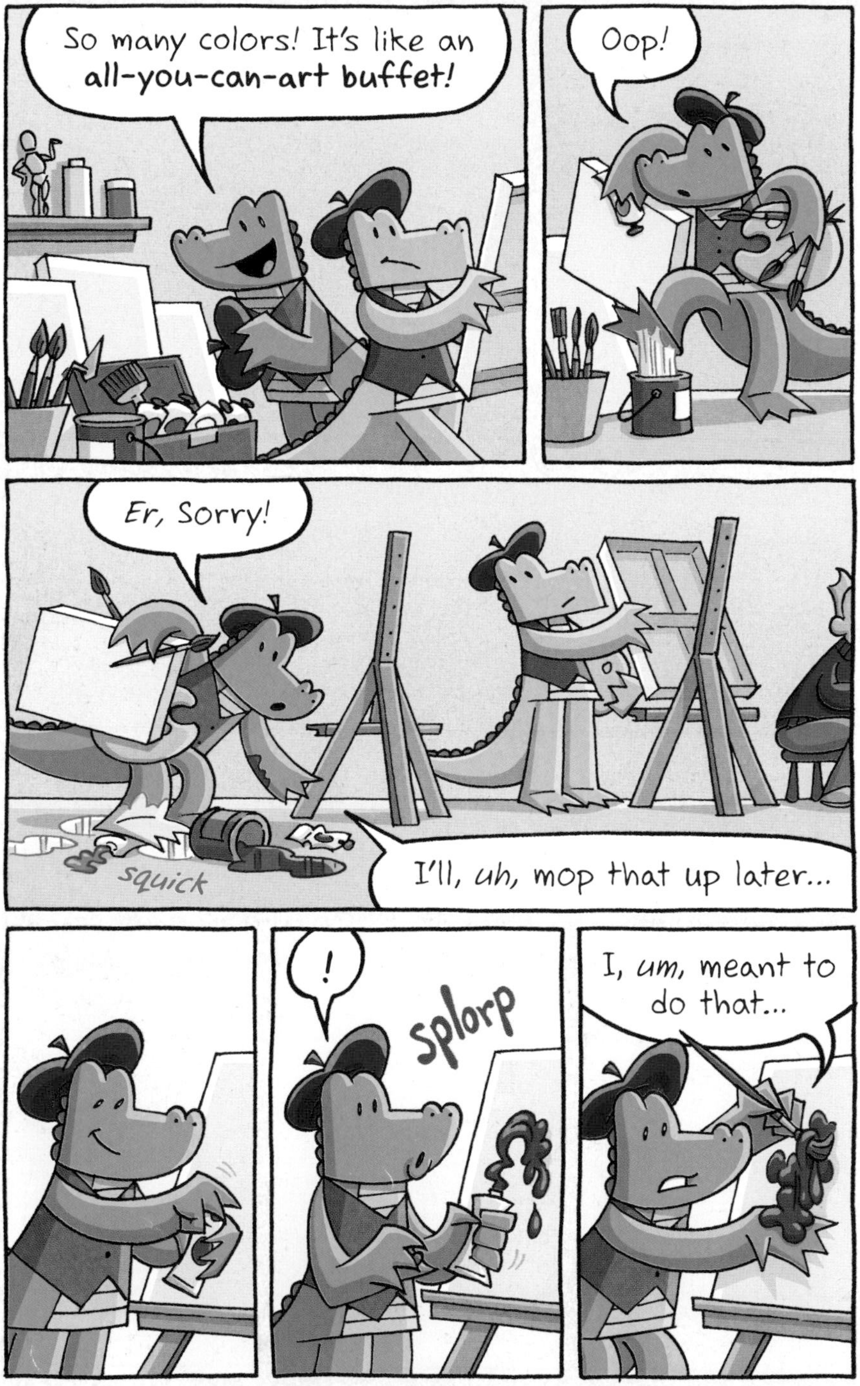

So many colors! It's like an **all-you-can-art buffet!**
Oop!
Er, Sorry!
squick
I'll, *uh*, mop that up later...
!
splorp
I, *um*, meant to do that...

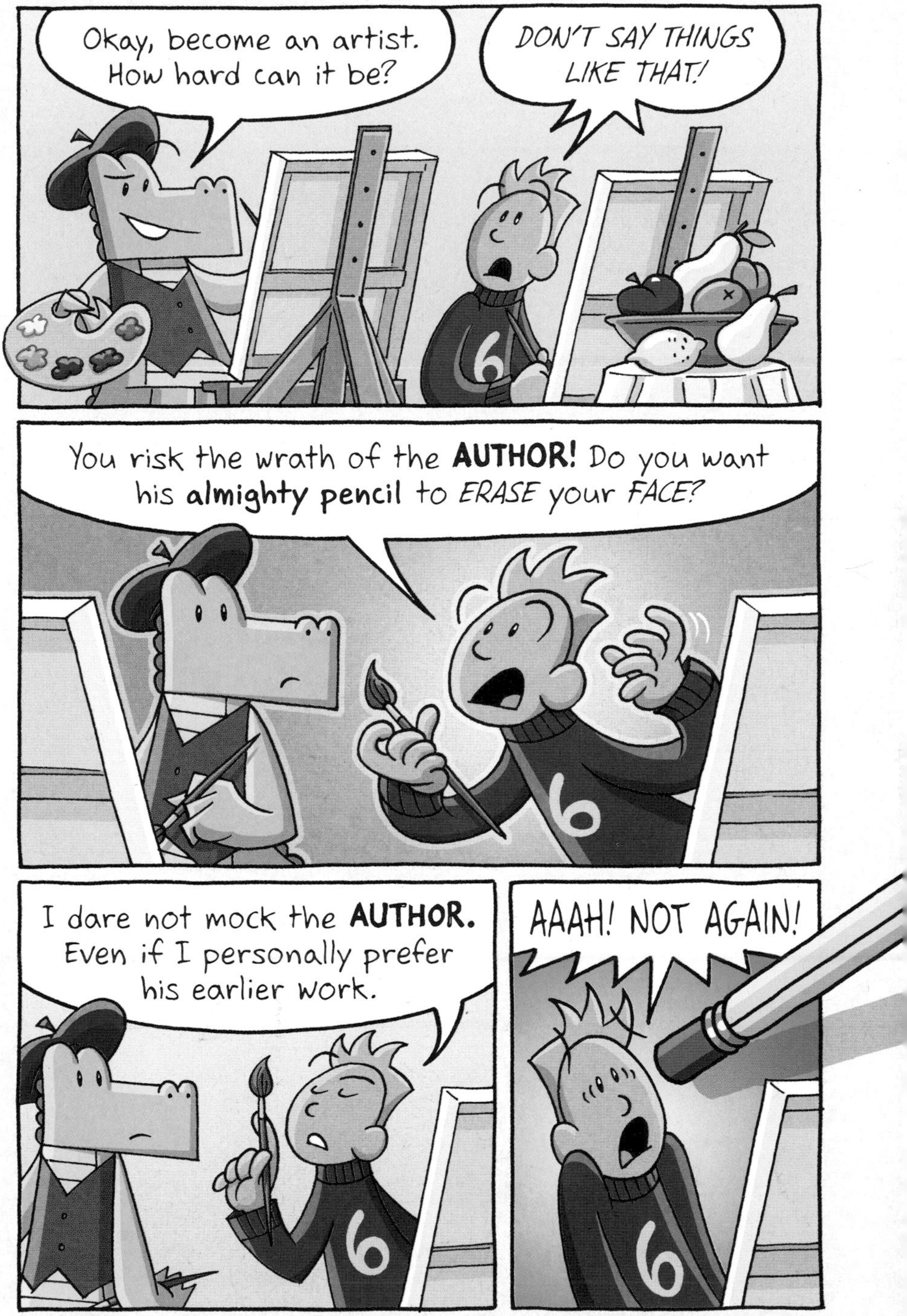
Okay, become an artist. How hard can it be?
DON'T SAY THINGS LIKE THAT!
You risk the wrath of the **AUTHOR!** Do you want his **almighty pencil** to *ERASE* your *FACE?*
I dare not mock the **AUTHOR.** Even if I personally prefer his earlier work.
AAAH! NOT AGAIN!

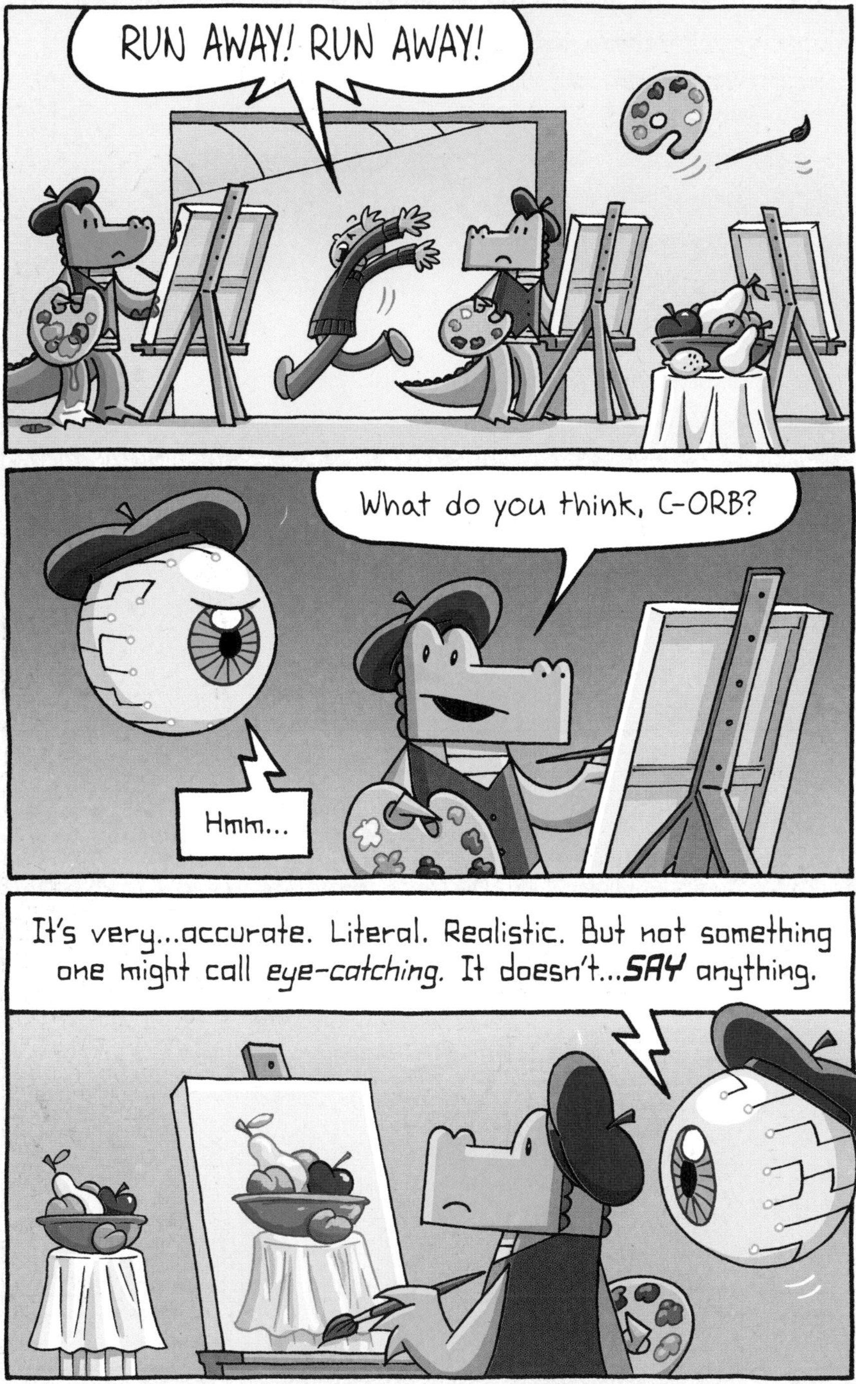
RUN AWAY! RUN AWAY!
What do you think, C-ORB?
Hmm...
It's very...accurate. Literal. Realistic. But not something one might call *eye-catching*. It doesn't...***SAY*** anything.

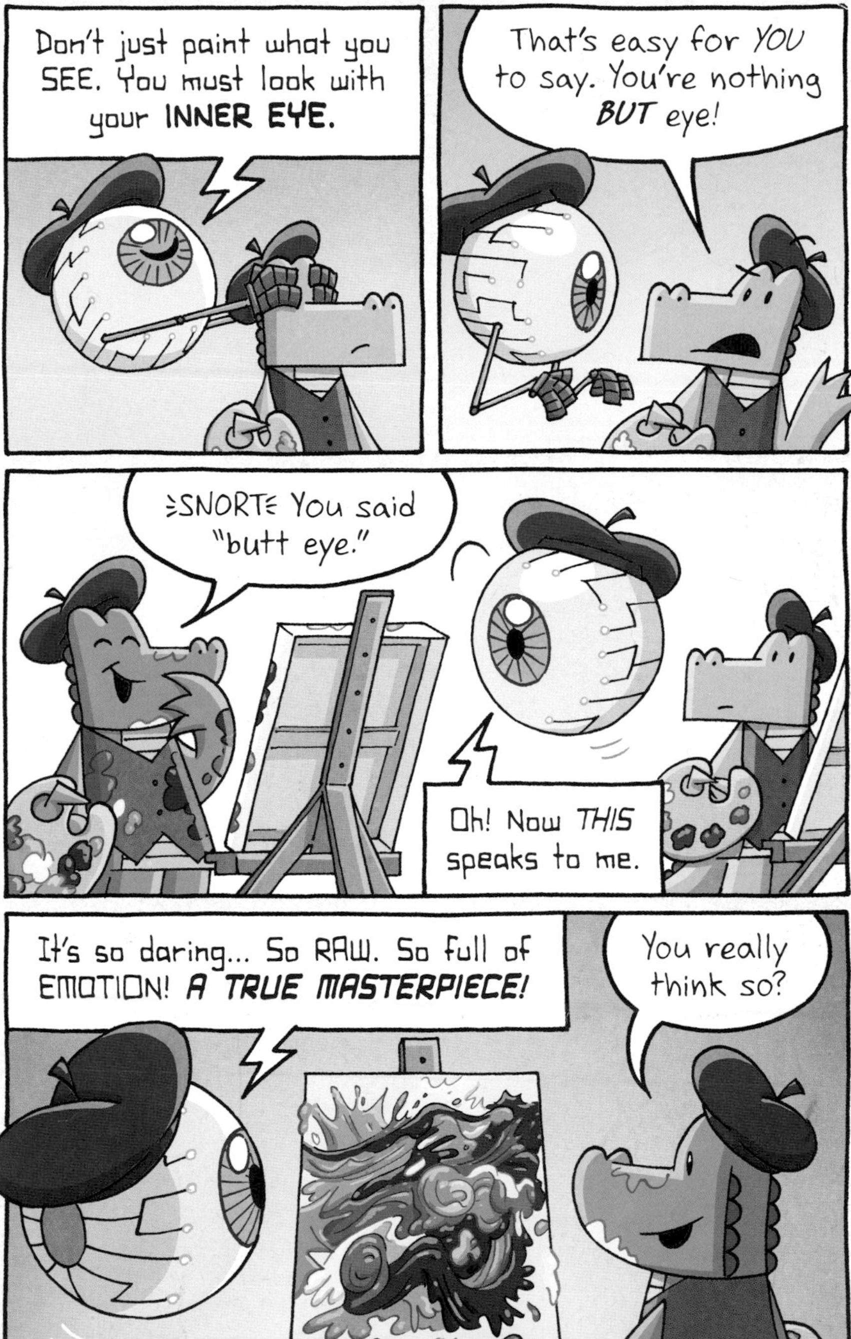
Don't just paint what you SEE. You must look with your INNER EYE.
That's easy for YOU to say. You're nothing BUT eye!
≥SNORT≤ You said "butt eye."
Oh! Now THIS speaks to me.
It's so daring... So RAW. So full of EMOTION! A TRUE MASTERPIECE!
You really think so?

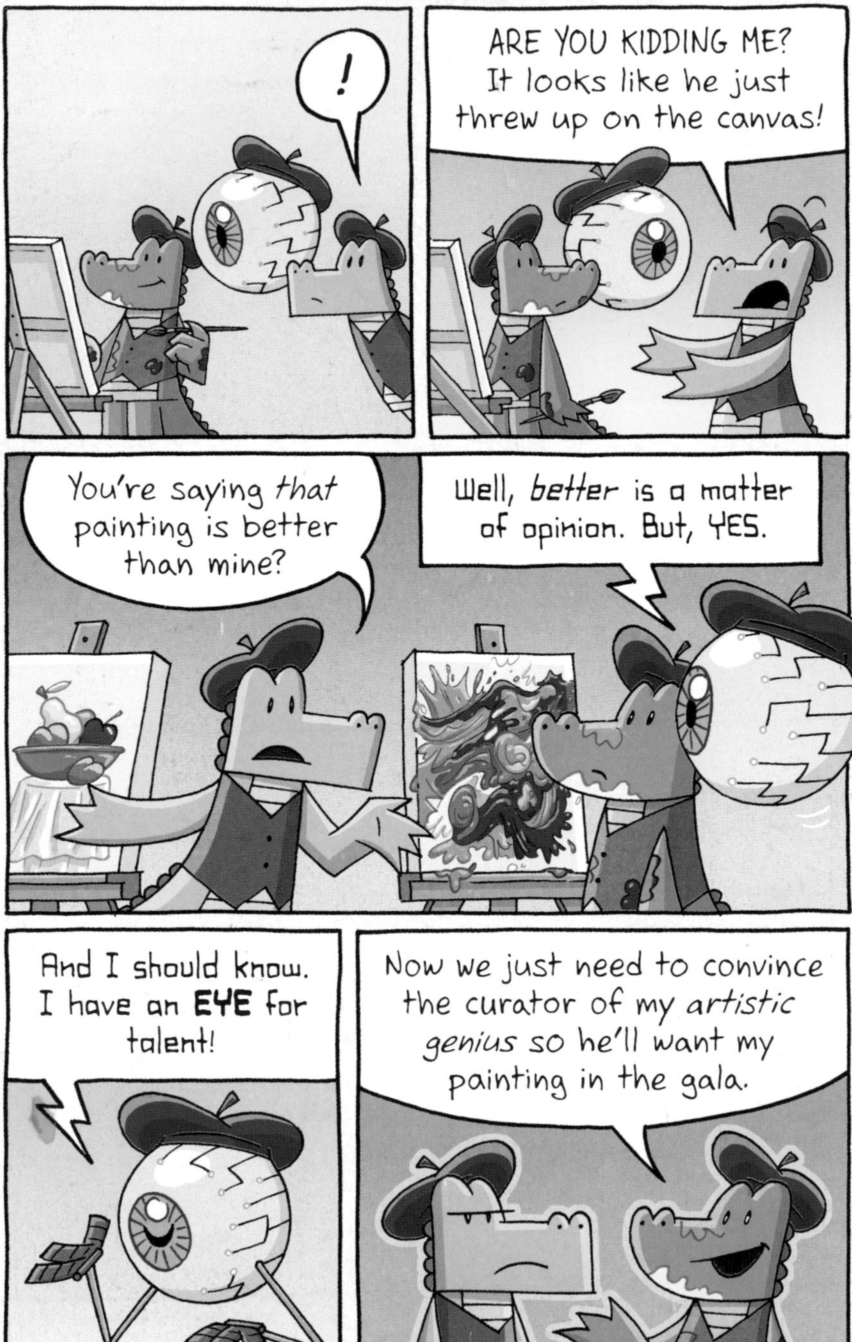
!
ARE YOU KIDDING ME? It looks like he just threw up on the canvas!
You're saying *that* painting is better than mine?
Well, *better* is a matter of opinion. But, YES.
And I should know. I have an **EYE** for talent!
Now we just need to convince the curator of my *artistic genius* so he'll want my painting in the gala.

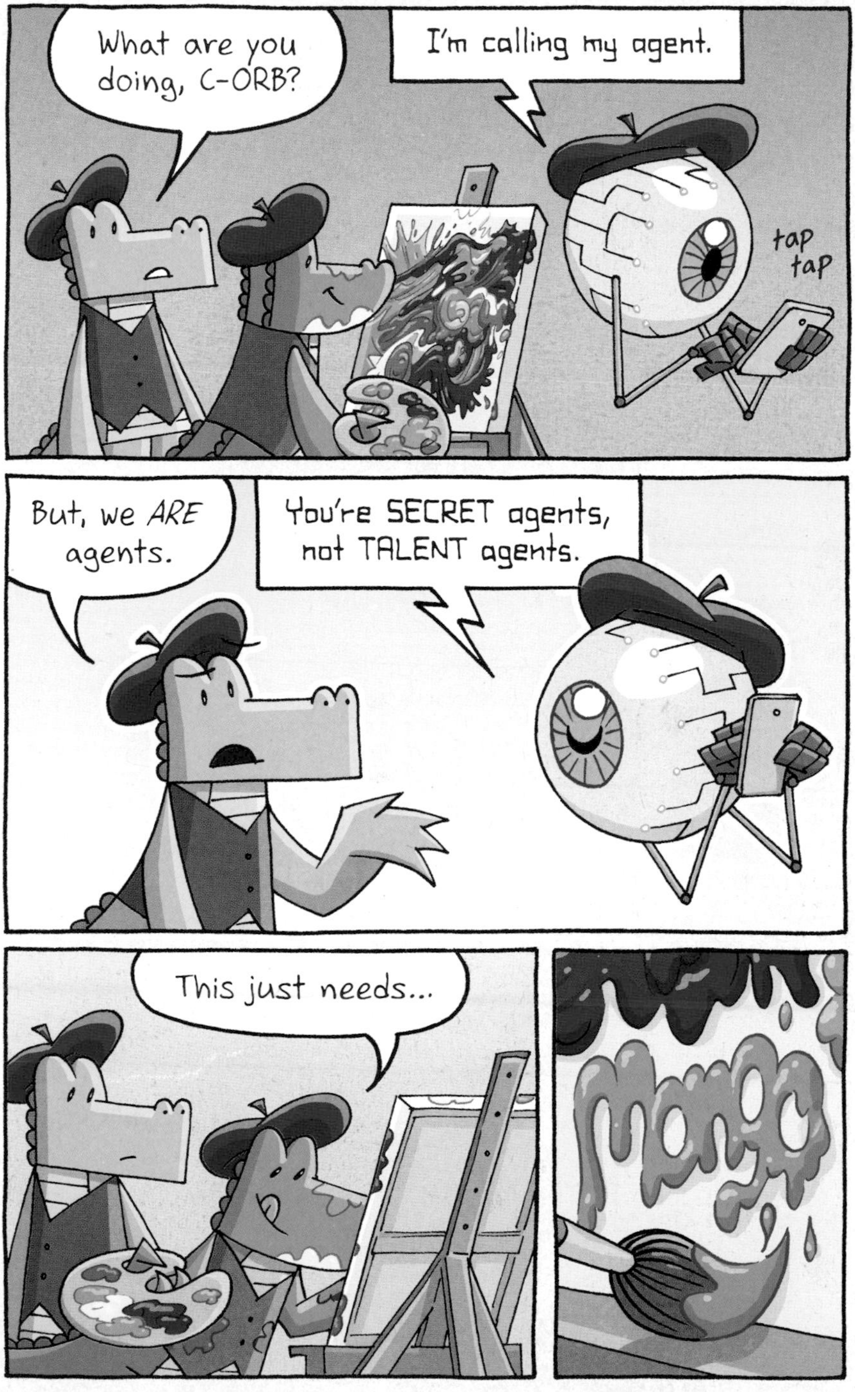
What are you doing, C-ORB?
I'm calling my agent.
tap tap
But, we ARE agents.
You're SECRET agents, not TALENT agents.
This just needs...
mango

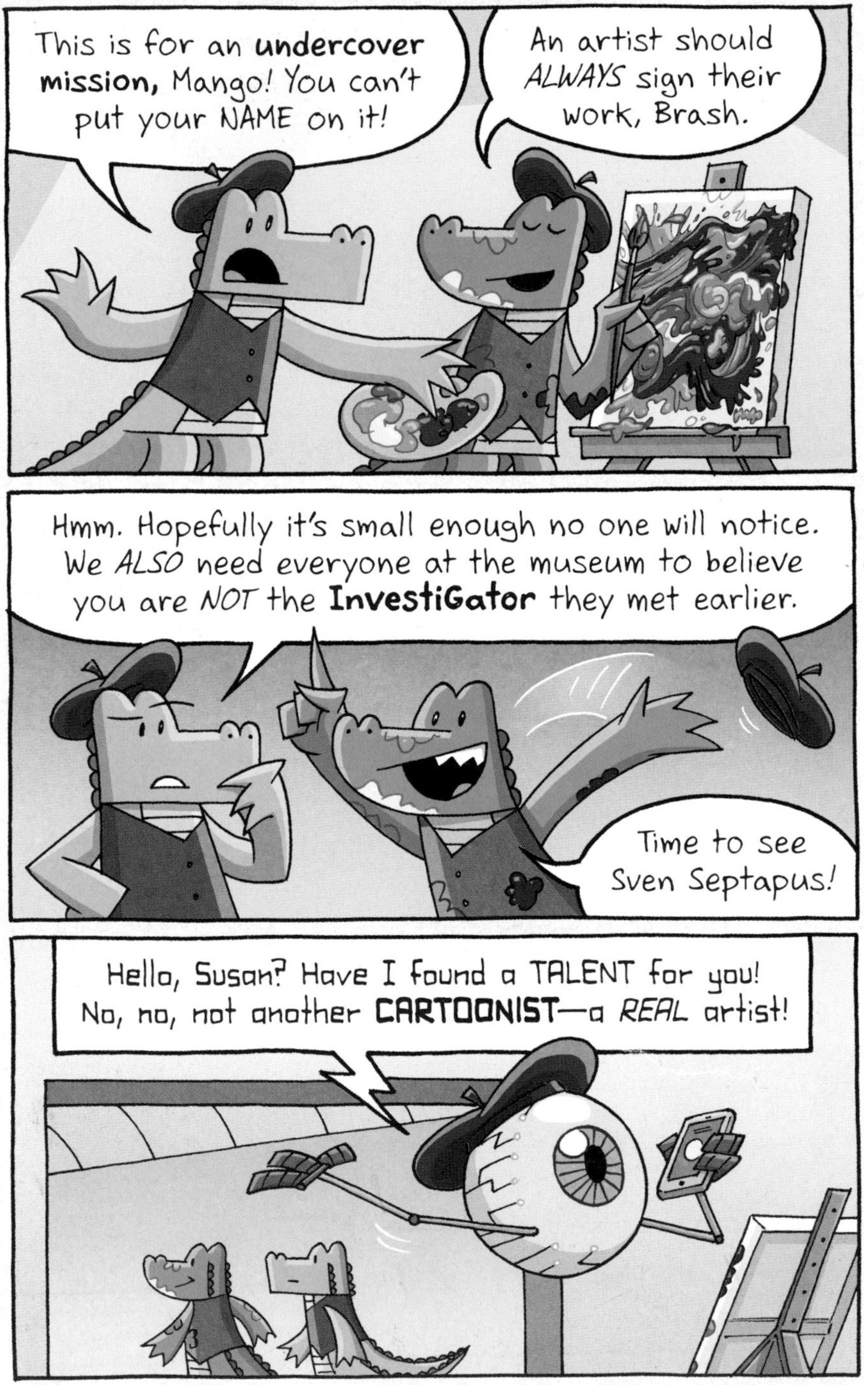
This is for an **undercover mission,** Mango! You can't put your NAME on it!
An artist should *ALWAYS* sign their work, Brash.
Hmm. Hopefully it's small enough no one will notice. We *ALSO* need everyone at the museum to believe you are *NOT* the **InvestiGator** they met earlier.
Time to see Sven Septapus!
Hello, Susan? Have I found a TALENT for you! No, no, not another **CARTOONIST**—a *REAL* artist!

Chapter 5

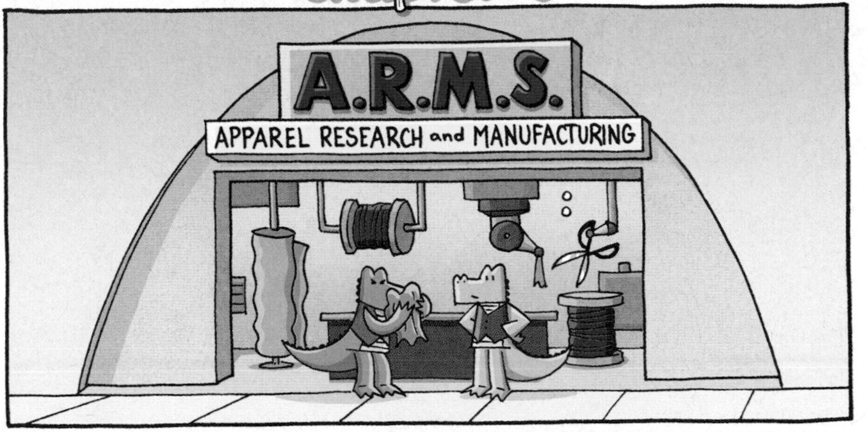
A.R.M.S.
APPAREL RESEARCH and MANUFACTURING

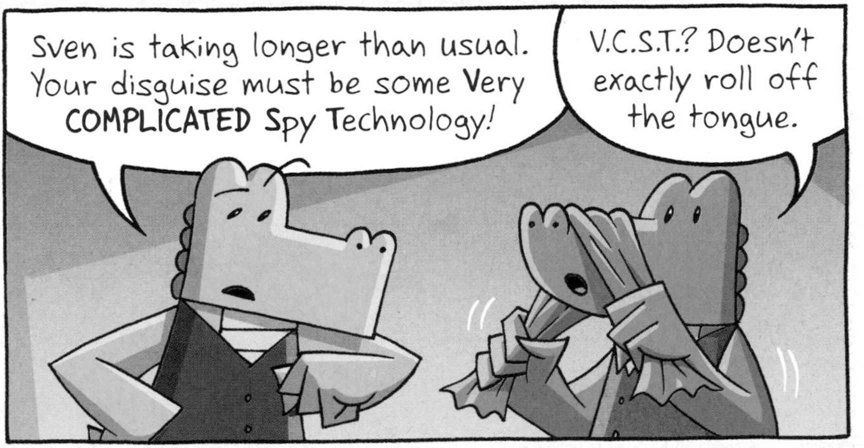
Sven is taking longer than usual. Your disguise must be some Very COMPLICATED Spy Technology!
V.C.S.T.? Doesn't exactly roll off the tongue.

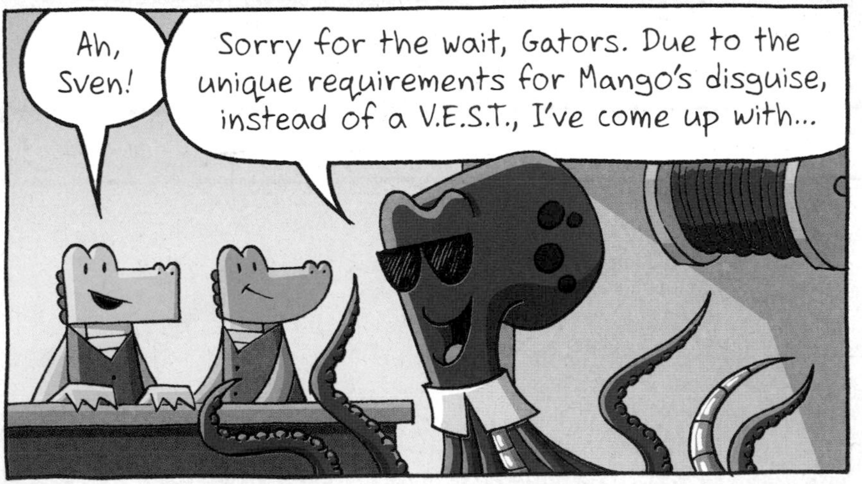
Ah, Sven!
Sorry for the wait, Gators. Due to the unique requirements for Mango's disguise, instead of a V.E.S.T., I've come up with...

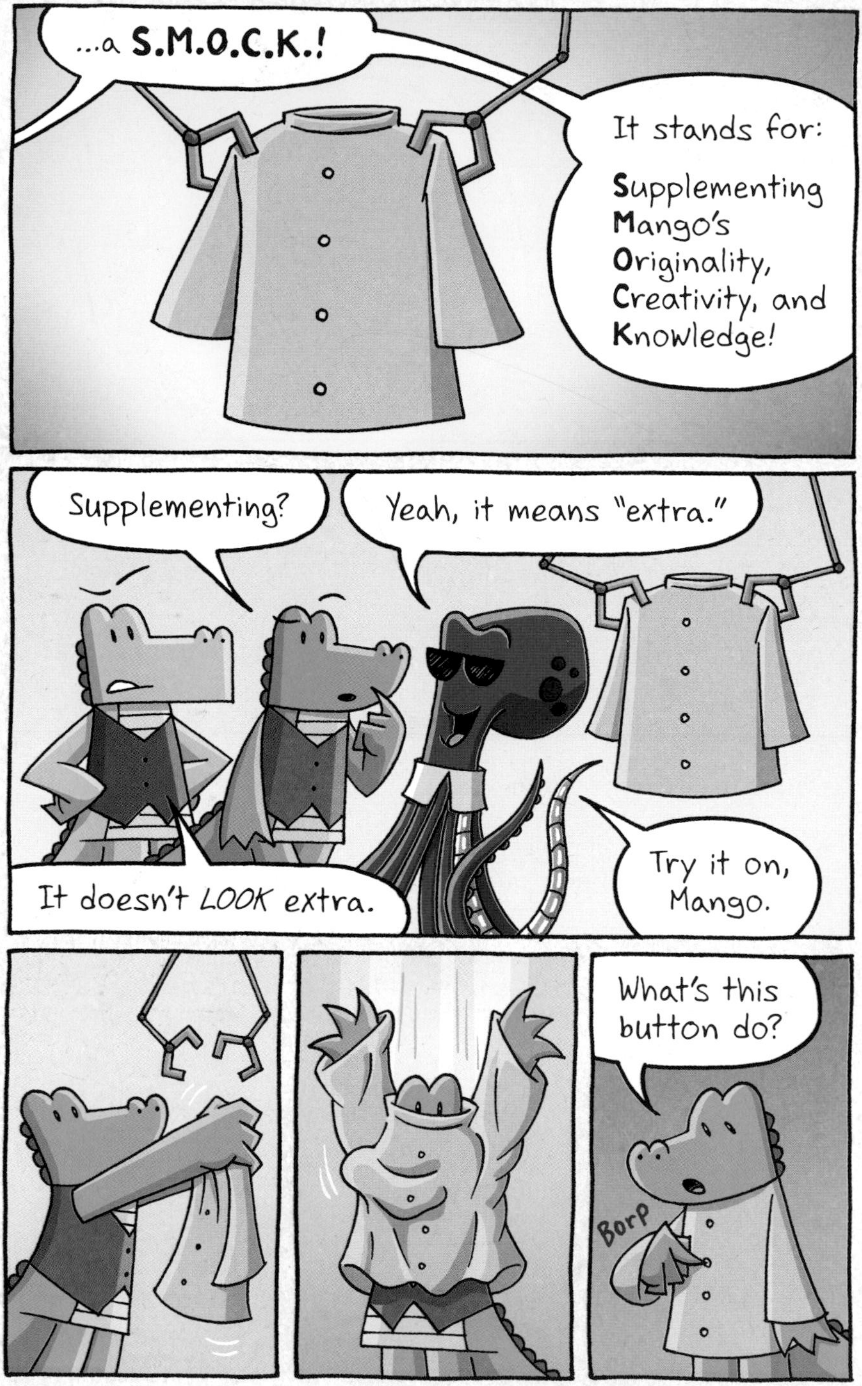
...a S.M.O.C.K.!
It stands for:
Supplementing Mango's Originality, Creativity, and Knowledge!
Supplementing?
Yeah, it means "extra."
It doesn't LOOK extra.
Try it on, Mango.
What's this button do?
Borp

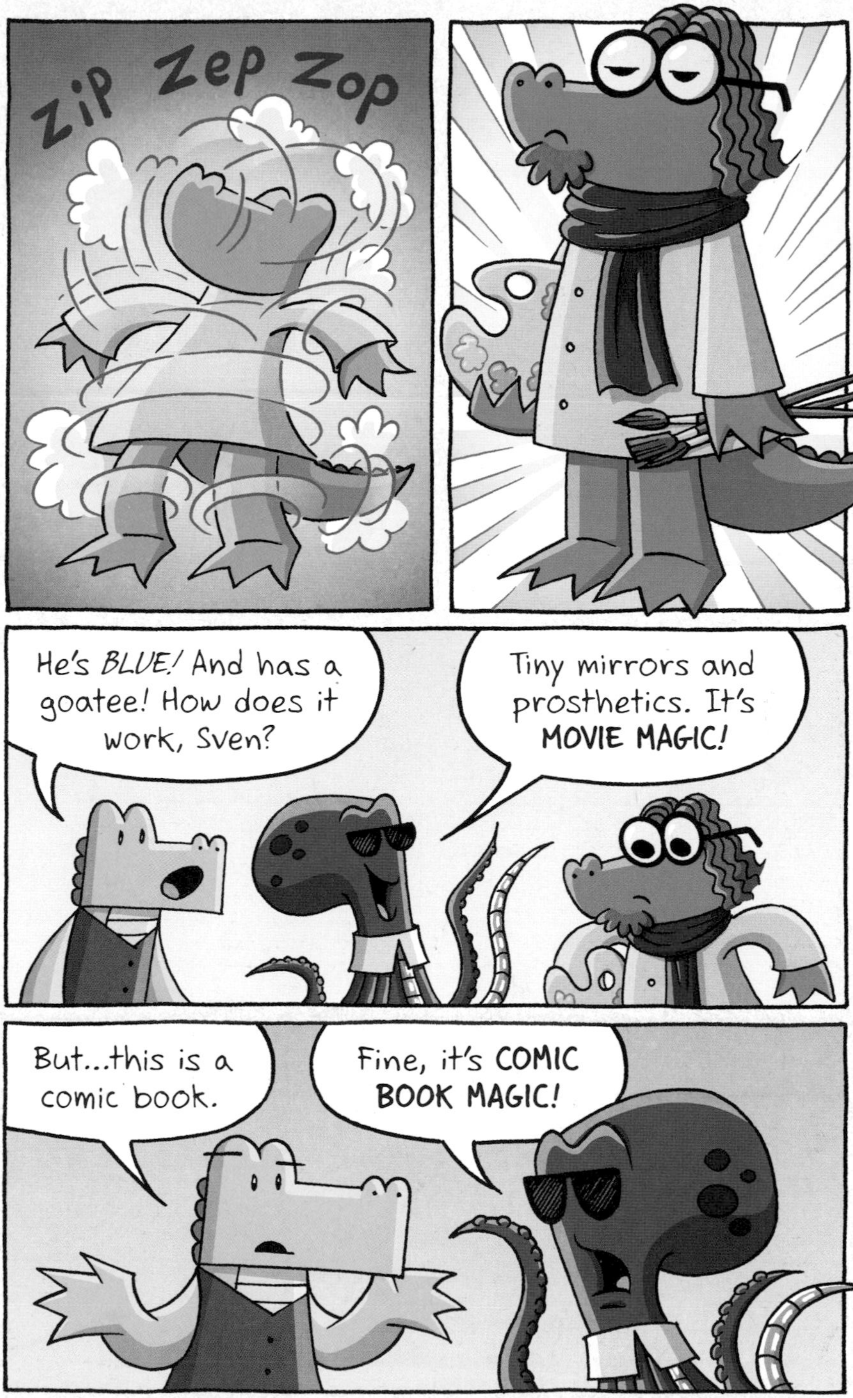
Zip Zep Zop
He's *BLUE!* And has a goatee! How does it work, Sven?
Tiny mirrors and prosthetics. It's **MOVIE MAGIC!**
But...this is a comic book.
Fine, it's **COMIC BOOK MAGIC!**

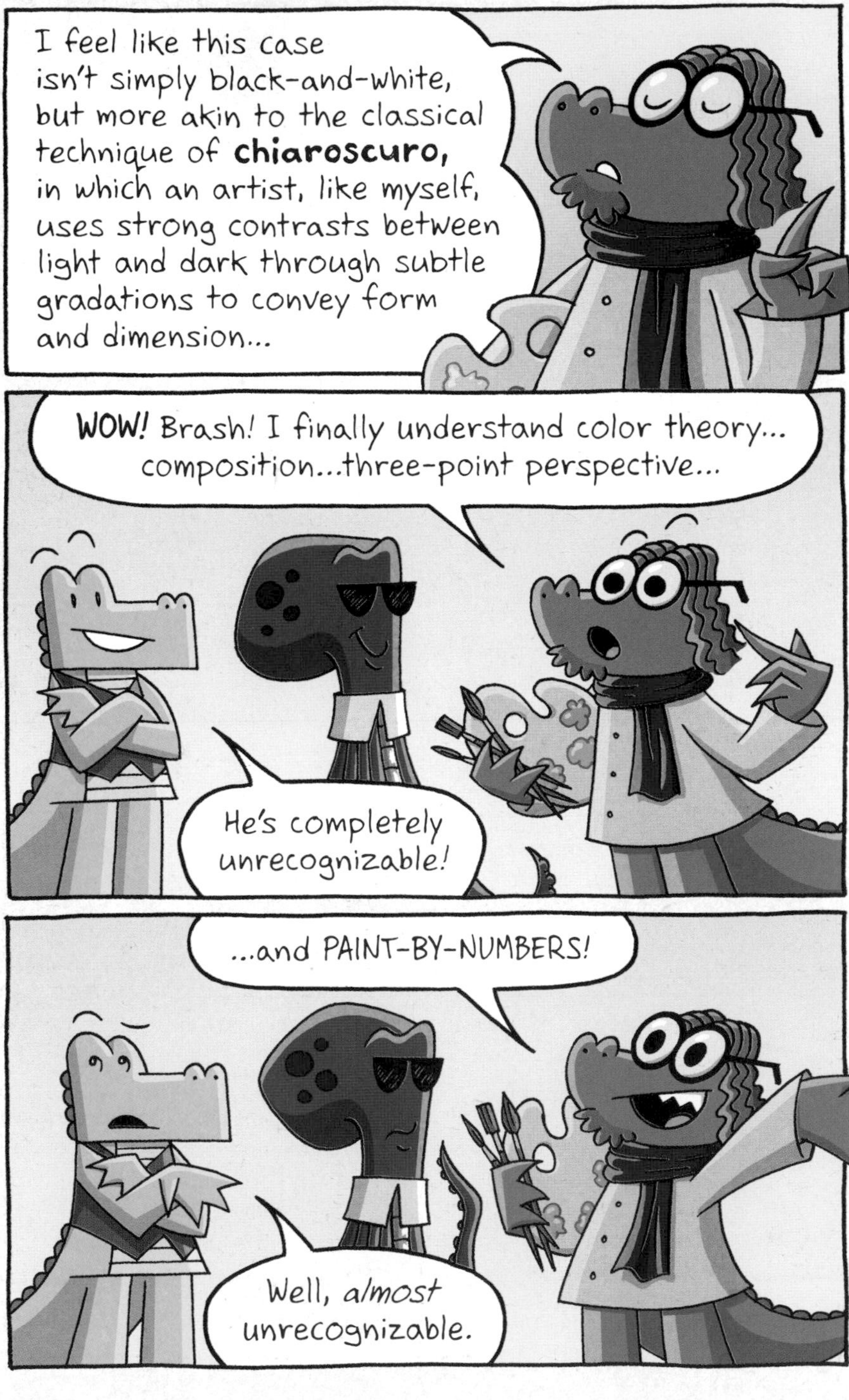

I feel like this case isn't simply black-and-white, but more akin to the classical technique of **chiaroscuro,** in which an artist, like myself, uses strong contrasts between light and dark through subtle gradations to convey form and dimension...
WOW! Brash! I finally understand color theory... composition...three-point perspective...
He's completely unrecognizable!
...and PAINT-BY-NUMBERS!
Well, *almost* unrecognizable.

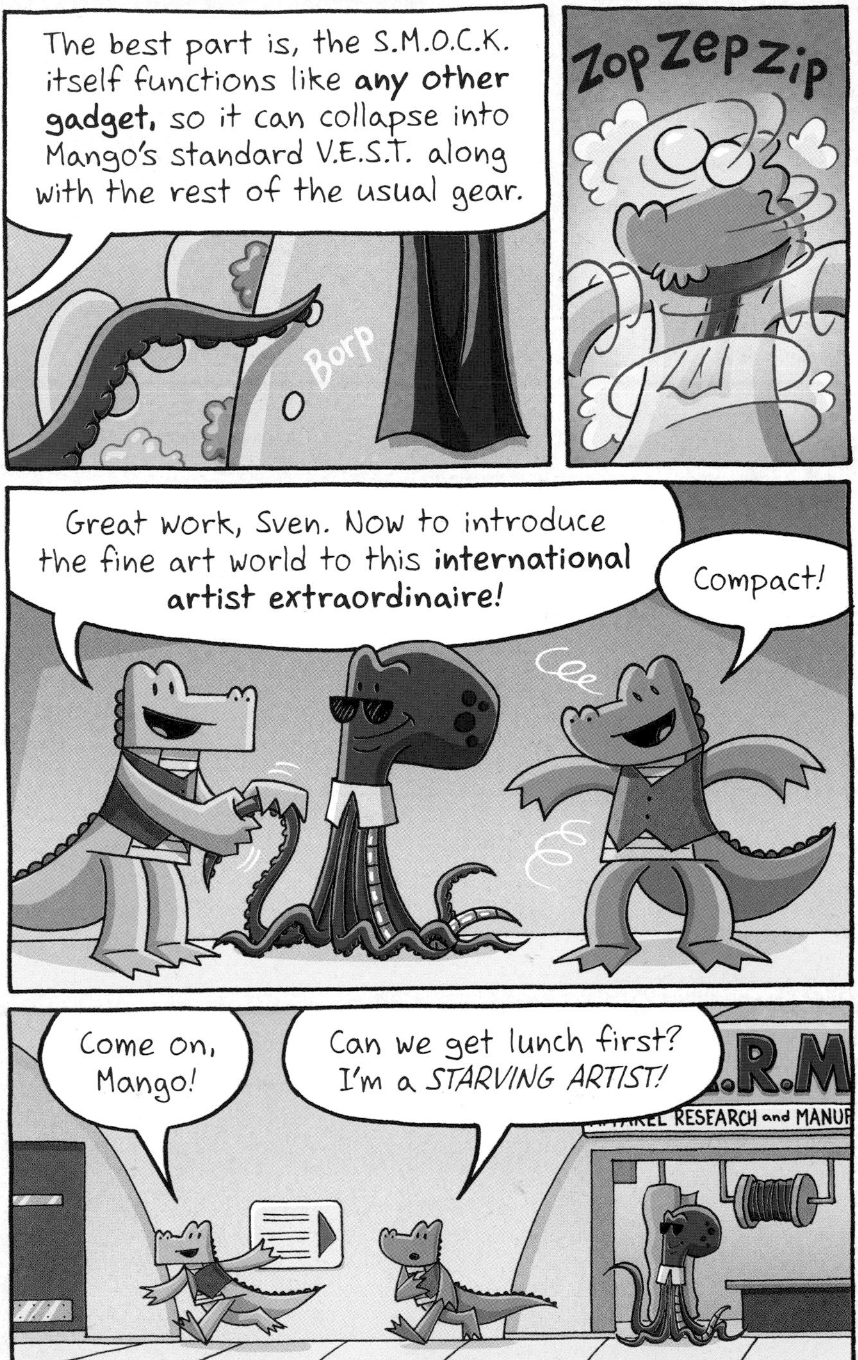

The best part is, the S.M.O.C.K. itself functions like **any other gadget,** so it can collapse into Mango's standard V.E.S.T. along with the rest of the usual gear.
Borp
Zop Zep Zip
Great work, Sven. Now to introduce the fine art world to this **international artist extraordinaire!**
Compact!
Come on, Mango!
Can we get lunch first? I'm a *STARVING ARTIST!*
RESEARCH and MANUF

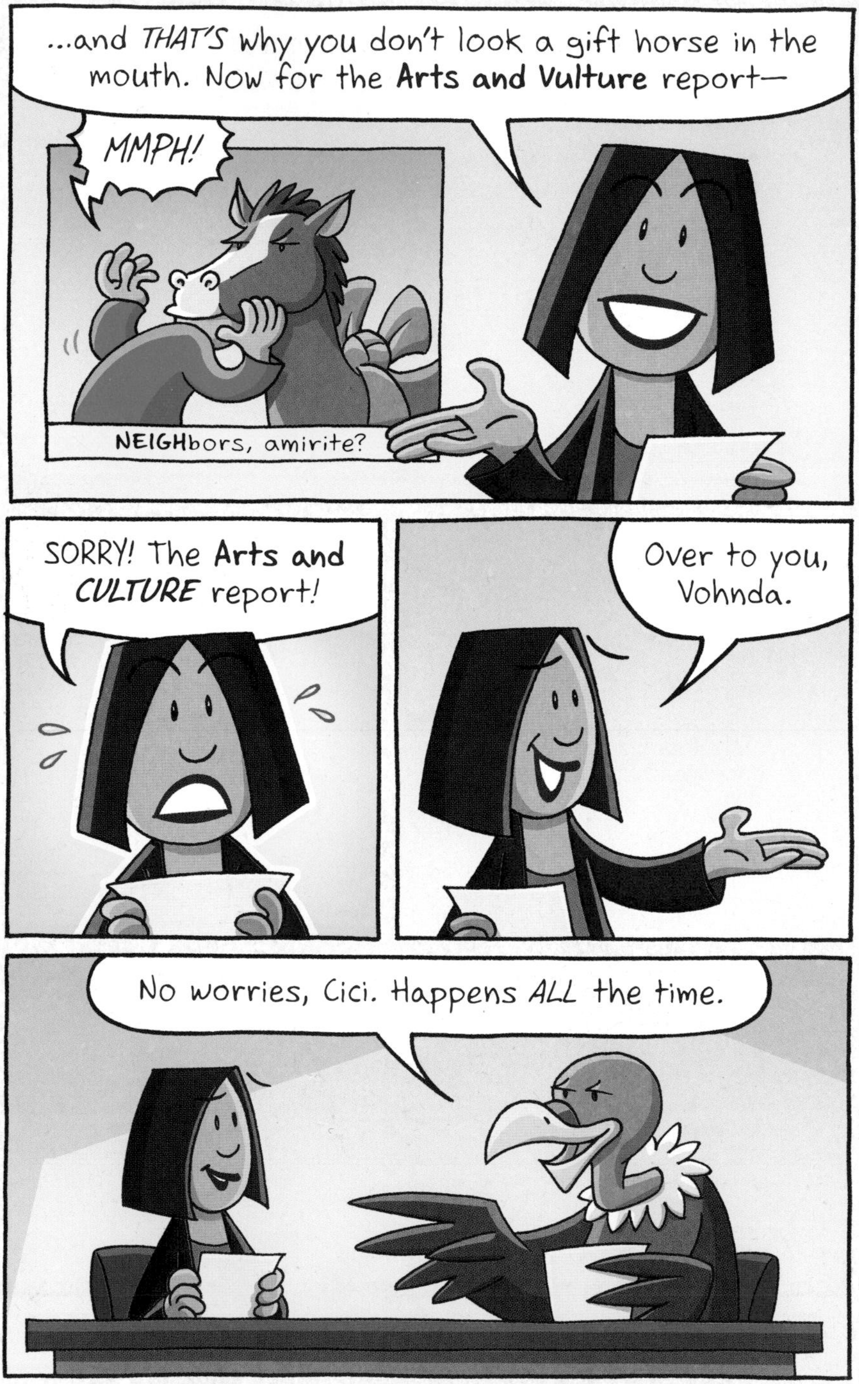
...and *THAT'S* why you don't look a gift horse in the mouth. Now for the **Arts and Vulture** report—
MMPH!
NEIGHbors, amirite?
SORRY! The **Arts and *CULTURE*** report!
Over to you, Vohnda.
No worries, Cici. Happens *ALL* the time.

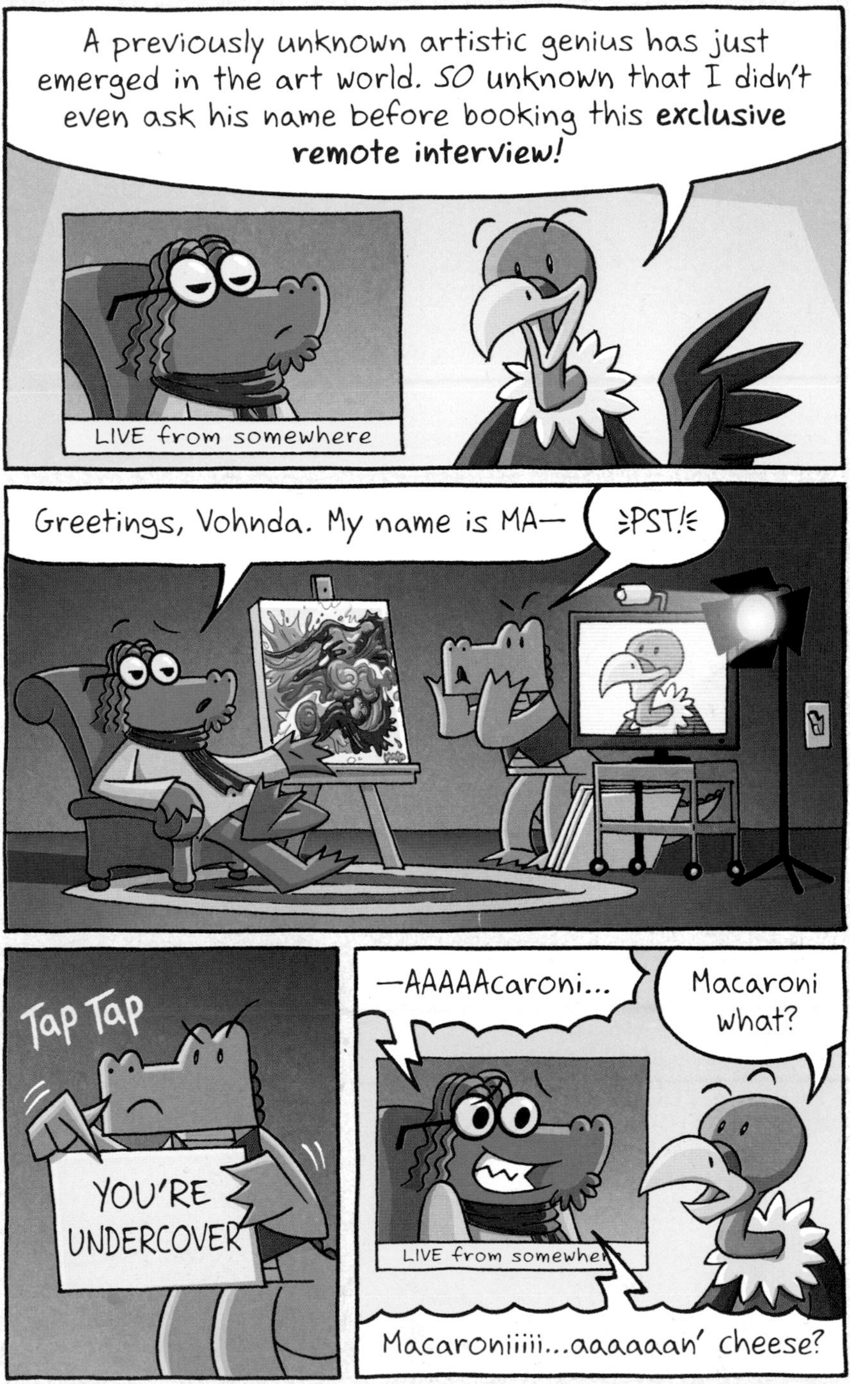
A previously unknown artistic genius has just emerged in the art world. *SO* unknown that I didn't even ask his name before booking this **exclusive remote interview!**
LIVE from somewhere
Greetings, Vohnda. My name is MA—
PST!
Tap Tap
YOU'RE UNDERCOVER
—AAAAAcaroni...
Macaroni what?
Macaroniiiii...aaaaaan' cheese?

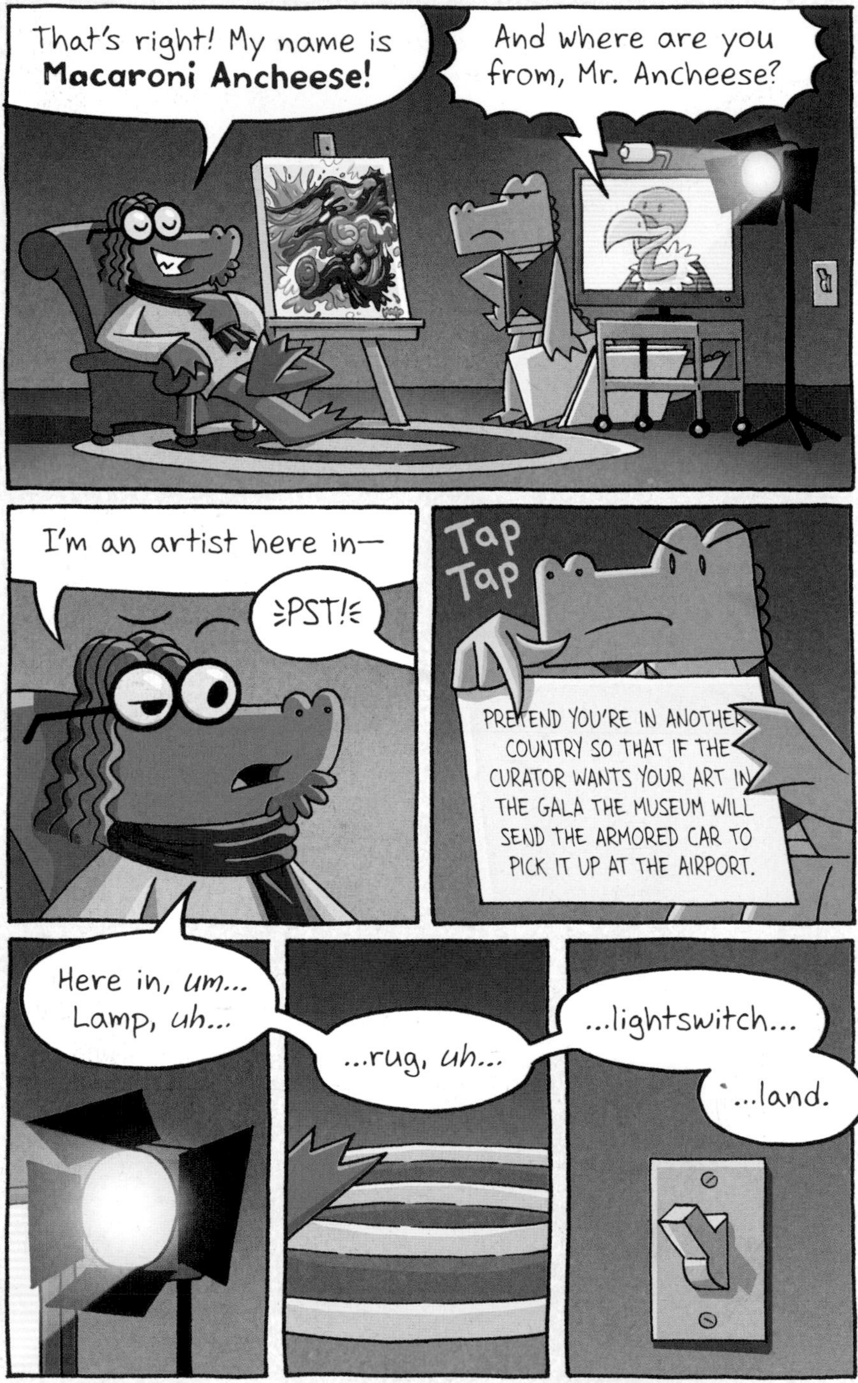
That's right! My name is **Macaroni Ancheese!**
And where are you from, Mr. Ancheese?
I'm an artist here in—
PST!
Tap Tap
PRETEND YOU'RE IN ANOTHER COUNTRY SO THAT IF THE CURATOR WANTS YOUR ART IN THE GALA THE MUSEUM WILL SEND THE ARMORED CAR TO PICK IT UP AT THE AIRPORT.
Here in, *um*... Lamp, *uh*...
...rug, *uh*...
...lightswitch...
...land.

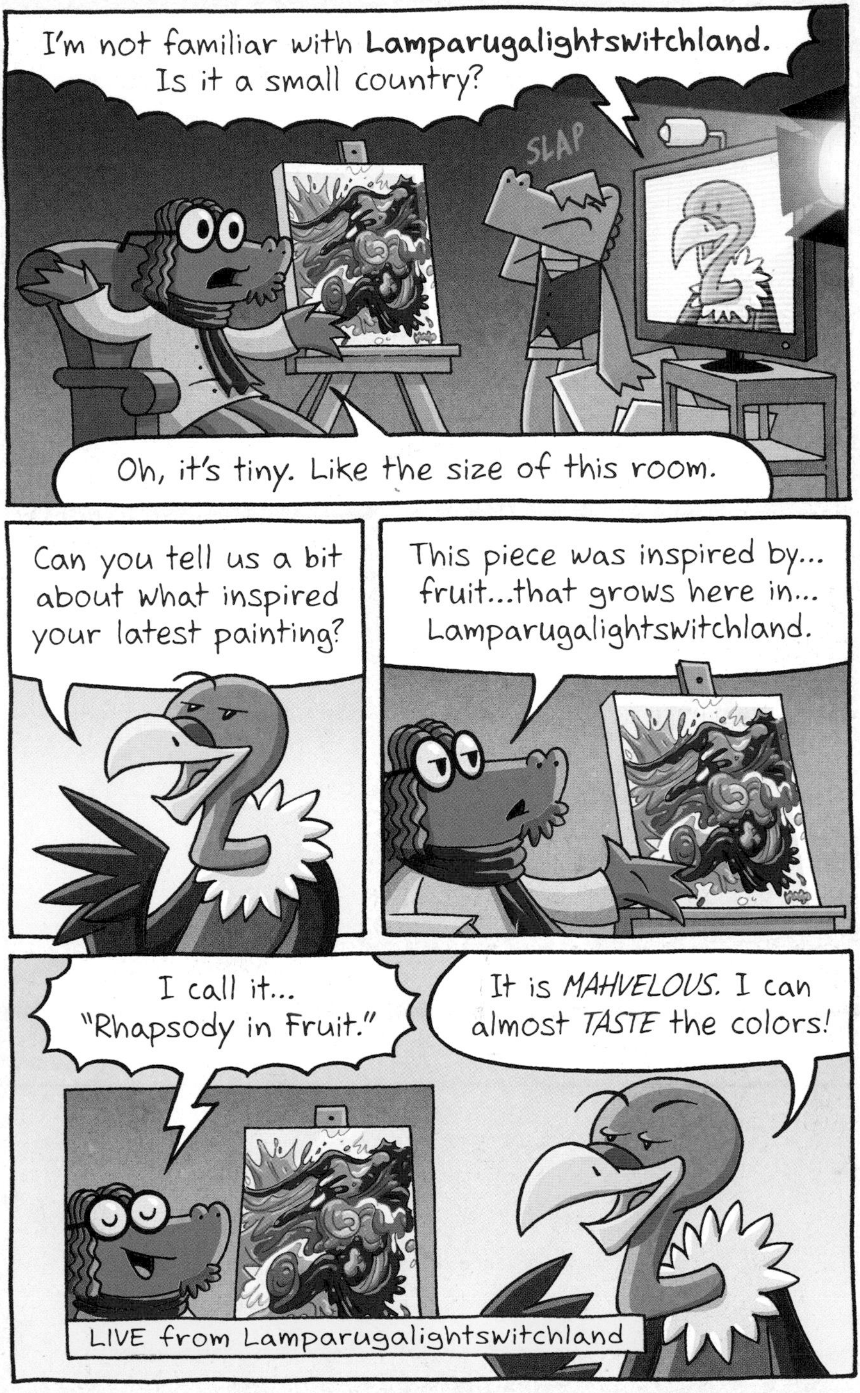
I'm not familiar with **Lamparugalightswitchland.** Is it a small country?
SLAP
Oh, it's tiny. Like the size of this room.
Can you tell us a bit about what inspired your latest painting?
This piece was inspired by... fruit...that grows here in... Lamparugalightswitchland.
I call it... "Rhapsody in Fruit."
It is *MAHVELOUS.* I can almost *TASTE* the colors!
LIVE from Lamparugalightswitchland

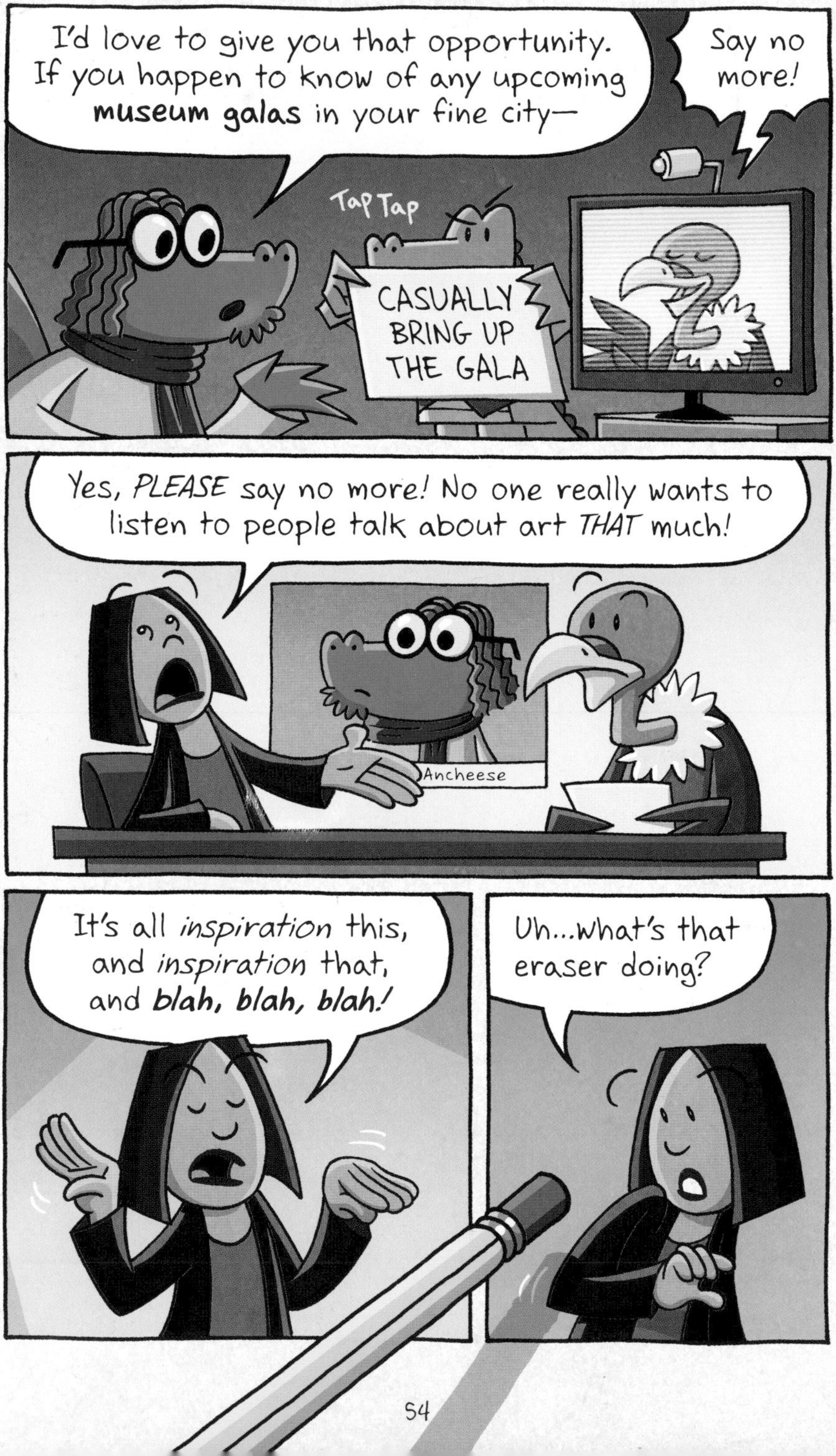
I'd love to give you that opportunity. If you happen to know of any upcoming **museum galas** in your fine city—
Say no more!
Tap Tap
CASUALLY BRING UP THE GALA
Yes, *PLEASE* say no more! No one really wants to listen to people talk about art *THAT* much!
Ancheese
It's all *inspiration* this, and *inspiration* that, and **blah, blah, blah!**
Uh...what's that eraser doing?

Chapter 6

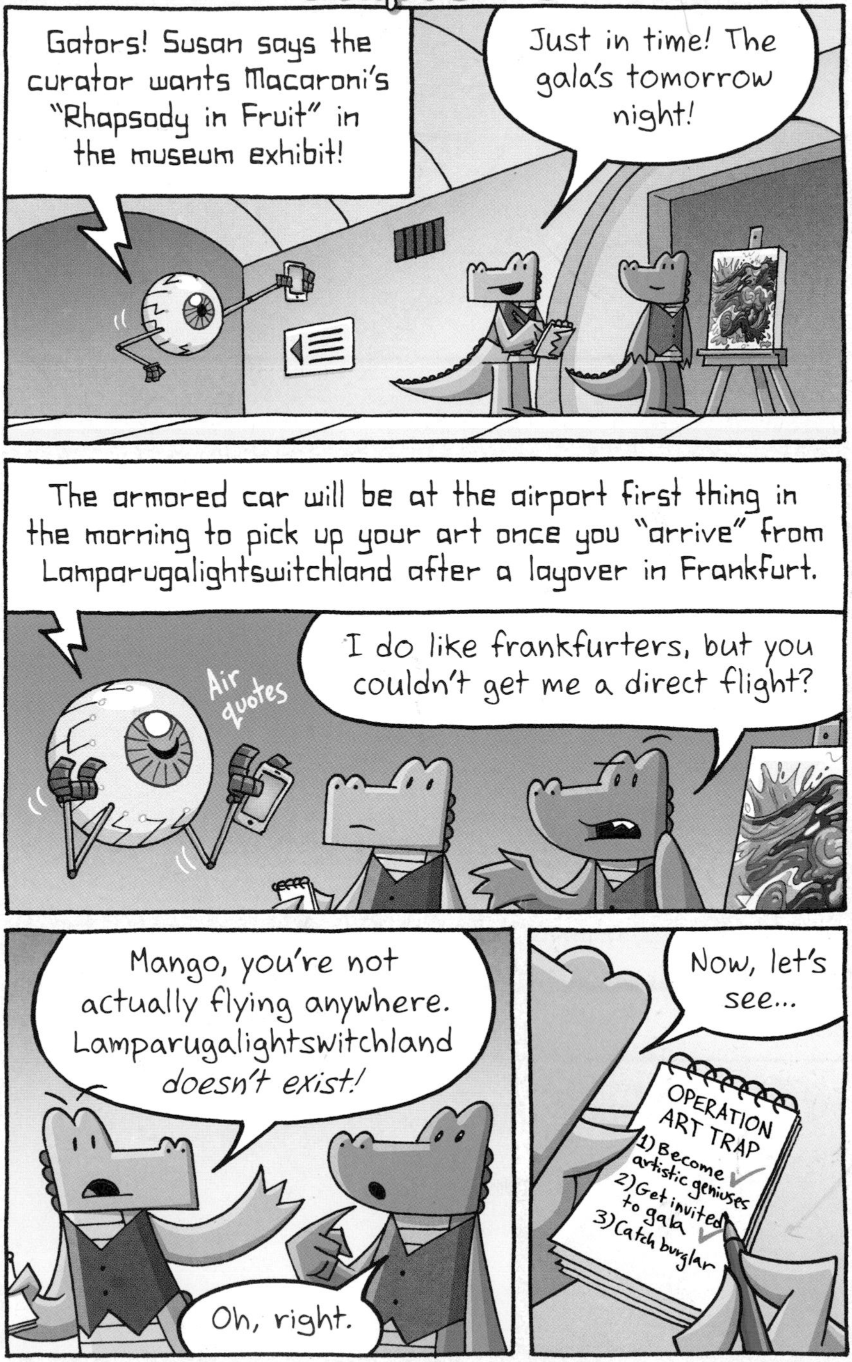
Gators! Susan says the curator wants Macaroni's "Rhapsody in Fruit" in the museum exhibit!
Just in time! The gala's tomorrow night!
The armored car will be at the airport first thing in the morning to pick up your art once you "arrive" from Lamparugalightswitchland after a layover in Frankfurt.
Air quotes
I do like frankfurters, but you couldn't get me a direct flight?
Mango, you're not actually flying anywhere. Lamparugalightswitchland *doesn't exist!*
Oh, right.
Now, let's see...
OPERATION ART TRAP
1) Become artistic geniuses
2) Get invited to gala
3) Catch burglar

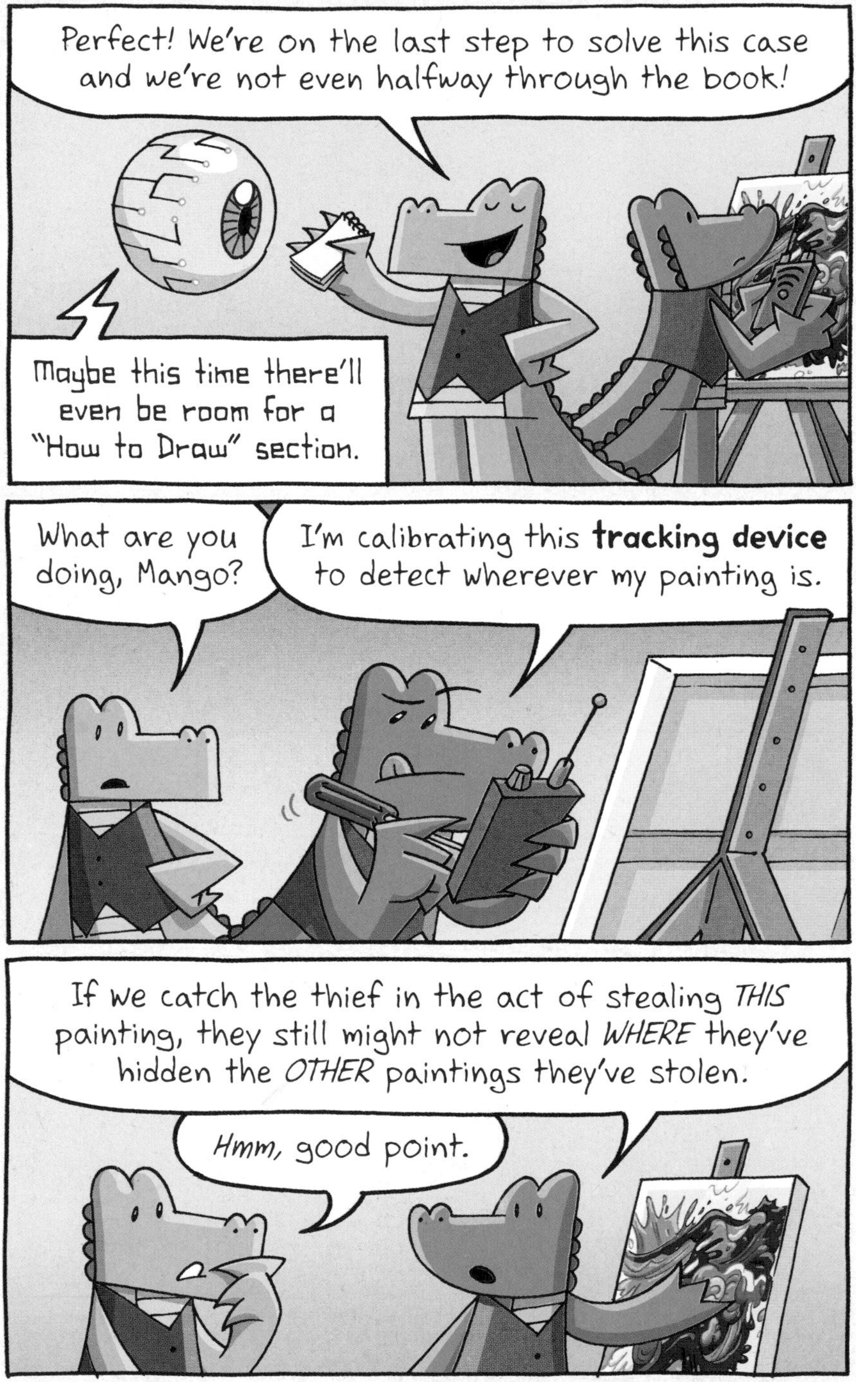
Perfect! We're on the last step to solve this case and we're not even halfway through the book!
Maybe this time there'll even be room for a "How to Draw" section.
What are you doing, Mango?
I'm calibrating this **tracking device** to detect wherever my painting is.
If we catch the thief in the act of stealing *THIS* painting, they still might not reveal *WHERE* they've hidden the *OTHER* paintings they've stolen.
Hmm, good point.

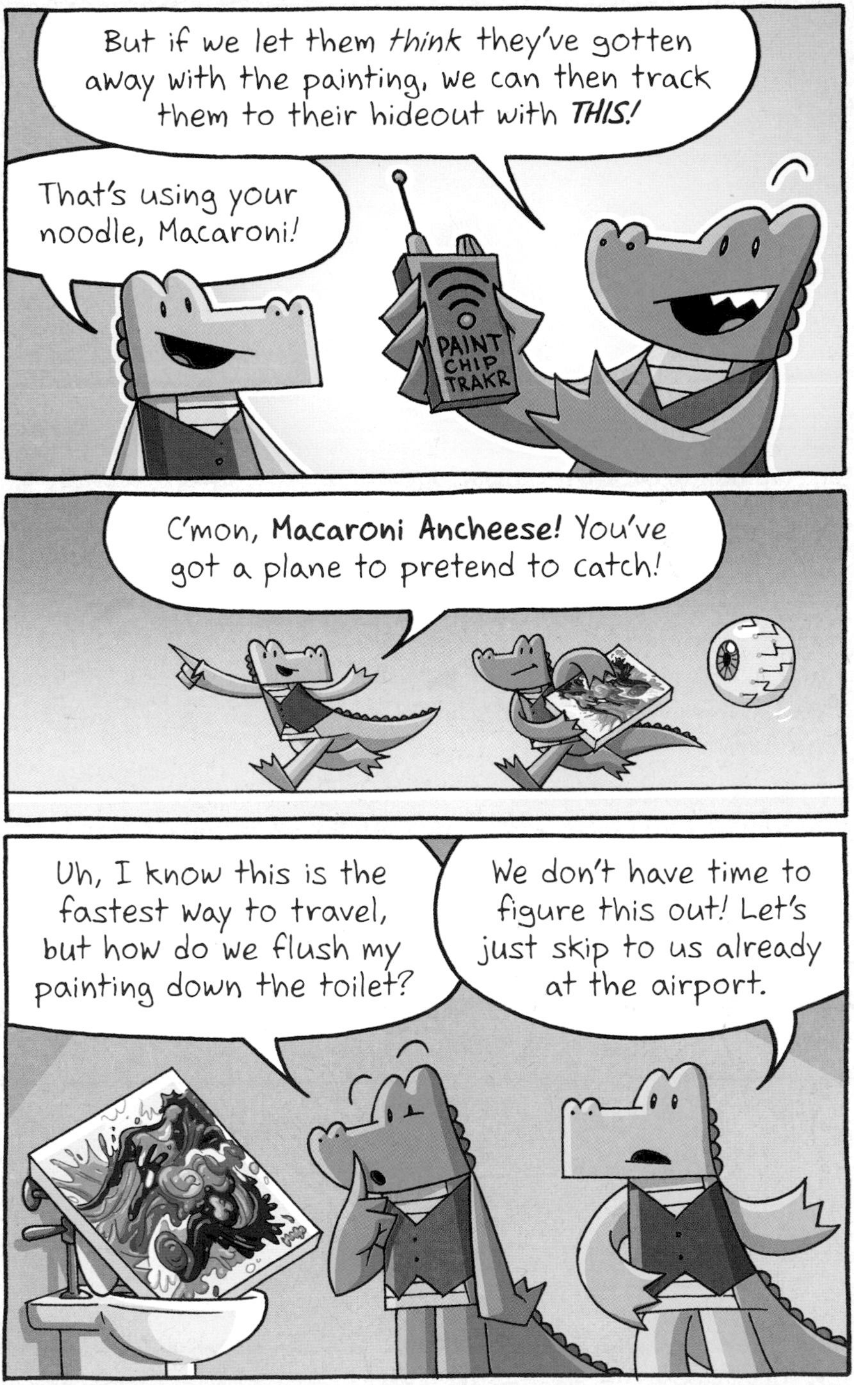
But if we let them *think* they've gotten away with the painting, we can then track them to their hideout with ***THIS!***
That's using your noodle, Macaroni!
PAINT CHIP TRAKR
C'mon, **Macaroni Ancheese!** You've got a plane to pretend to catch!
Uh, I know this is the fastest way to travel, but how do we flush my painting down the toilet?
We don't have time to figure this out! Let's just skip to us already at the airport.

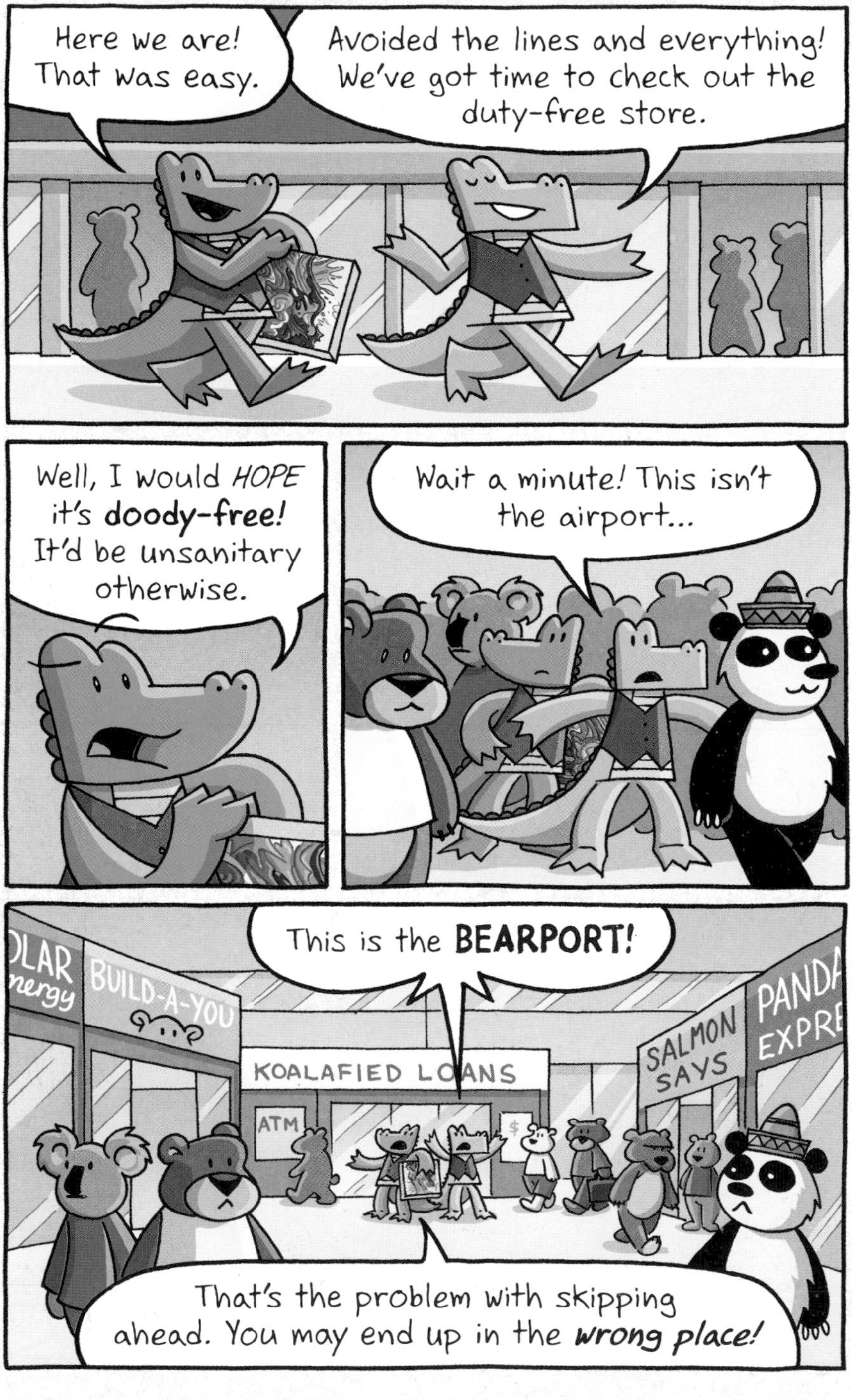
Here we are! That was easy.
Avoided the lines and everything! We've got time to check out the duty-free store.
Well, I would *HOPE* it's **doody-free!** It'd be unsanitary otherwise.
Wait a minute! This isn't the airport...
This is the **BEARPORT!**
BUILD-A-YOU
KOALAFIED LOANS
ATM
SALMON SAYS
That's the problem with skipping ahead. You may end up in the ***wrong place!***

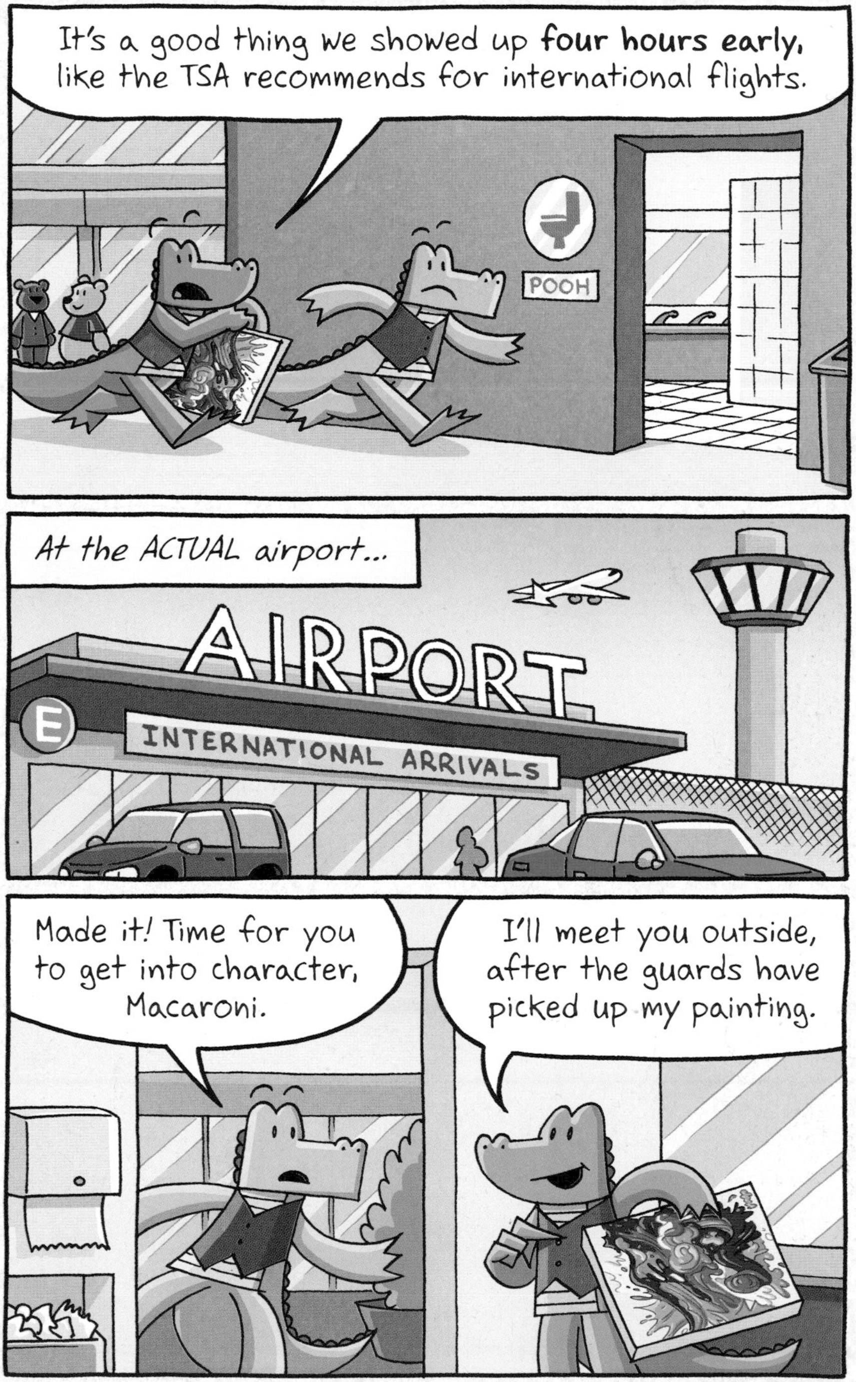
It's a good thing we showed up **four hours early,** like the TSA recommends for international flights.
POOH
At the ACTUAL airport...
AIRPORT
E
INTERNATIONAL ARRIVALS
Made it! Time for you to get into character, Macaroni.
I'll meet you outside, after the guards have picked up my painting.

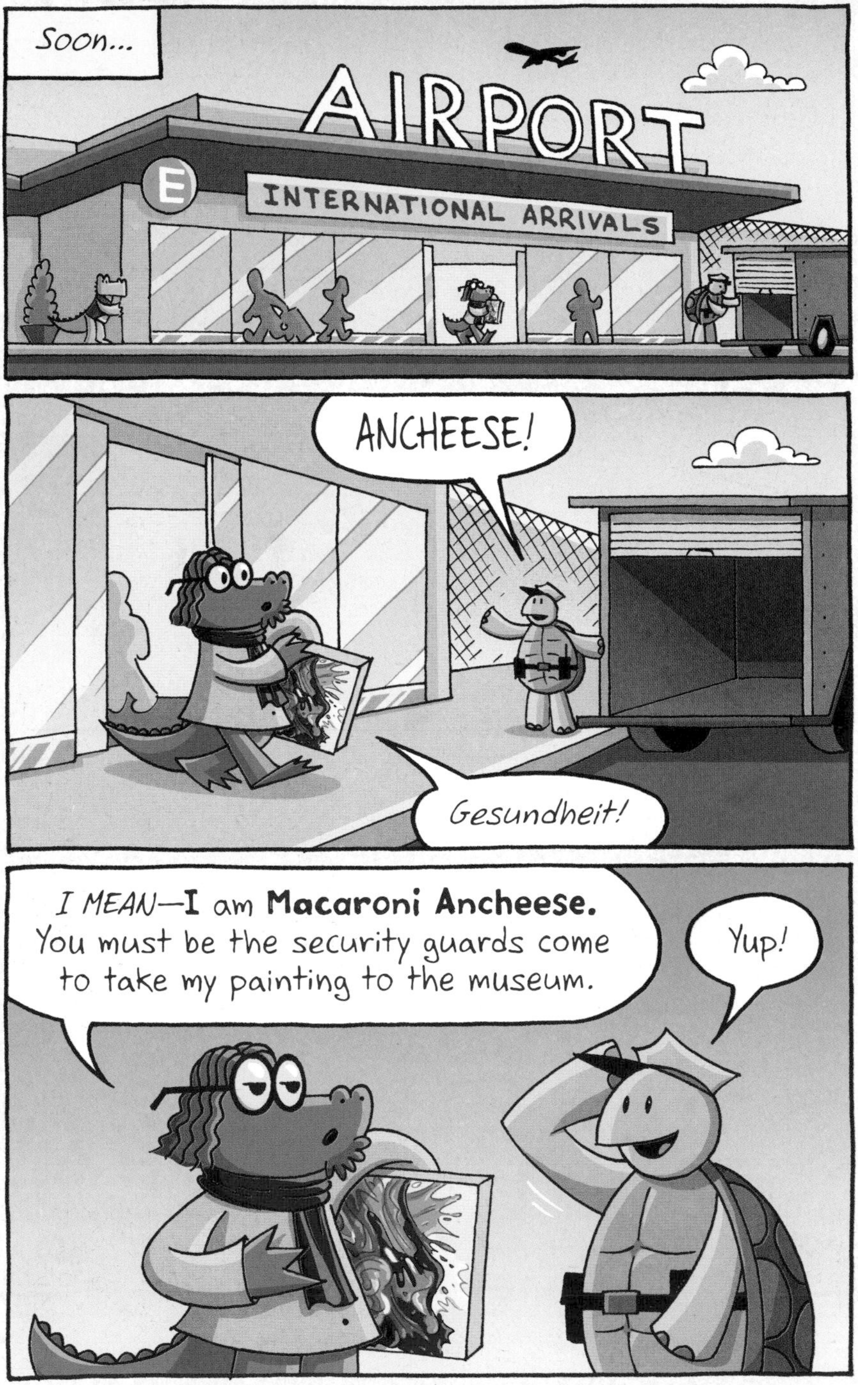
Soon...
AIRPORT
E
INTERNATIONAL ARRIVALS
ANCHEESE!
Gesundheit!
I MEAN—I am Macaroni Ancheese. You must be the security guards come to take my painting to the museum.
Yup!

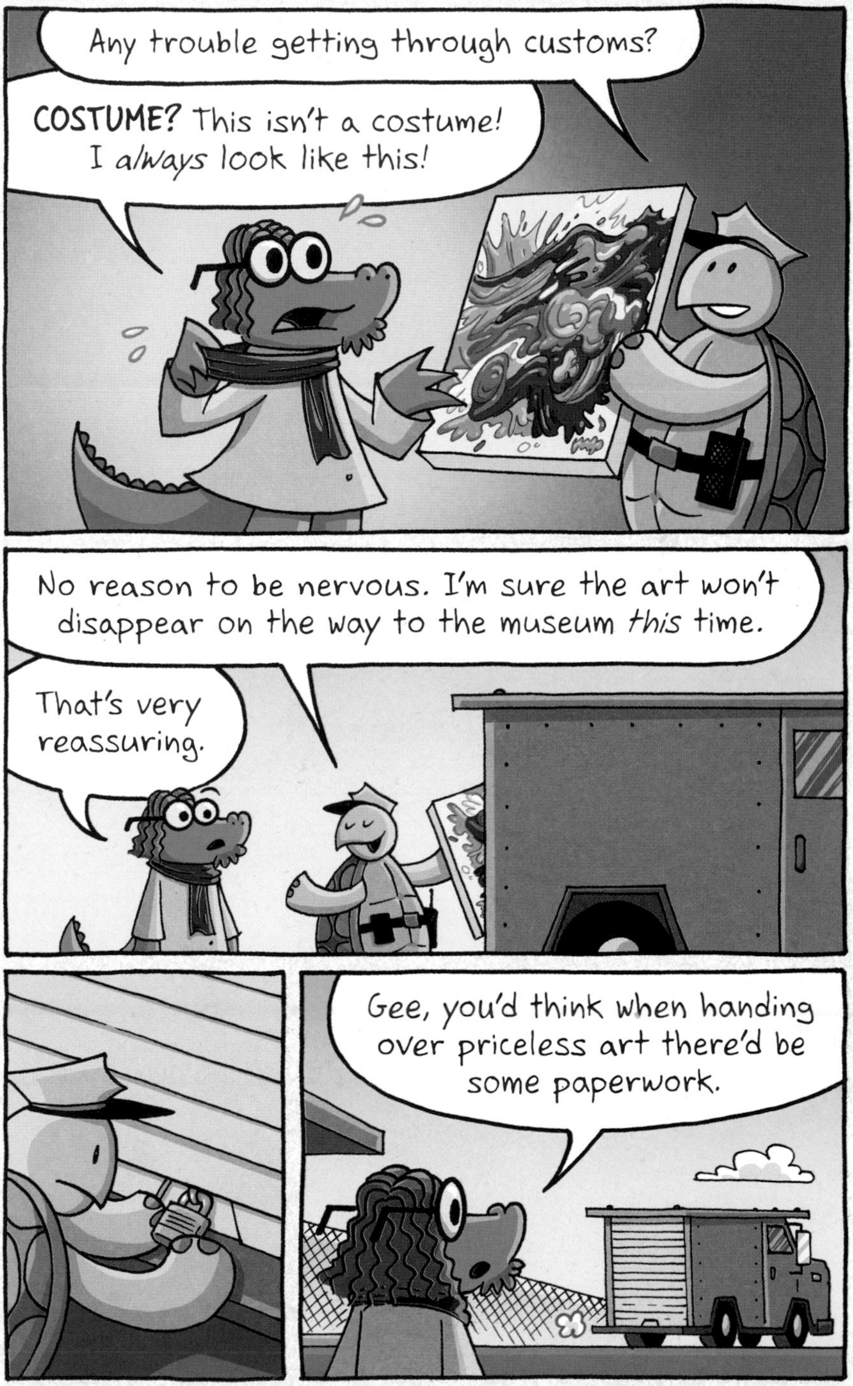
Any trouble getting through customs?
COSTUME? This isn't a costume! I *always* look like this!
No reason to be nervous. I'm sure the art won't disappear on the way to the museum *this* time.
That's very reassuring.
Gee, you'd think when handing over priceless art there'd be some paperwork.

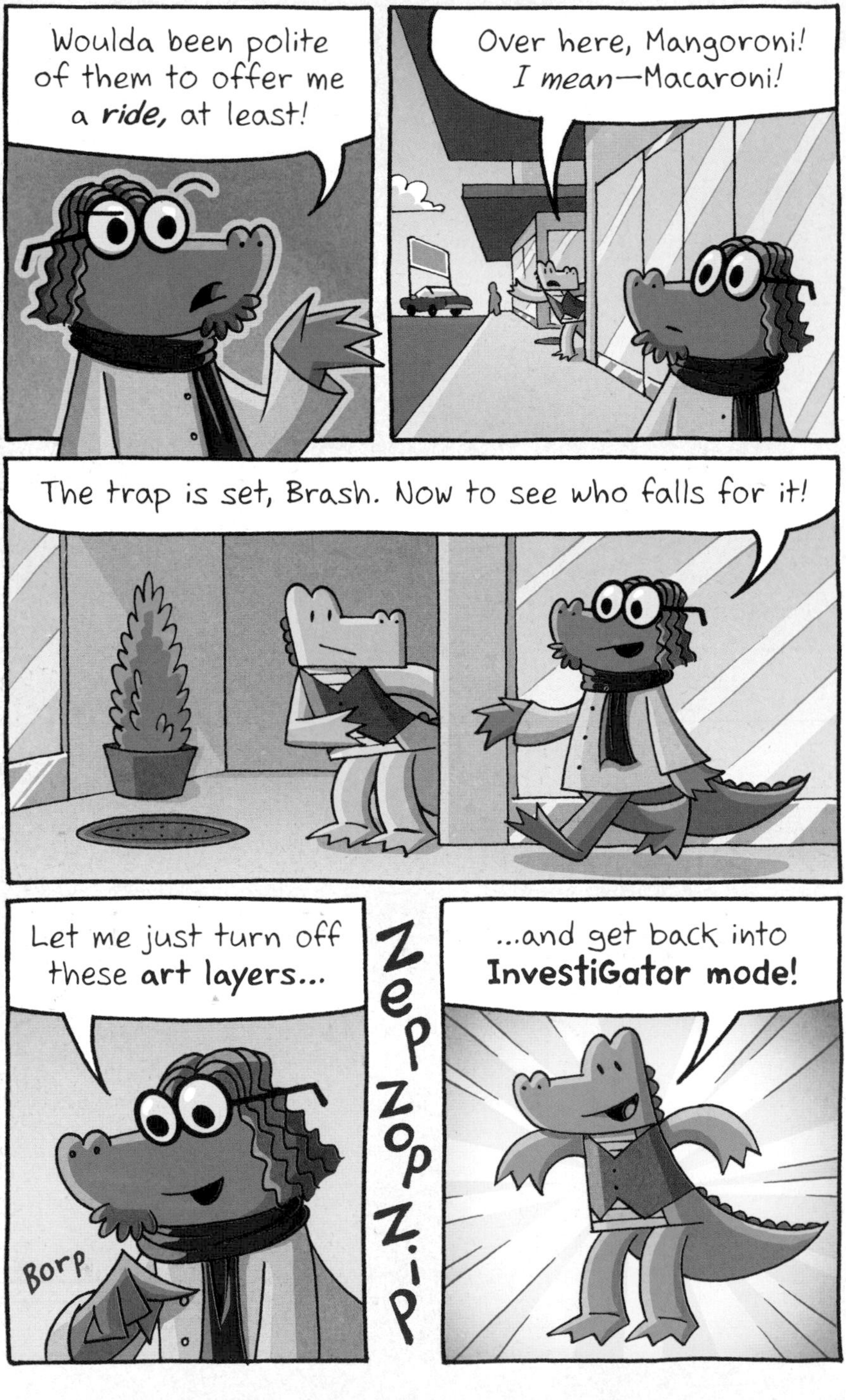
Woulda been polite of them to offer me a *ride,* at least!
Over here, Mangoroni! *I mean*—Macaroni!
The trap is set, Brash. Now to see who falls for it!
Let me just turn off these **art layers...**
Borp
Zep Zop Zip
...and get back into **InvestiGator mode!**

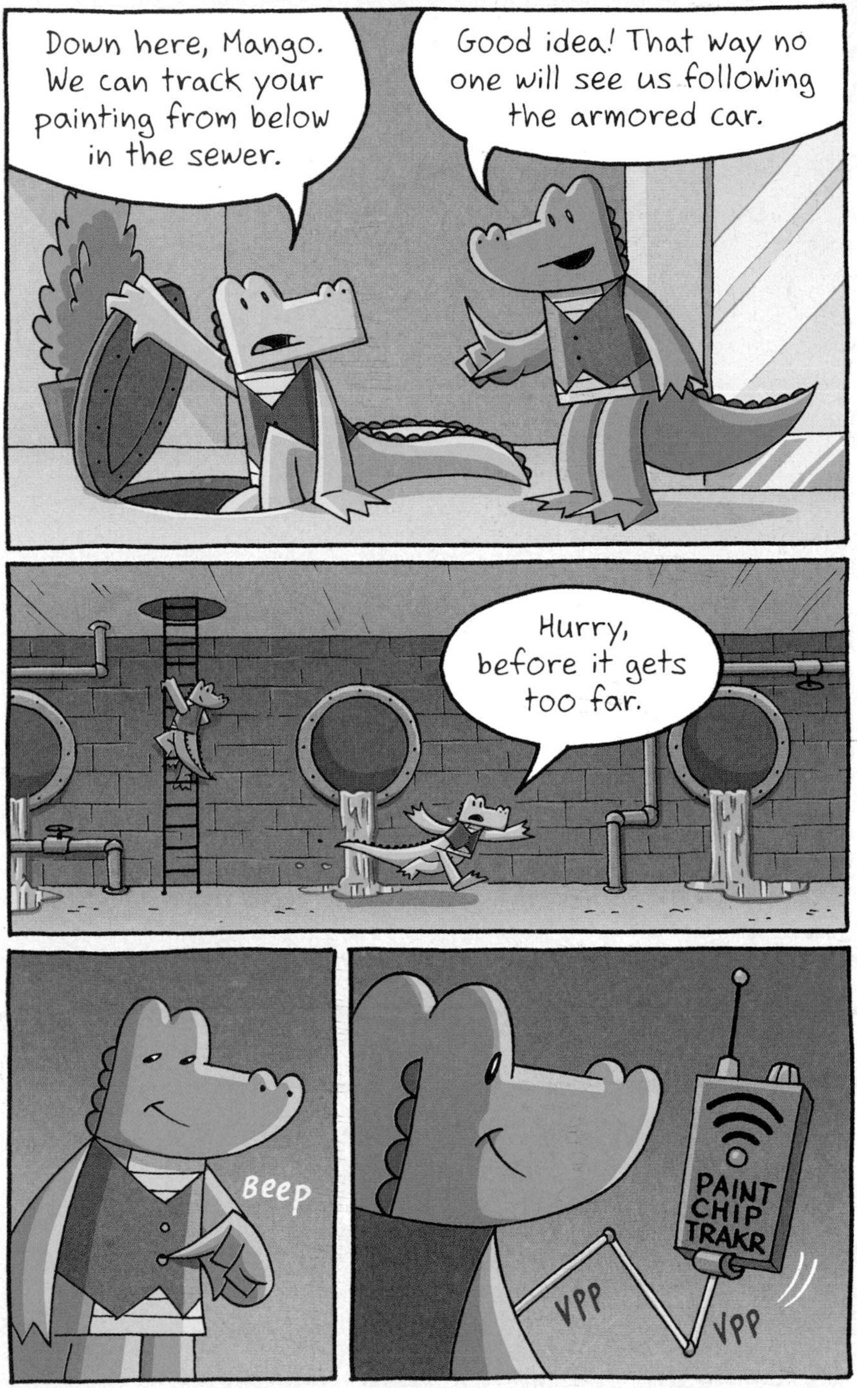

Down here, Mango. We can track your painting from below in the sewer.
Good idea! That way no one will see us following the armored car.
Hurry, before it gets too far.
Beep
PAINT CHIP TRAKR
VPP
VPP

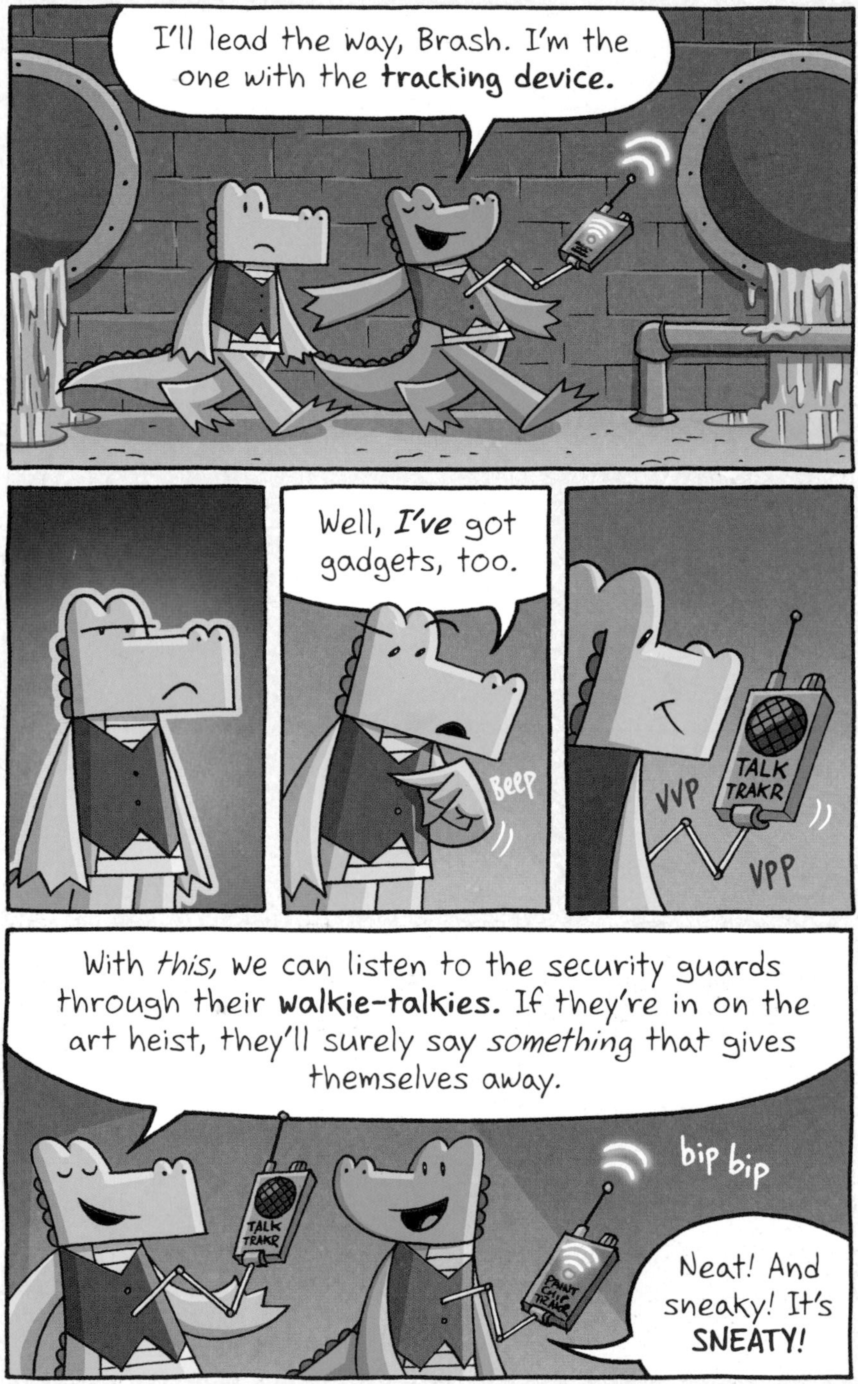

I'll lead the way, Brash. I'm the one with the **tracking device.**
Well, ***I've*** got gadgets, too.
Beep
TALK TRAKR
VVP
VPP
With *this,* we can listen to the security guards through their **walkie-talkies.** If they're in on the art heist, they'll surely say *something* that gives themselves away.
TALK TRAKR
bip bip
Neat! And sneaky! It's **SNEATY!**

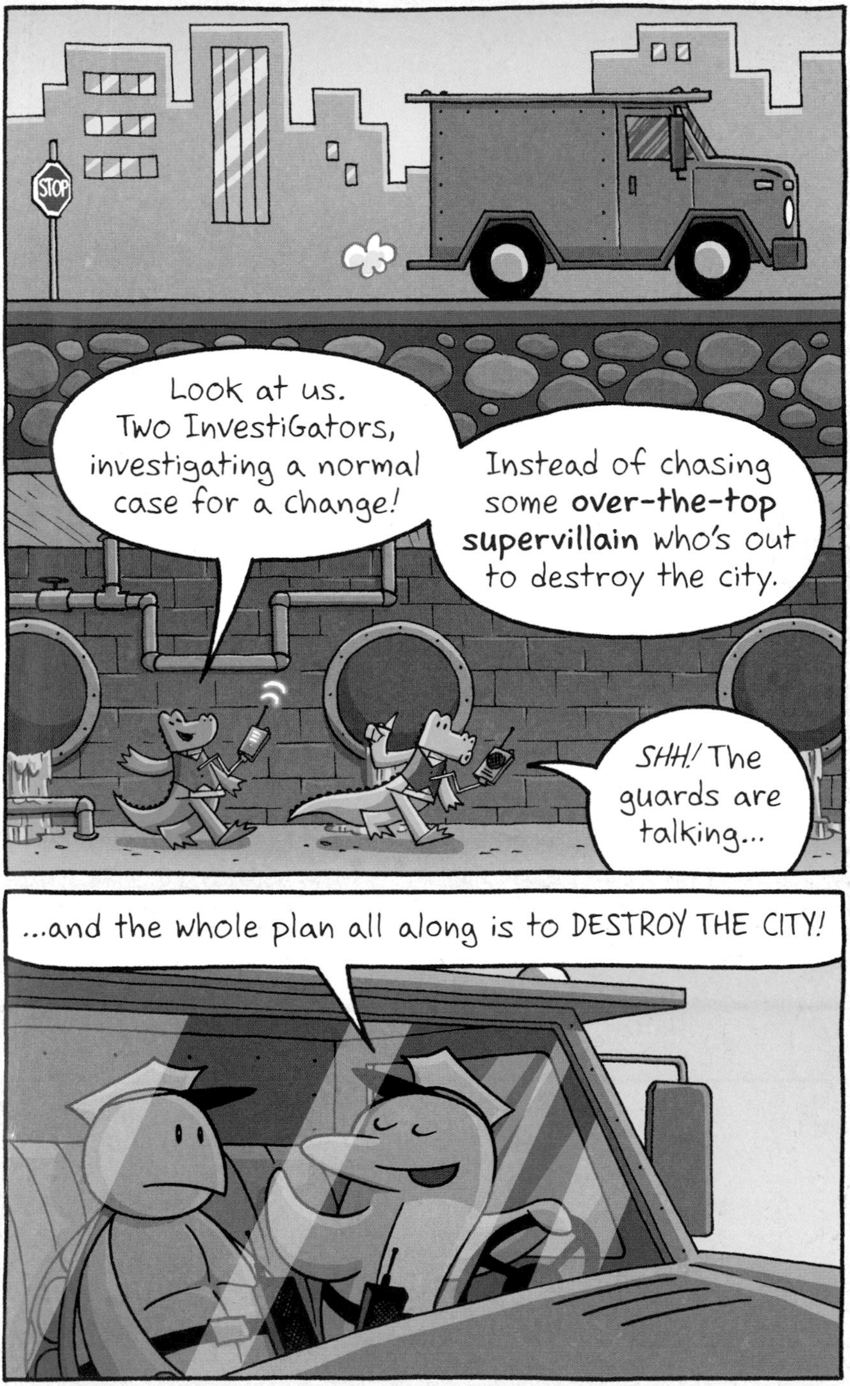
STOP
Look at us. Two InvestiGators, investigating a normal case for a change!
Instead of chasing some **over-the-top supervillain** who's out to destroy the city.
SHH! The guards are talking...
...and the whole plan all along is to DESTROY THE CITY!

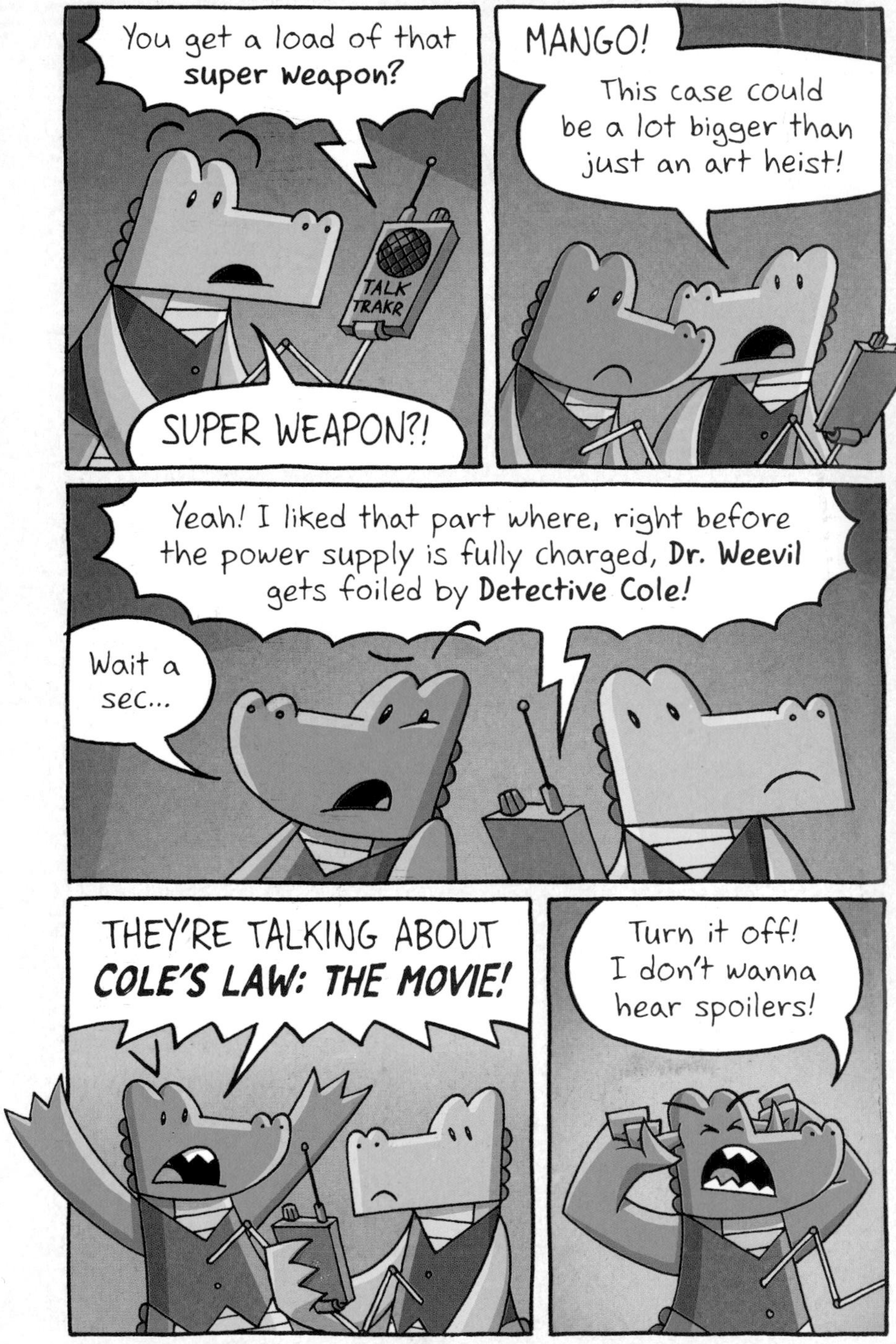
You get a load of that **super weapon?**
TALK TRAKR
SUPER WEAPON?!
MANGO!
This case could be a lot bigger than just an art heist!
Yeah! I liked that part where, right before the power supply is fully charged, **Dr. Weevil** gets foiled by **Detective Cole!**
Wait a sec...
THEY'RE TALKING ABOUT **COLE'S LAW: THE MOVIE!**
Turn it off! I don't wanna hear spoilers!

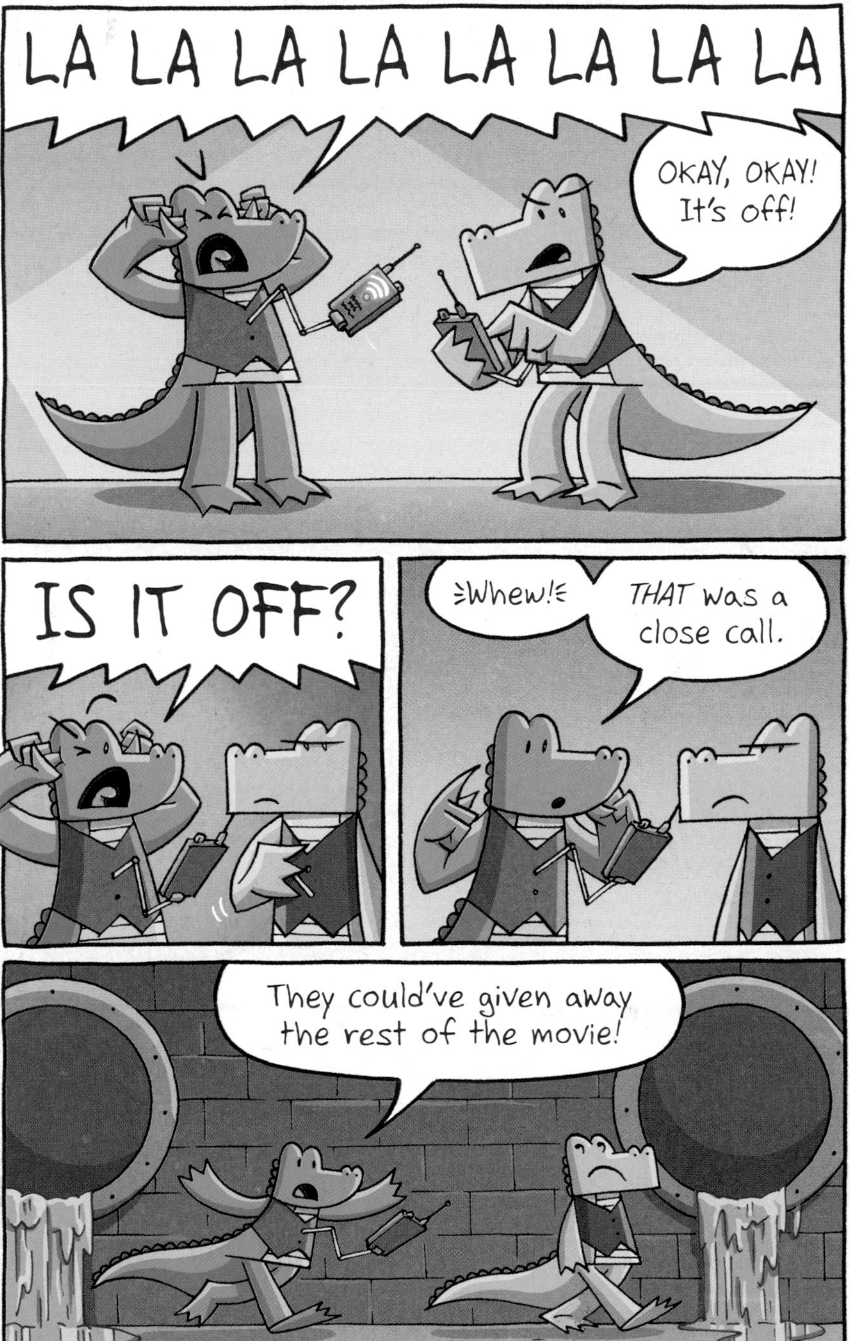
LA LA LA LA LA LA LA LA
OKAY, OKAY! It's off!
IS IT OFF?
Whew!
THAT was a close call.
They could've given away the rest of the movie!

Chapter 7

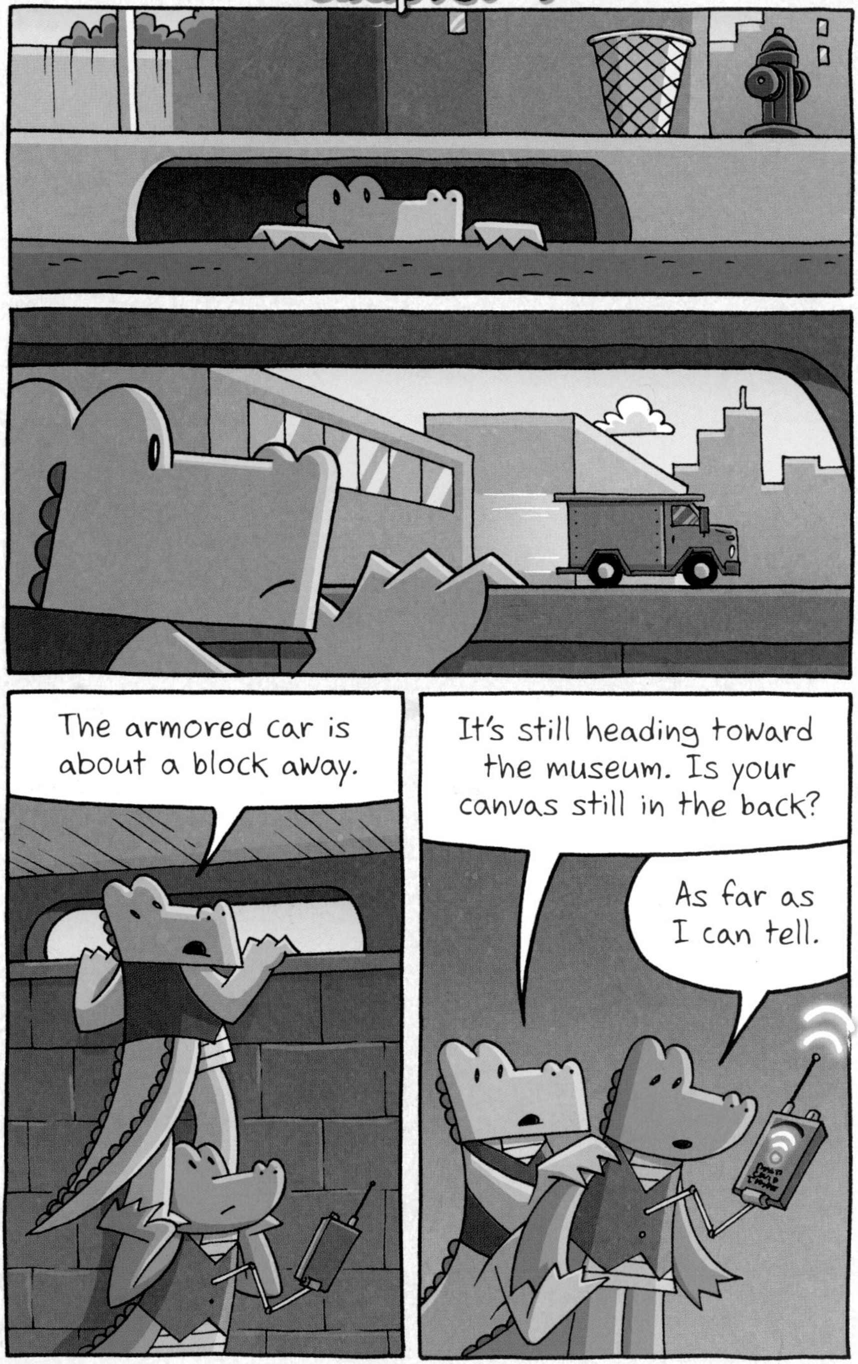
The armored car is about a block away.
It's still heading toward the museum. Is your canvas still in the back?
As far as I can tell.

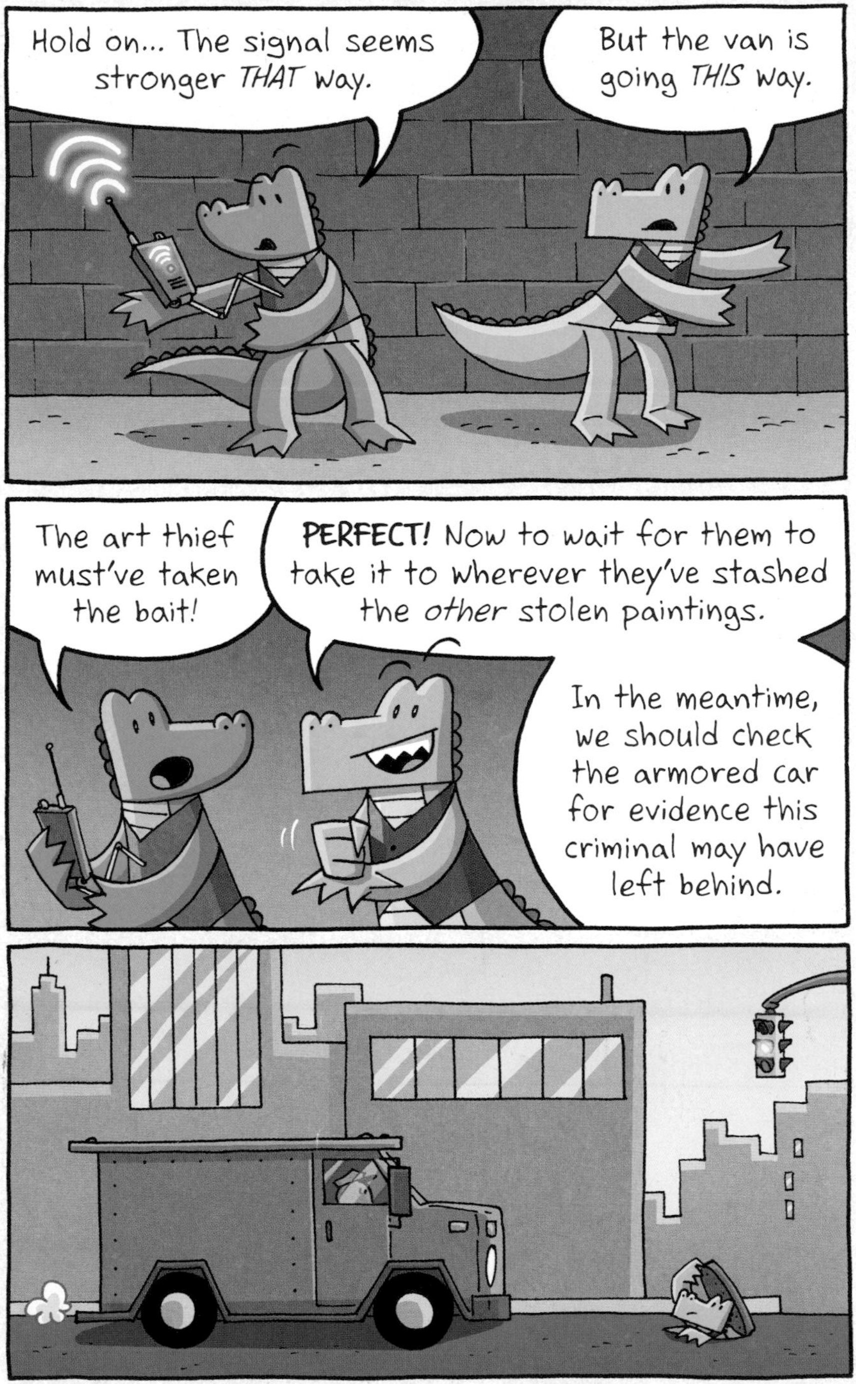
Hold on... The signal seems stronger *THAT* way.
But the van is going *THIS* way.
The art thief must've taken the bait!
PERFECT! Now to wait for them to take it to wherever they've stashed the *other* stolen paintings.
In the meantime, we should check the armored car for evidence this criminal may have left behind.

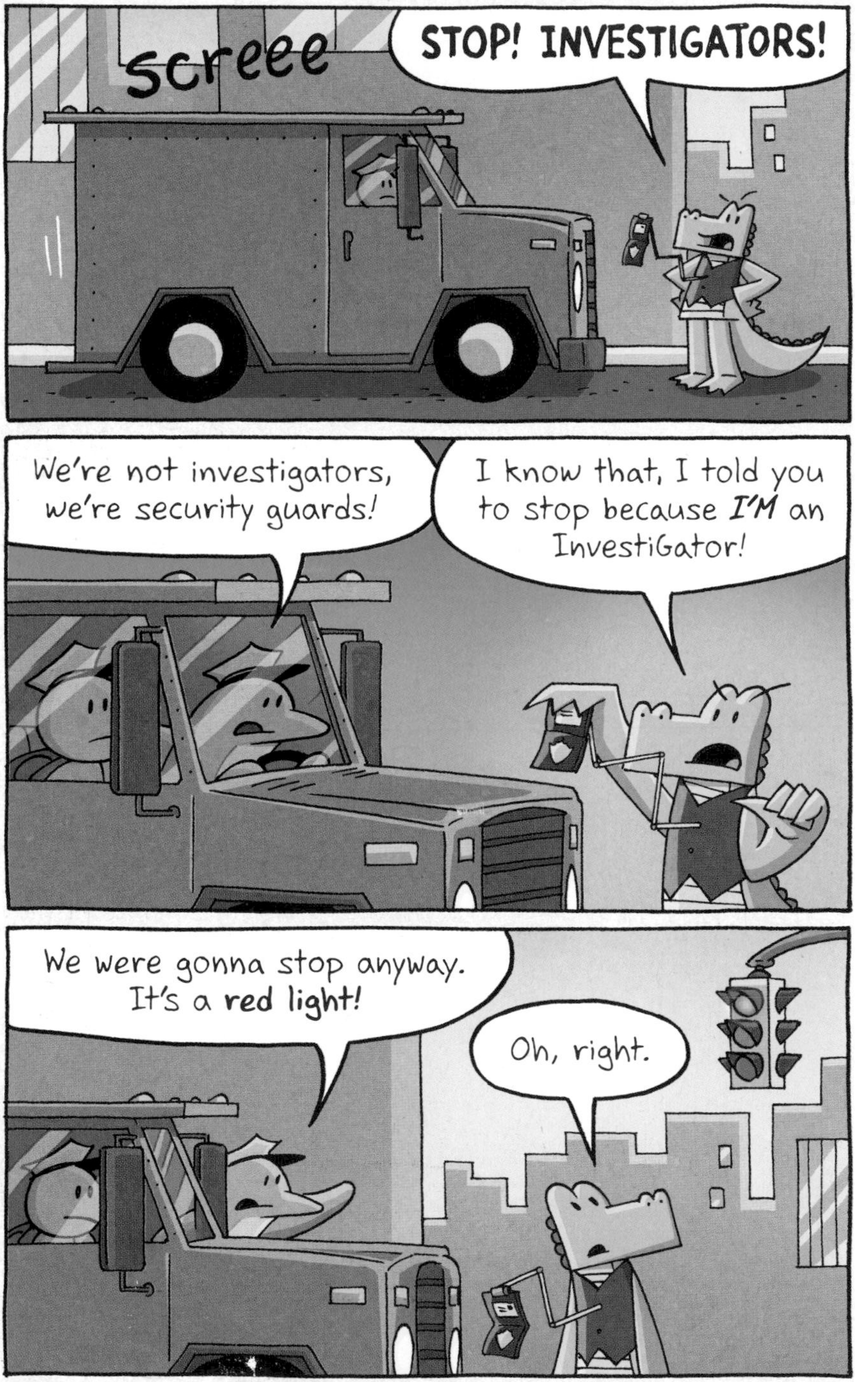
Screee
STOP! INVESTIGATORS!
We're not investigators, we're security guards!
I know that, I told you to stop because *I'M* an InvestiGator!
We were gonna stop anyway. It's a **red light!**
Oh, right.

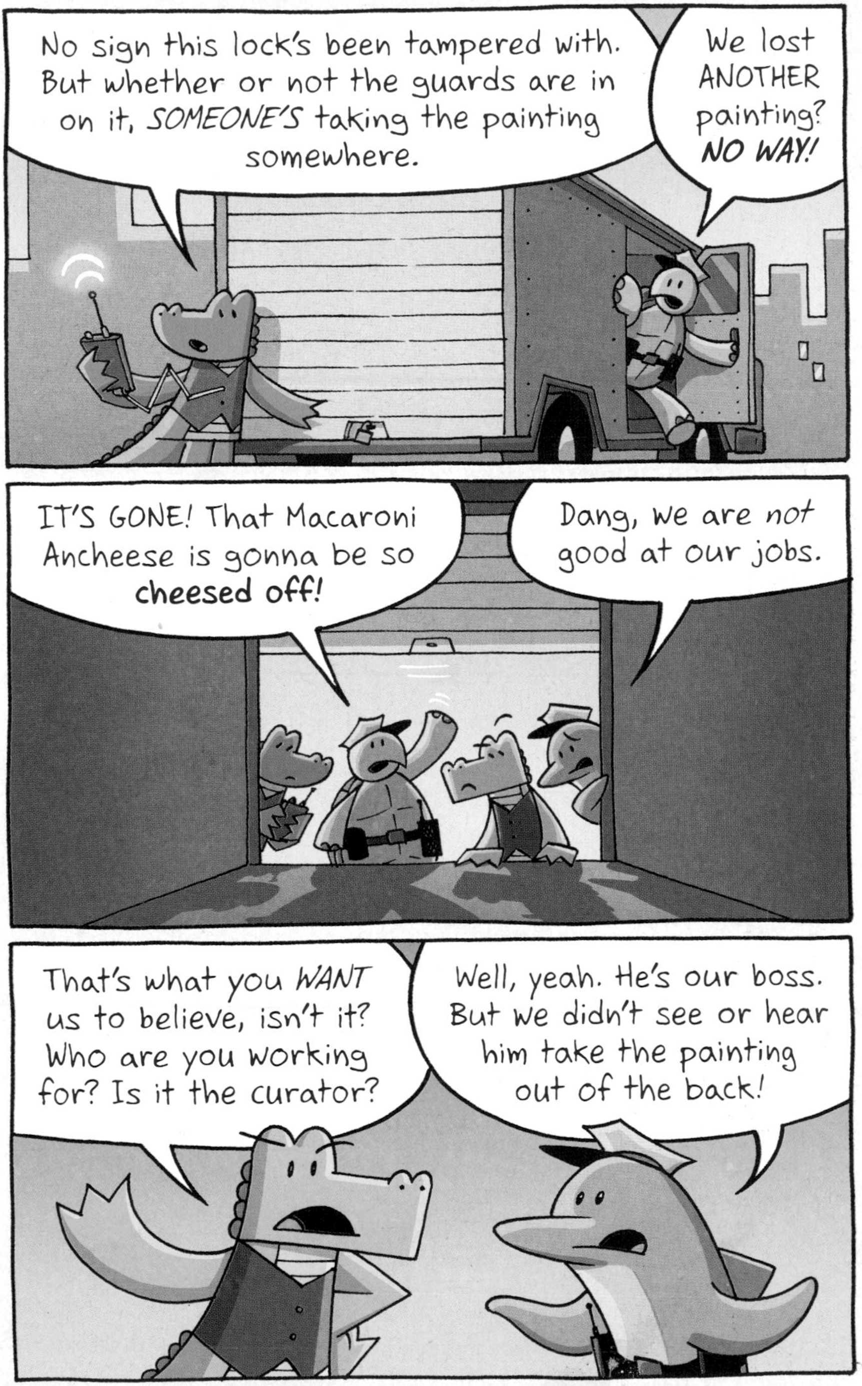
No sign this lock's been tampered with. But whether or not the guards are in on it, *SOMEONE'S* taking the painting somewhere.
We lost ANOTHER painting? ***NO WAY!***
IT'S GONE! That Macaroni Ancheese is gonna be so **cheesed off!**
Dang, we are *not* good at our jobs.
That's what you *WANT* us to believe, isn't it? Who are you working for? Is it the curator?
Well, yeah. He's our boss. But we didn't see or hear him take the painting out of the back!

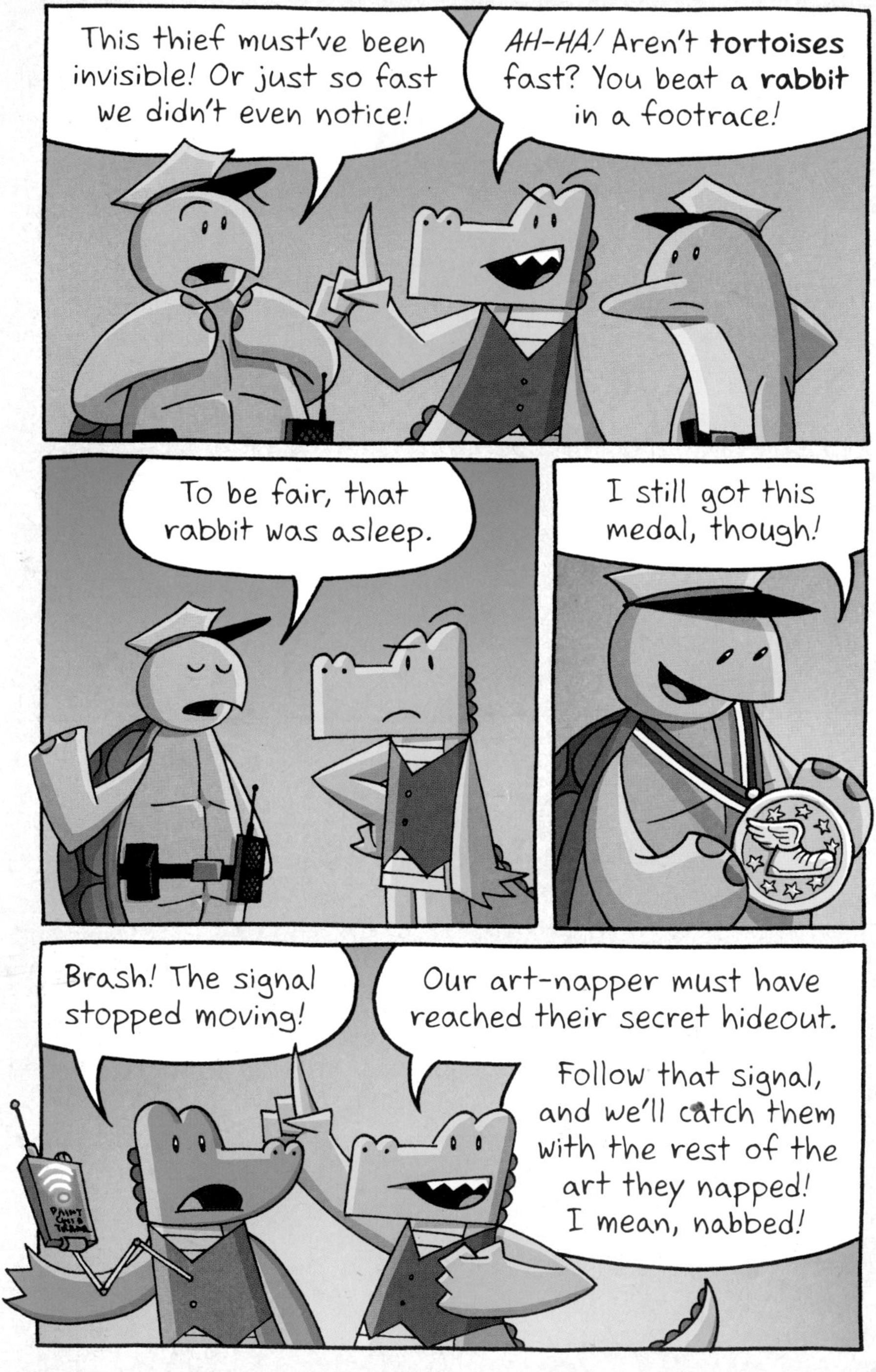
This thief must've been invisible! Or just so fast we didn't even notice!
AH-HA! Aren't **tortoises** fast? You beat a **rabbit** in a footrace!
To be fair, that rabbit was asleep.
I still got this medal, though!
Brash! The signal stopped moving!
Our art-napper must have reached their secret hideout.
Follow that signal, and we'll catch them with the rest of the art they napped! I mean, nabbed!

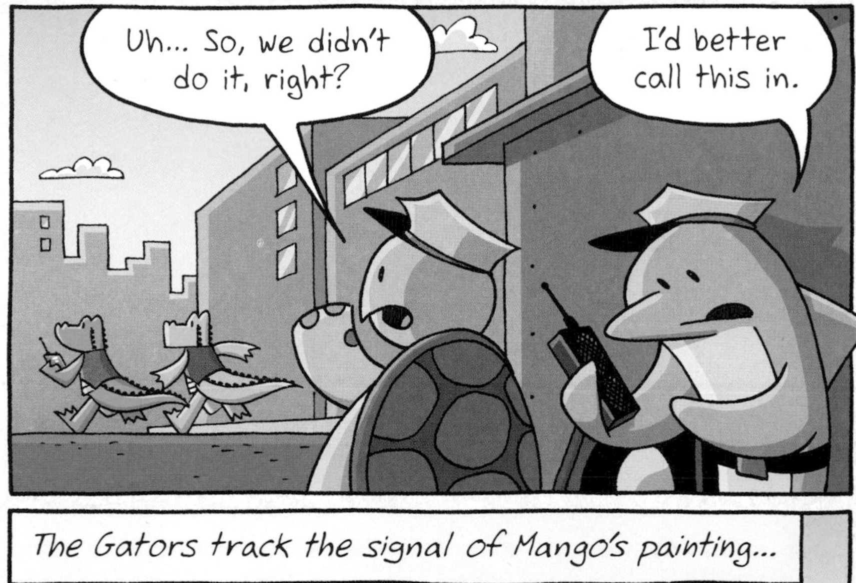
Uh... So, we didn't do it, right?
I'd better call this in.

The Gators track the signal of Mango's painting...

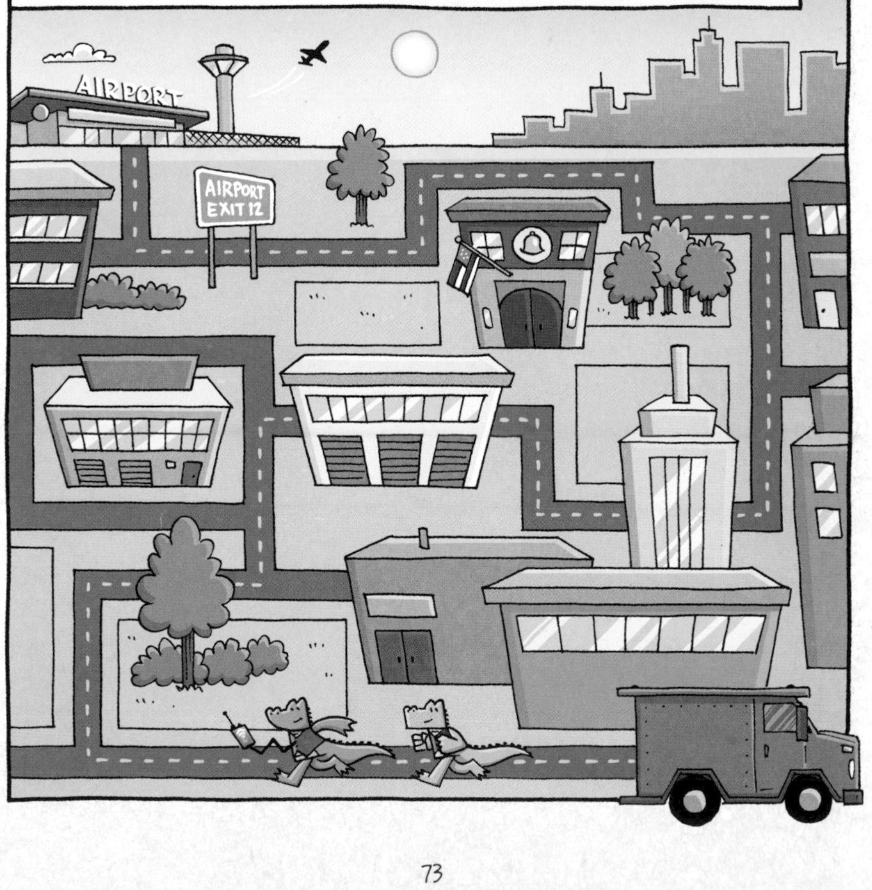
AIRPORT
AIRPORT EXIT 12

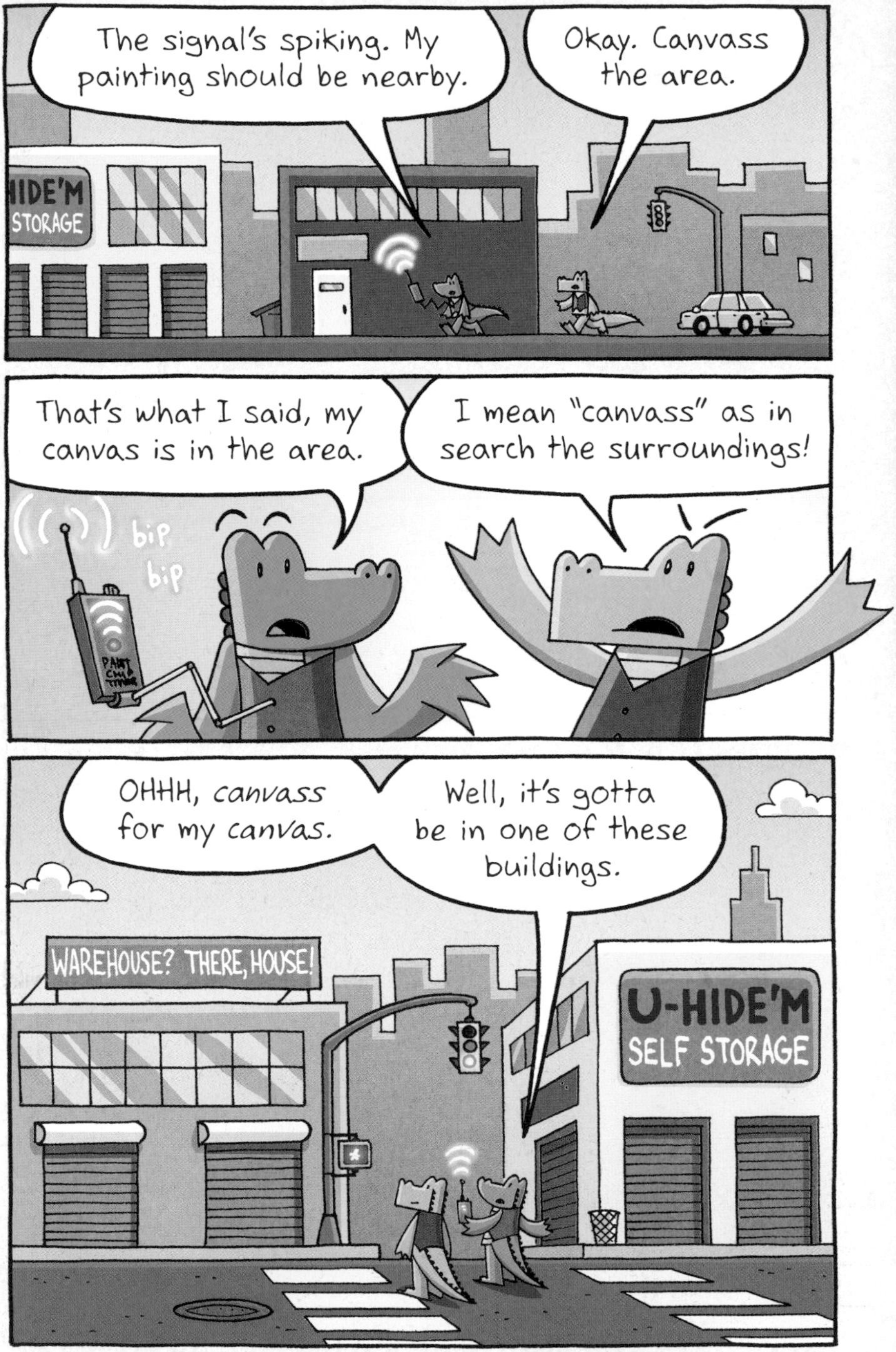

The signal's spiking. My painting should be nearby.
Okay. Canvass the area.
HIDE'M STORAGE
That's what I said, my canvas is in the area.
I mean "canvass" as in search the surroundings!
bip bip
OHHH, *canvass* for my canvas.
Well, it's gotta be in one of these buildings.
WAREHOUSE? THERE, HOUSE!
U-HIDE'M SELF STORAGE

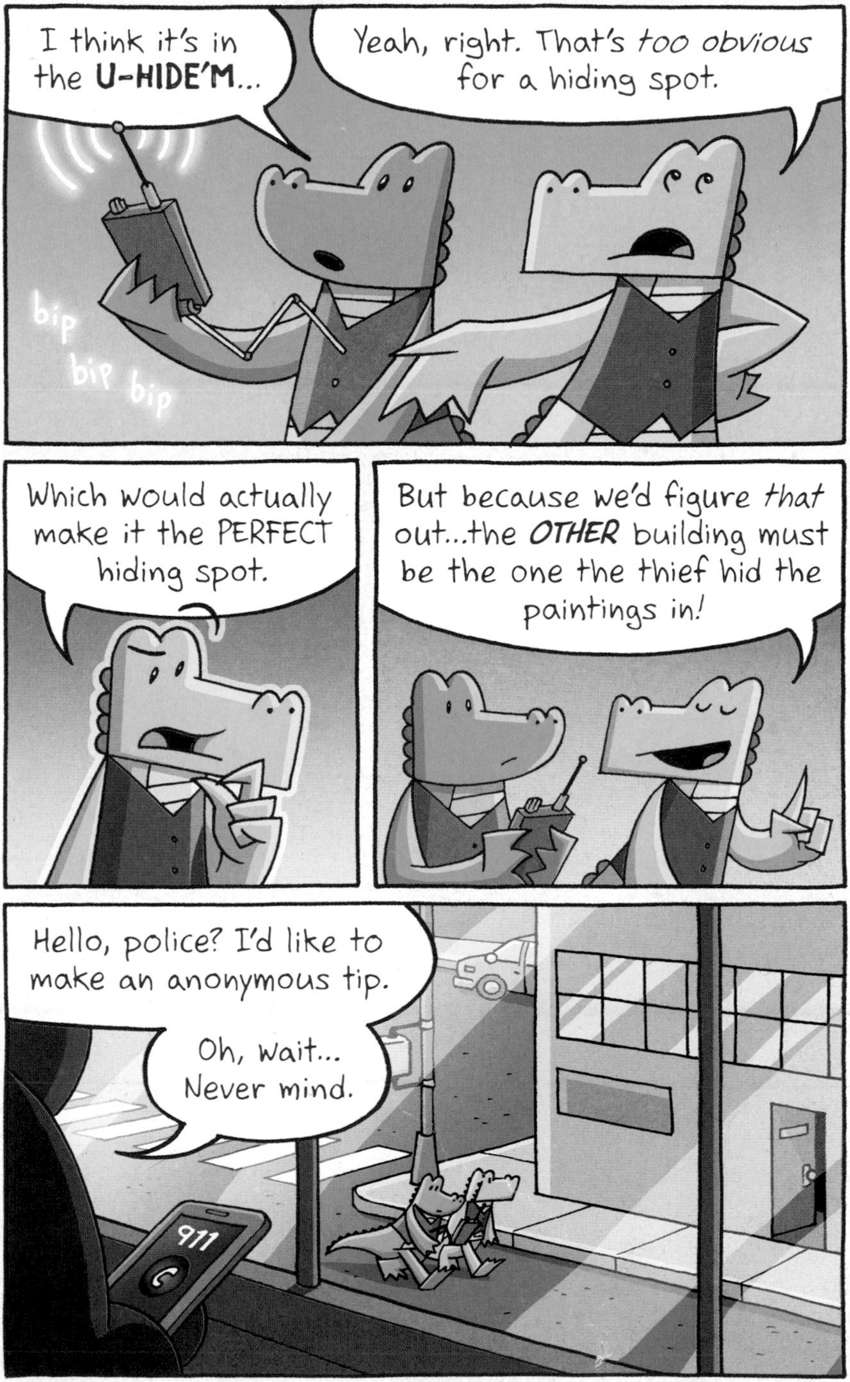
I think it's in the **U-HIDE'M**...
Yeah, right. That's *too obvious* for a hiding spot.
bip bip bip
Which would actually make it the PERFECT hiding spot.
But because we'd figure *that* out...the ***OTHER*** building must be the one the thief hid the paintings in!
Hello, police? I'd like to make an anonymous tip.
Oh, wait... Never mind.
911

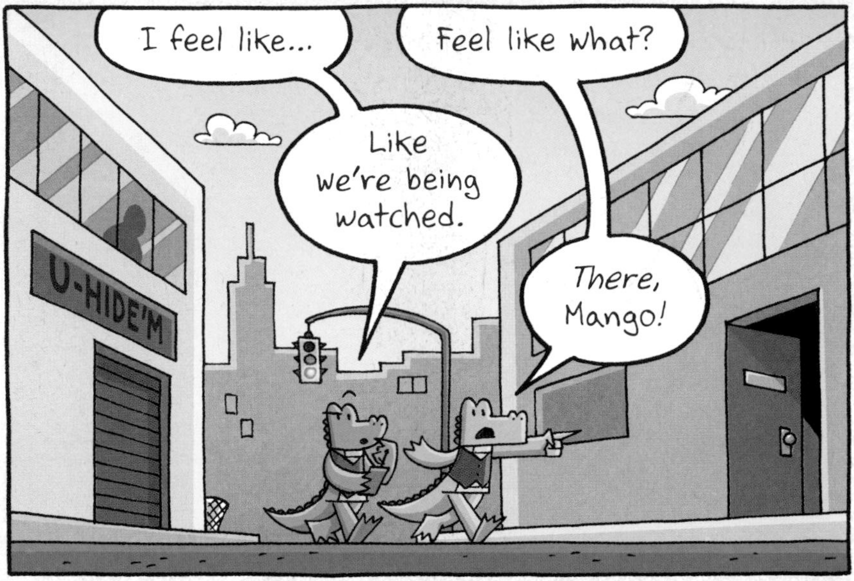
I feel like...
Feel like what?
Like we're being watched.
There, Mango!
U-HIDE'M

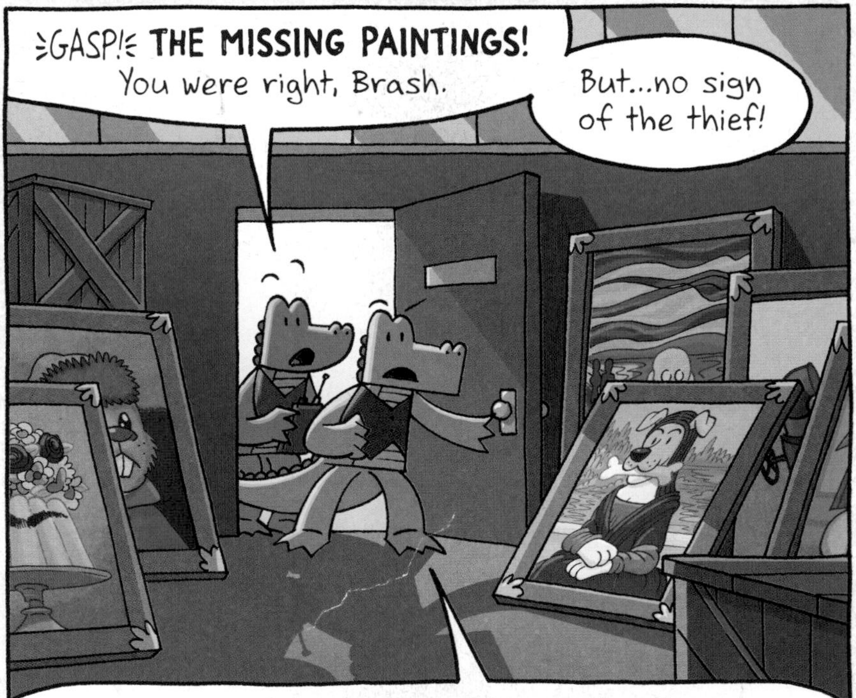
GASP! THE MISSING PAINTINGS! You were right, Brash.
But...no sign of the thief!
We must've scared them off. Our plan for them to lead us to these masterpieces worked, though!

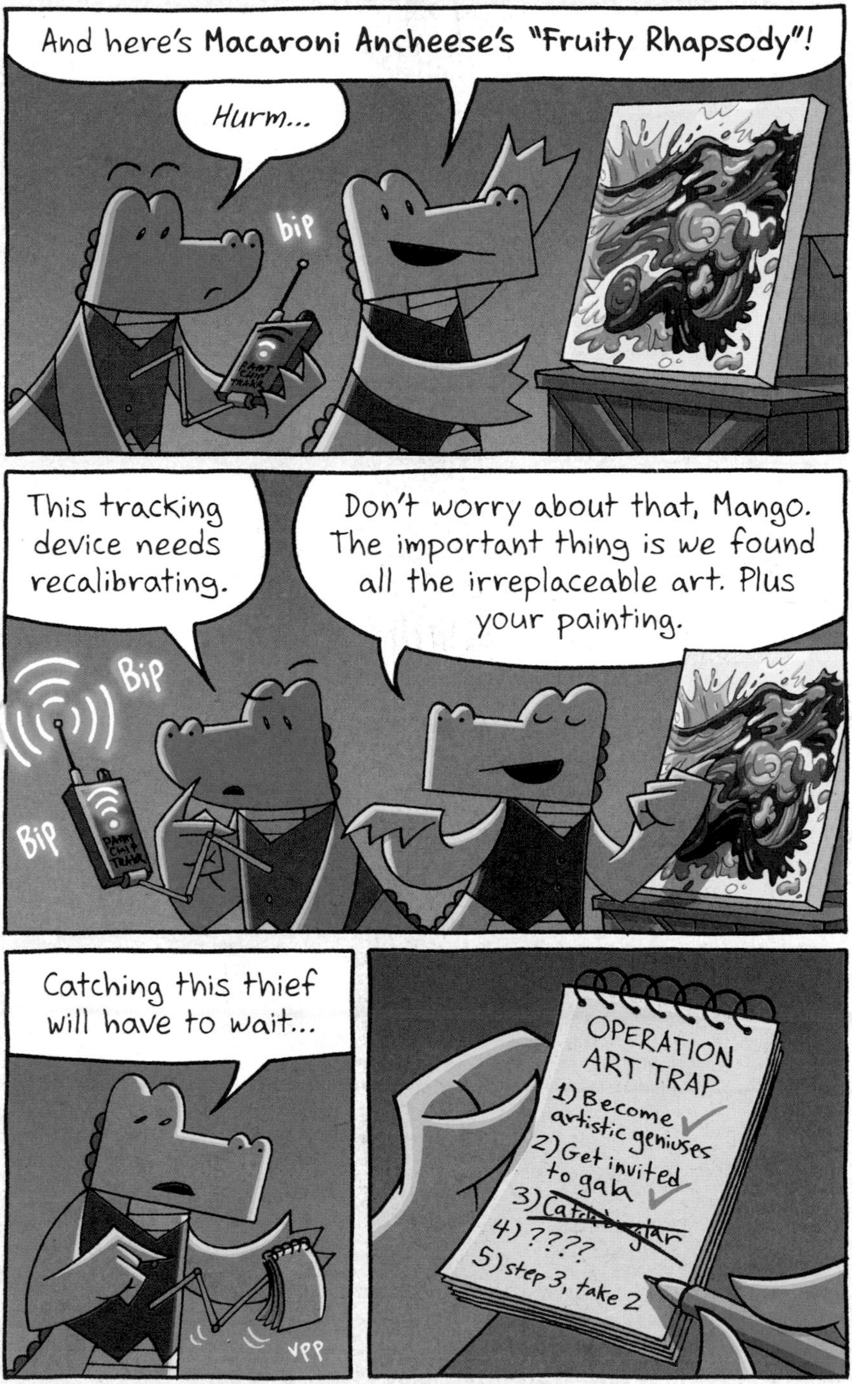
And here's Macaroni Ancheese's "Fruity Rhapsody"!
Hurm...
bip
This tracking device needs recalibrating.
Don't worry about that, Mango. The important thing is we found all the irreplaceable art. Plus your painting.
Bip
Bip
Catching this thief will have to wait...
vpp
OPERATION ART TRAP
1) Become artistic geniuses
2) Get invited to gala
3)
4) ????
5) step 3, take 2

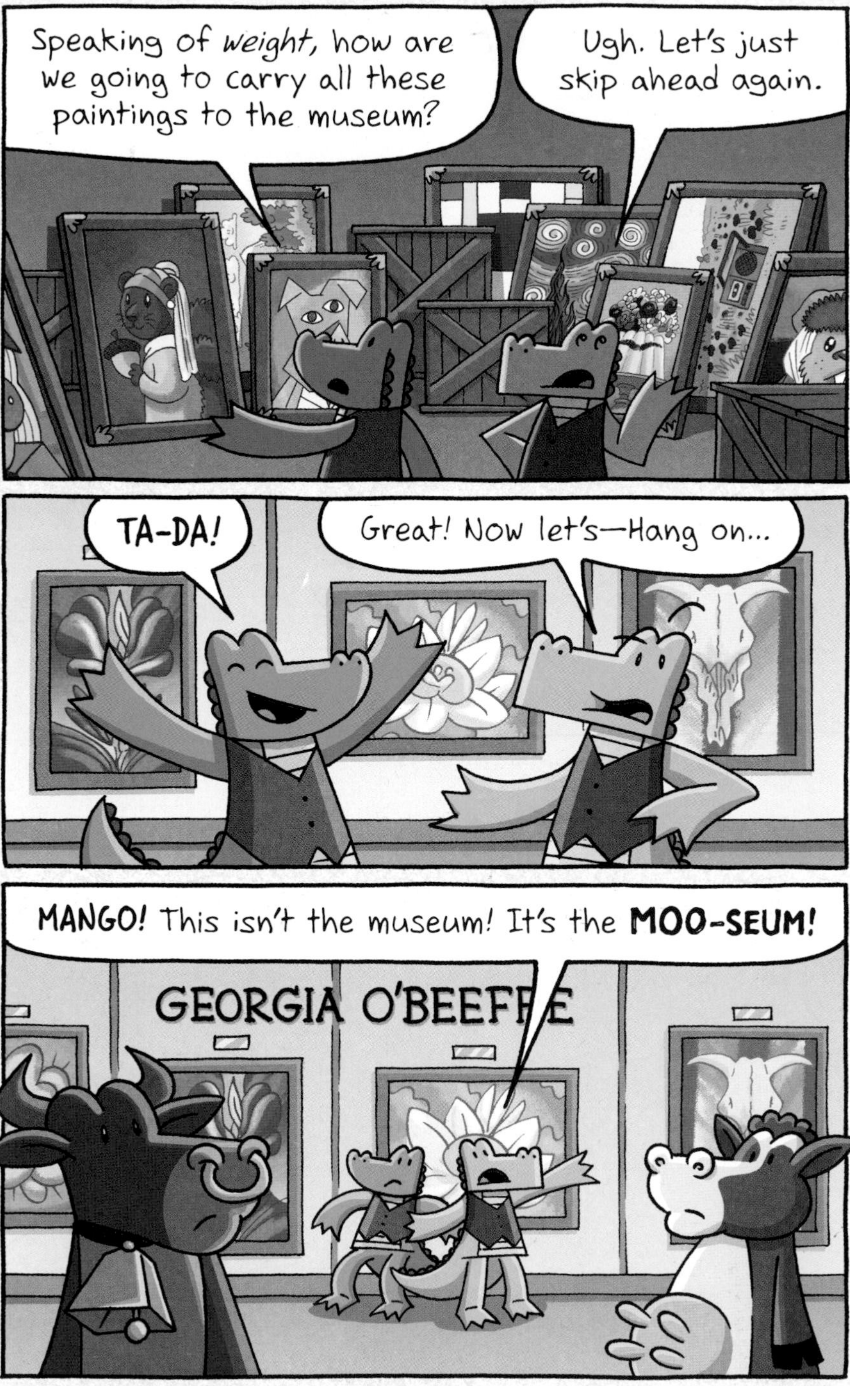
Speaking of *weight*, how are we going to carry all these paintings to the museum?
Ugh. Let's just skip ahead again.
TA-DA!
Great! Now let's—Hang on...
MANGO! This isn't the museum! It's the MOO-SEUM!
GEORGIA O'BEEFFE

Chapter 8

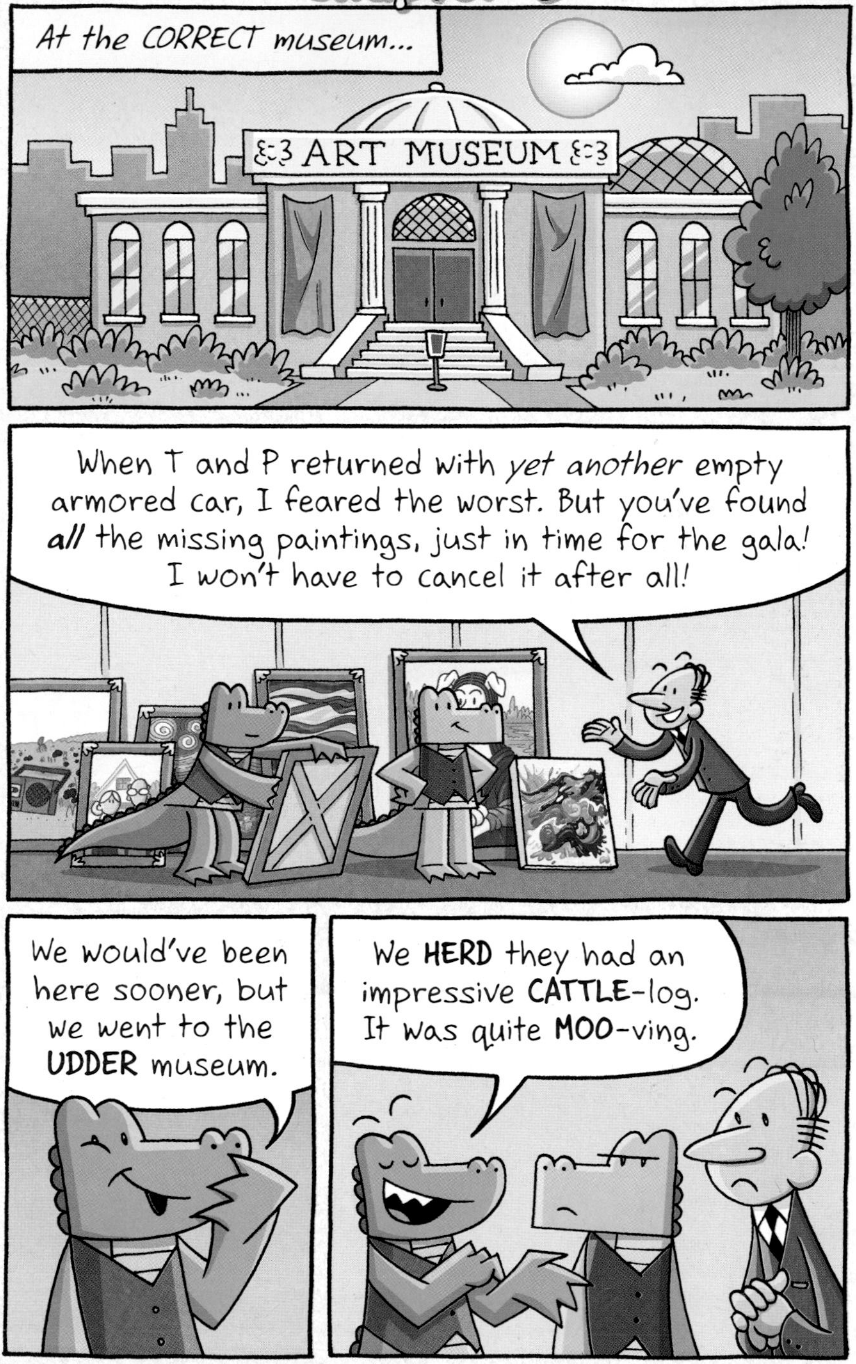
At the CORRECT museum...
ART MUSEUM
When T and P returned with *yet another* empty armored car, I feared the worst. But you've found ***all*** the missing paintings, just in time for the gala! I won't have to cancel it after all!
We would've been here sooner, but we went to the **UDDER** museum.
We **HERD** they had an impressive **CATTLE**-log. It was quite **MOO**-ving.

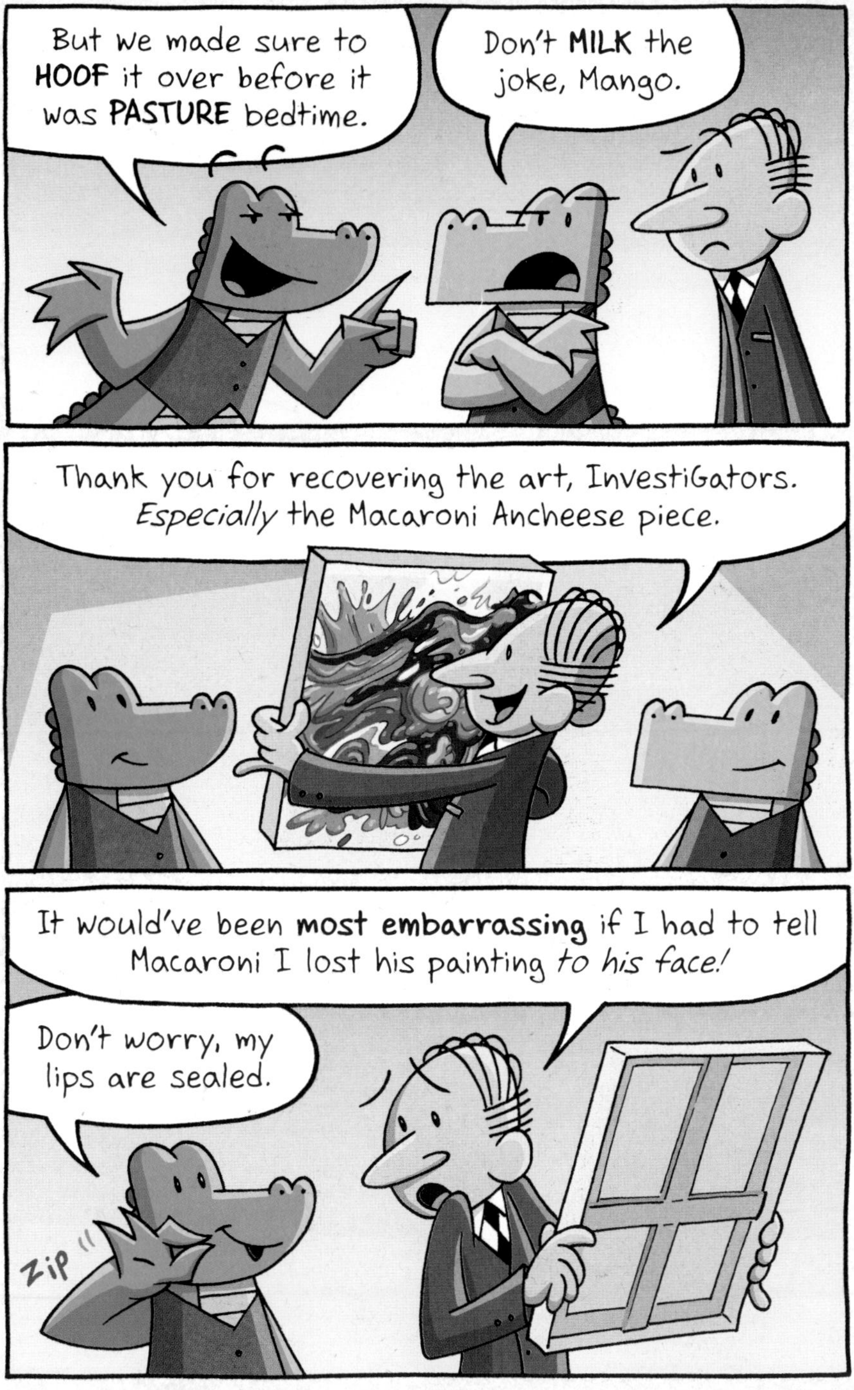
But we made sure to **HOOF** it over before it was **PASTURE** bedtime.
Don't **MILK** the joke, Mango.
Thank you for recovering the art, InvestiGators. *Especially* the Macaroni Ancheese piece.
It would've been **most embarrassing** if I had to tell Macaroni I lost his painting *to his face!*
Don't worry, my lips are sealed.
ZIP

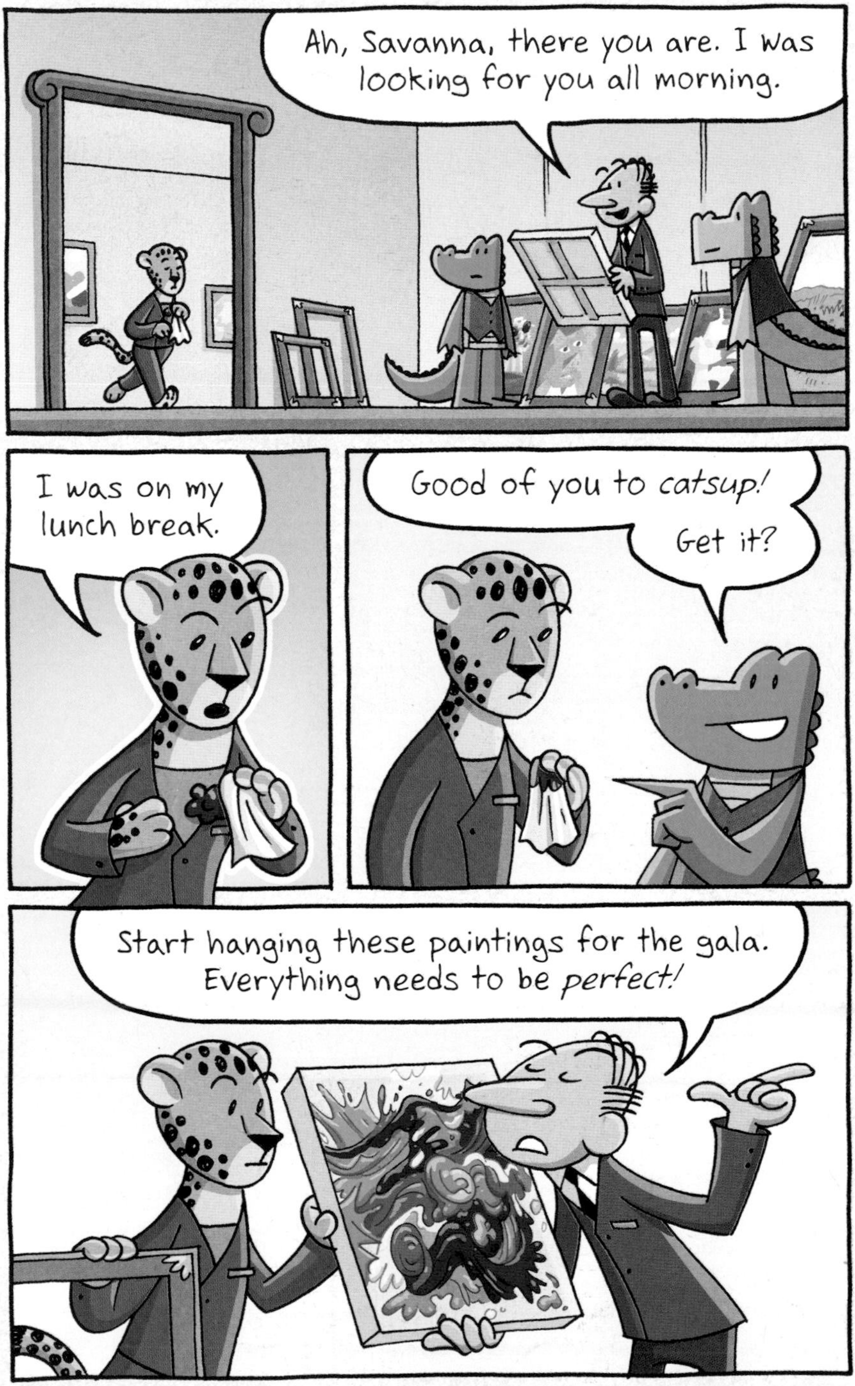
Ah, Savanna, there you are. I was looking for you all morning.
I was on my lunch break.
Good of you to *catsup!*
Get it?
Start hanging these paintings for the gala. Everything needs to be *perfect!*

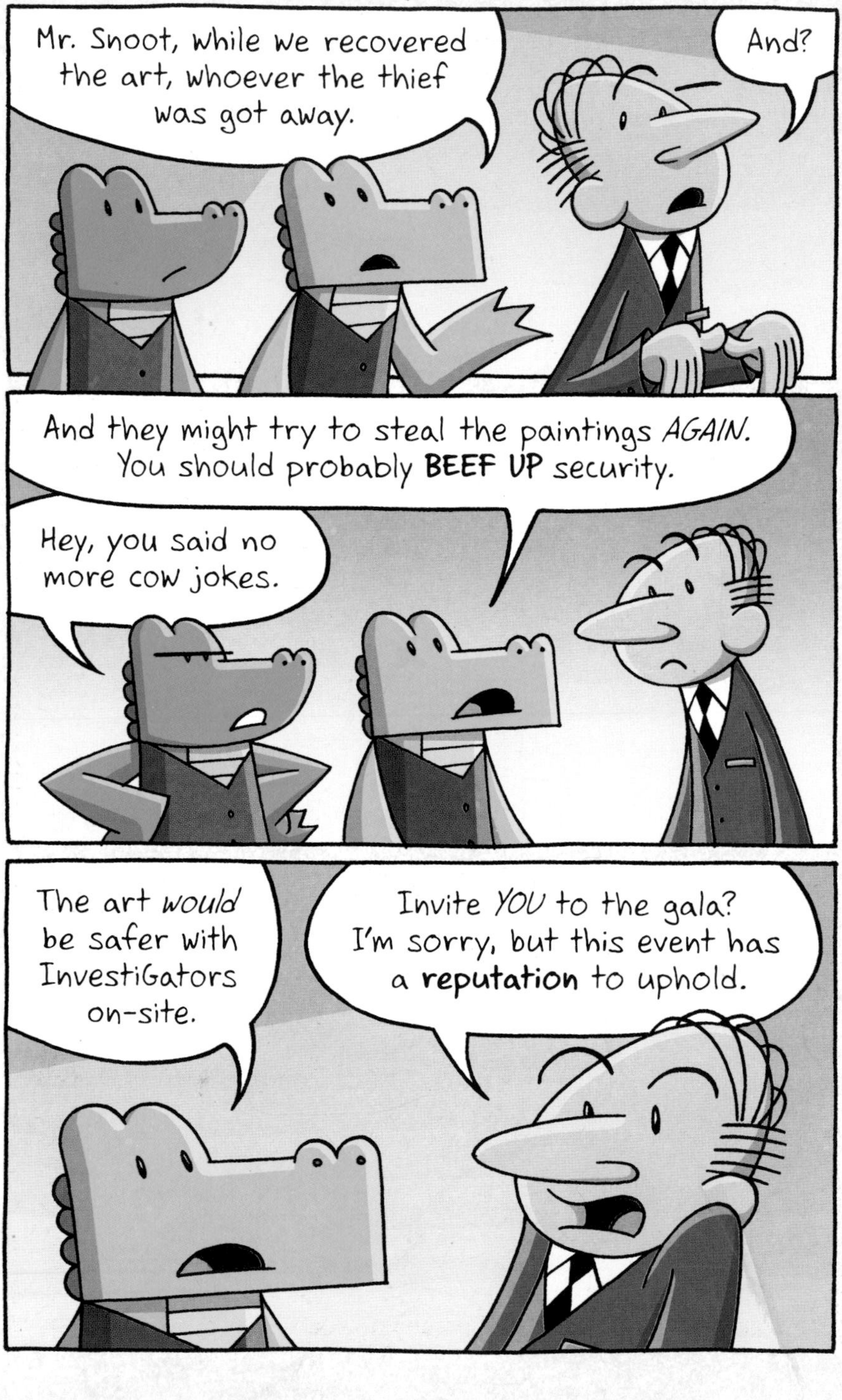
Mr. Snoot, while we recovered the art, whoever the thief was got away.
And?
And they might try to steal the paintings *AGAIN*. You should probably **BEEF UP** security.
Hey, you said no more cow jokes.
The art *would* be safer with InvestiGators on-site.
Invite *YOU* to the gala? I'm sorry, but this event has a **reputation** to uphold.

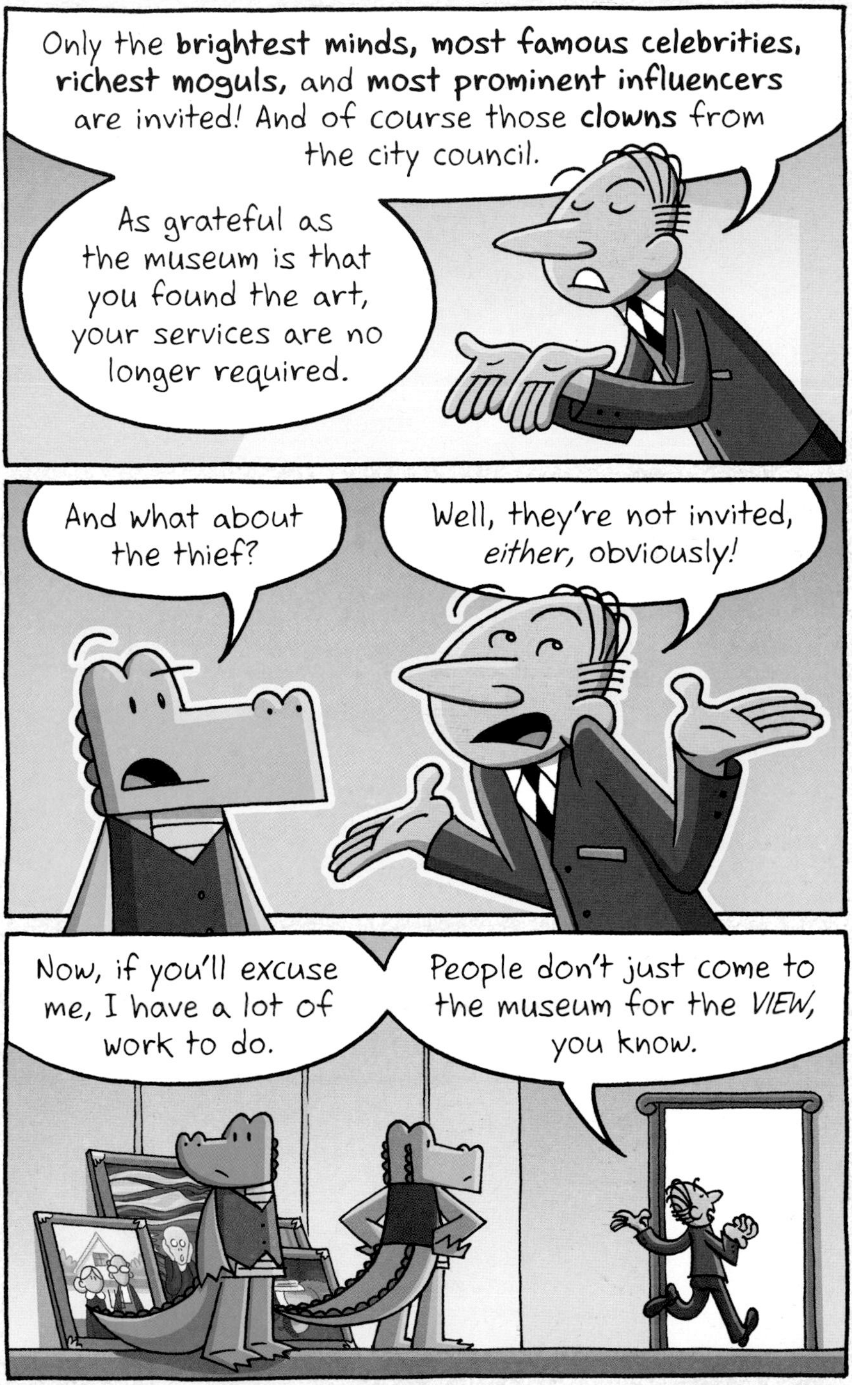
Only the **brightest minds, most famous celebrities, richest moguls,** and **most prominent influencers** are invited! And of course those **clowns** from the city council.
As grateful as the museum is that you found the art, your services are no longer required.
And what about the thief?
Well, they're not invited, *either,* obviously!
Now, if you'll excuse me, I have a lot of work to do.
People don't just come to the museum for the *VIEW,* you know.

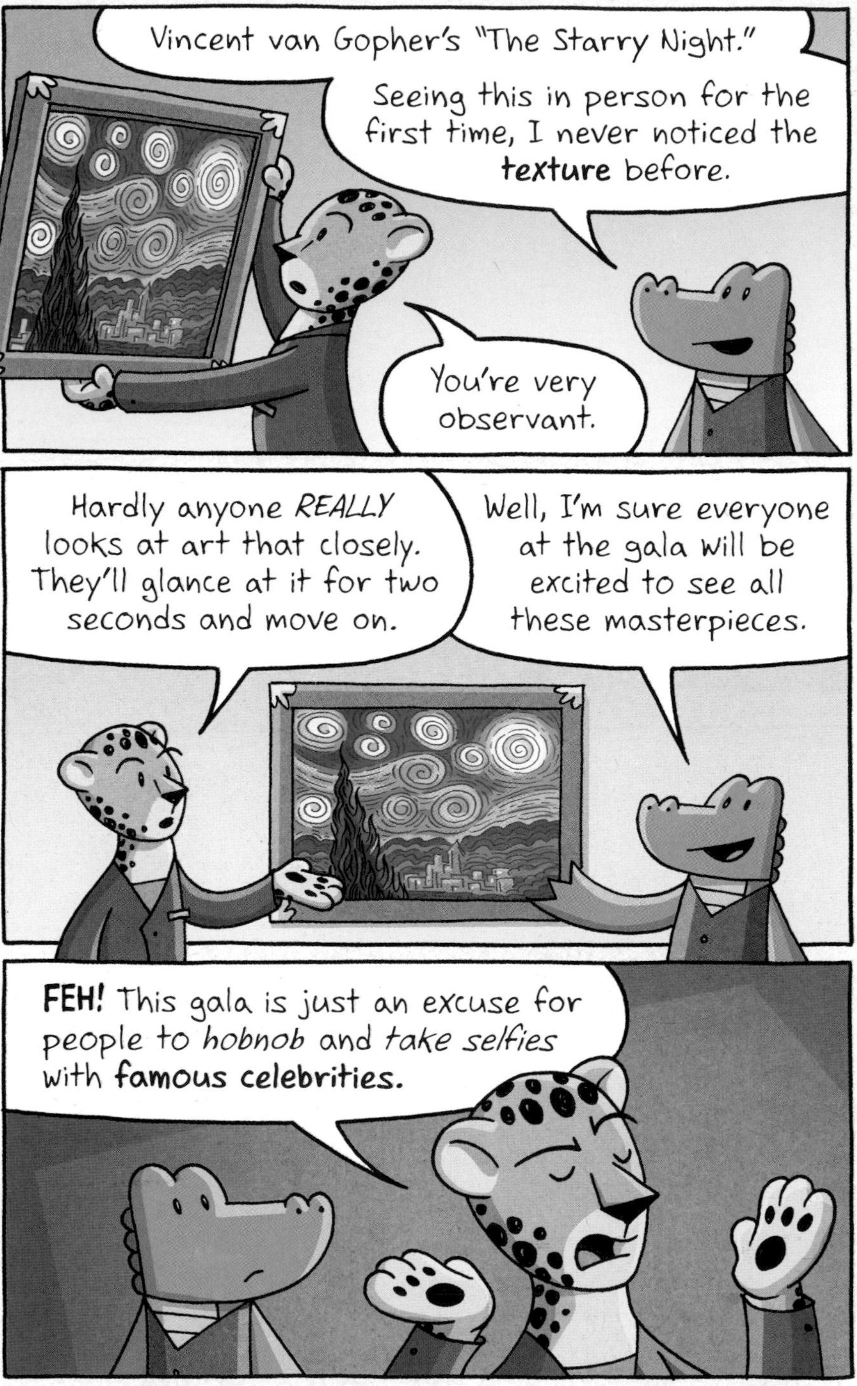

Vincent van Gopher's "The Starry Night."
Seeing this in person for the first time, I never noticed the **texture** before.
You're very observant.
Hardly anyone *REALLY* looks at art that closely. They'll glance at it for two seconds and move on.
Well, I'm sure everyone at the gala will be excited to see all these masterpieces.
FEH! This gala is just an excuse for people to *hobnob* and *take selfies* with **famous celebrities.**

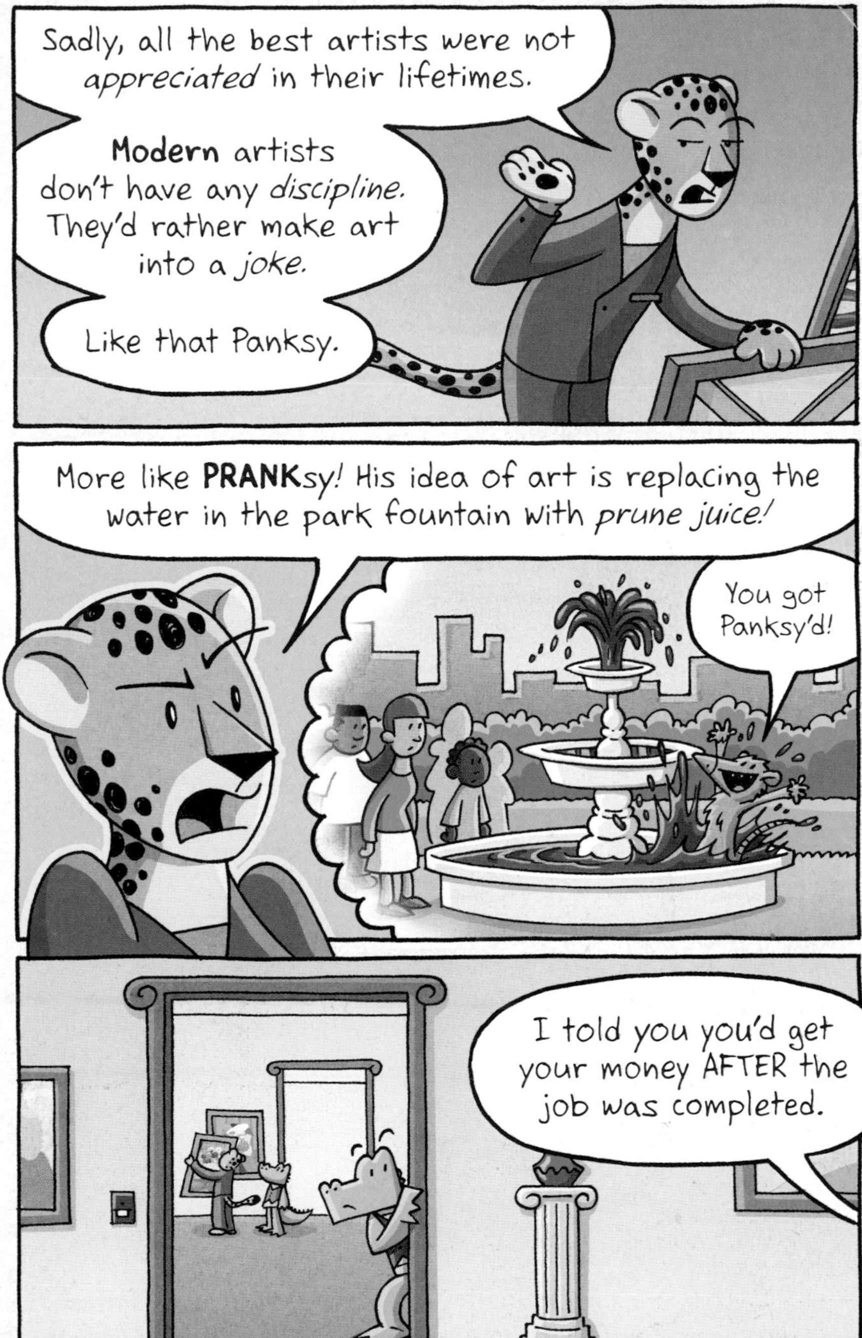
Sadly, all the best artists were not *appreciated* in their lifetimes.
Modern artists don't have any *discipline.* They'd rather make art into a *joke.*
Like that Panksy.
More like **PRANK**sy! His idea of art is replacing the water in the park fountain with *prune juice!*
You got Panksy'd!
I told you you'd get your money AFTER the job was completed.

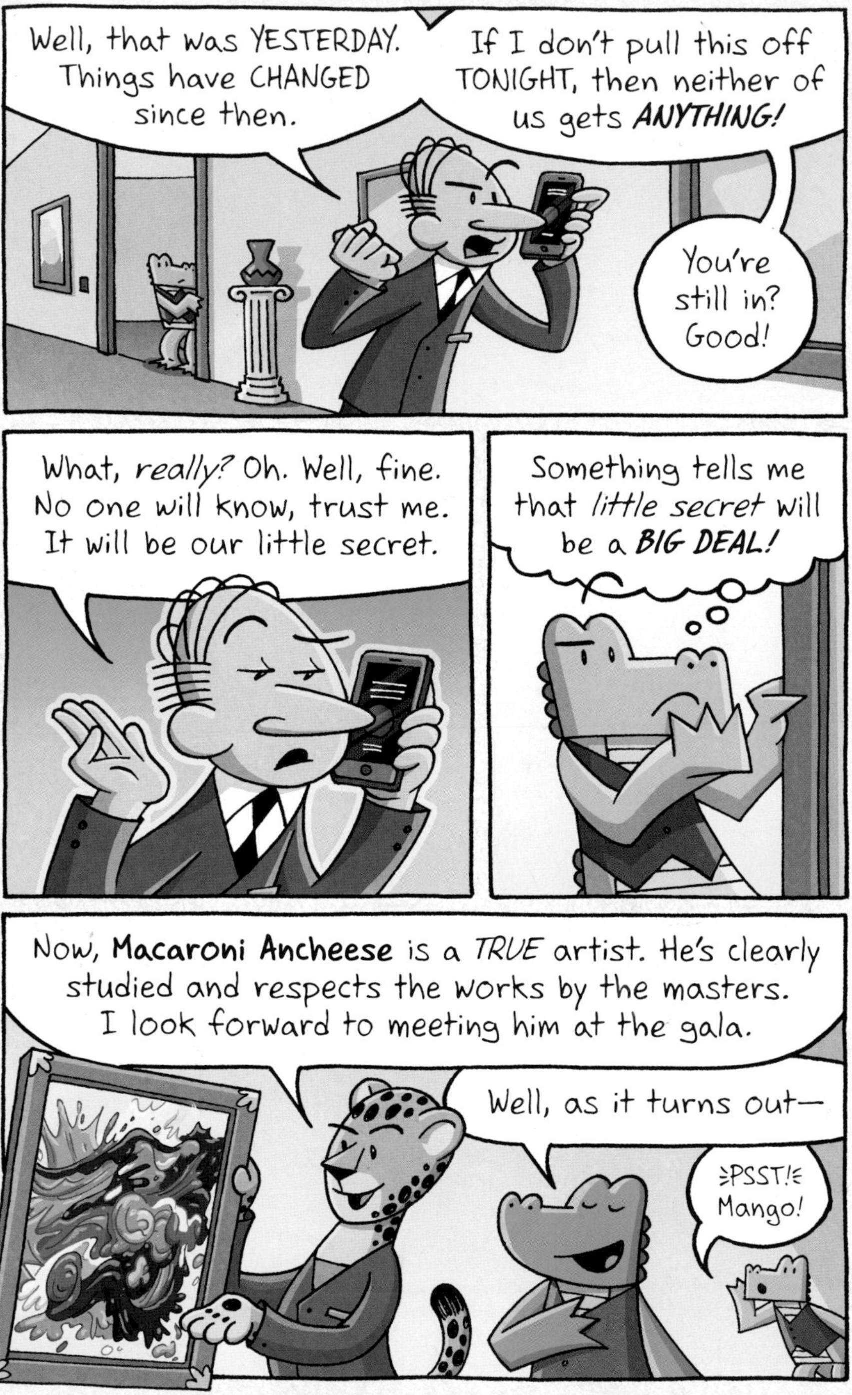
Well, that was YESTERDAY. Things have CHANGED since then.
If I don't pull this off TONIGHT, then neither of us gets ***ANYTHING!***
You're still in? Good!
What, *really?* Oh. Well, fine. No one will know, trust me. It will be our little secret.
Something tells me that *little secret* will be a ***BIG DEAL!***
Now, **Macaroni Ancheese** is a *TRUE* artist. He's clearly studied and respects the works by the masters. I look forward to meeting him at the gala.
Well, as it turns out—
PSST! Mango!

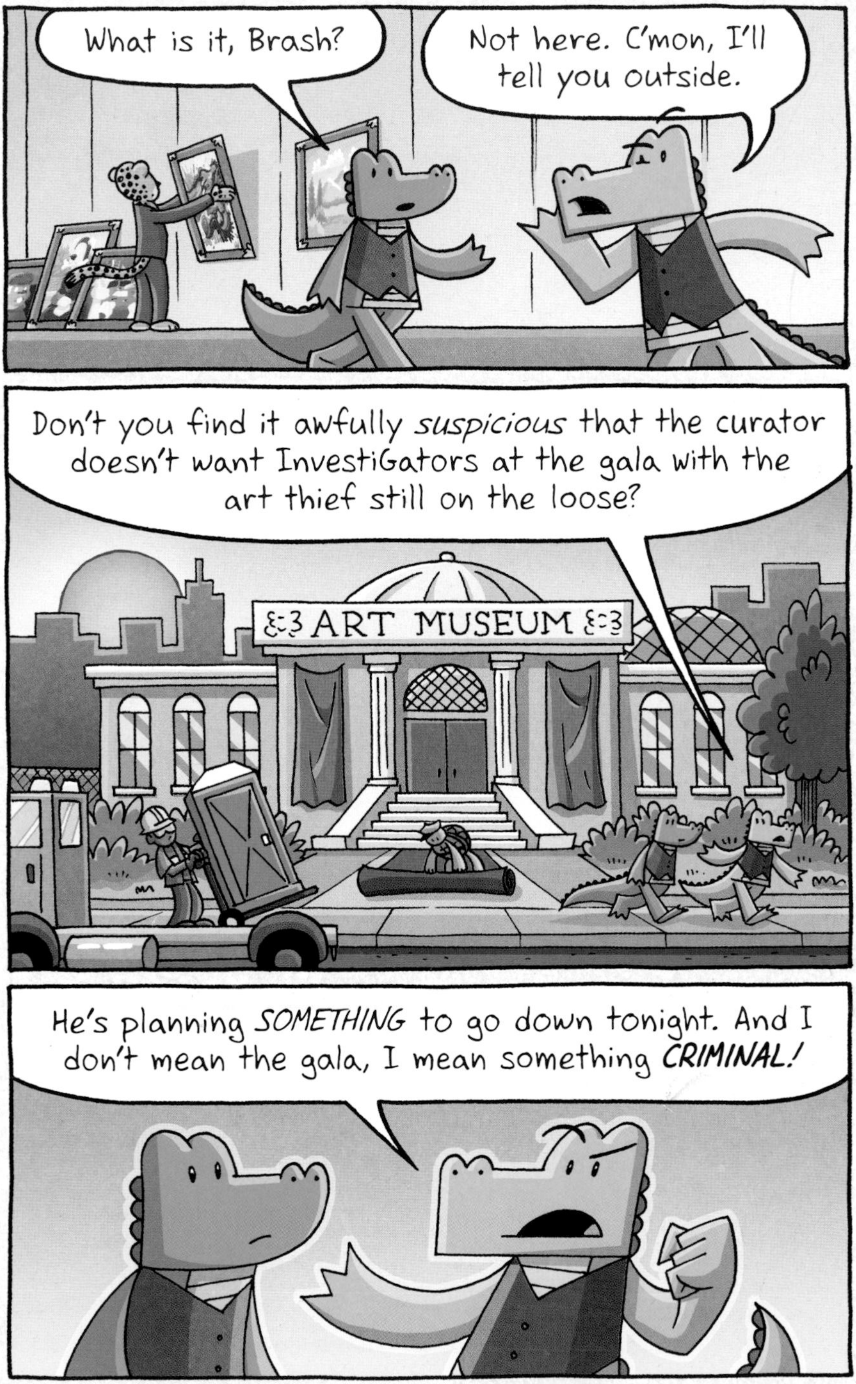
What is it, Brash?
Not here. C'mon, I'll tell you outside.
Don't you find it awfully *suspicious* that the curator doesn't want InvestiGators at the gala with the art thief still on the loose?
ART MUSEUM
He's planning *SOMETHING* to go down tonight. And I don't mean the gala, I mean something *CRIMINAL!*

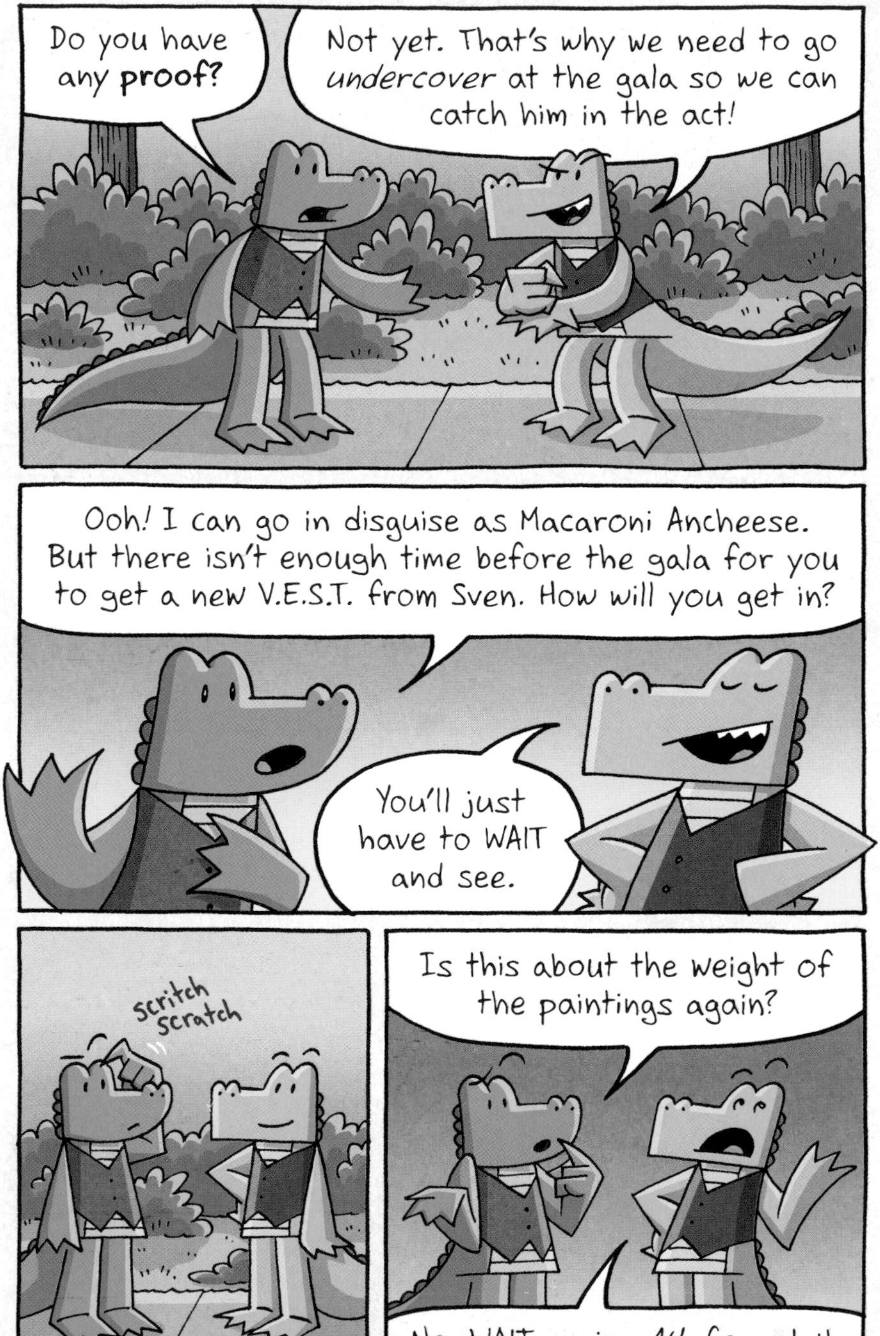
Do you have any **proof?**
Not yet. That's why we need to go *undercover* at the gala so we can catch him in the act!
Ooh! I can go in disguise as Macaroni Ancheese. But there isn't enough time before the gala for you to get a new V.E.S.T. from Sven. How will you get in?
You'll just have to WAIT and see.
scritch scratch
Is this about the weight of the paintings again?
No, WAIT as in—*AH,* forget it.

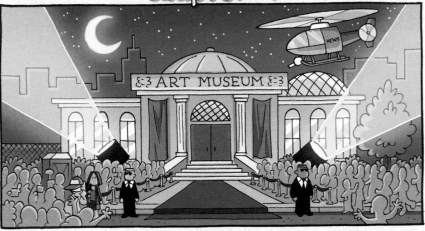

Chapter 9

ART MUSEUM
This is Cici Boringstories with *Action News Now*, reporting LIVE from outside the city **Art Museum Gala**! I'm filling in for Vohnda, the Culture Vulture, who's out sick with **avian flu.**
ART MUSEUM
I don't care much for *boring old art*, but I'll never pass up an opportunity for **celebrity gawking.** Catching a glimpse of a famous face is quite a competition amongst the **paparazzi!**

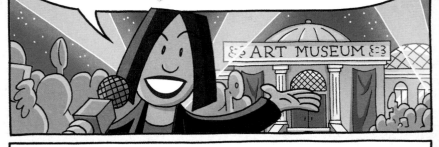

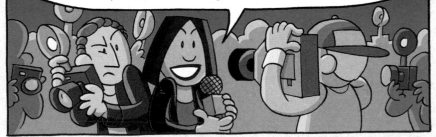

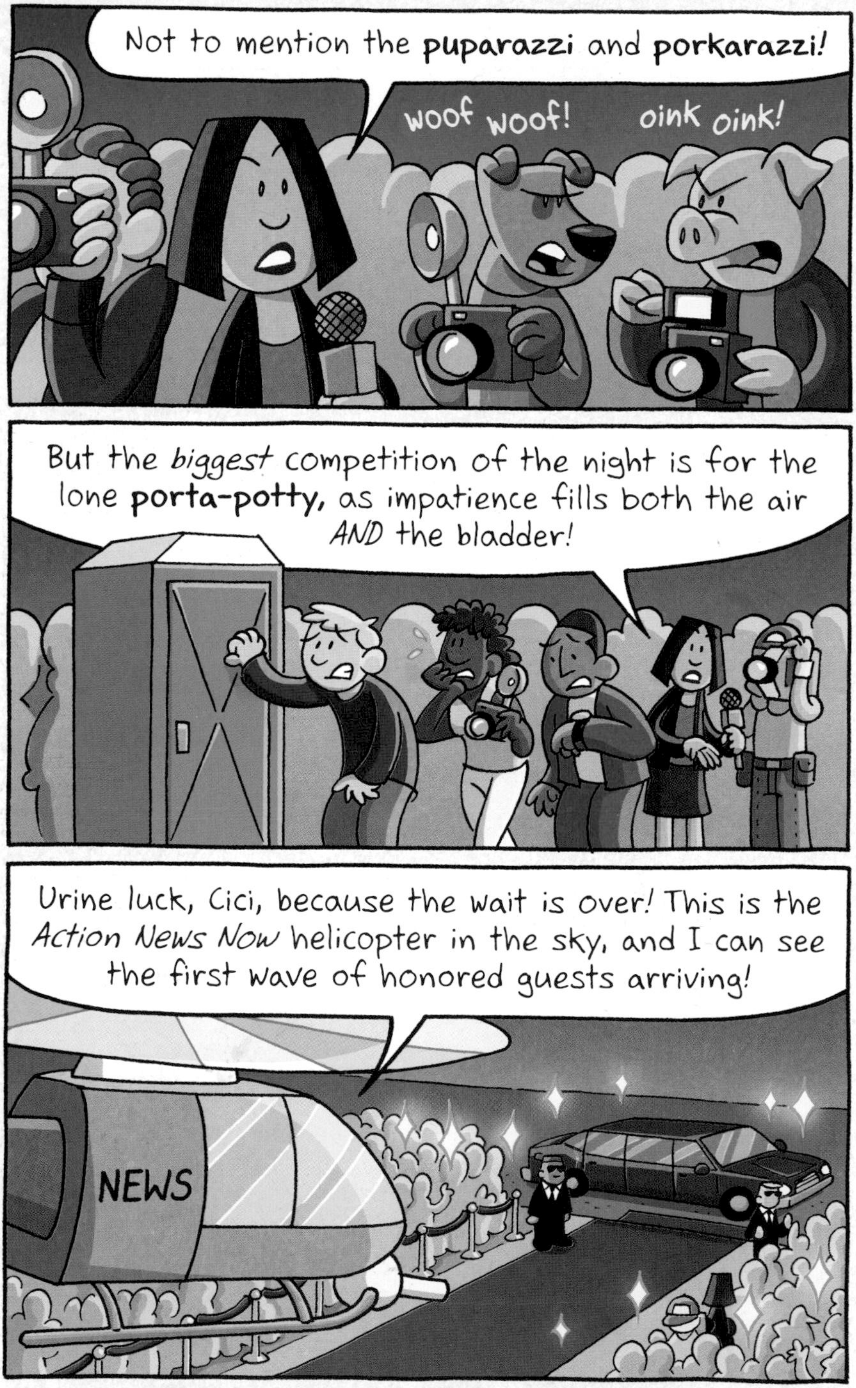

Not to mention the **puparazzi** and **porkarazzi!**
woof woof!
oink oink!
But the *biggest* competition of the night is for the lone **porta-potty,** as impatience fills both the air *AND* the bladder!
Urine luck, Cici, because the wait is over! This is the *Action News Now* helicopter in the sky, and I can see the first wave of honored guests arriving!
NEWS

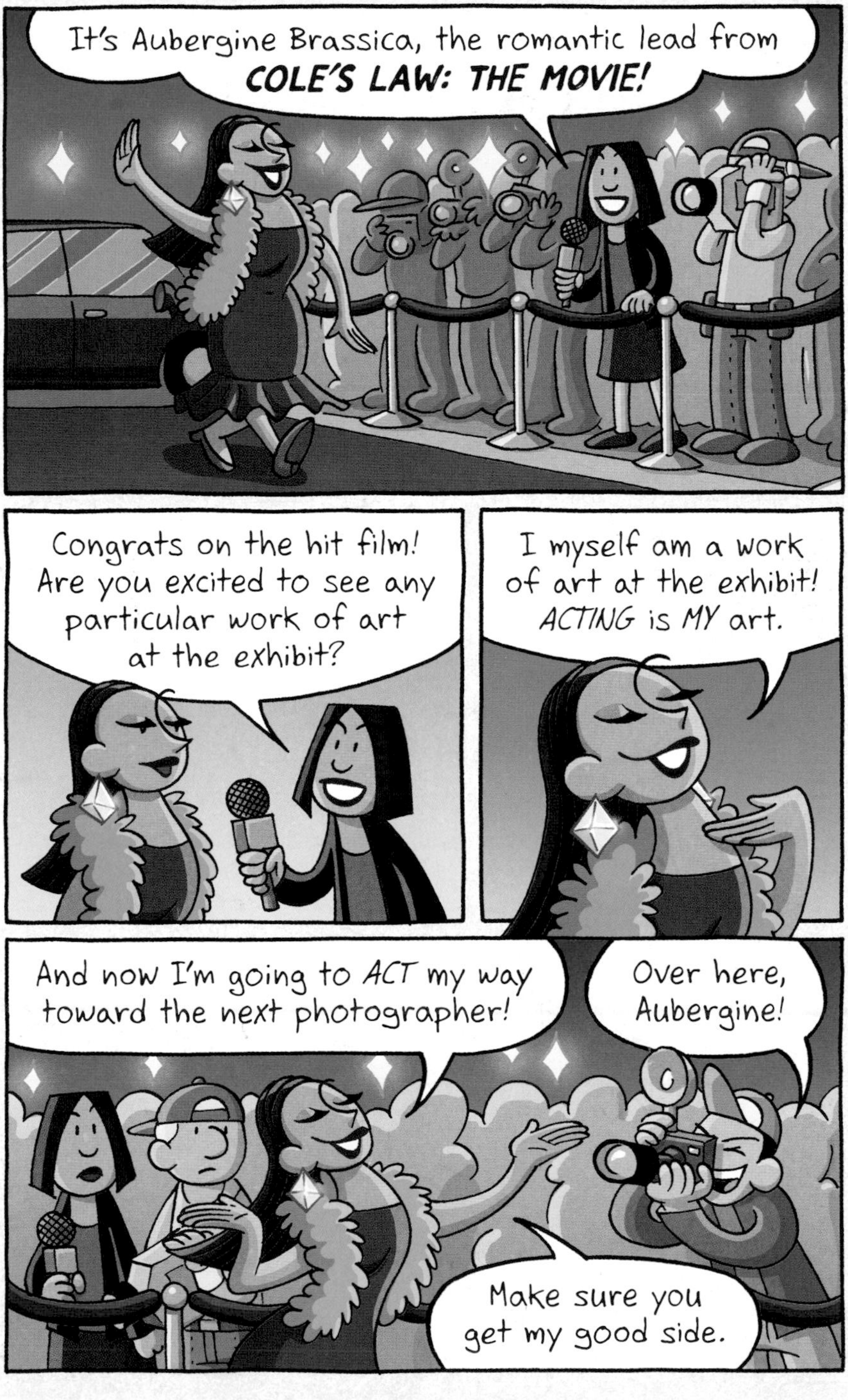
It's Aubergine Brassica, the romantic lead from **COLE'S LAW: THE MOVIE!**
Congrats on the hit film! Are you excited to see any particular work of art at the exhibit?
I myself am a work of art at the exhibit! *ACTING* is *MY* art.
And now I'm going to *ACT* my way toward the next photographer!
Over here, Aubergine!
Make sure you get my good side.

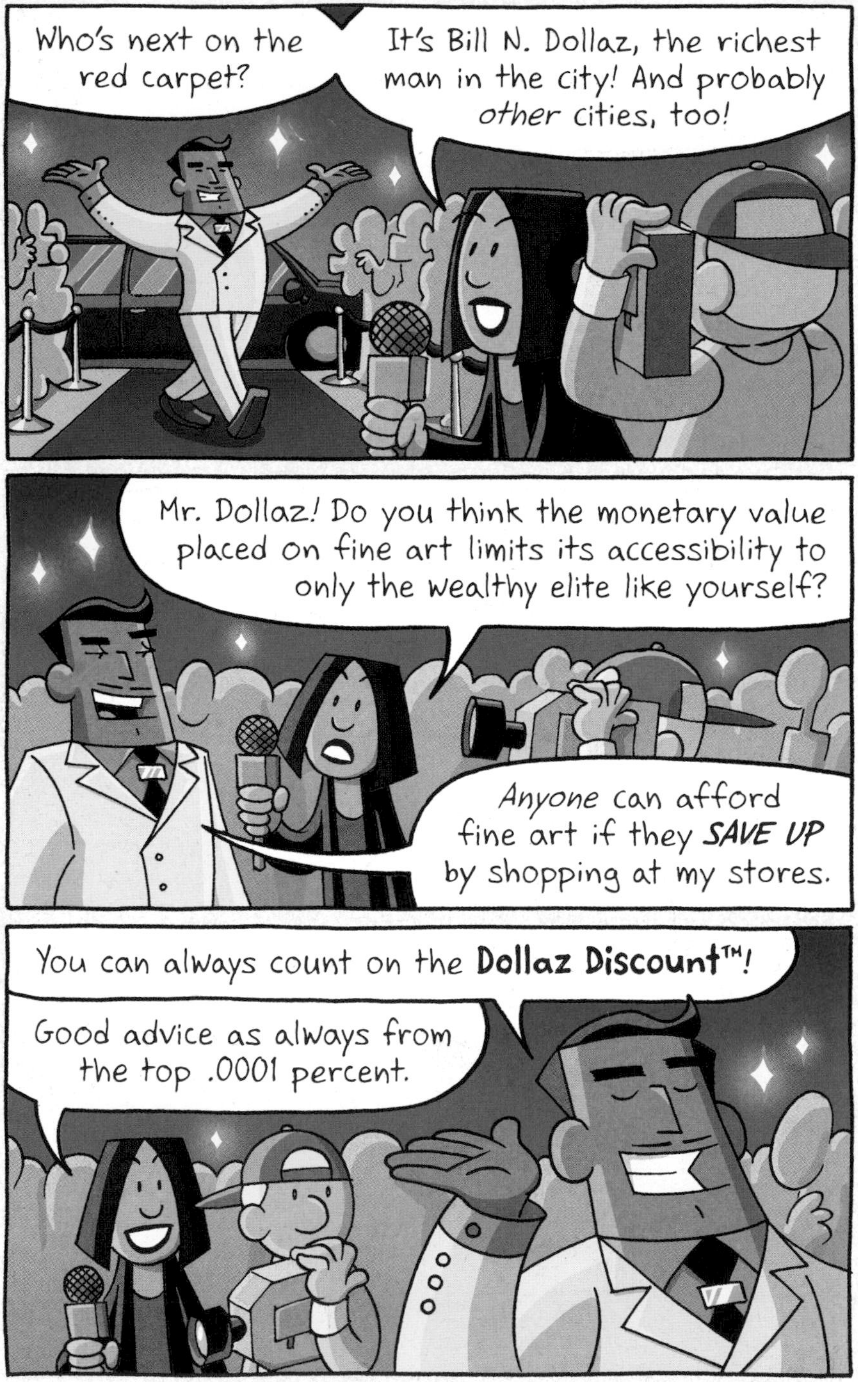
Who's next on the red carpet?
It's Bill N. Dollaz, the richest man in the city! And probably *other* cities, too!
Mr. Dollaz! Do you think the monetary value placed on fine art limits its accessibility to only the wealthy elite like yourself?
Anyone can afford fine art if they ***SAVE UP*** by shopping at my stores.
You can always count on the **Dollaz Discount™**!
Good advice as always from the top .0001 percent.

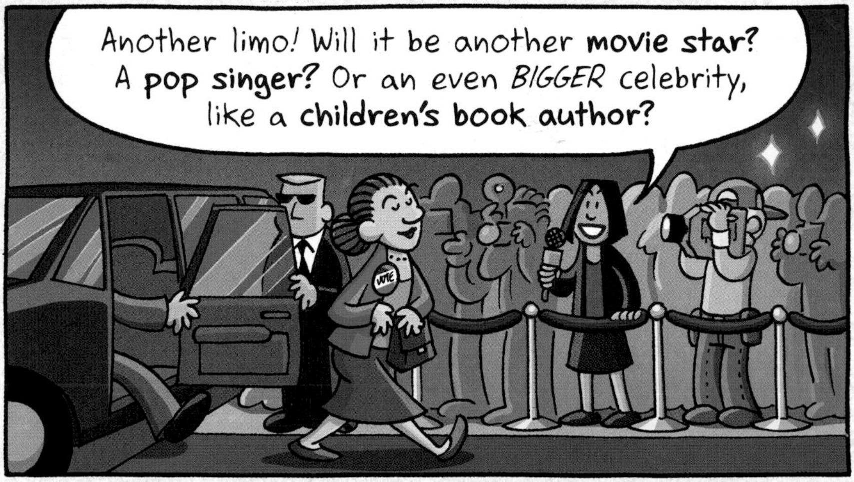
Another limo! Will it be another **movie star?** A **pop singer?** Or an even *BIGGER* celebrity, like a **children's book author?**
VOTE

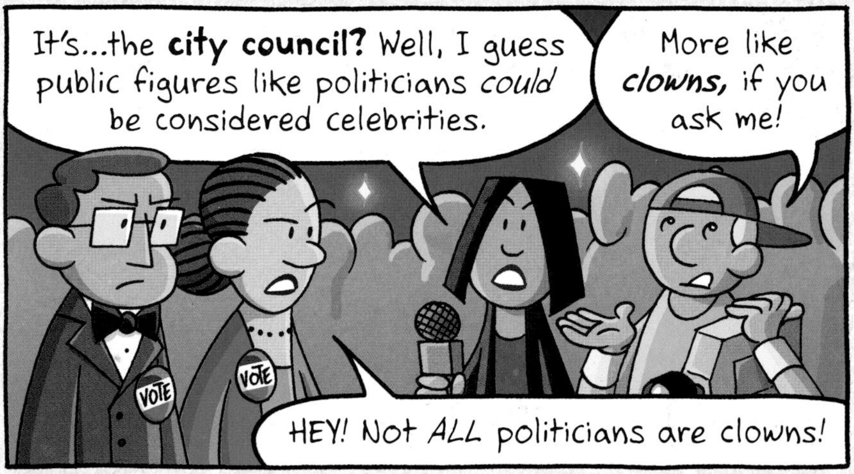
It's...the **city council?** Well, I guess public figures like politicians *could* be considered celebrities.
More like ***clowns,*** if you ask me!
VOTE
VOTE
HEY! Not *ALL* politicians are clowns!

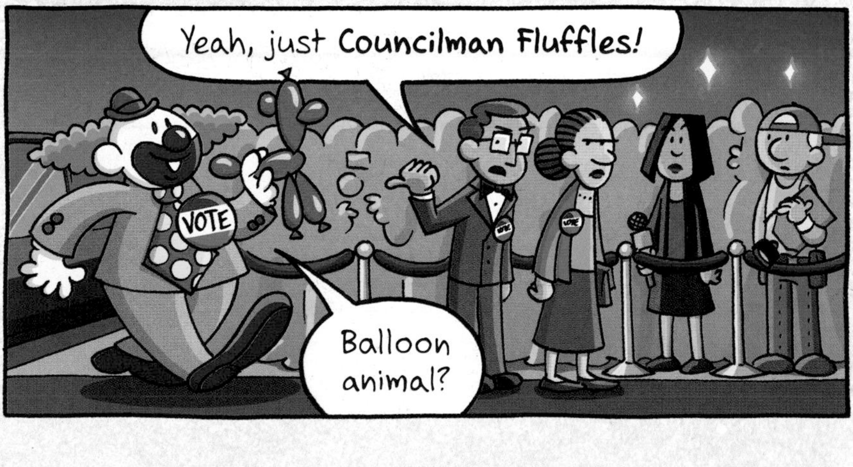
Yeah, just **Councilman Fluffles!**
VOTE
Balloon animal?

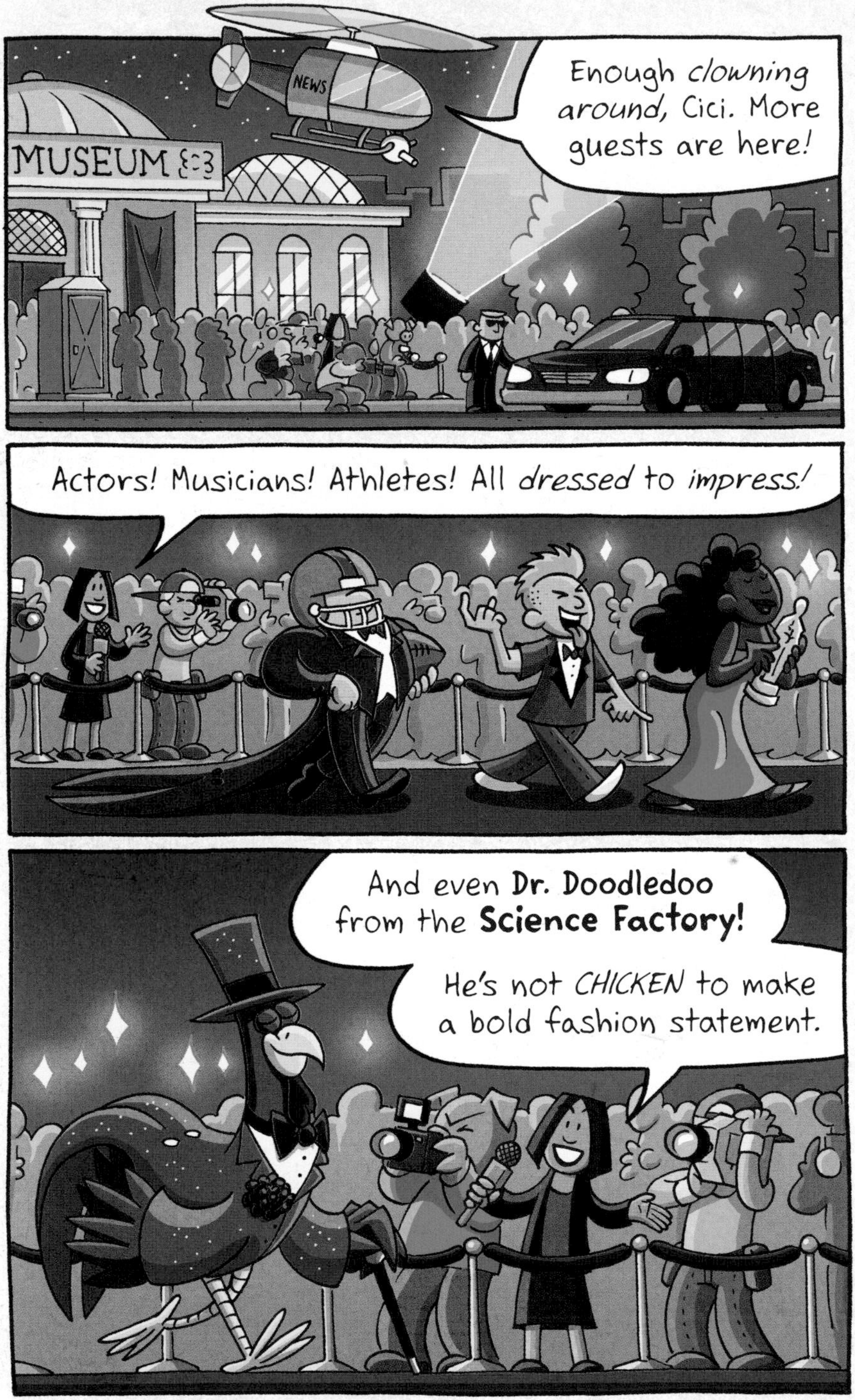
MUSEUM
NEWS
Enough *clowning* around, Cici. More guests are here!
Actors! Musicians! Athletes! All *dressed* to *impress*!
And even **Dr. Doodledoo** from the **Science Factory**!
He's not *CHICKEN* to make a bold fashion statement.

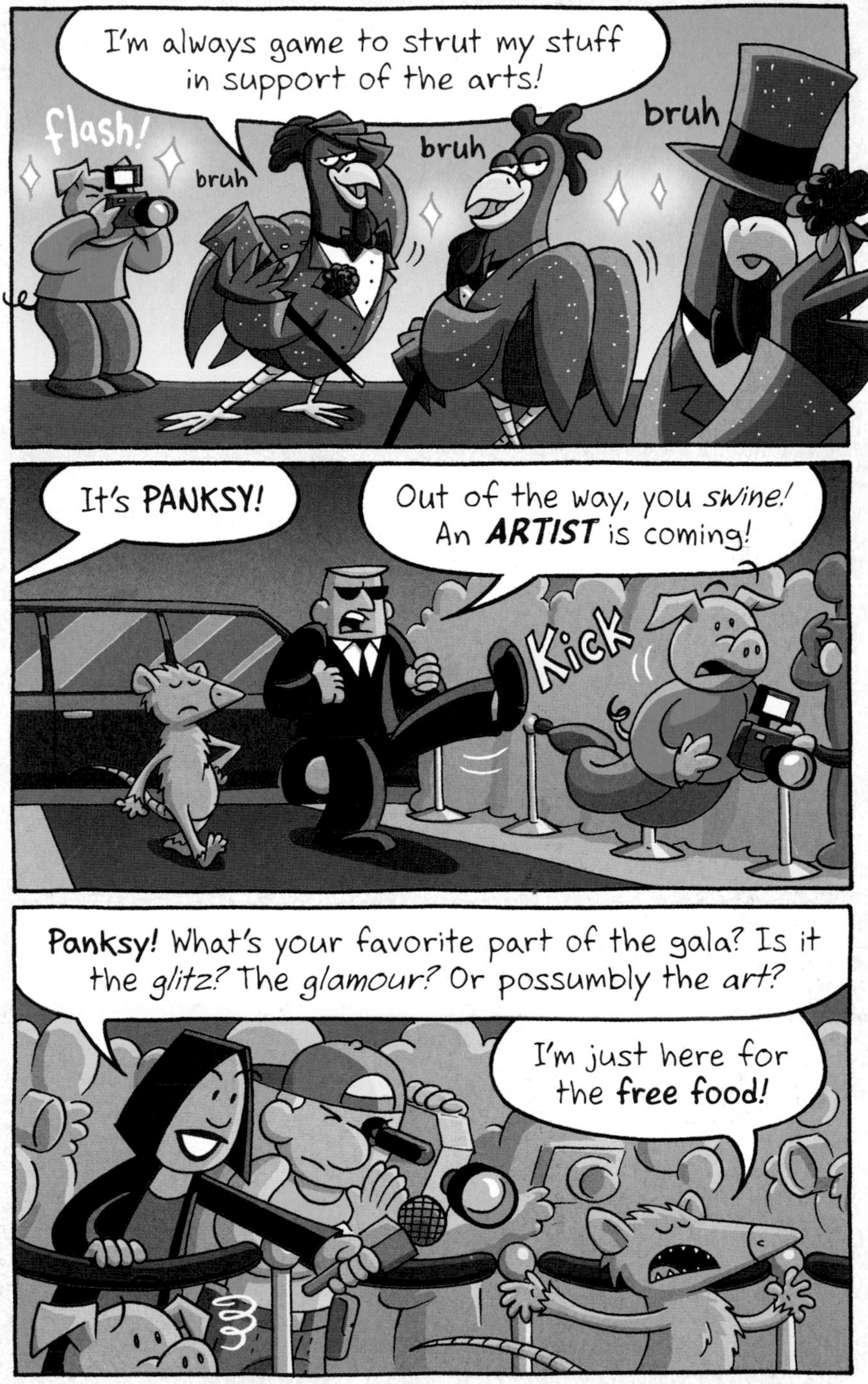
I'm always game to strut my stuff in support of the arts!
flash!
bruh
bruh
bruh
It's PANKSY!
Out of the way, you *swine!* An ***ARTIST*** is coming!
Kick
Panksy! What's your favorite part of the gala? Is it the *glitz?* The *glamour?* Or possumbly the *art?*
I'm just here for the **free food!**

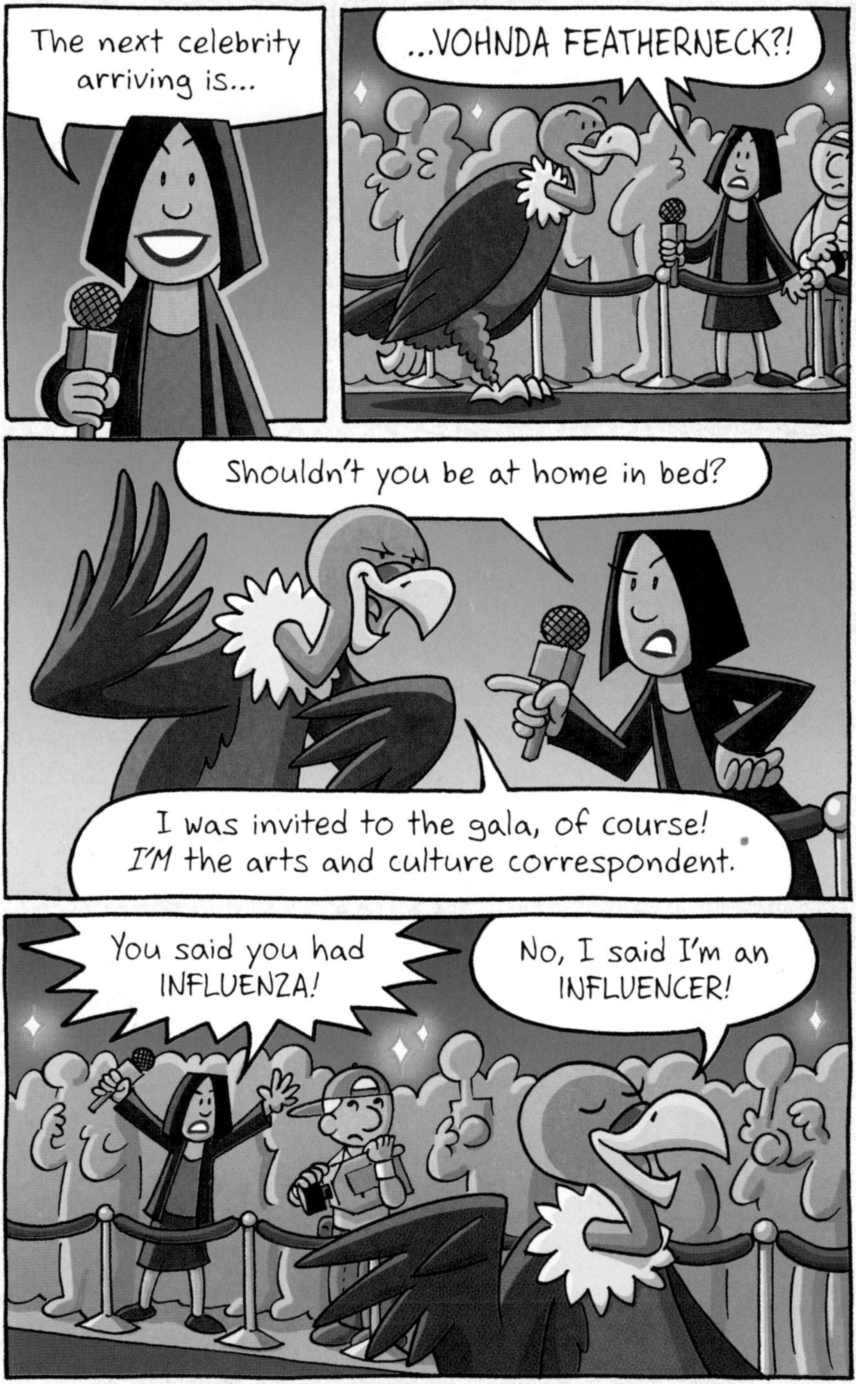
The next celebrity arriving is...
...VOHNDA FEATHERNECK?!
Shouldn't you be at home in bed?
I was invited to the gala, of course! *I'M* the arts and culture correspondent.
You said you had INFLUENZA!
No, I said I'm an INFLUENCER!

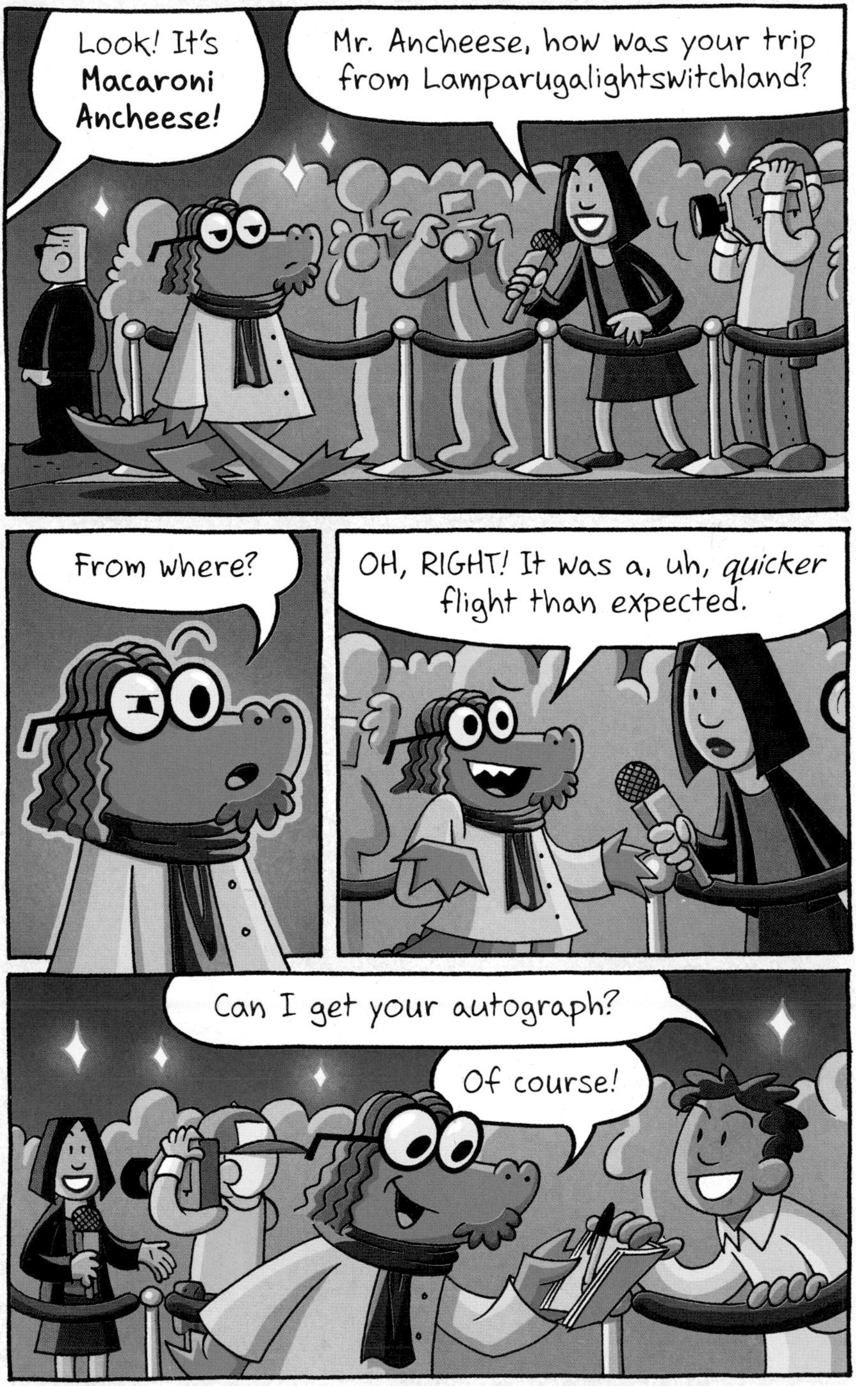
Look! It's **Macaroni Ancheese!**
Mr. Ancheese, how was your trip from Lamparugalightswitchland?
From where?
OH, RIGHT! It was a, uh, *quicker* flight than expected.
Can I get your autograph?
Of course!

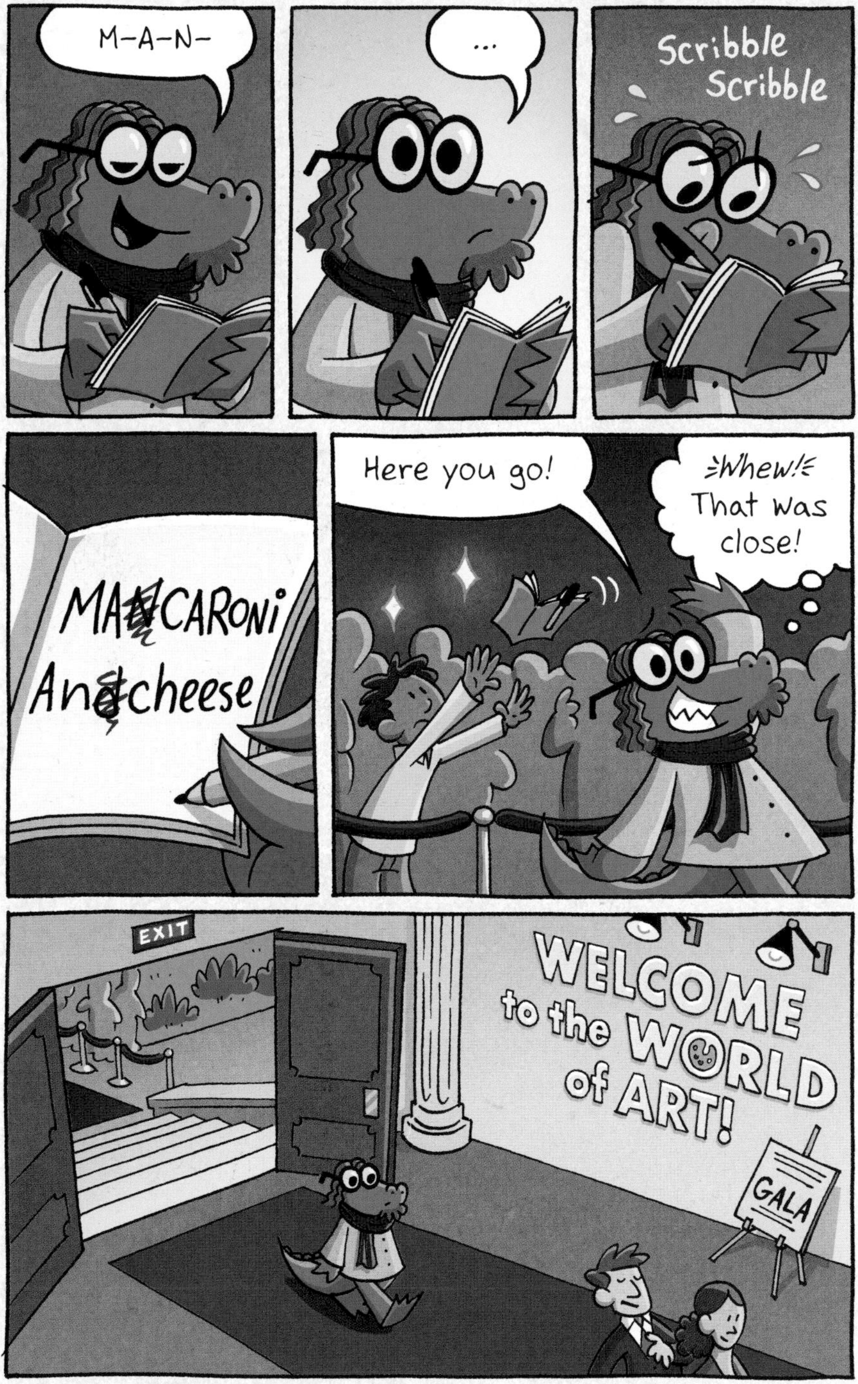
M-A-N-
...
Scribble Scribble
MANCARONI
Anecheese
Here you go!
Whew! That was close!
EXIT
WELCOME to the WORLD of ART!
GALA

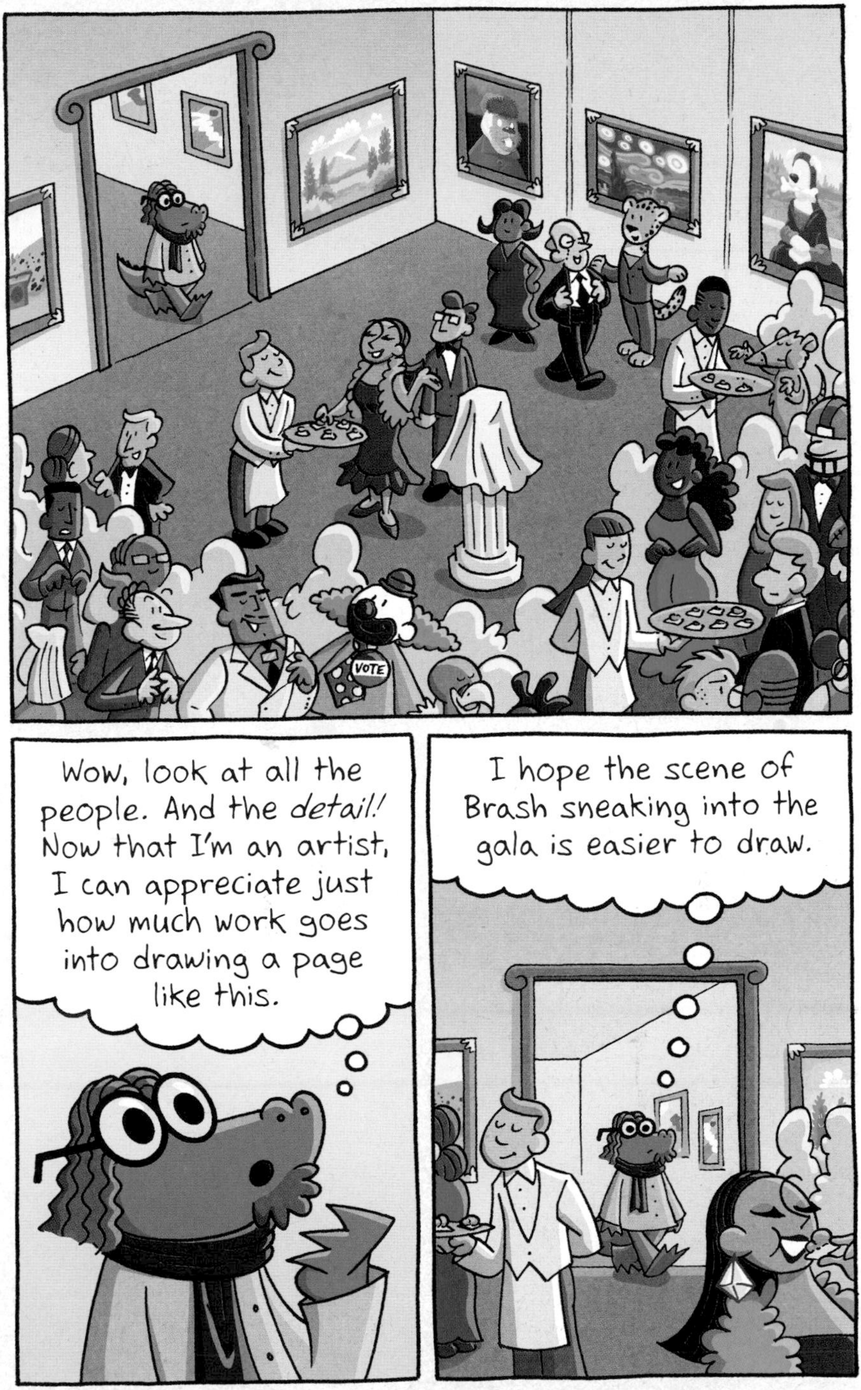
VOTE
Wow, look at all the people. And the *detail!* Now that I'm an artist, I can appreciate just how much work goes into drawing a page like this.
I hope the scene of Brash sneaking into the gala is easier to draw.

Chapter 10

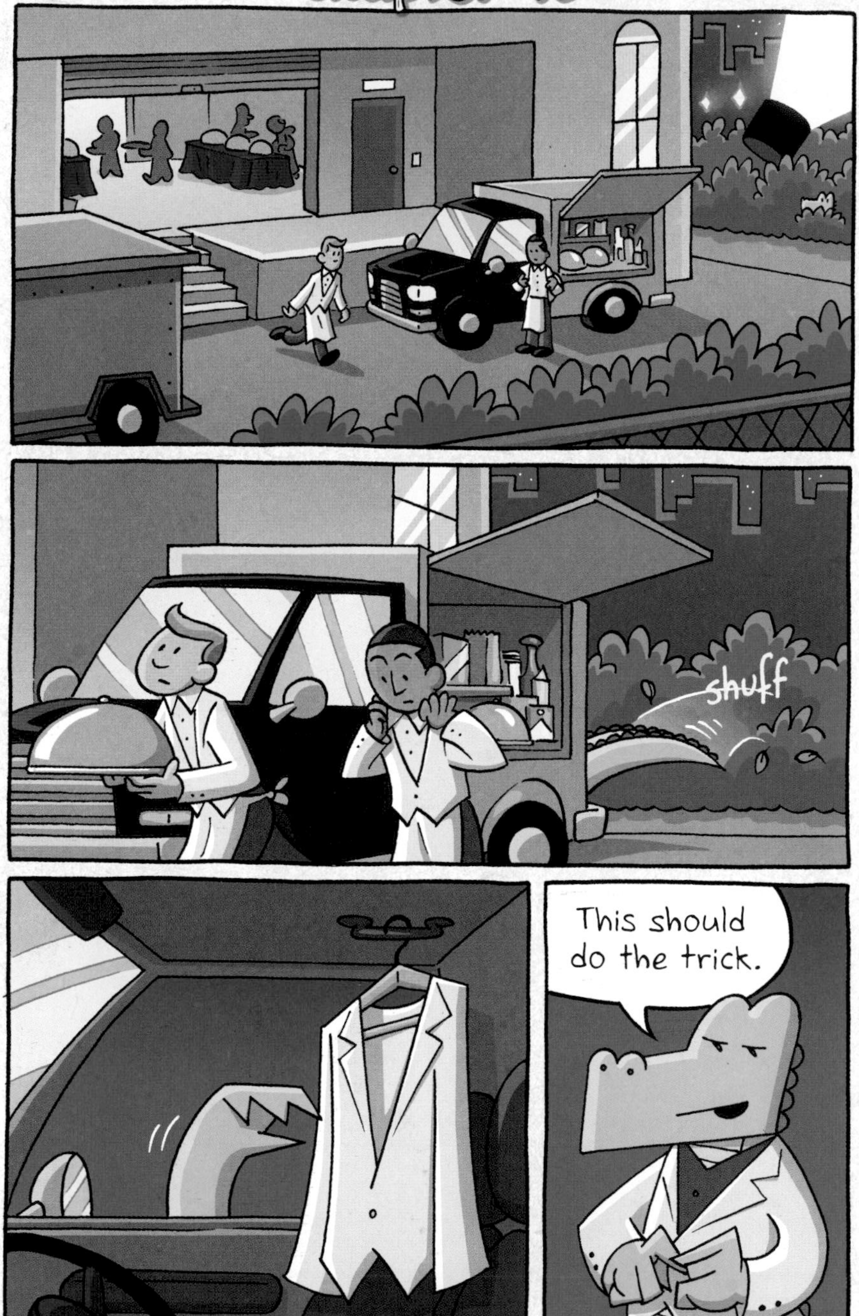
shuff
This should do the trick.

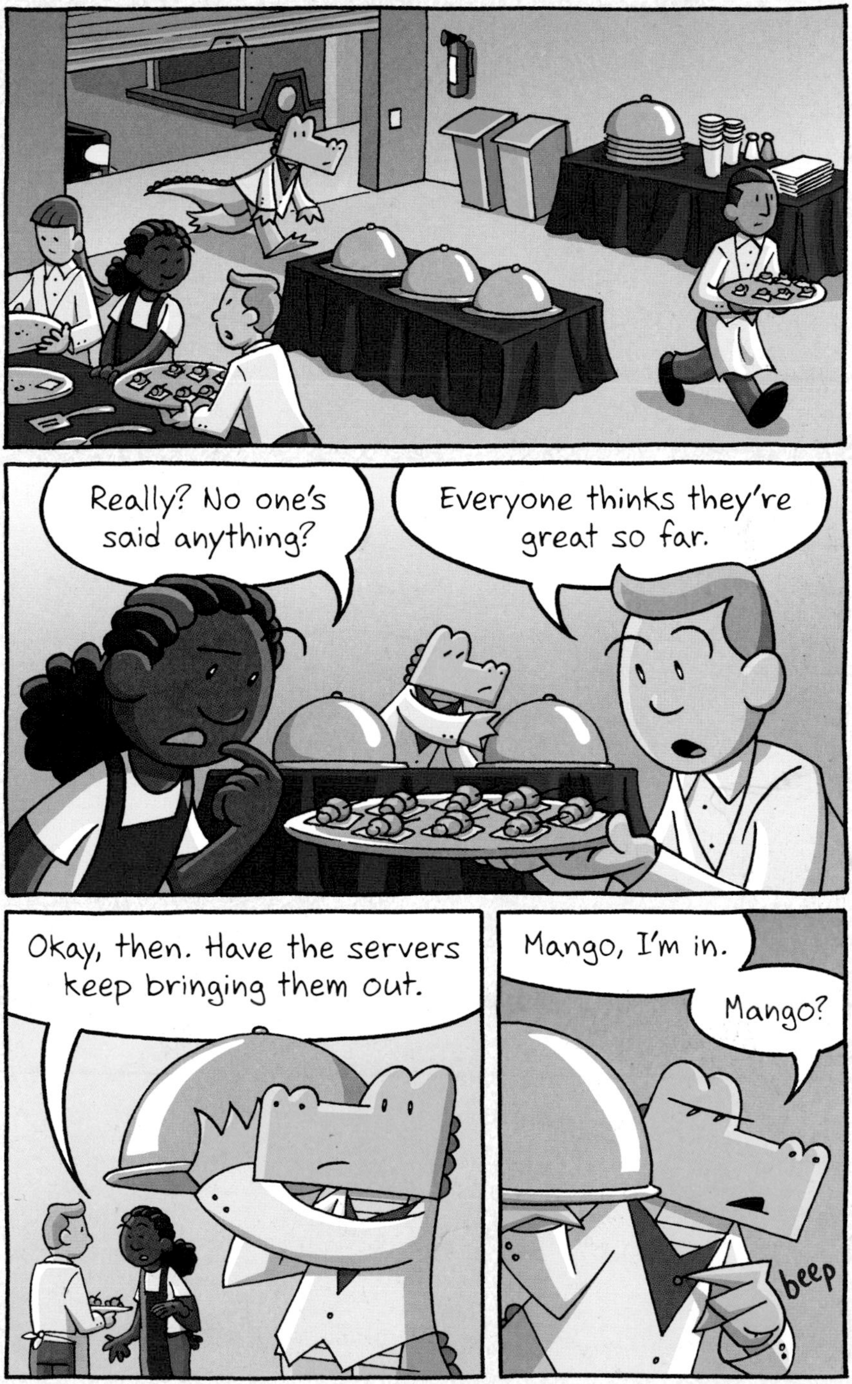
Really? No one's said anything?
Everyone thinks they're great so far.
Okay, then. Have the servers keep bringing them out.
Mango, I'm in.
Mango?
beep

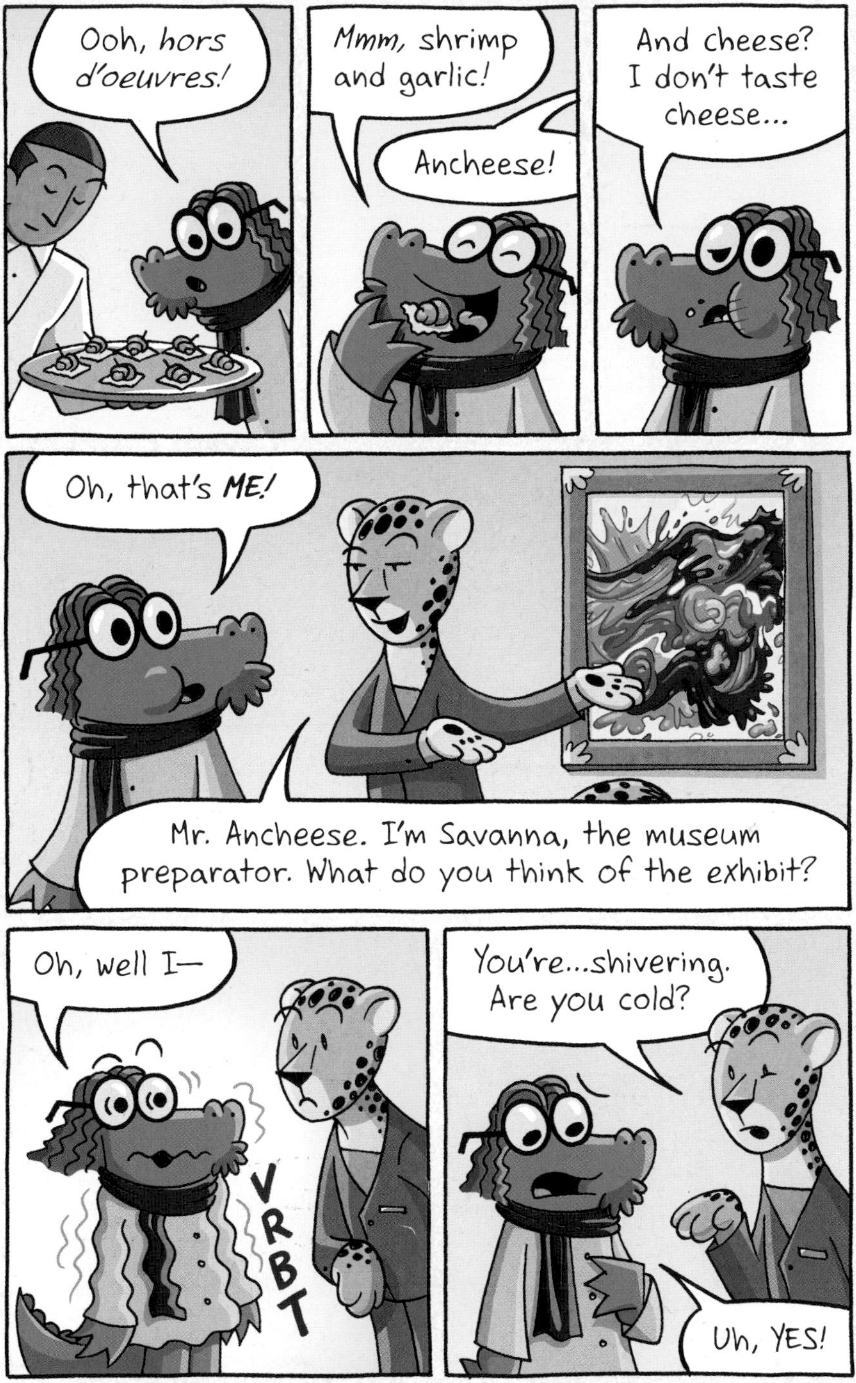
Ooh, hors d'oeuvres!
Mmm, shrimp and garlic!
Ancheese!
And cheese? I don't taste cheese...
Oh, that's **ME!**
Mr. Ancheese. I'm Savanna, the museum preparator. What do you think of the exhibit?
Oh, well I—
VRBT
You're...shivering. Are you cold?
Uh, YES!

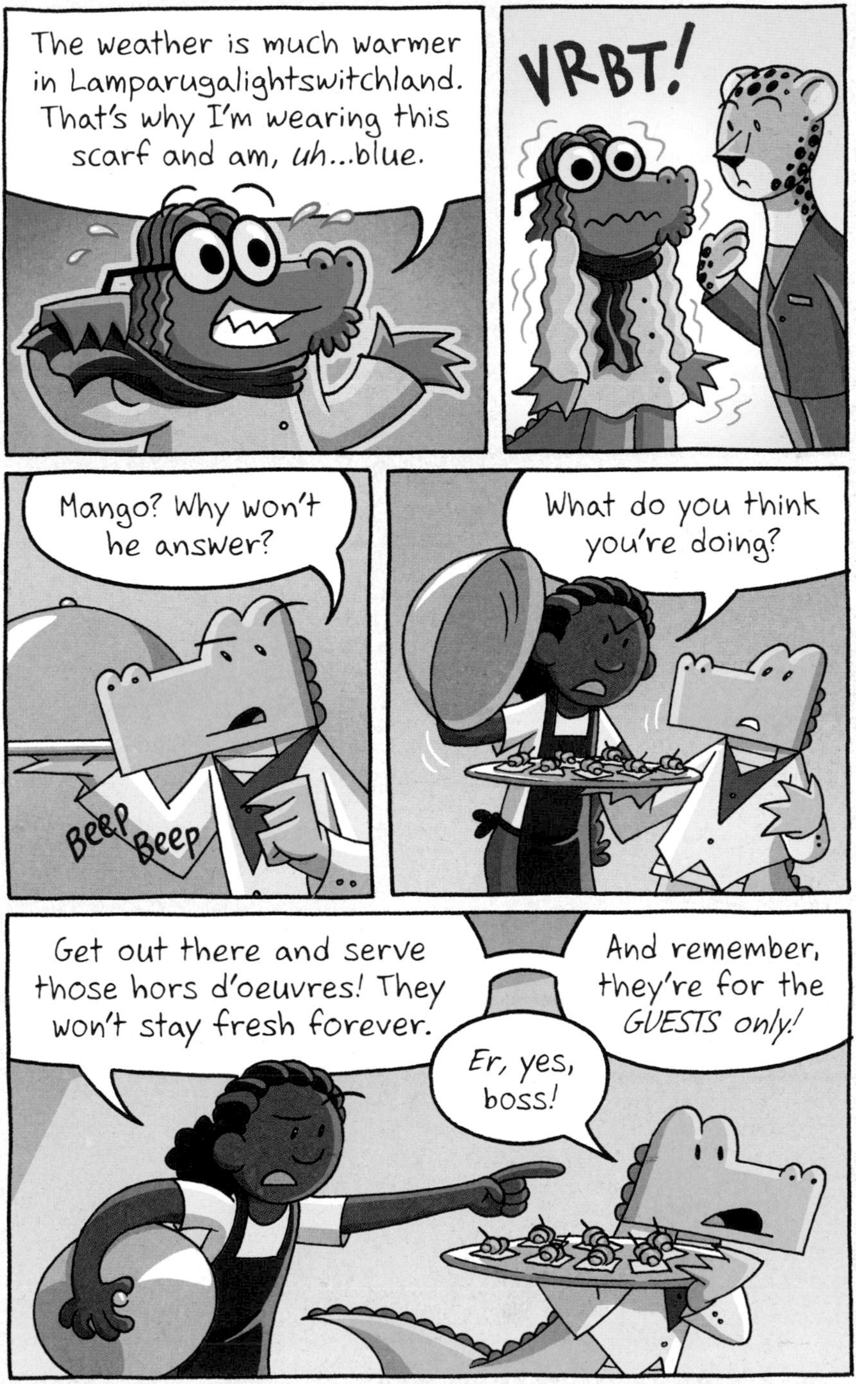

The weather is much warmer in Lamparugalightswitchland. That's why I'm wearing this scarf and am, *uh*...blue.
VRBT!
Mango? Why won't he answer?
BEEP BEEP
What do you think you're doing?
Get out there and serve those hors d'oeuvres! They won't stay fresh forever.
And remember, they're for the *GUESTS* only!
Er, yes, boss!

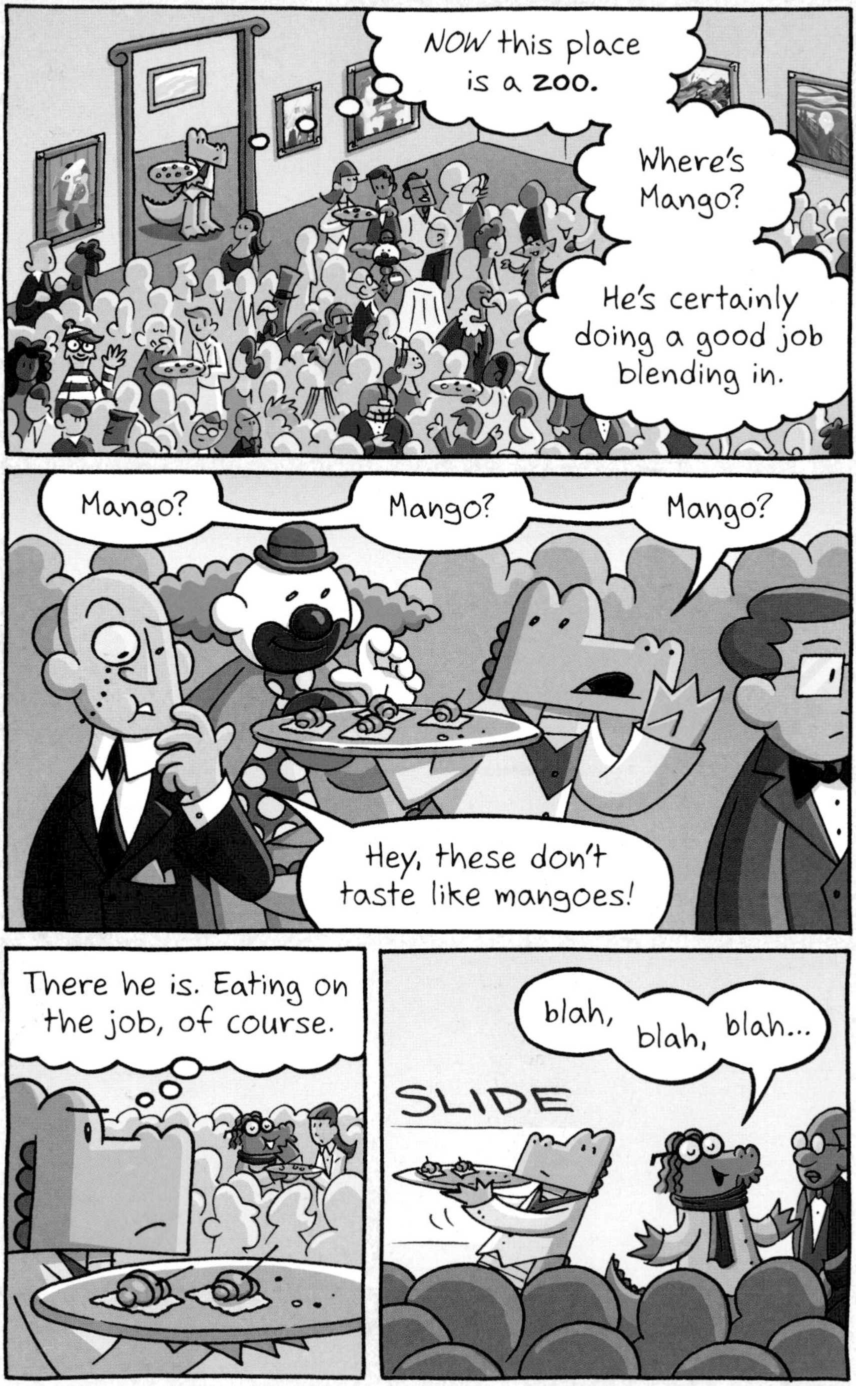
NOW this place is a zoo.
Where's Mango?
He's certainly doing a good job blending in.
Mango?
Mango?
Mango?
Hey, these don't taste like mangoes!
There he is. Eating on the job, of course.
blah, blah, blah...
SLIDE

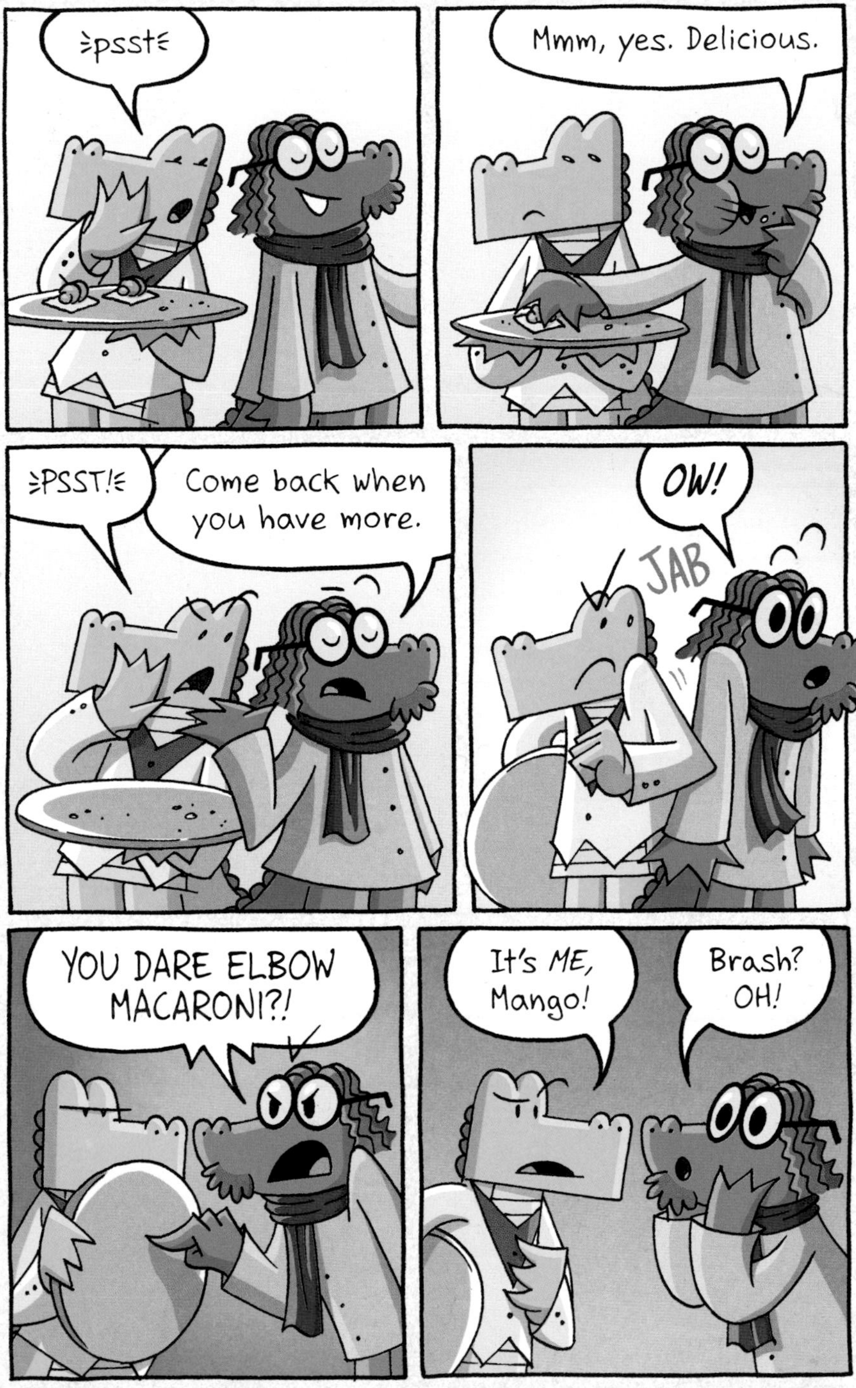
psst
Mmm, yes. Delicious.
PSST!
Come back when you have more.
OW!
JAB
YOU DARE ELBOW MACARONI?!
It's ME, Mango!
Brash? OH!

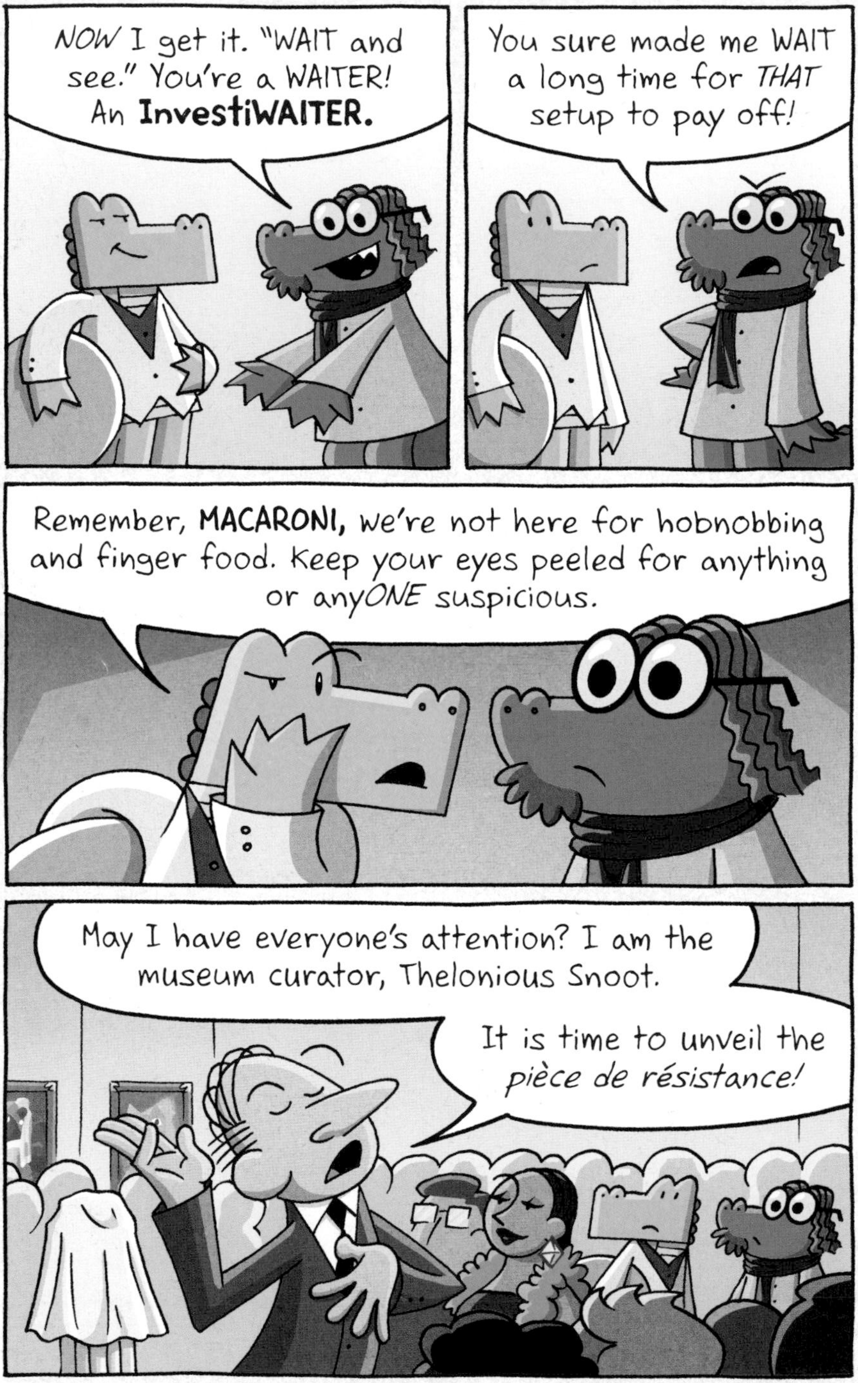
NOW I get it. "WAIT and see." You're a WAITER! An **InvestiWAITER.**
You sure made me WAIT a long time for *THAT* setup to pay off!
Remember, **MACARONI,** we're not here for hobnobbing and finger food. Keep your eyes peeled for anything or any*ONE* suspicious.
May I have everyone's attention? I am the museum curator, Thelonious Snoot.
It is time to unveil the *pièce de résistance!*

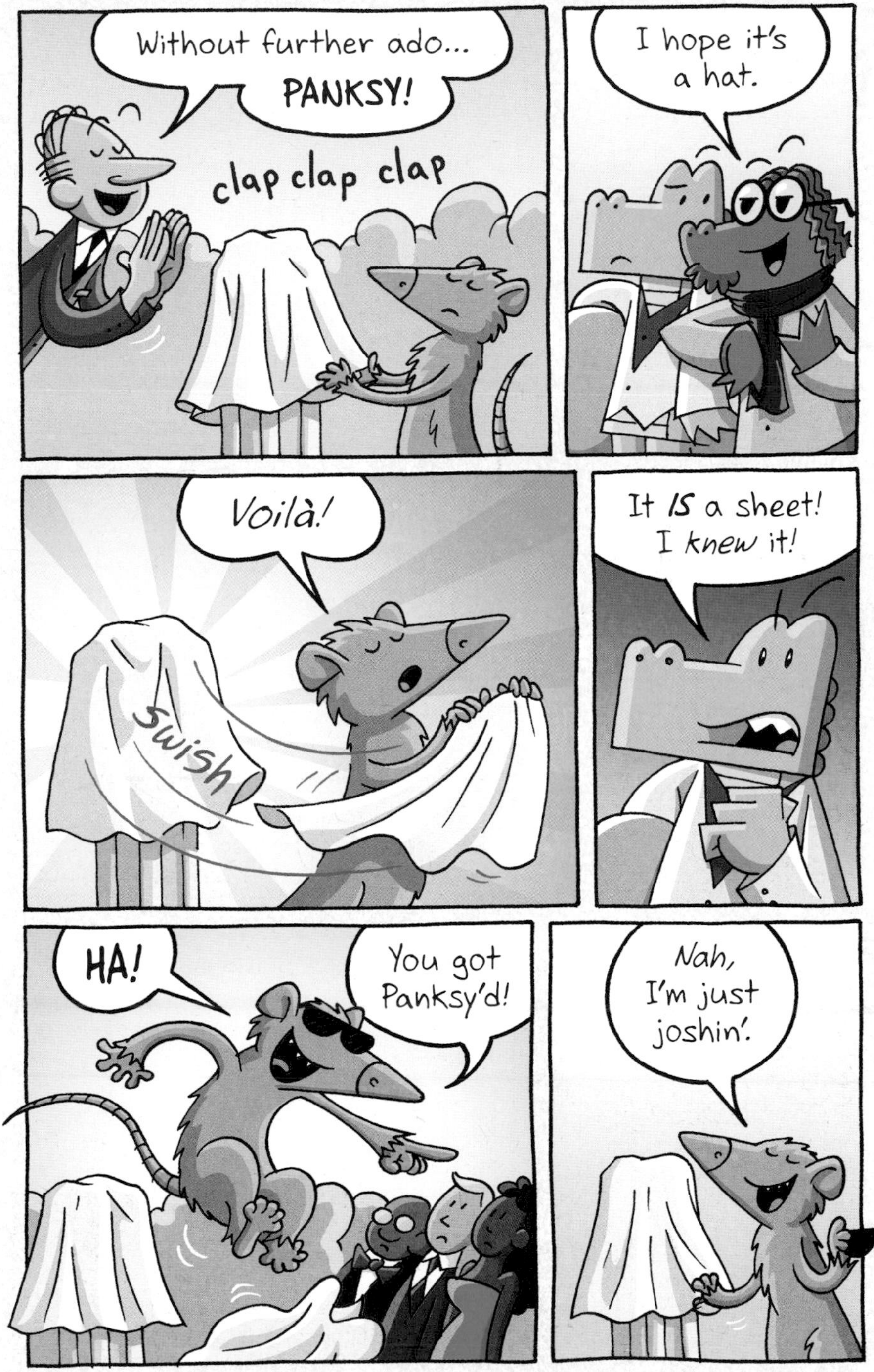
Without further ado...
PANKSY!
clap clap clap
I hope it's a hat.
Voilà!
Swish
It IS a sheet! I knew it!
HA!
You got Panksy'd!
Nah, I'm just joshin'.

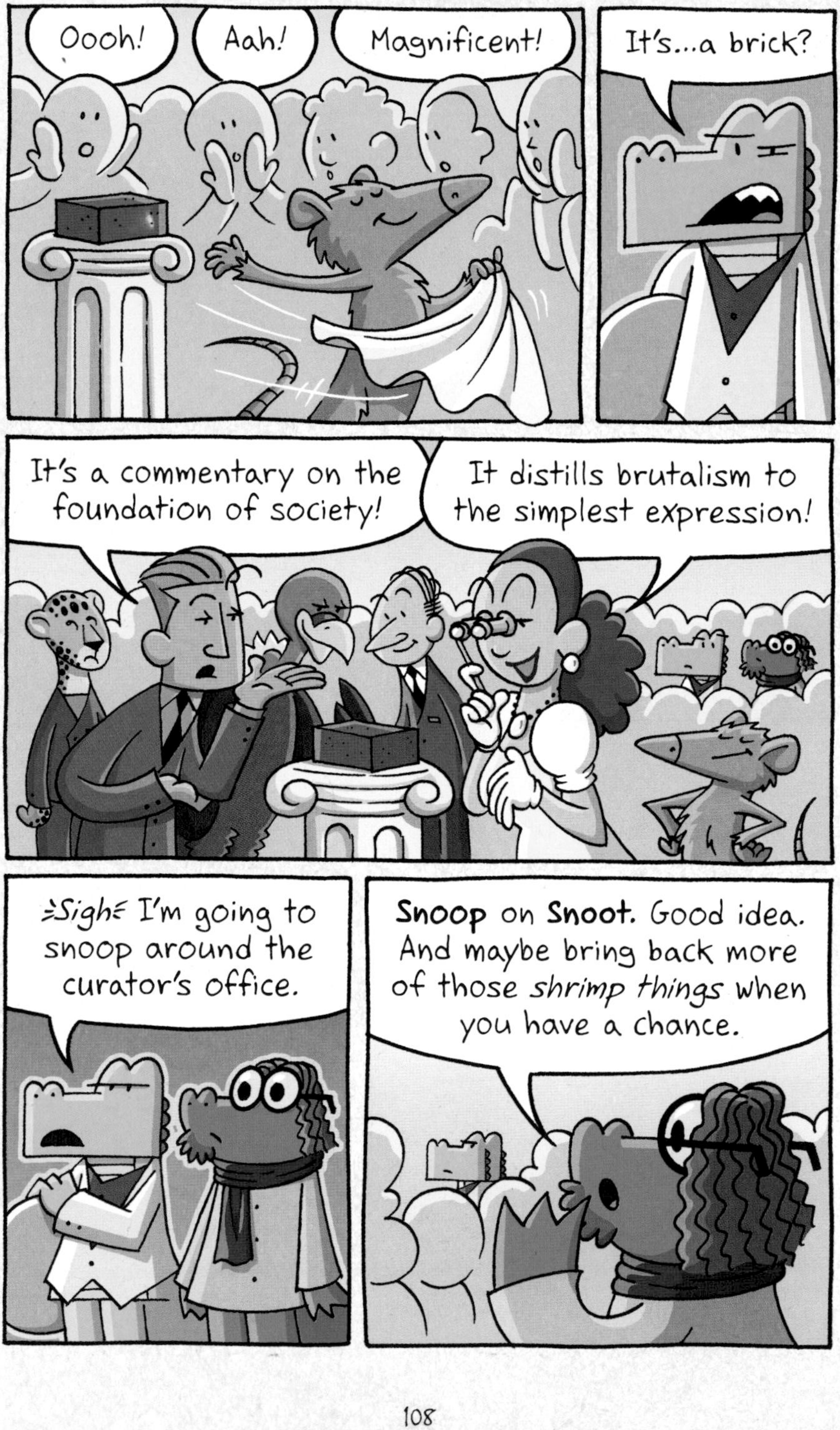
Oooh!
Aah!
Magnificent!
It's...a brick?
It's a commentary on the foundation of society!
It distills brutalism to the simplest expression!
Sigh I'm going to snoop around the curator's office.
Snoop on **Snoot**. Good idea. And maybe bring back more of those *shrimp things* when you have a chance.

Chapter 11

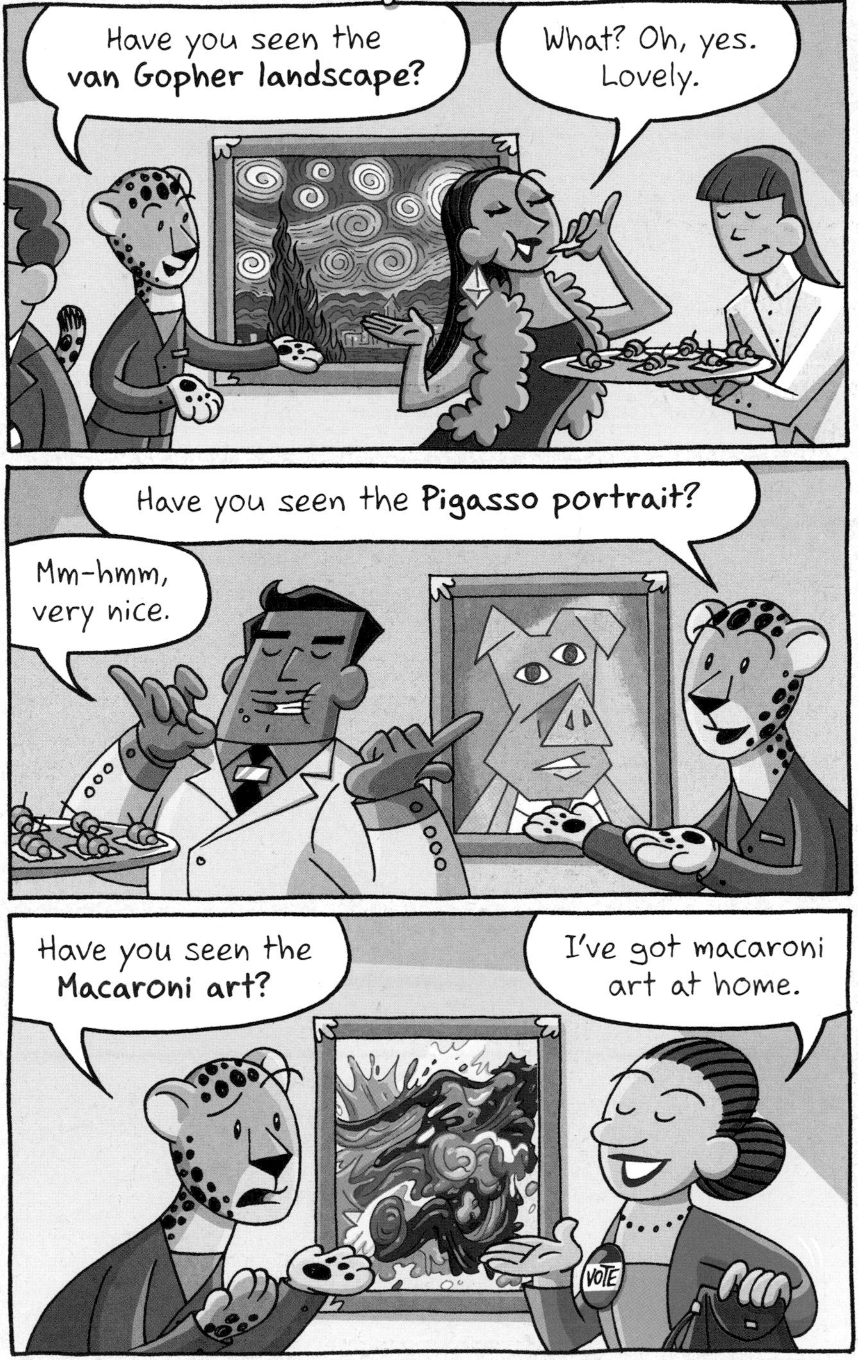
Have you seen the van Gopher landscape?
What? Oh, yes. Lovely.
Have you seen the Pigasso portrait?
Mm-hmm, very nice.
Have you seen the Macaroni art?
I've got macaroni art at home.
VOTE

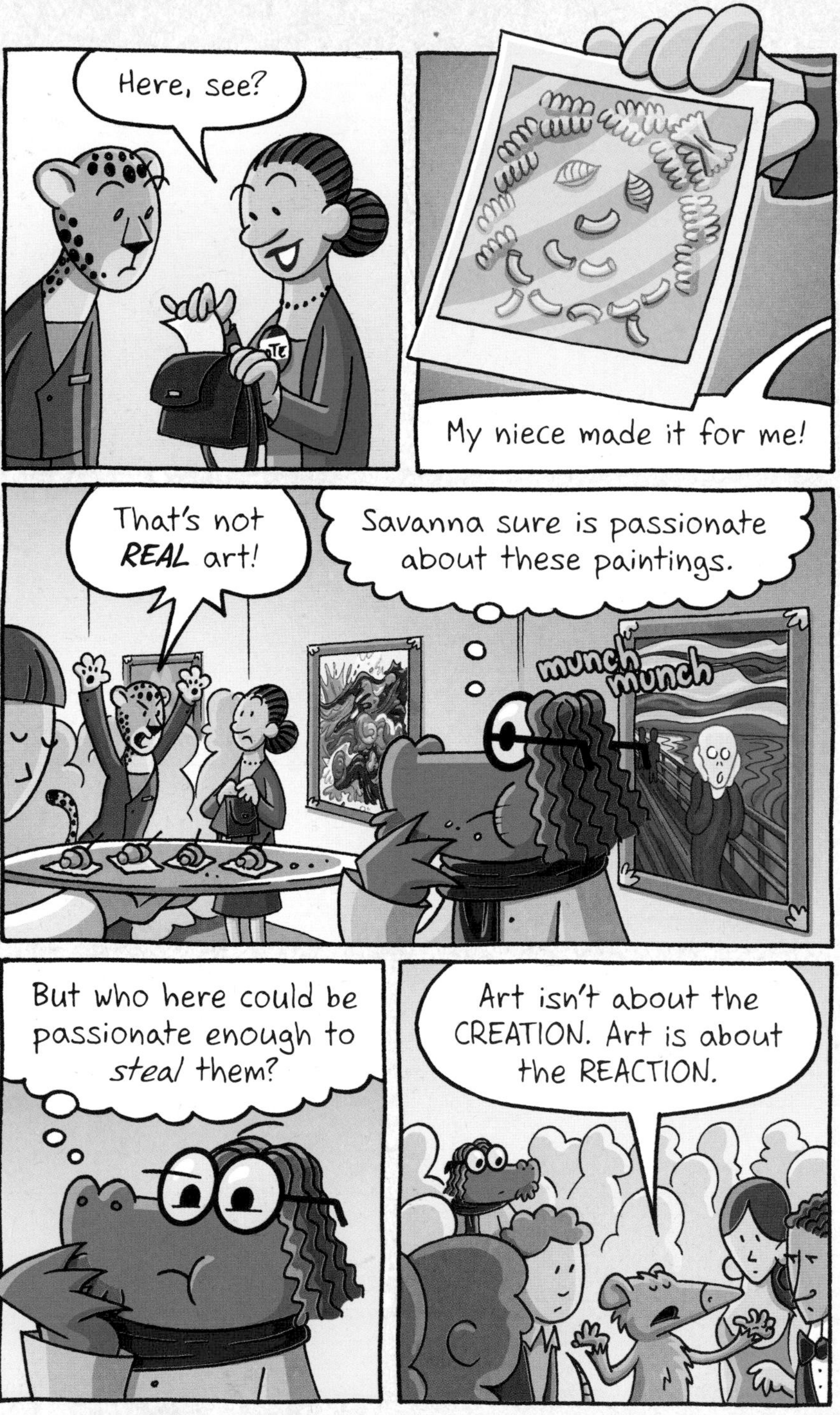
Here, see?
My niece made it for me!
That's not *REAL* art!
Savanna sure is passionate about these paintings.
munch munch
But who here could be passionate enough to *steal* them?
Art isn't about the CREATION. Art is about the REACTION.

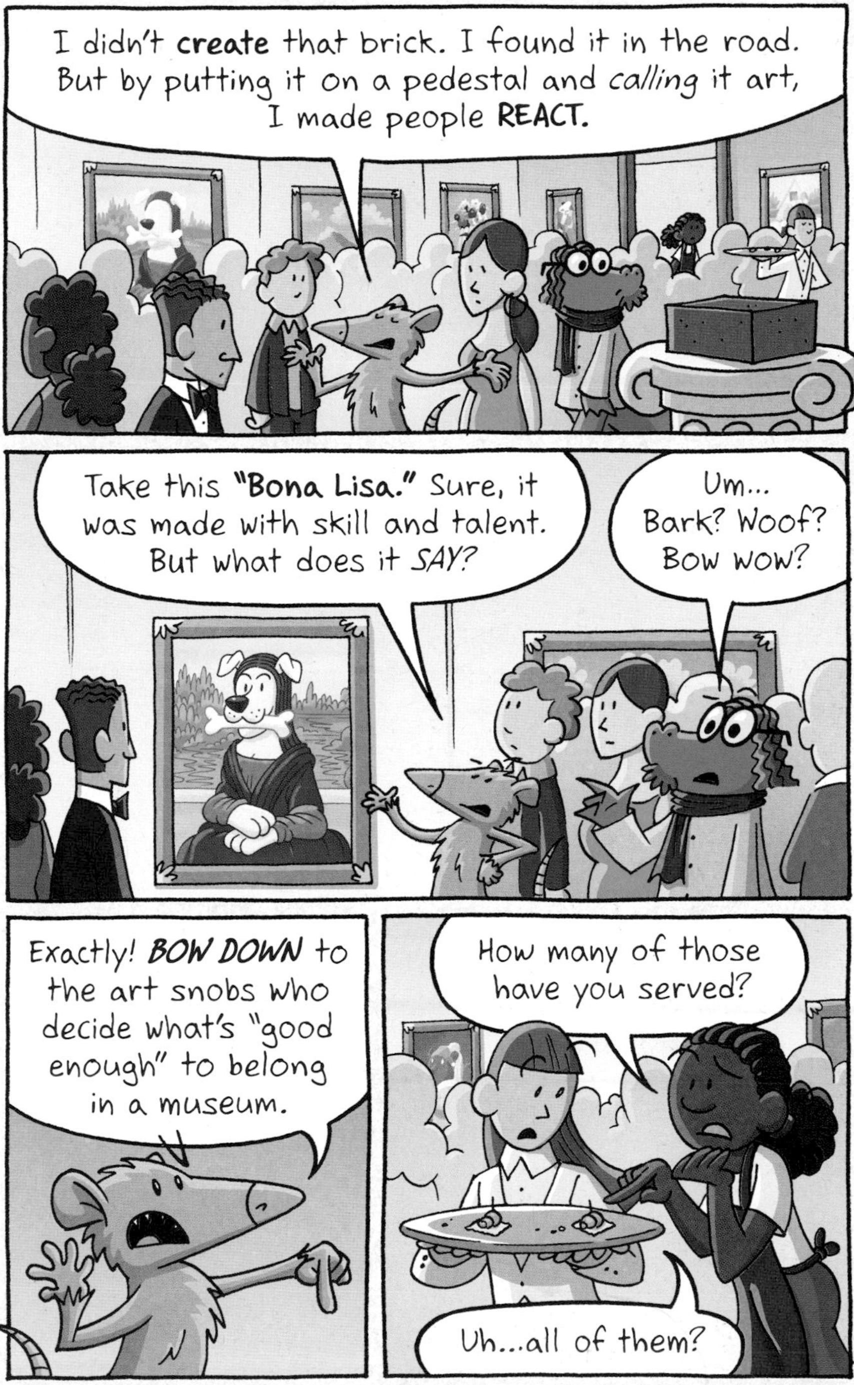
I didn't **create** that brick. I found it in the road. But by putting it on a pedestal and *calling* it art, I made people **REACT.**
Take this **"Bona Lisa."** Sure, it was made with skill and talent. But what does it *SAY?*
Um... Bark? Woof? Bow wow?
Exactly! ***BOW DOWN*** to the art snobs who decide what's "good enough" to belong in a museum.
How many of those have you served?
Uh...all of them?

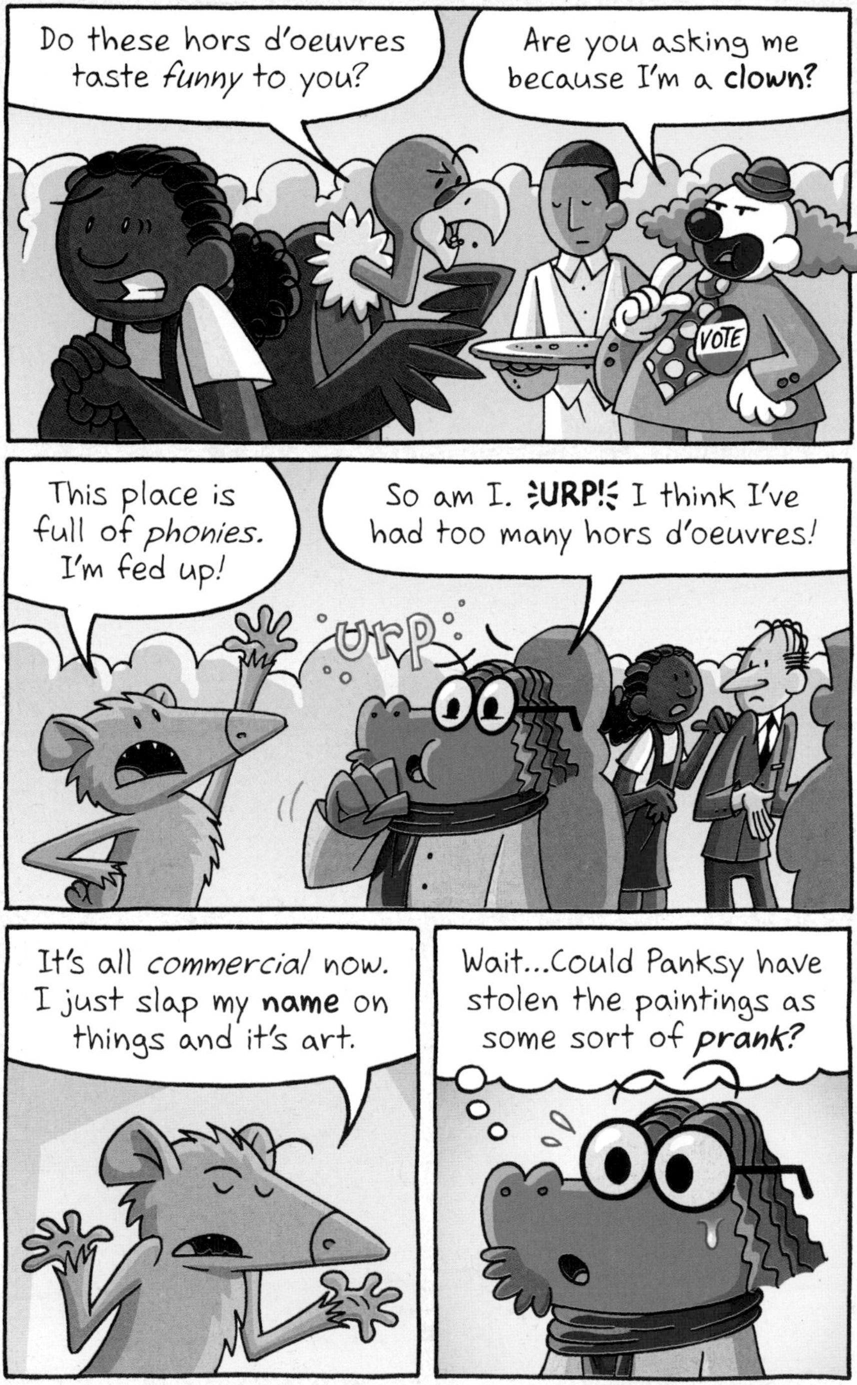
Do these hors d'oeuvres taste *funny* to you?
Are you asking me because I'm a **clown?**
VOTE
This place is full of *phonies.* I'm fed up!
So am I. **URP!** I think I've had too many hors d'oeuvres!
URP
It's all *commercial* now. I just slap my **name** on things and it's art.
Wait...Could Panksy have stolen the paintings as some sort of *prank?*

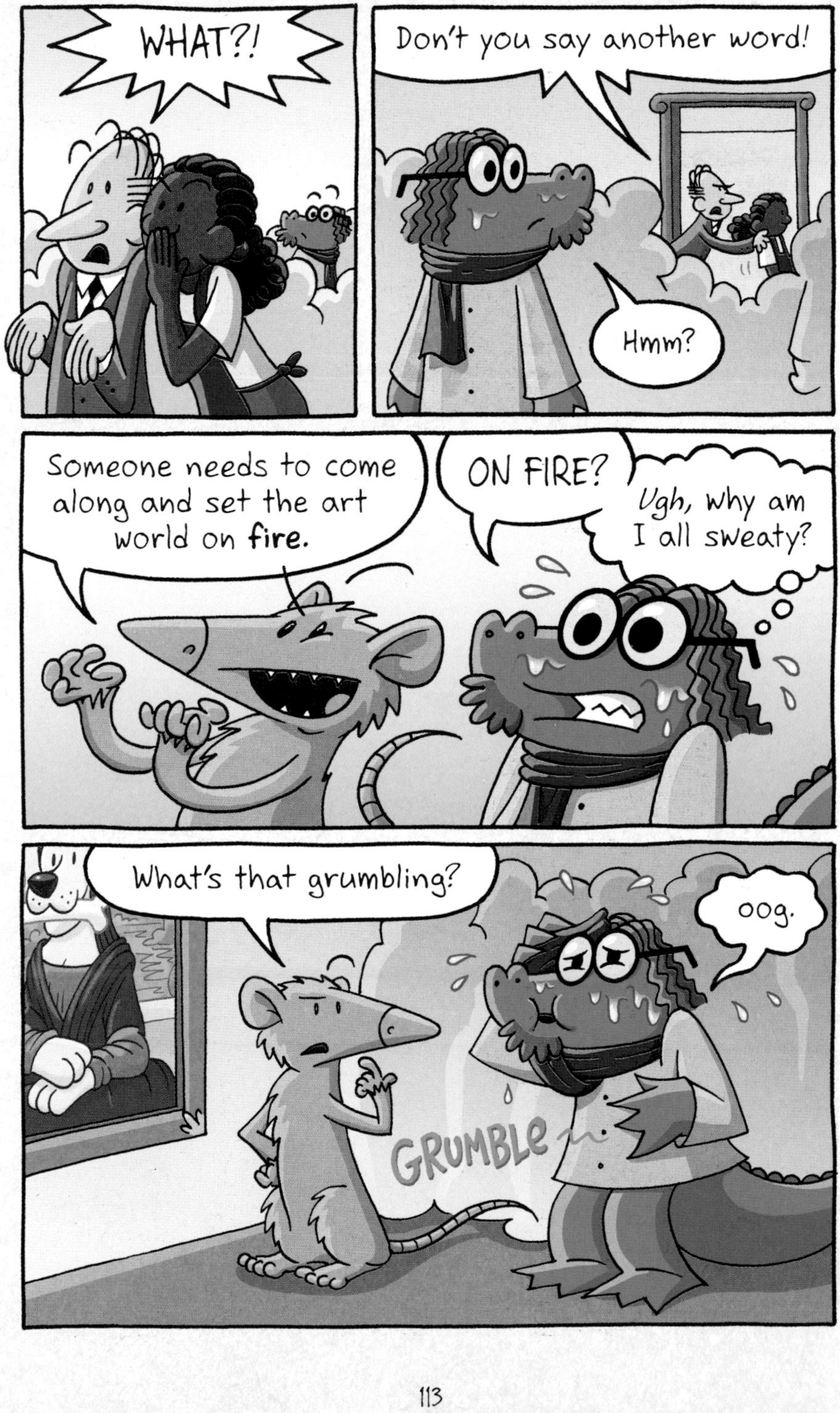
WHAT?!
Don't you say another word!
Hmm?
Someone needs to come along and set the art world on **fire.**
ON FIRE?
Ugh, why am I all sweaty?
What's that grumbling?
oog.
GRUMBLE

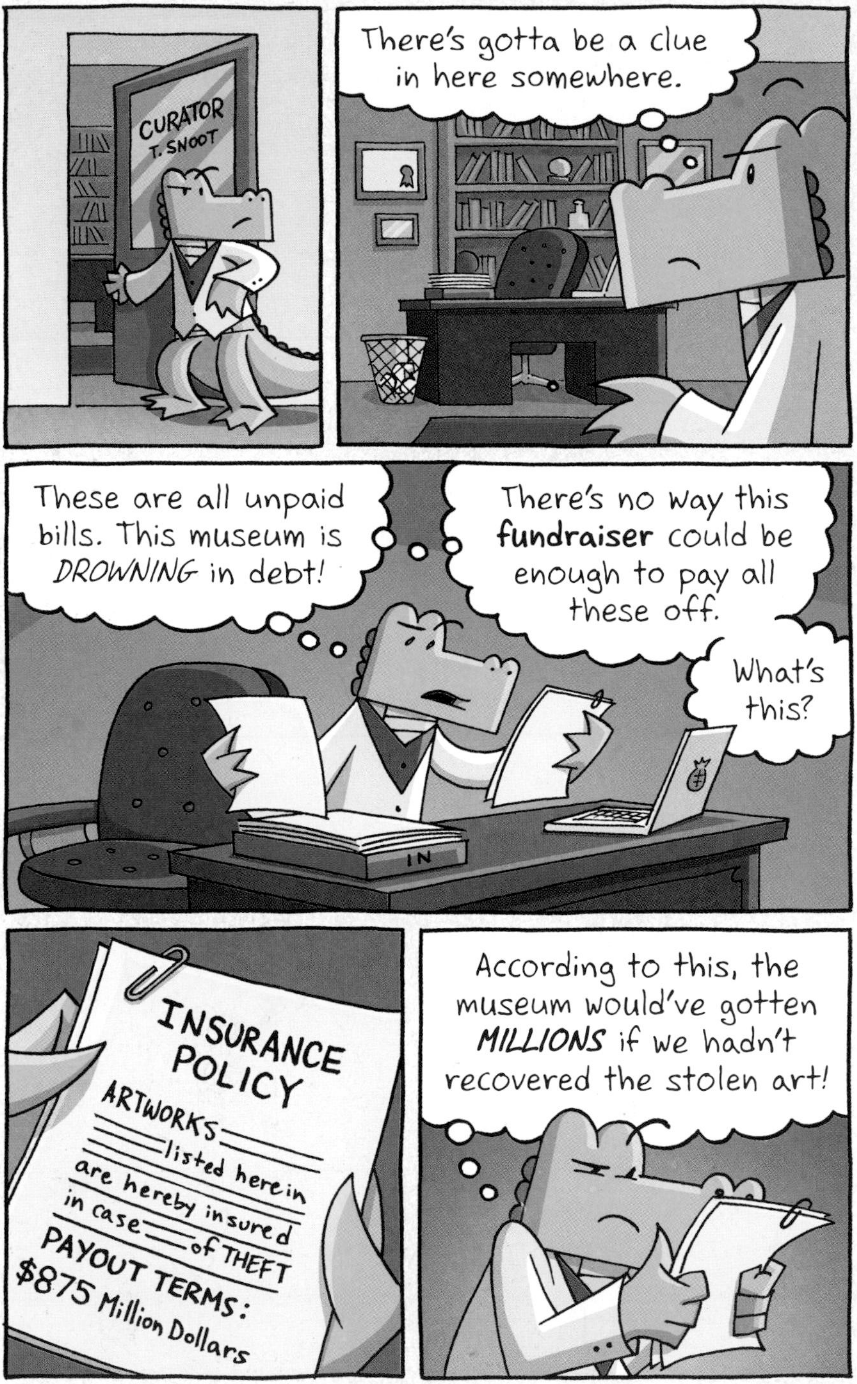

CURATOR
T. SNOOT
There's gotta be a clue in here somewhere.
These are all unpaid bills. This museum is DROWNING in debt!
There's no way this fundraiser could be enough to pay all these off.
What's this?
IN
INSURANCE POLICY
ARTWORKS listed herein are hereby insured in case of THEFT
PAYOUT TERMS:
$875 Million Dollars
According to this, the museum would've gotten MILLIONS if we hadn't recovered the stolen art!

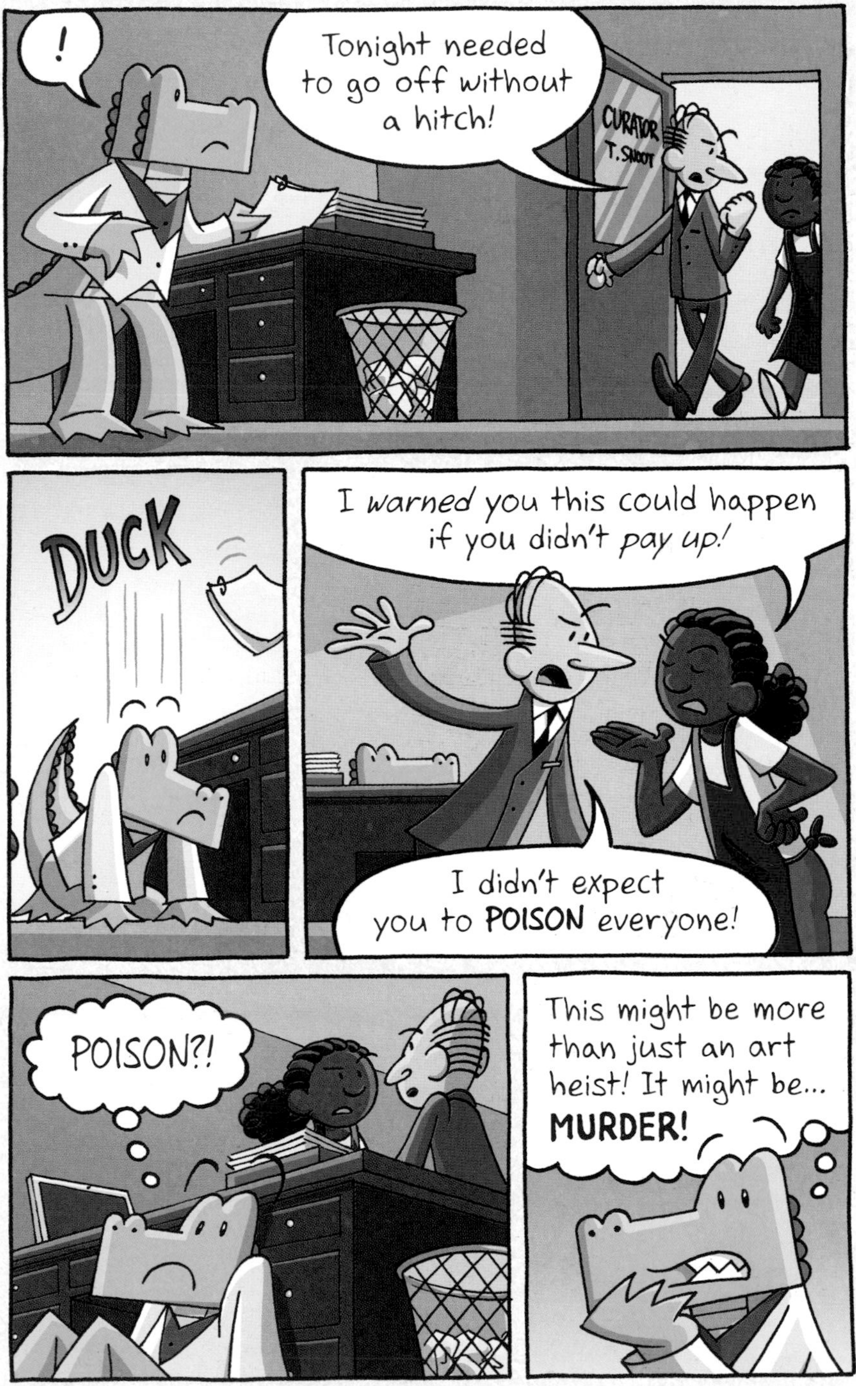
!
Tonight needed to go off without a hitch!
CURATOR T. SNOOT
DUCK
I *warned* you this could happen if you didn't *pay up!*
I didn't expect you to **POISON** everyone!
POISON?!
This might be more than just an art heist! It might be... **MURDER!**

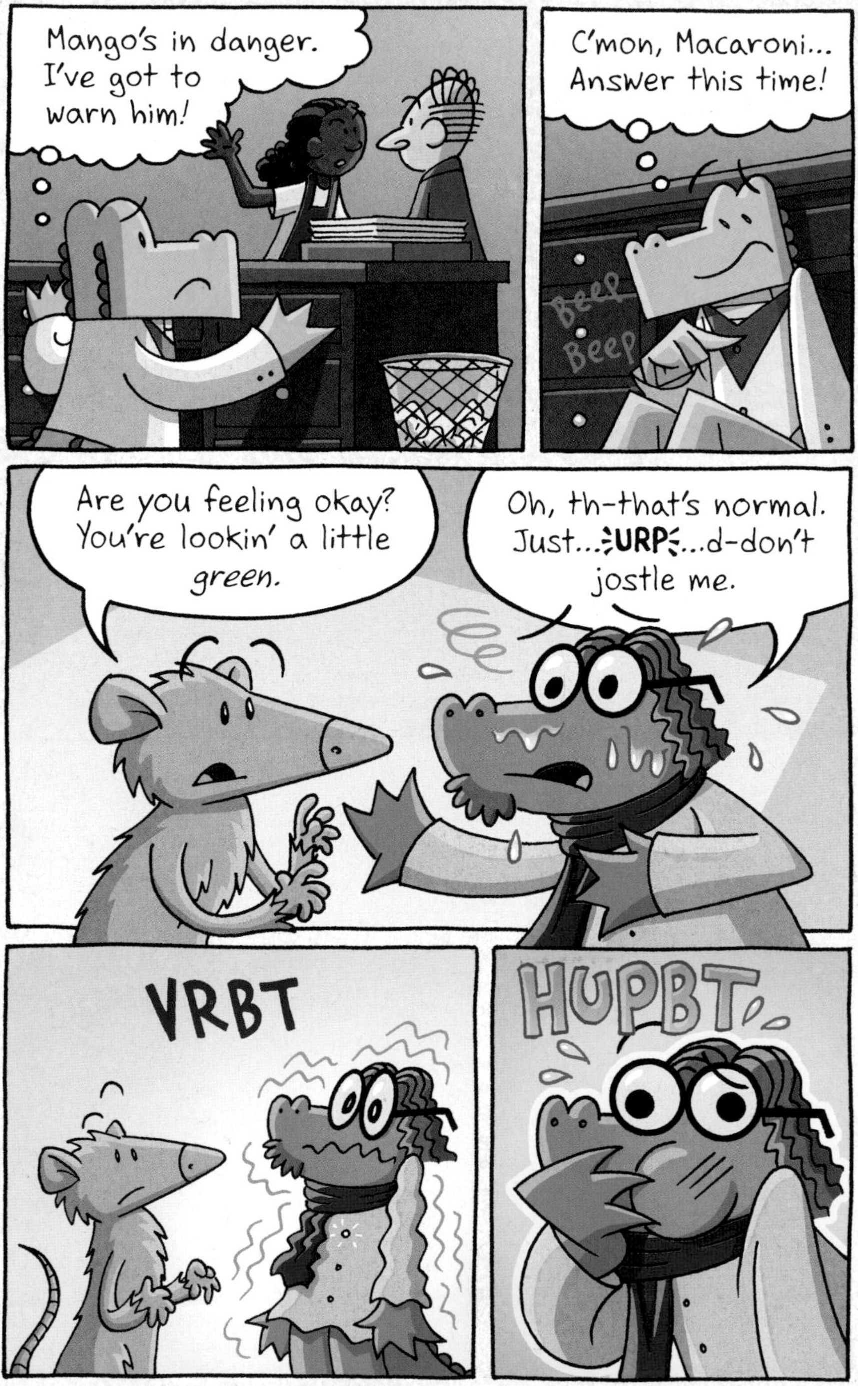
Mango's in danger. I've got to warn him!
C'mon, Macaroni... Answer this time!
Beep Beep
Are you feeling okay? You're lookin' a little green.
Oh, th-that's normal. Just... URP ...d-don't jostle me.
VRBT
HUPBT

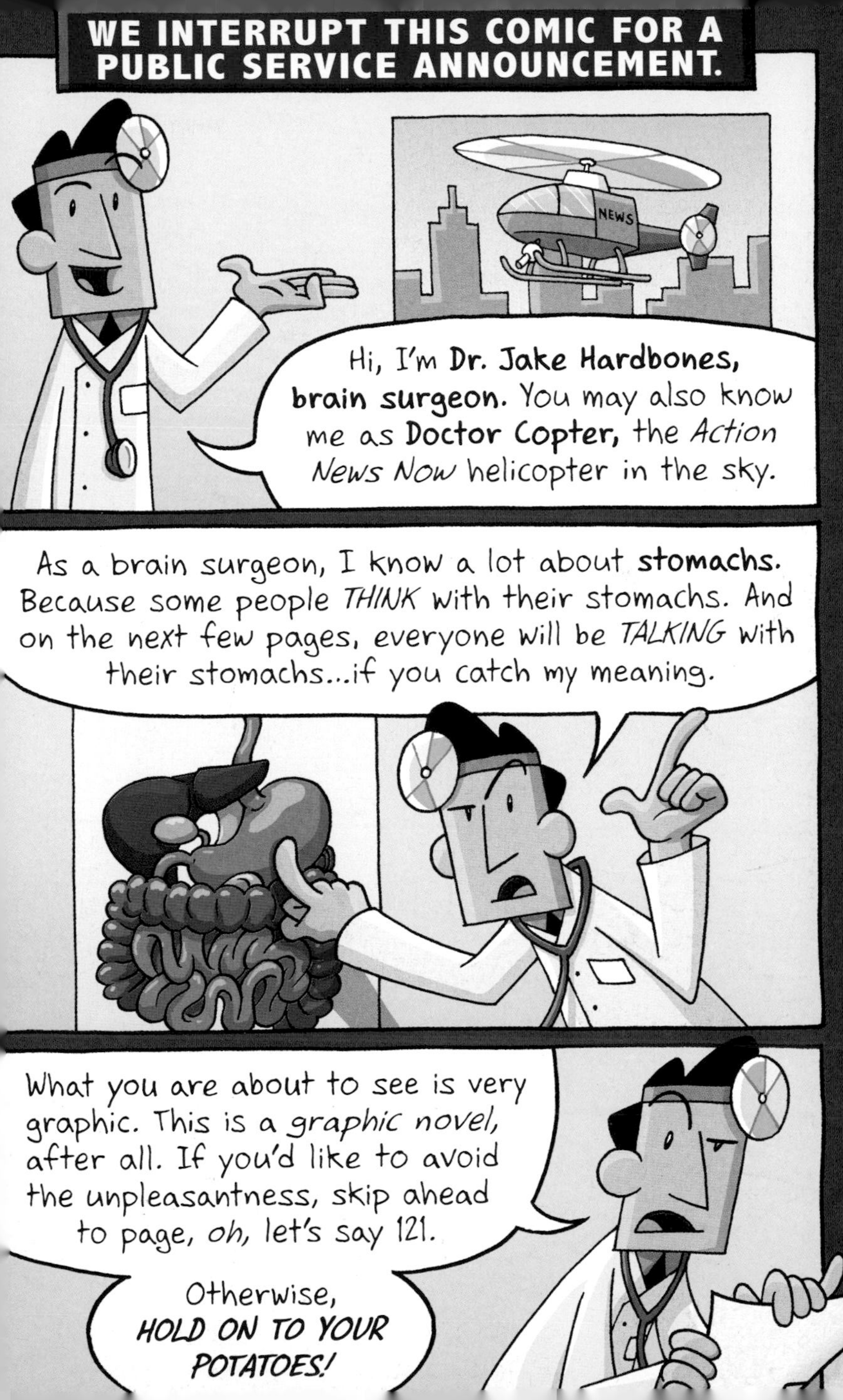
WE INTERRUPT THIS COMIC FOR A PUBLIC SERVICE ANNOUNCEMENT.
NEWS
Hi, I'm Dr. Jake Hardbones, brain surgeon. You may also know me as Doctor Copter, the Action News Now helicopter in the sky.
As a brain surgeon, I know a lot about stomachs. Because some people THINK with their stomachs. And on the next few pages, everyone will be TALKING with their stomachs...if you catch my meaning.
What you are about to see is very graphic. This is a graphic novel, after all. If you'd like to avoid the unpleasantness, skip ahead to page, oh, let's say 121.
Otherwise, HOLD ON TO YOUR POTATOES!

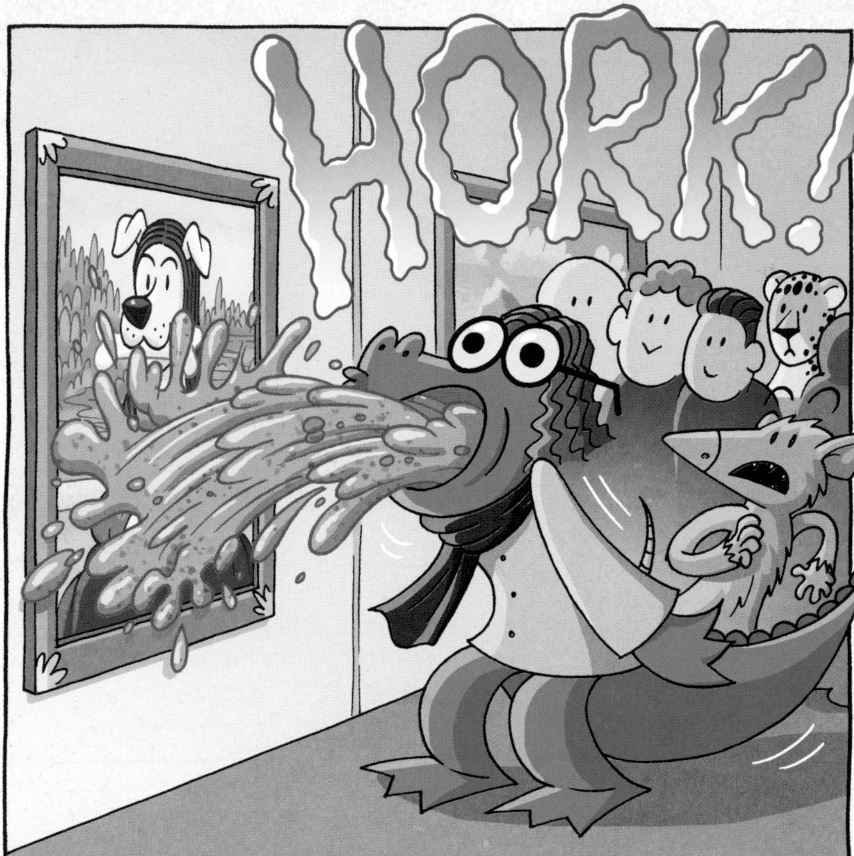
HORK!

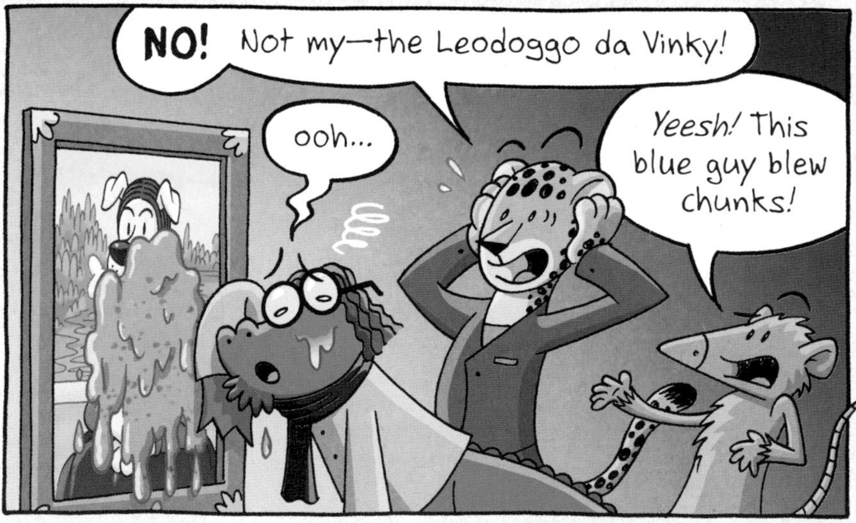
NO! Not my—the Leodoggo da Vinky!
ooh...
Yeesh! This blue guy blew chunks!

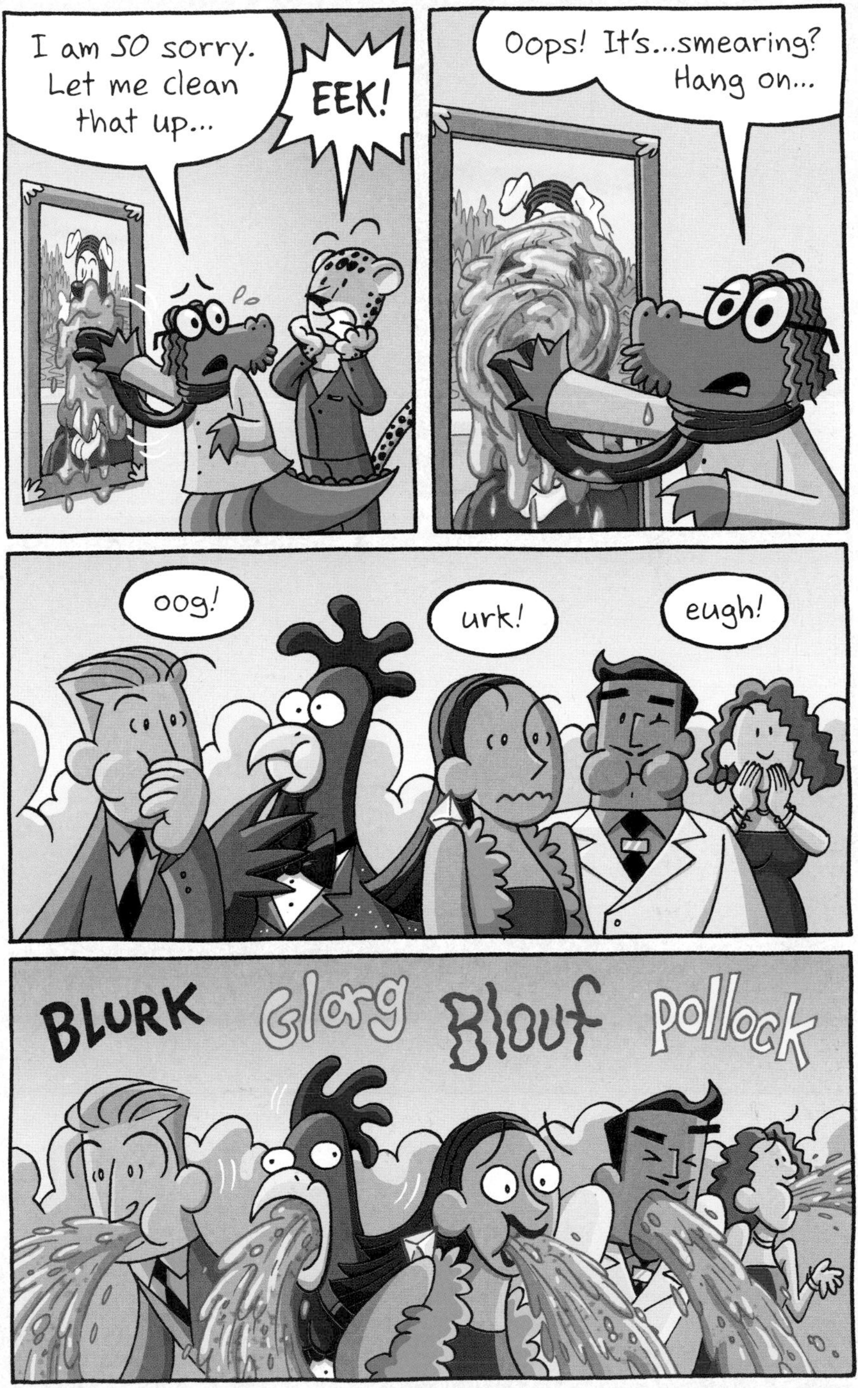
I am SO sorry. Let me clean that up...
EEK!
Oops! It's...smearing? Hang on...
oog!
urk!
eugh!
BLURK
Glorg
Blouf
pollock

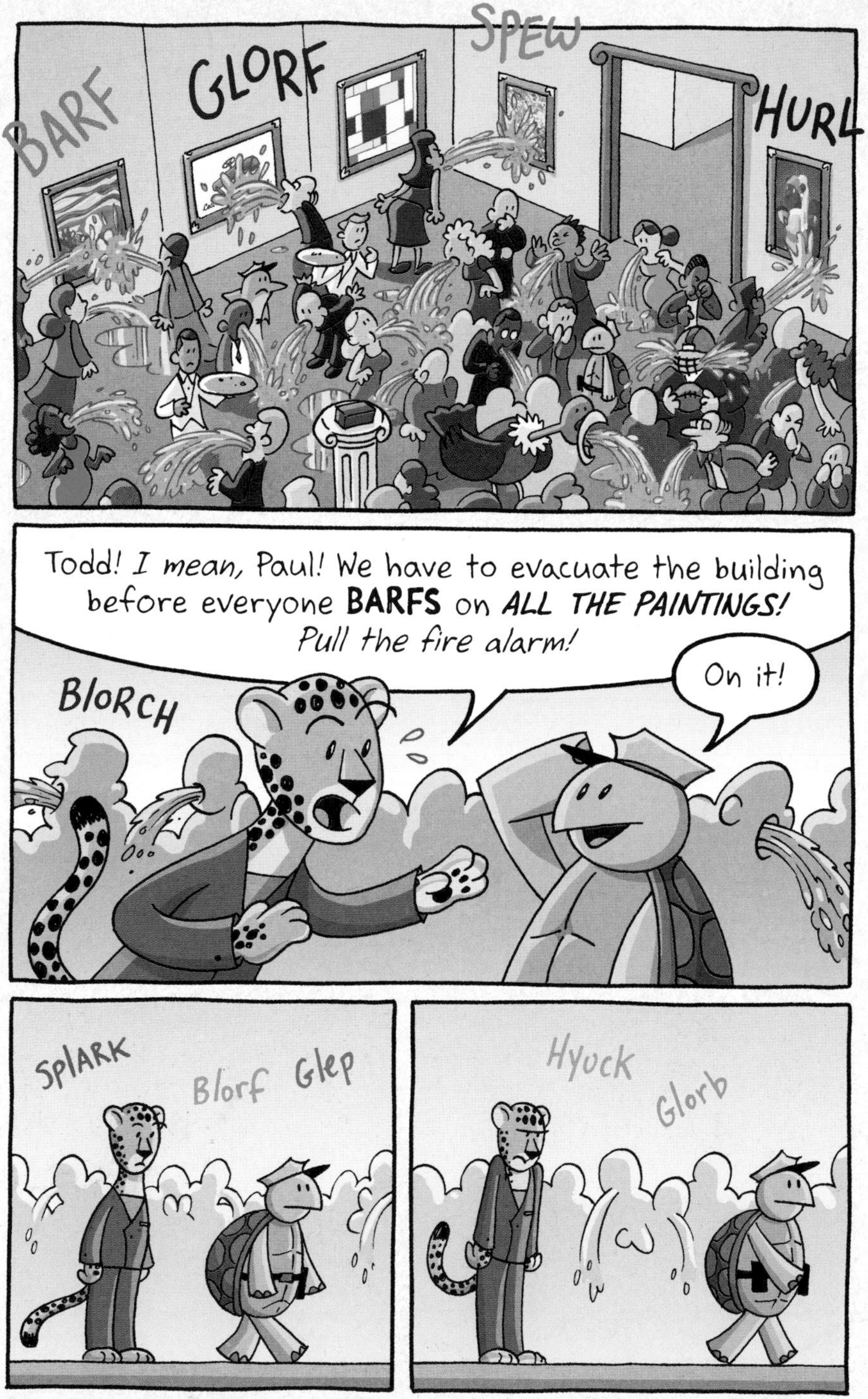
BARF
GLORF
SPEW
HURL
Todd! I mean, Paul! We have to evacuate the building before everyone BARFS on ALL THE PAINTINGS! Pull the fire alarm!
BLORCH
On it!
SPLARK
Blorf
Glep
Hyuck
Glorb

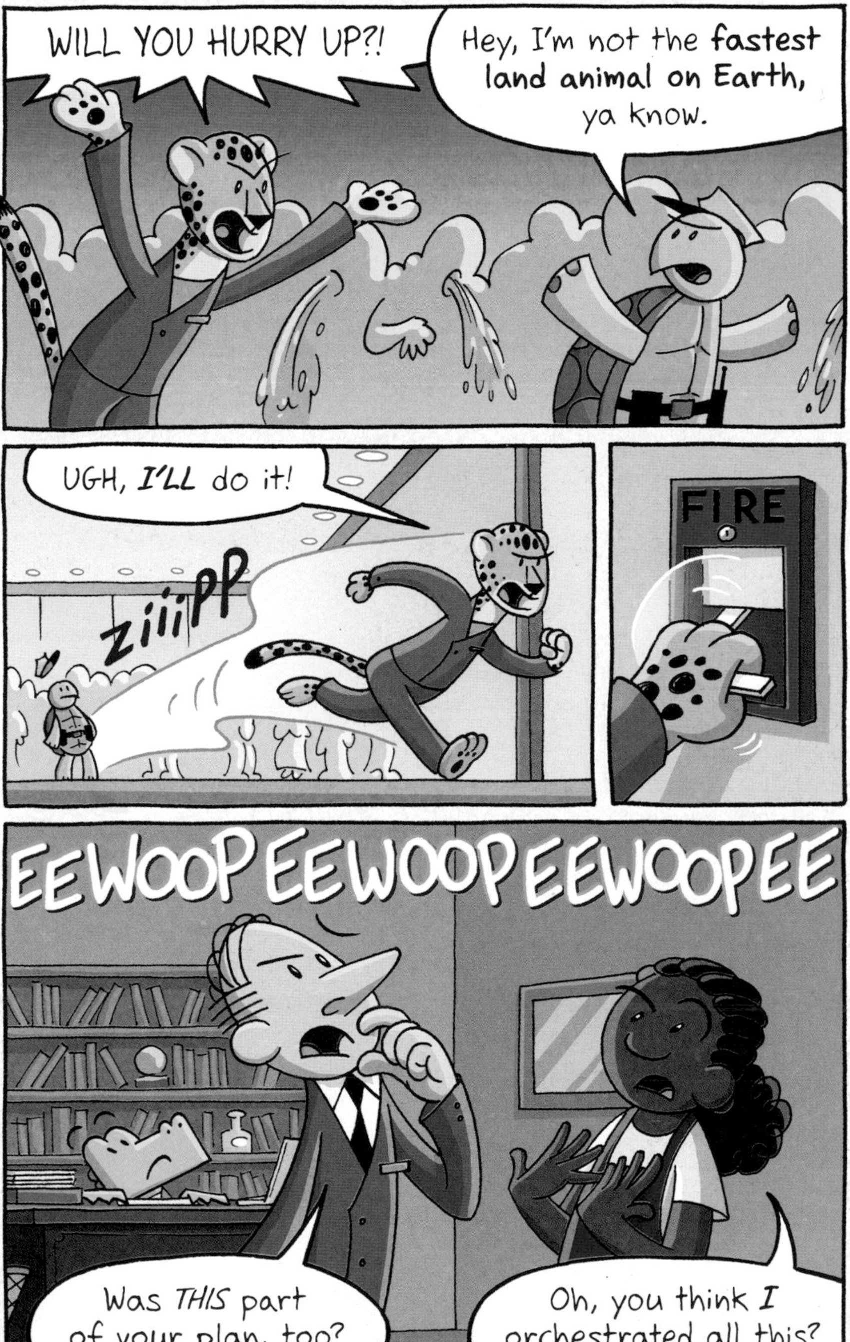
WILL YOU HURRY UP?!
Hey, I'm not the **fastest land animal on Earth,** ya know.
UGH, *I'LL* do it!
ziiiPP
FIRE
EEWOOPEEWOOPEEWOOPEE
Was *THIS* part of your plan, too?
Oh, you think *I* orchestrated all this?

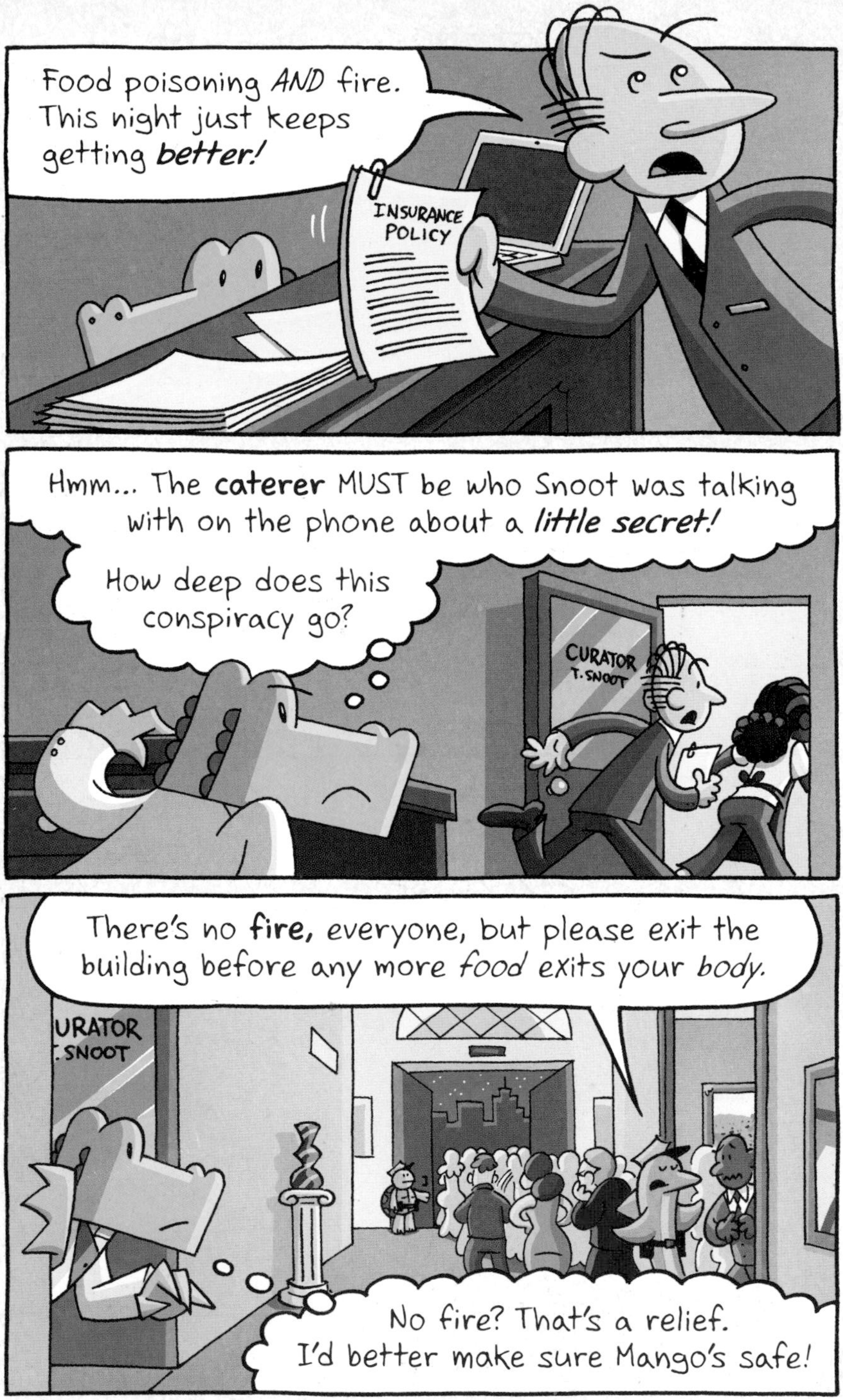
Food poisoning AND fire. This night just keeps getting better!
INSURANCE POLICY
Hmm... The caterer MUST be who Snoot was talking with on the phone about a little secret!
How deep does this conspiracy go?
CURATOR T. SNOOT
There's no fire, everyone, but please exit the building before any more food exits your body.
URATOR T. SNOOT
No fire? That's a relief. I'd better make sure Mango's safe!

Chapter 12

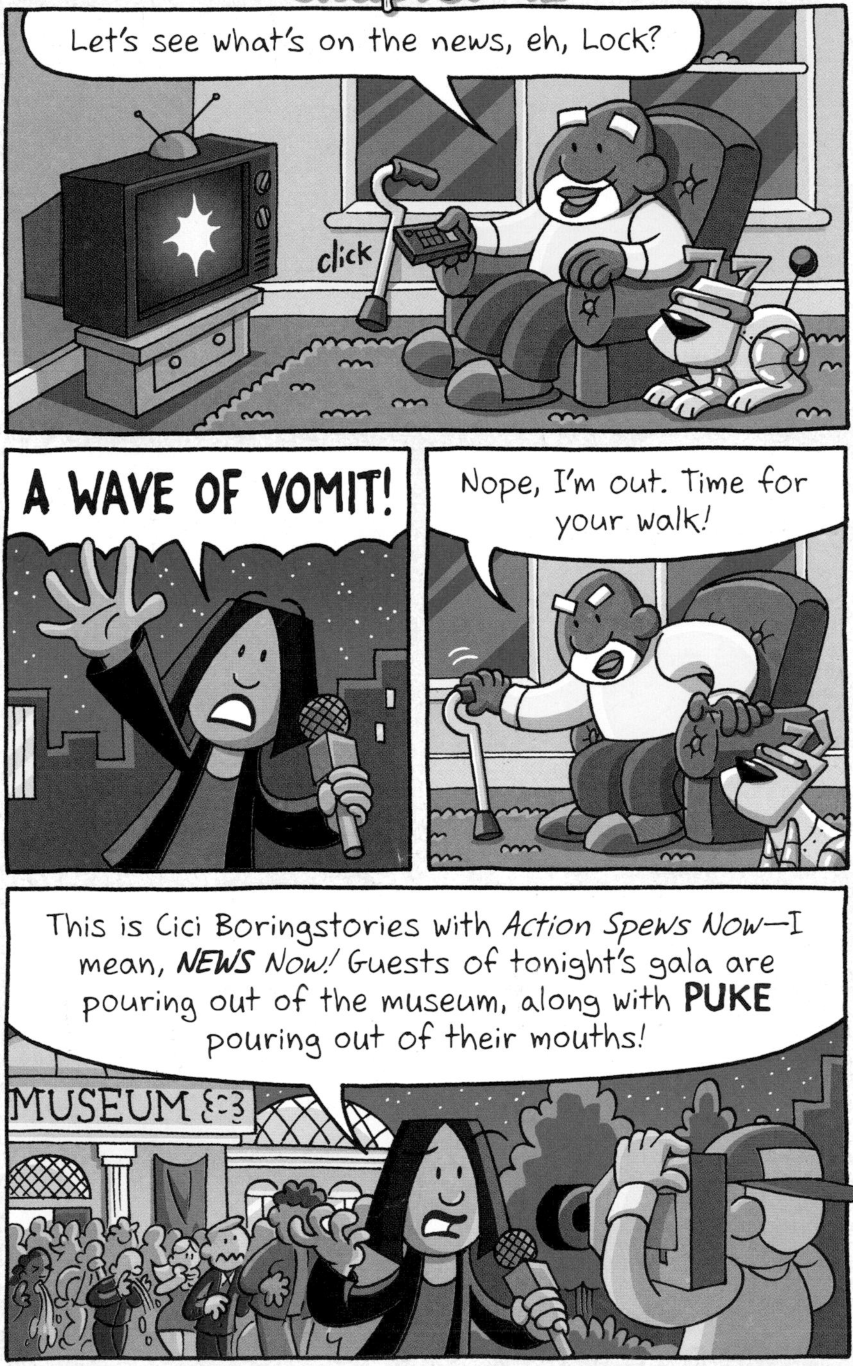

Let's see what's on the news, eh, Lock?
click
A WAVE OF VOMIT!
Nope, I'm out. Time for your walk!
This is Cici Boringstories with *Action Spews Now*—I mean, ***NEWS** Now!* Guests of tonight's gala are pouring out of the museum, along with **PUKE** pouring out of their mouths!
MUSEUM

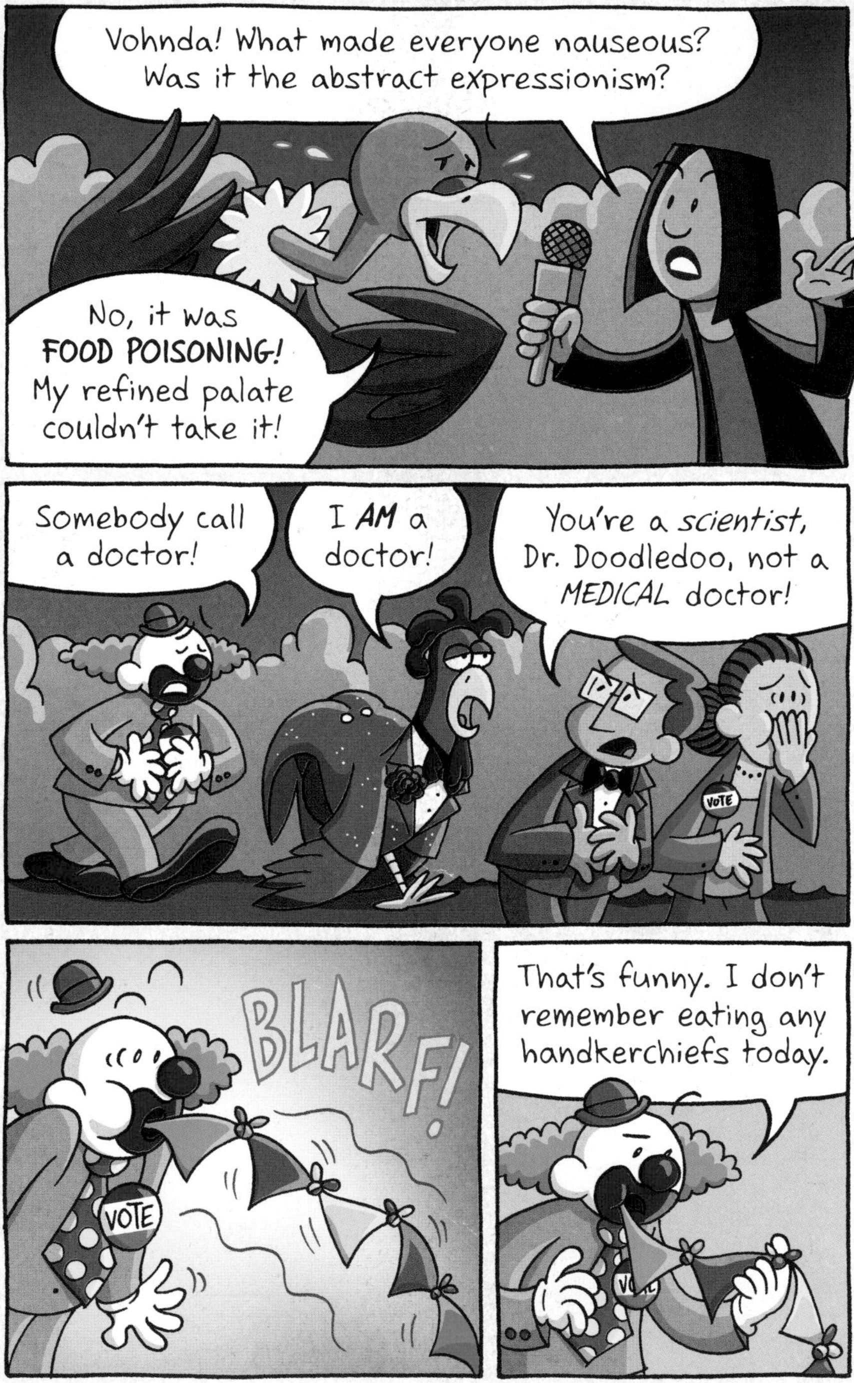
Vohnda! What made everyone nauseous? Was it the abstract expressionism?
No, it was FOOD POISONING! My refined palate couldn't take it!
Somebody call a doctor!
I AM a doctor!
You're a scientist, Dr. Doodledoo, not a MEDICAL doctor!
VOTE
BLARF!
VOTE
That's funny. I don't remember eating any handkerchiefs today.

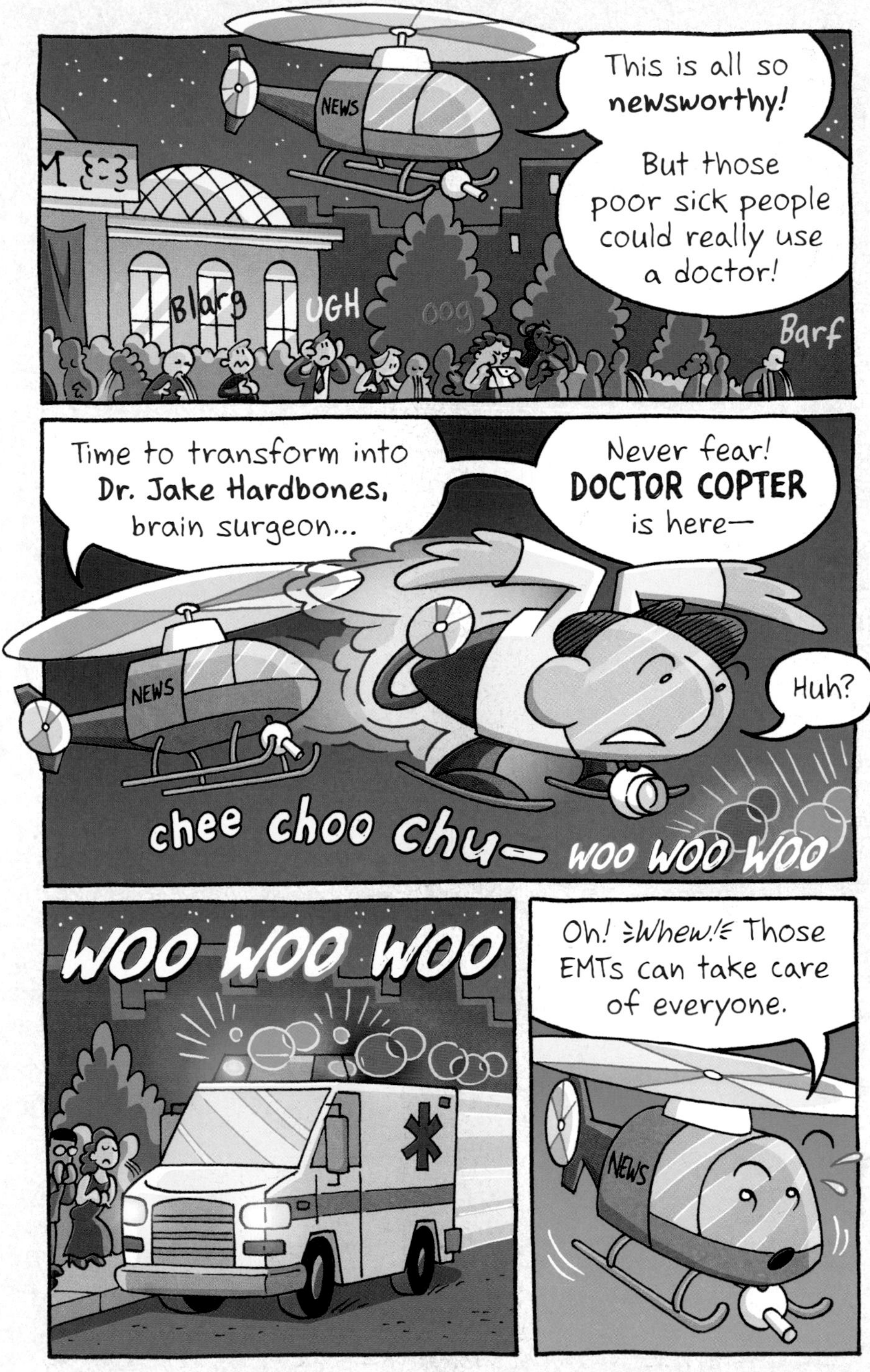
This is all so newsworthy!
But those poor sick people could really use a doctor!
Blarg
UGH
oog
Barf
Time to transform into Dr. Jake Hardbones, brain surgeon...
Never fear! DOCTOR COPTER is here—
Huh?
chee choo chu— WOO WOO WOO
WOO WOO WOO
Oh! Whew! Those EMTs can take care of everyone.
NEWS

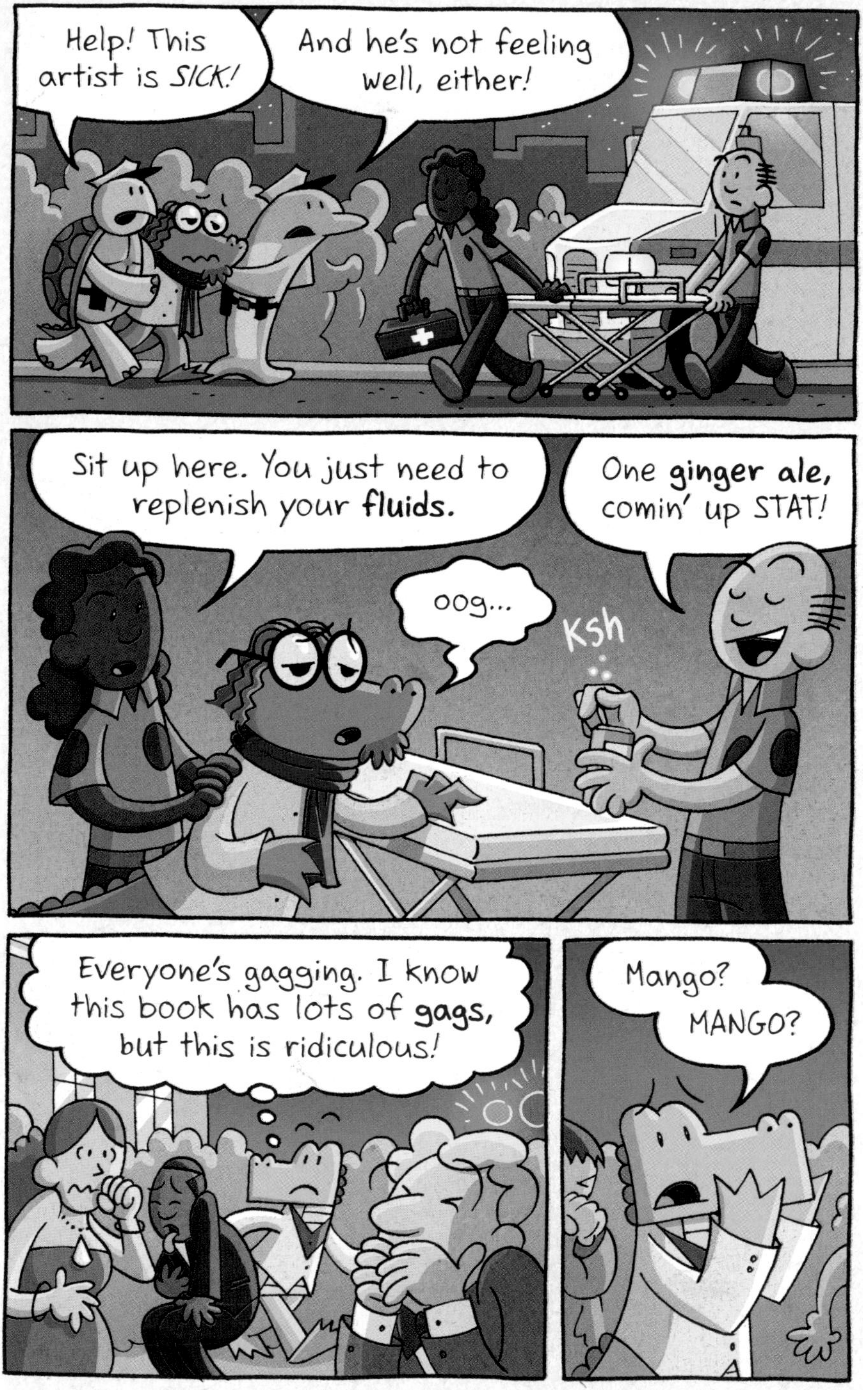
Help! This artist is SICK!
And he's not feeling well, either!
Sit up here. You just need to replenish your **fluids.**
oog...
One **ginger ale,** comin' up STAT!
KSH
Everyone's gagging. I know this book has lots of **gags,** but this is ridiculous!
Mango? MANGO?

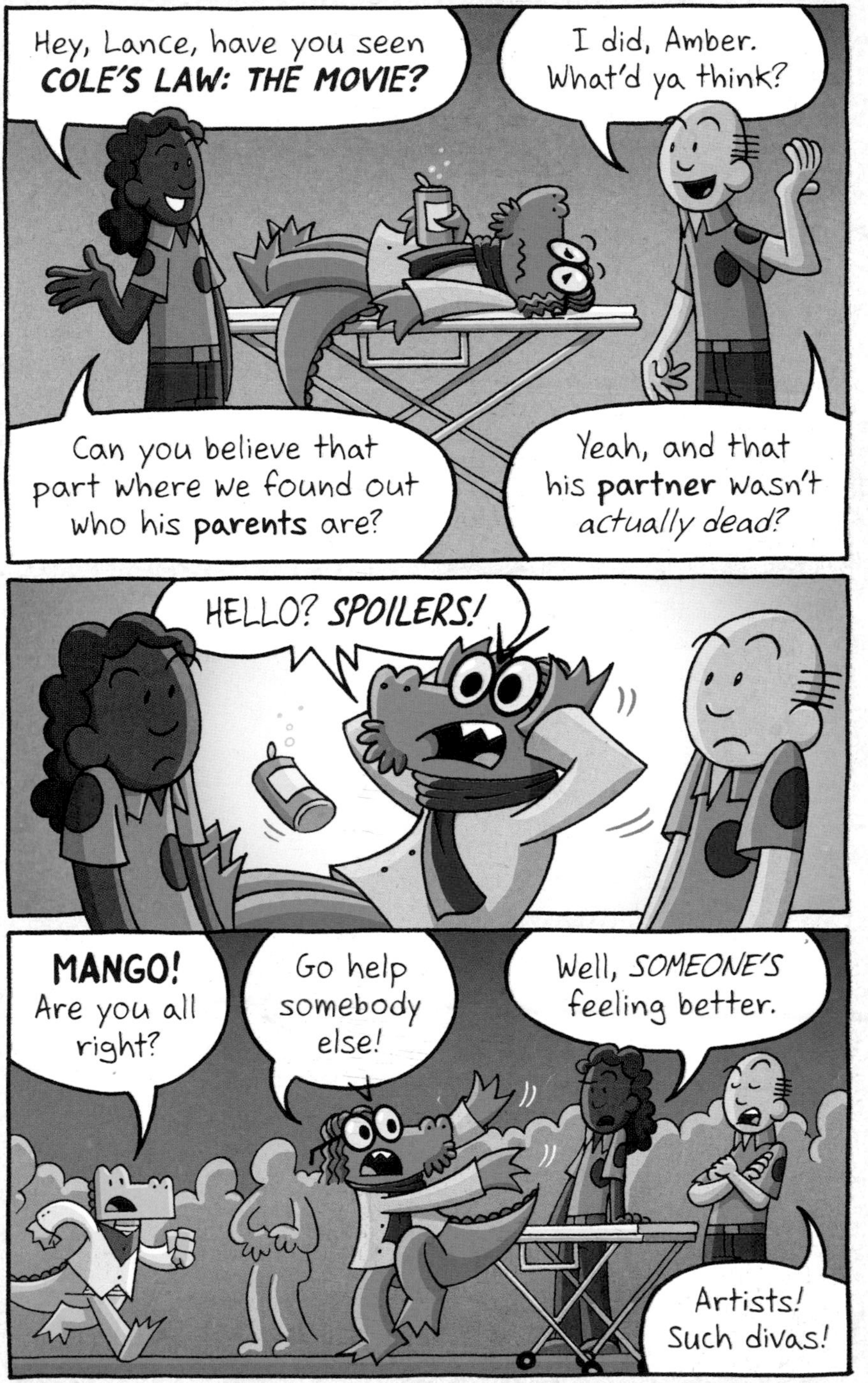
Hey, Lance, have you seen **COLE'S LAW: THE MOVIE?**
I did, Amber. What'd ya think?
Can you believe that part where we found out who his **parents** are?
Yeah, and that his **partner** wasn't *actually dead?*
HELLO? *SPOILERS!*
MANGO! Are you all right?
Go help somebody else!
Well, *SOMEONE'S* feeling better.
Artists! Such divas!

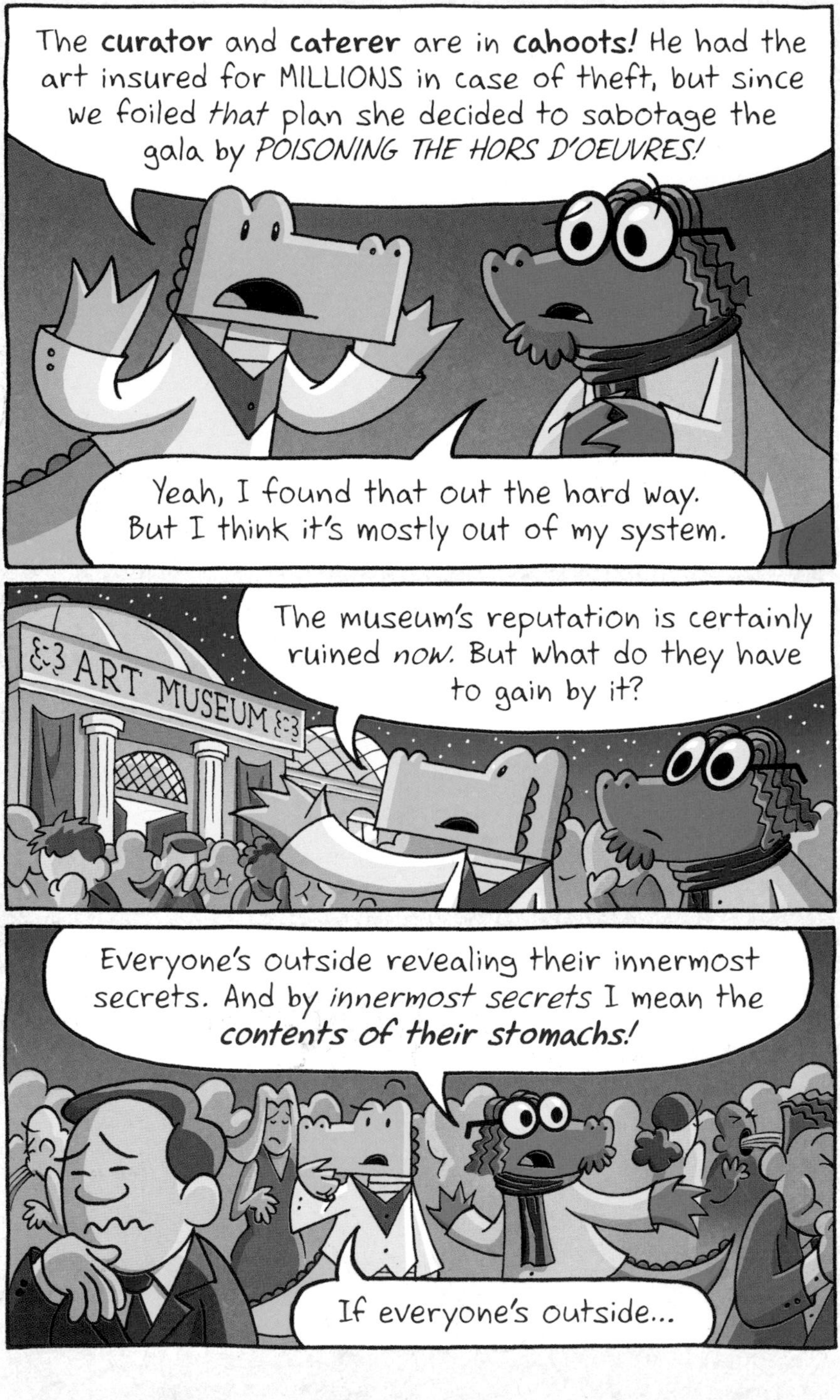
The **curator** and **caterer** are in **cahoots!** He had the art insured for MILLIONS in case of theft, but since we foiled *that* plan she decided to sabotage the gala by *POISONING THE HORS D'OEUVRES!*
Yeah, I found that out the hard way. But I think it's mostly out of my system.
ART MUSEUM
The museum's reputation is certainly ruined *now*. But what do they have to gain by it?
Everyone's outside revealing their innermost secrets. And by *innermost secrets* I mean the ***contents of their stomachs!***
If everyone's outside...

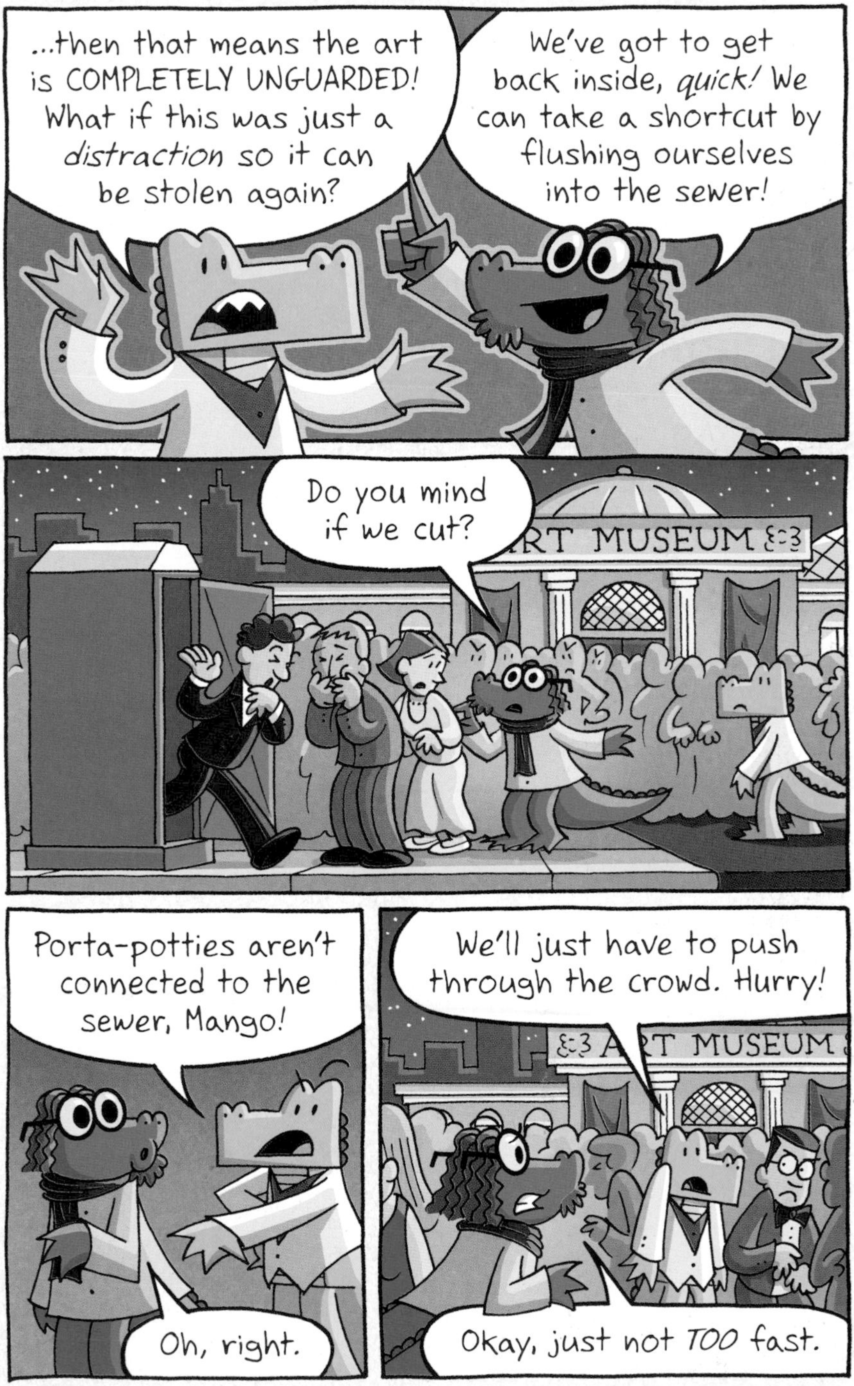
...then that means the art is COMPLETELY UNGUARDED! What if this was just a *distraction* so it can be stolen again?
We've got to get back inside, *quick!* We can take a shortcut by flushing ourselves into the sewer!
Do you mind if we cut?
ART MUSEUM
Porta-potties aren't connected to the sewer, Mango!
Oh, right.
We'll just have to push through the crowd. Hurry!
ART MUSEUM
Okay, just not *TOO* fast.

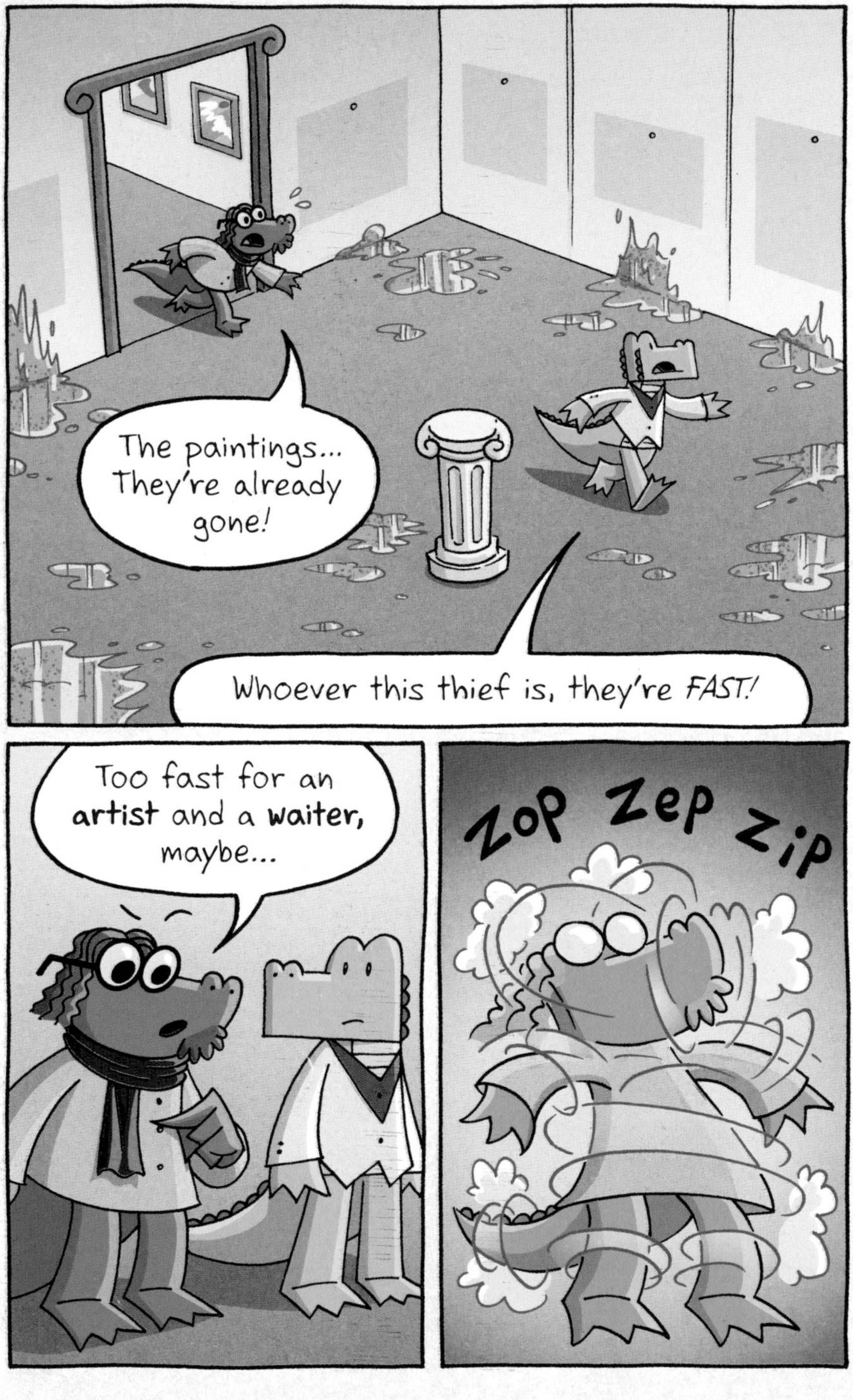
The paintings... They're already gone!
Whoever this thief is, they're FAST!
Too fast for an **artist** and a **waiter**, maybe...
ZOP ZEP ZIP

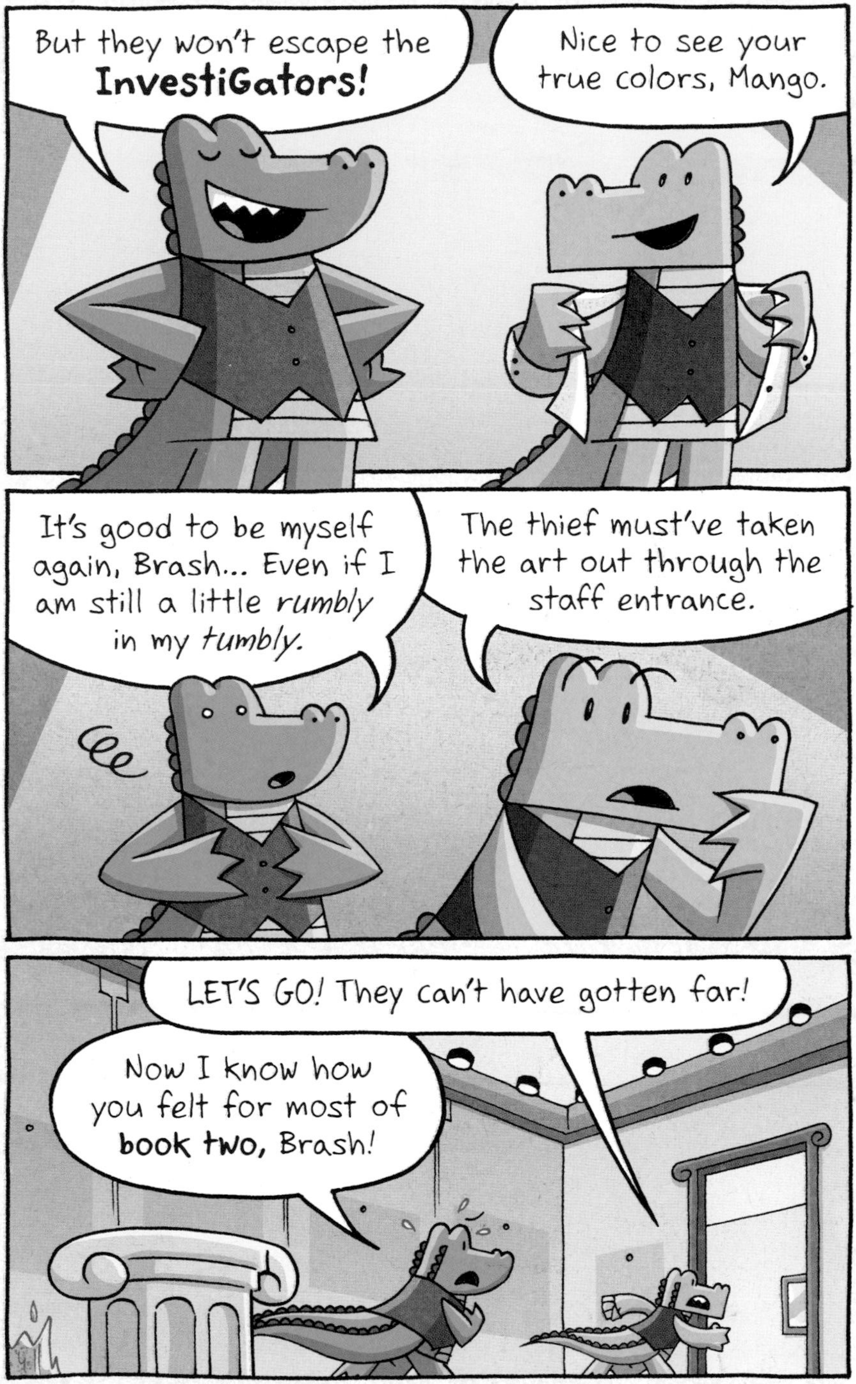
But they won't escape the **InvestiGators!**
Nice to see your true colors, Mango.
It's good to be myself again, Brash... Even if I am still a little *rumbly* in my *tumbly*.
The thief must've taken the art out through the staff entrance.
LET'S GO! They can't have gotten far!
Now I know how you felt for most of **book two,** Brash!

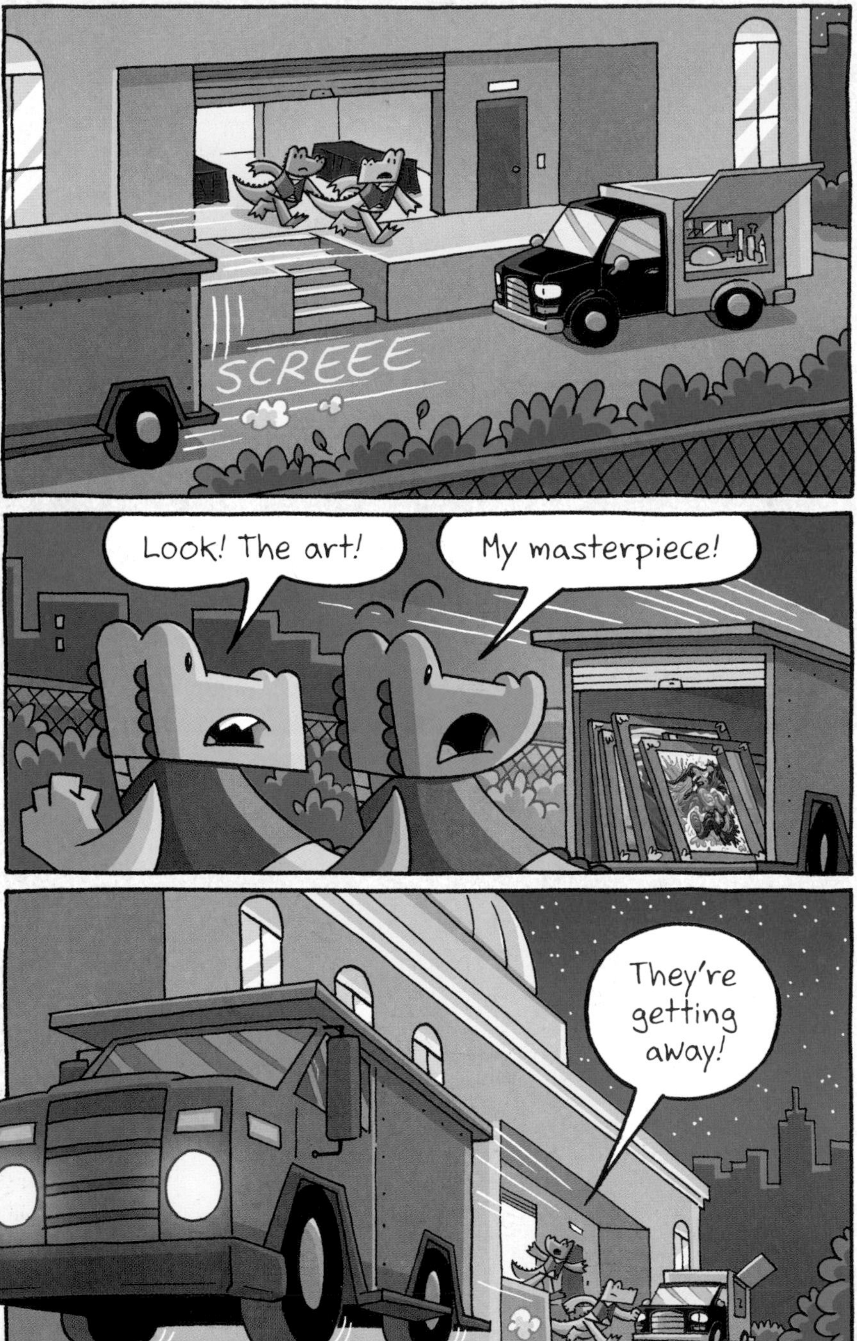
SCREEE
Look! The art!
My masterpiece!
They're getting away!

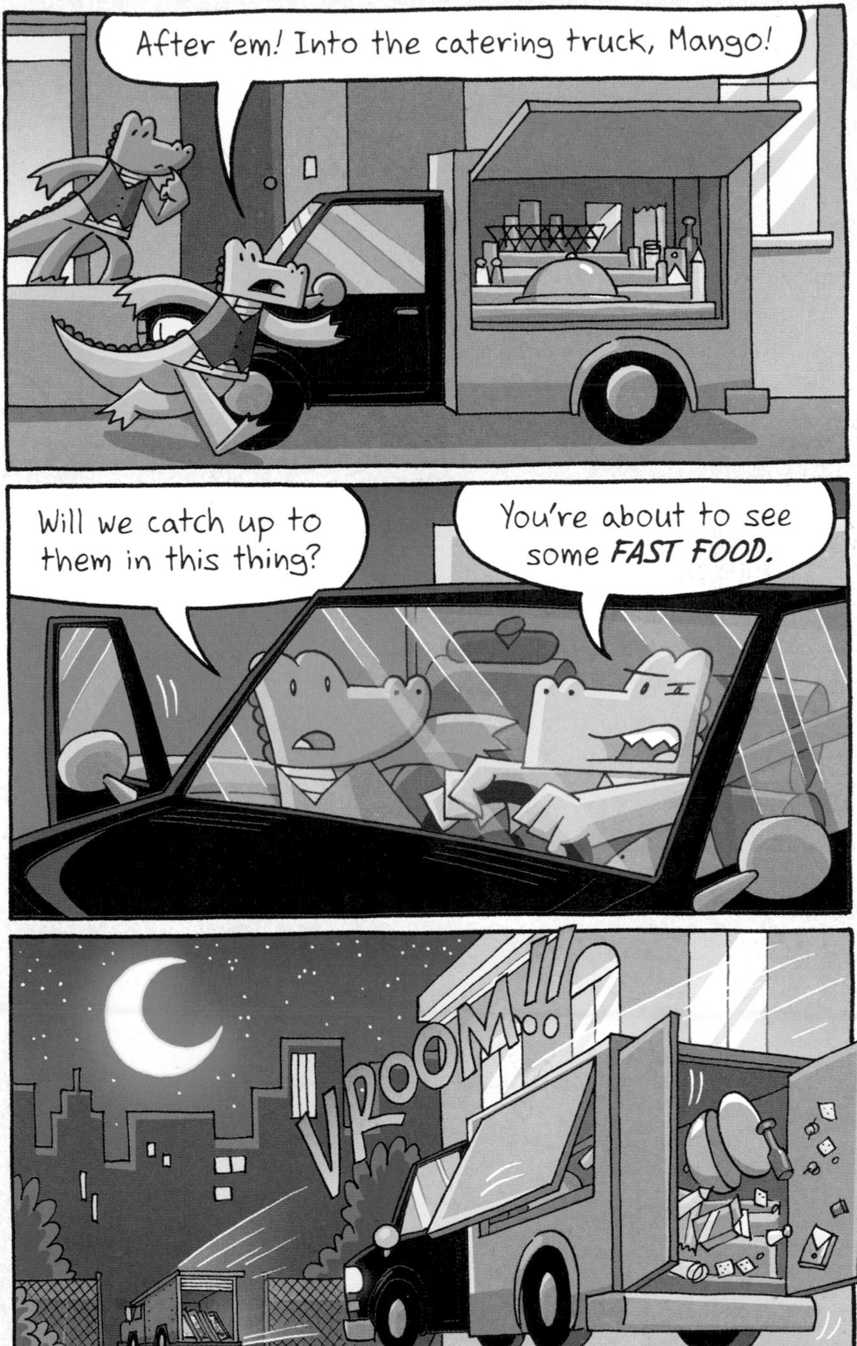
After 'em! Into the catering truck, Mango!
Will we catch up to them in this thing?
You're about to see some FAST FOOD.
VROOM!!

Chapter 13

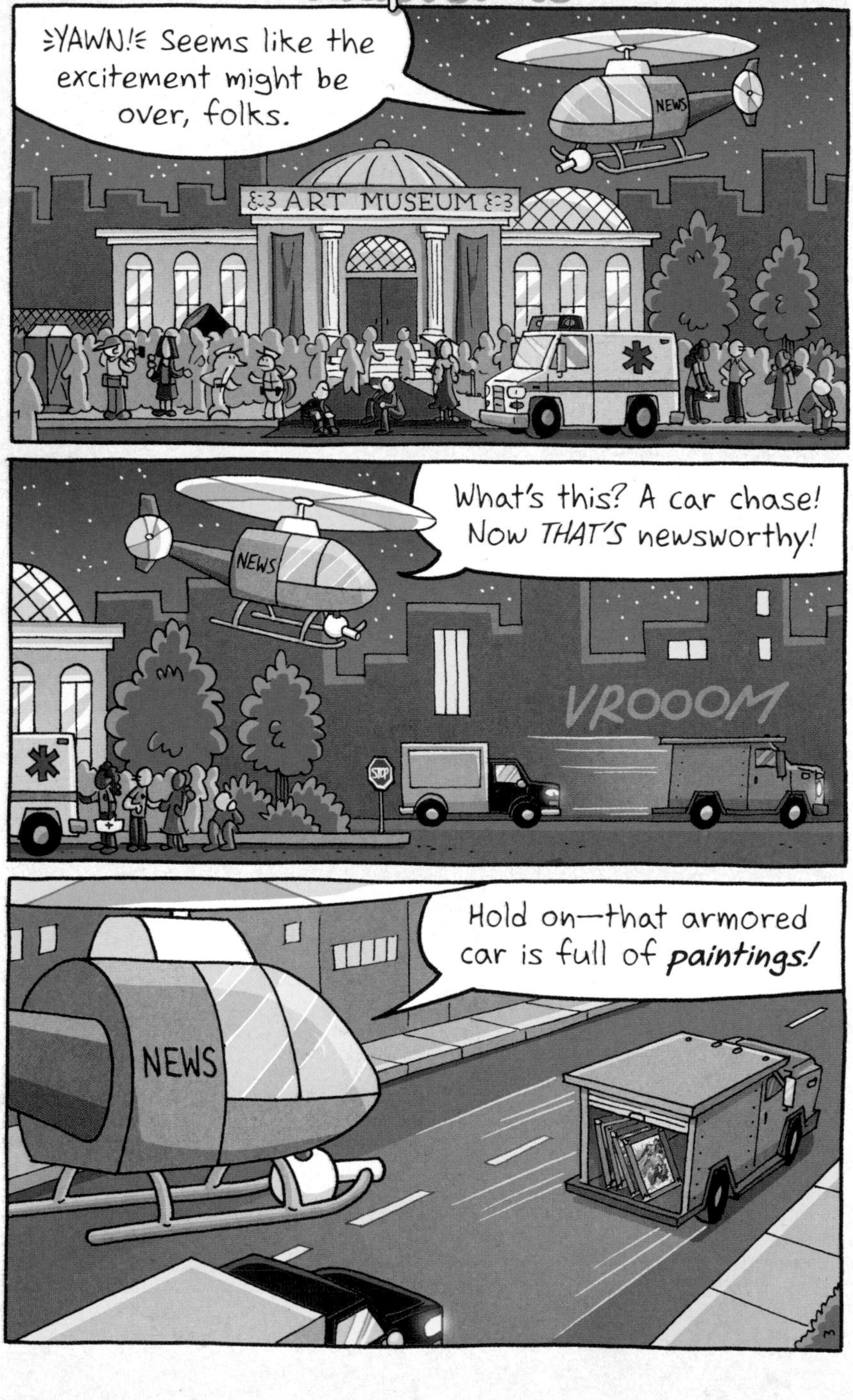

⋛YAWN!⋚ Seems like the excitement might be over, folks.
NEWS
ART MUSEUM
What's this? A car chase! Now *THAT'S* newsworthy!
NEWS
STOP
VROOOM
Hold on—that armored car is full of ***paintings!***
NEWS

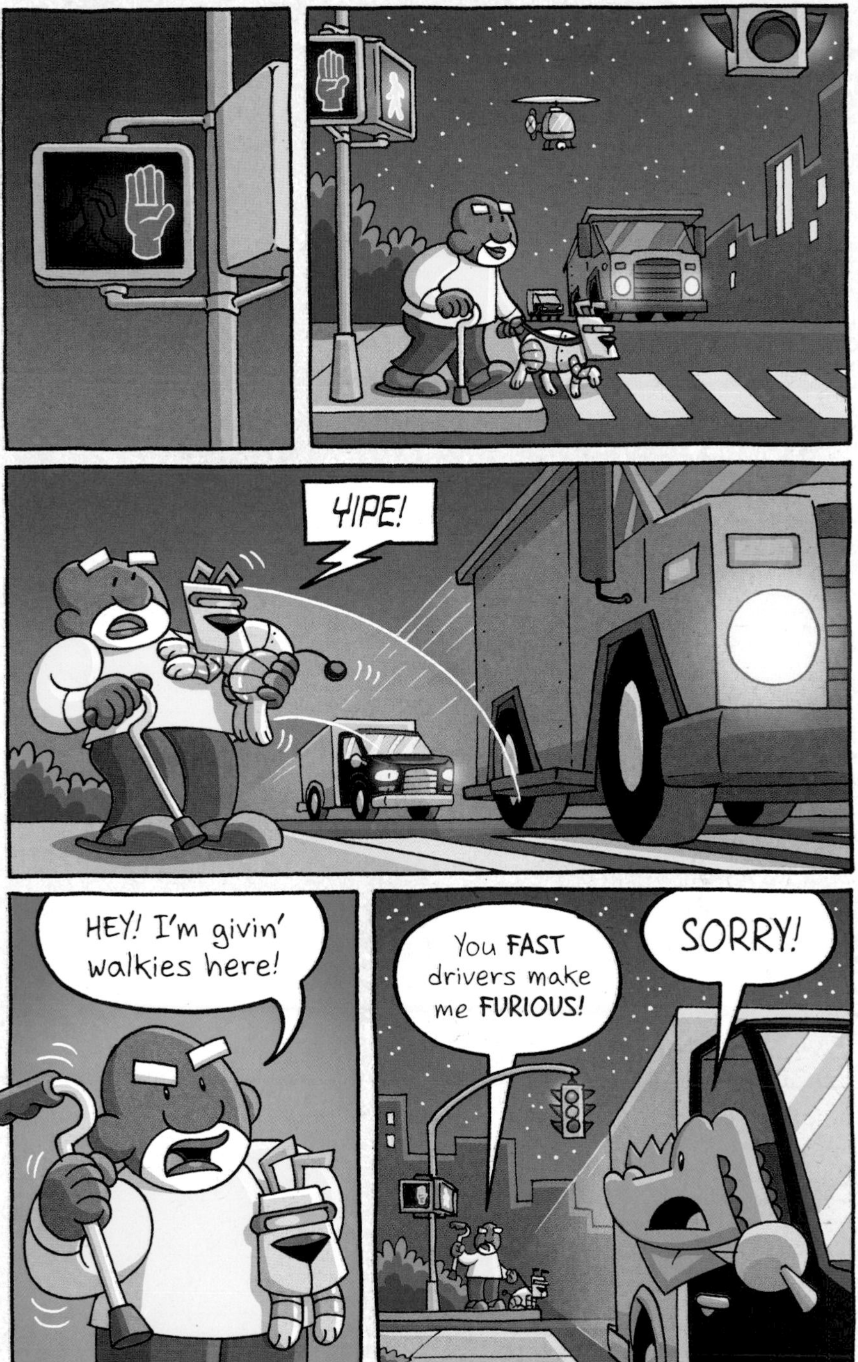
YIPE!
HEY! I'm givin' walkies here!
You FAST drivers make me FURIOUS!
SORRY!

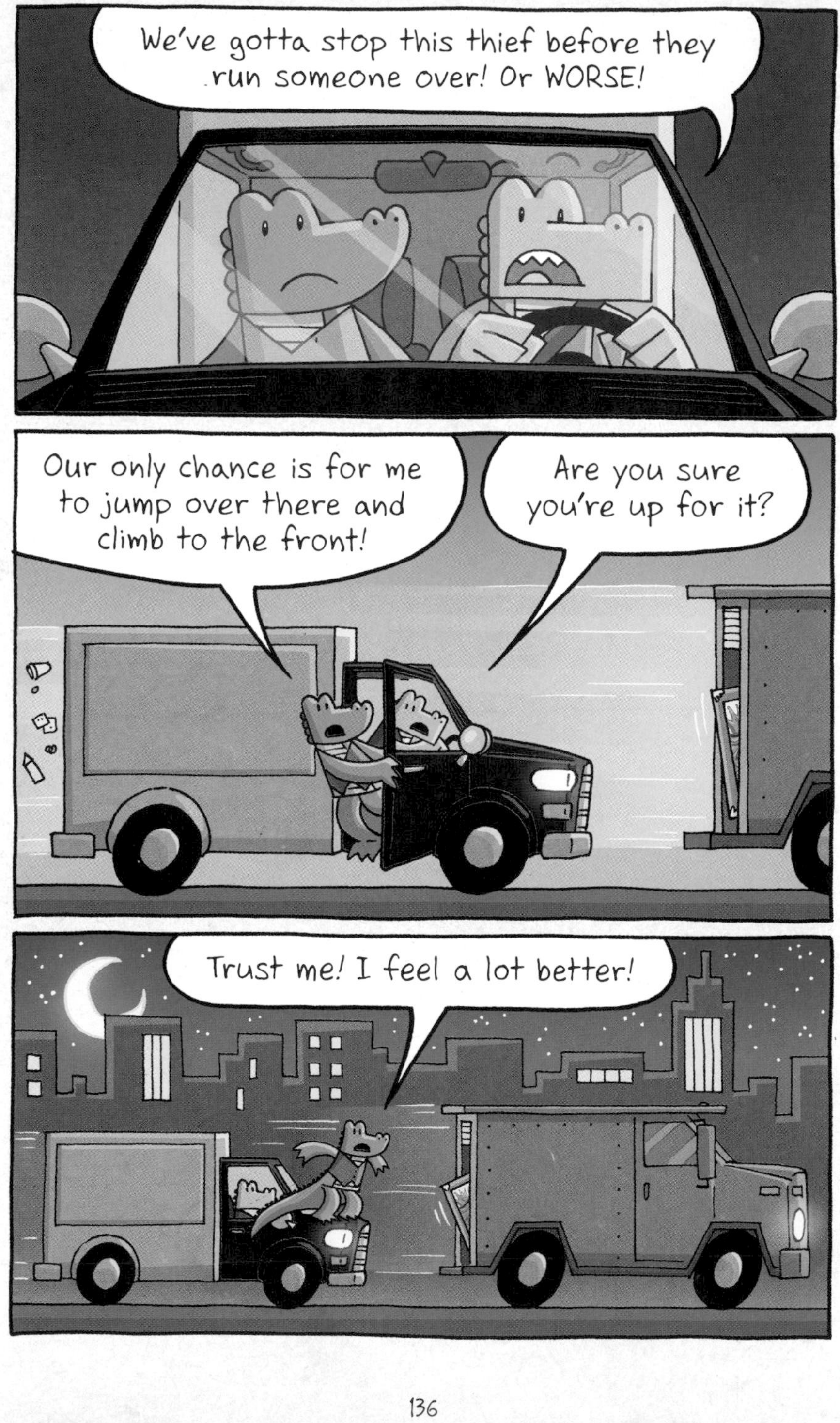
We've gotta stop this thief before they run someone over! Or WORSE!
Our only chance is for me to jump over there and climb to the front!
Are you sure you're up for it?
Trust me! I feel a lot better!

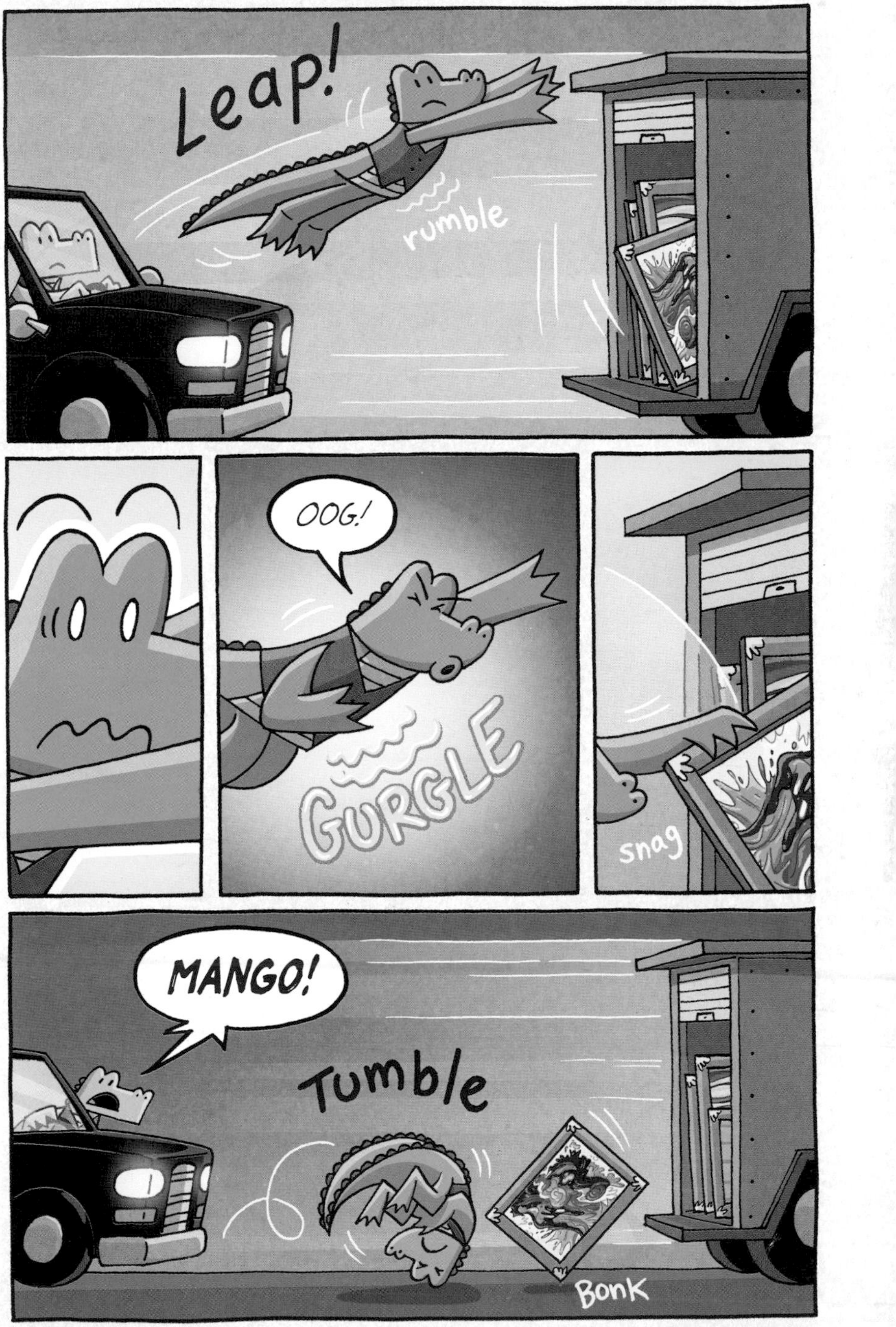
Leap!
rumble
OOG!
GURGLE
snag
MANGO!
Tumble
Bonk

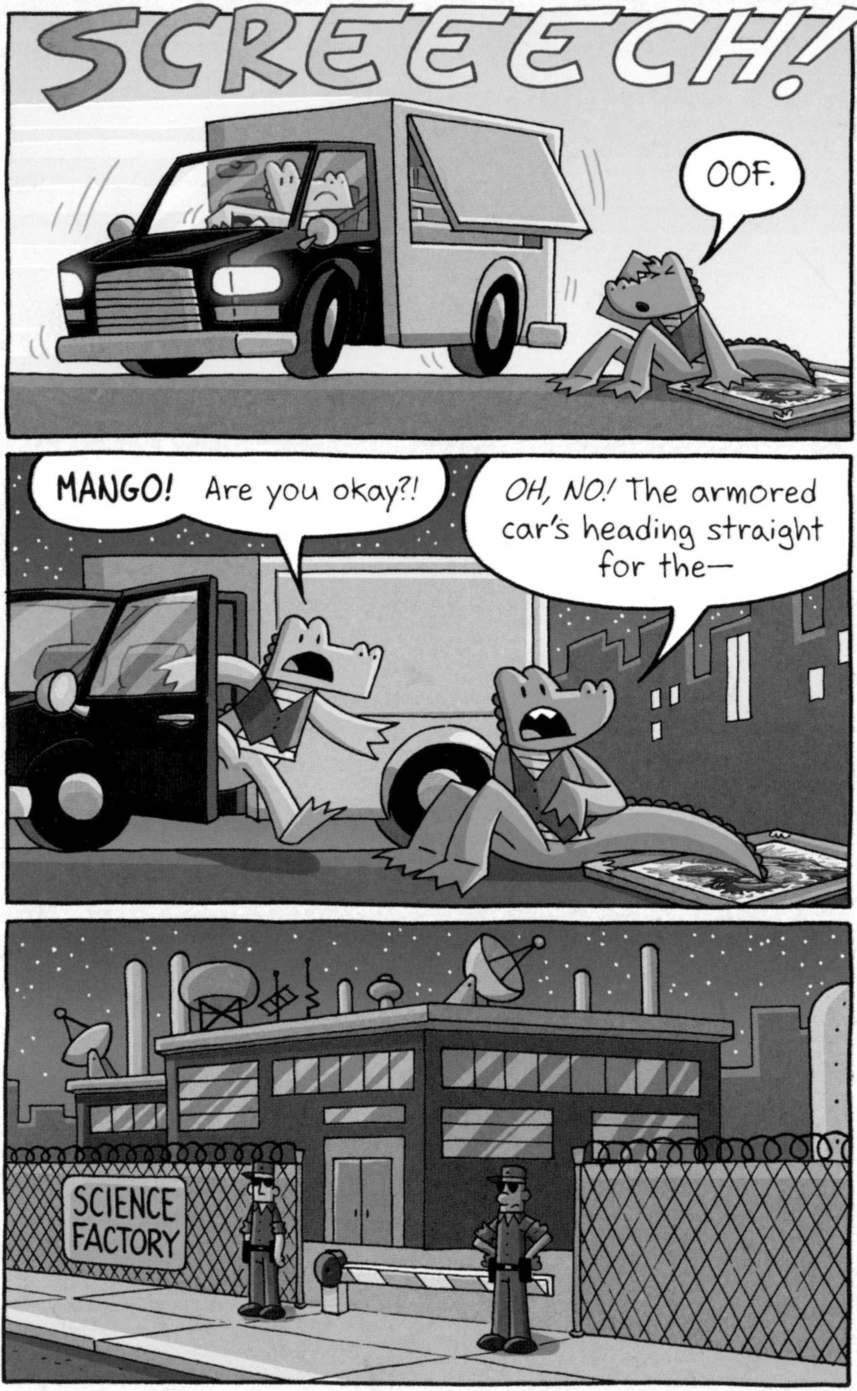
SCREEECH!
OOF.
MANGO! Are you okay?!
OH, NO! The armored car's heading straight for the—
SCIENCE FACTORY

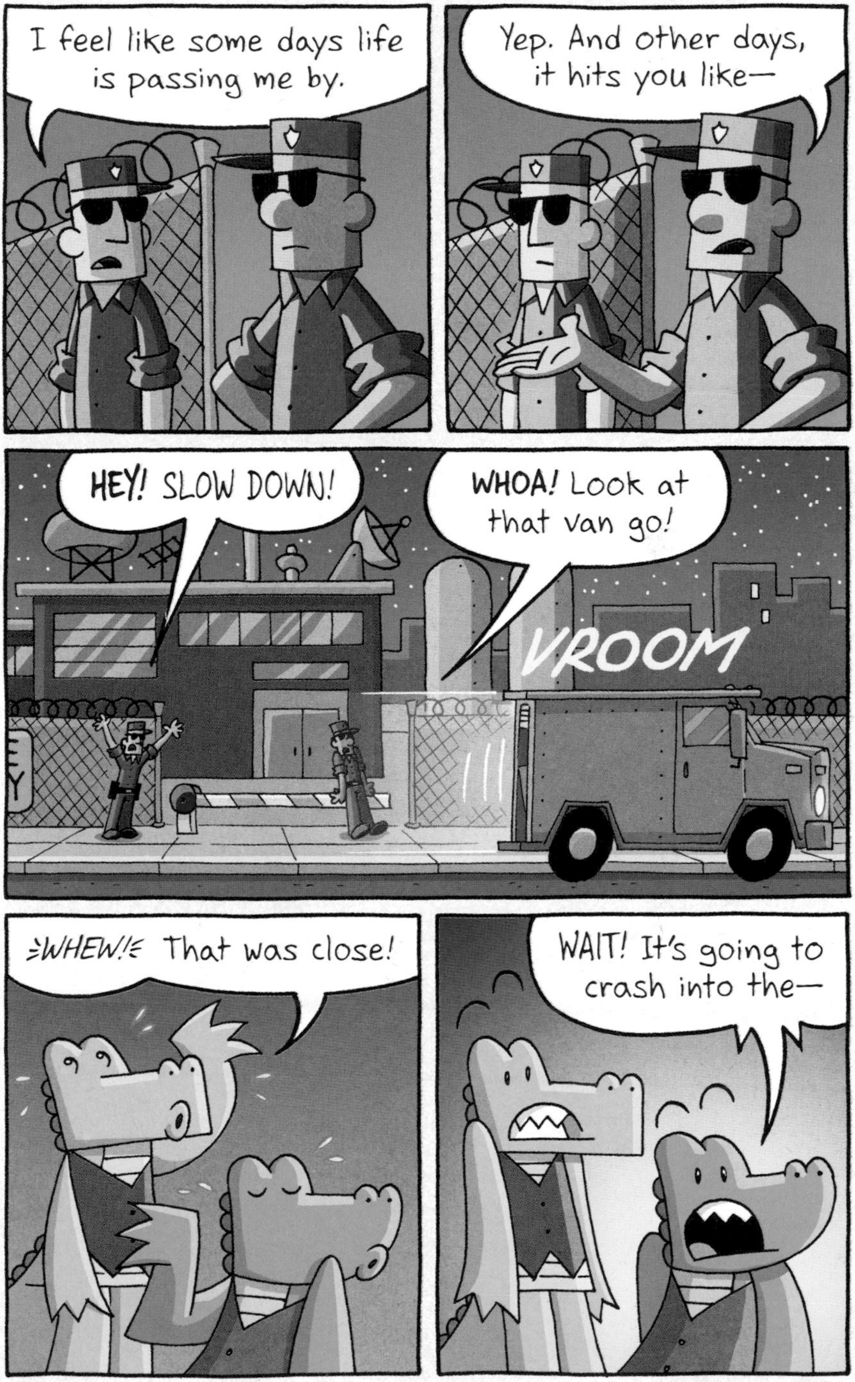
I feel like some days life is passing me by.
Yep. And other days, it hits you like—
HEY! SLOW DOWN!
WHOA! Look at that van go!
VROOM
WHEW! That was close!
WAIT! It's going to crash into the—

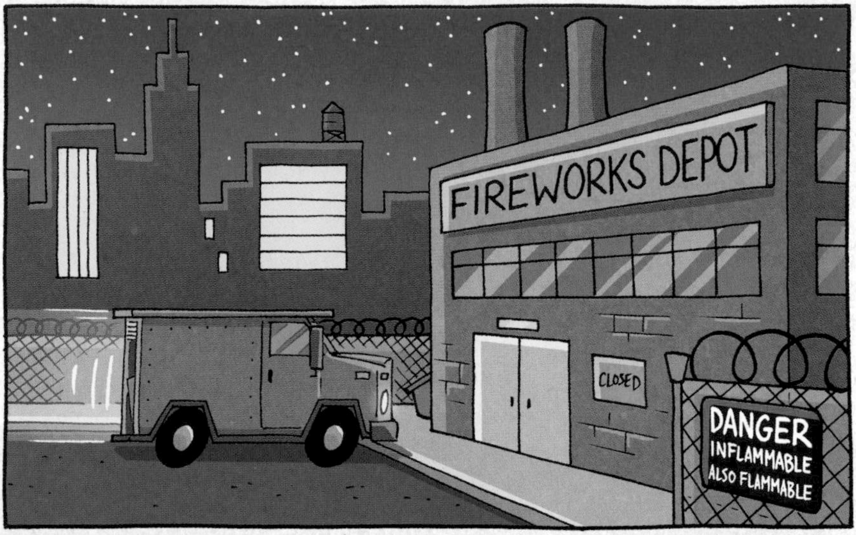
FIREWORKS DEPOT
CLOSED
DANGER
INFLAMMABLE
ALSO FLAMMABLE

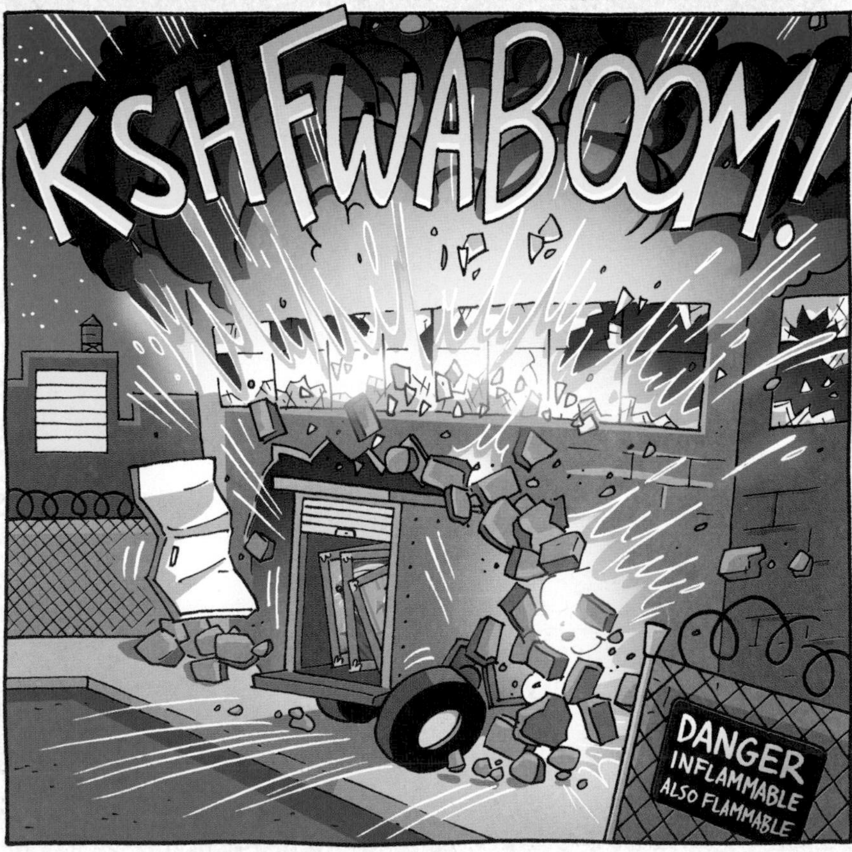
KSHFWABOOM!
DANGER
INFLAMMABLE
ALSO FLAMMABLE

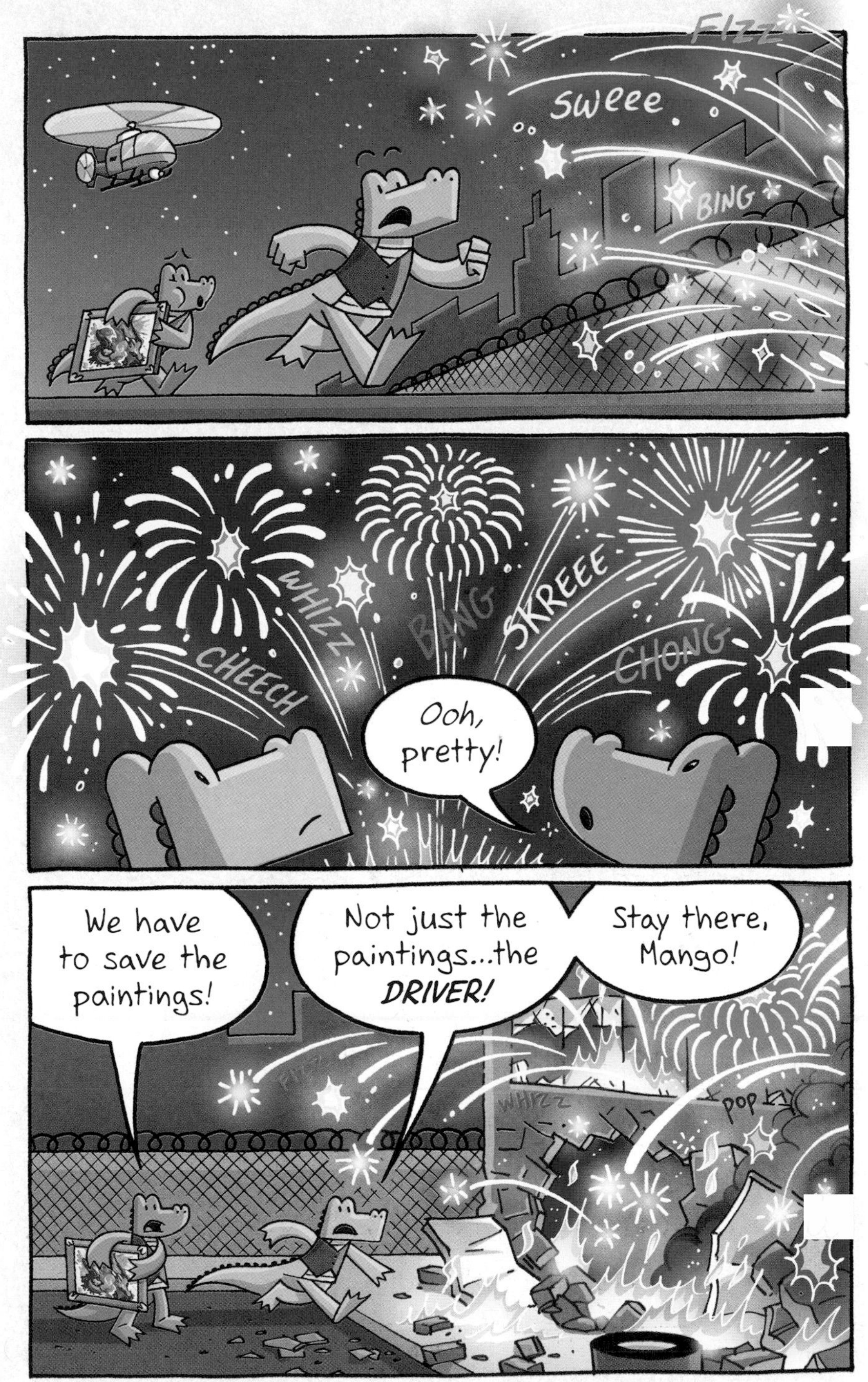
FIZZ
SWEEE
BING
WHIZZ
BANG
SKREEE
CHEECH
CHONG
Ooh, pretty!
We have to save the paintings!
Not just the paintings...the **DRIVER!**
Stay there, Mango!
WHIZZ
POP

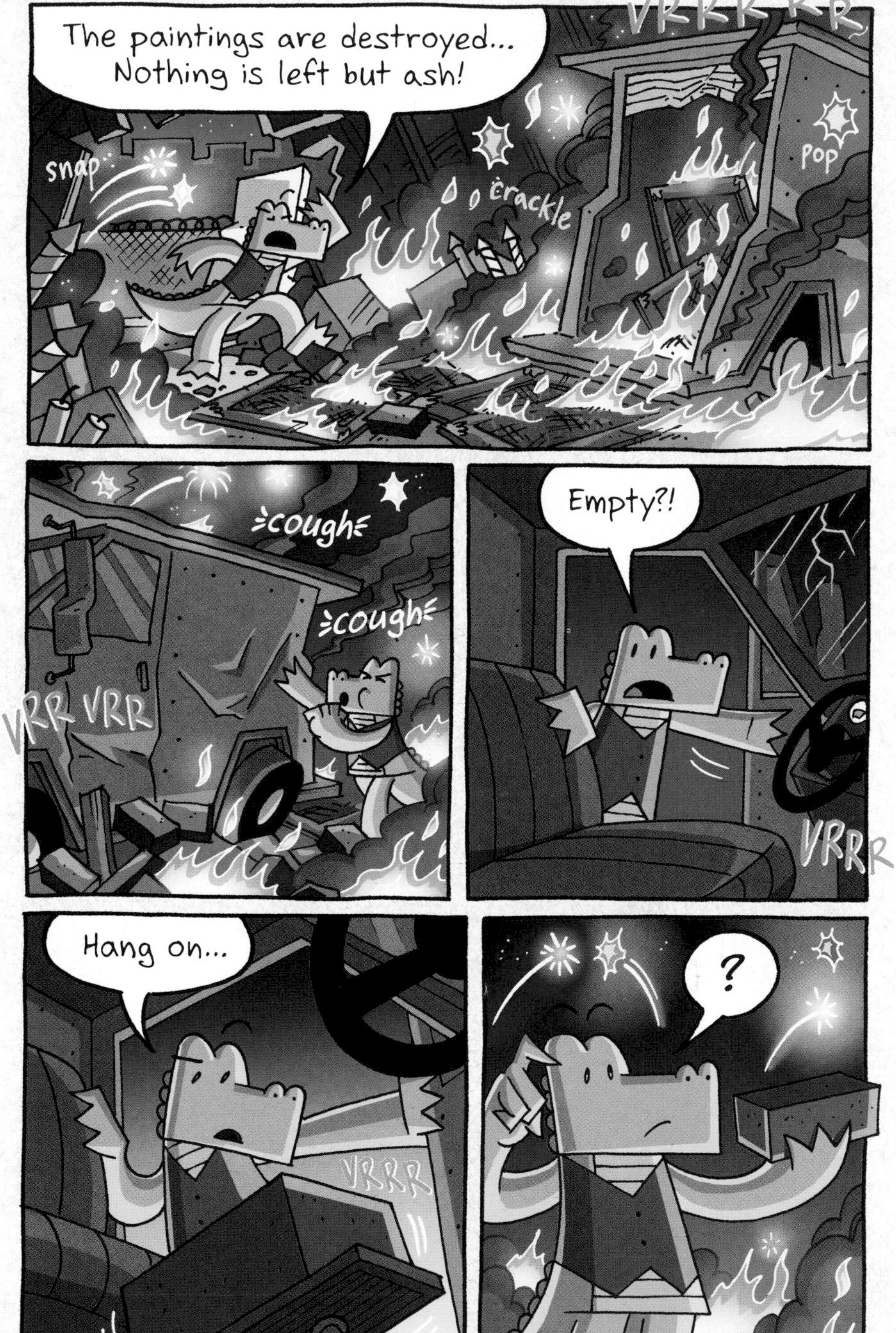
The paintings are destroyed... Nothing is left but ash!
VRRRRRR
snap
crackle
pop
cough
cough
VRR VRR
Empty?!
VRRR
Hang on...
VRRR
?

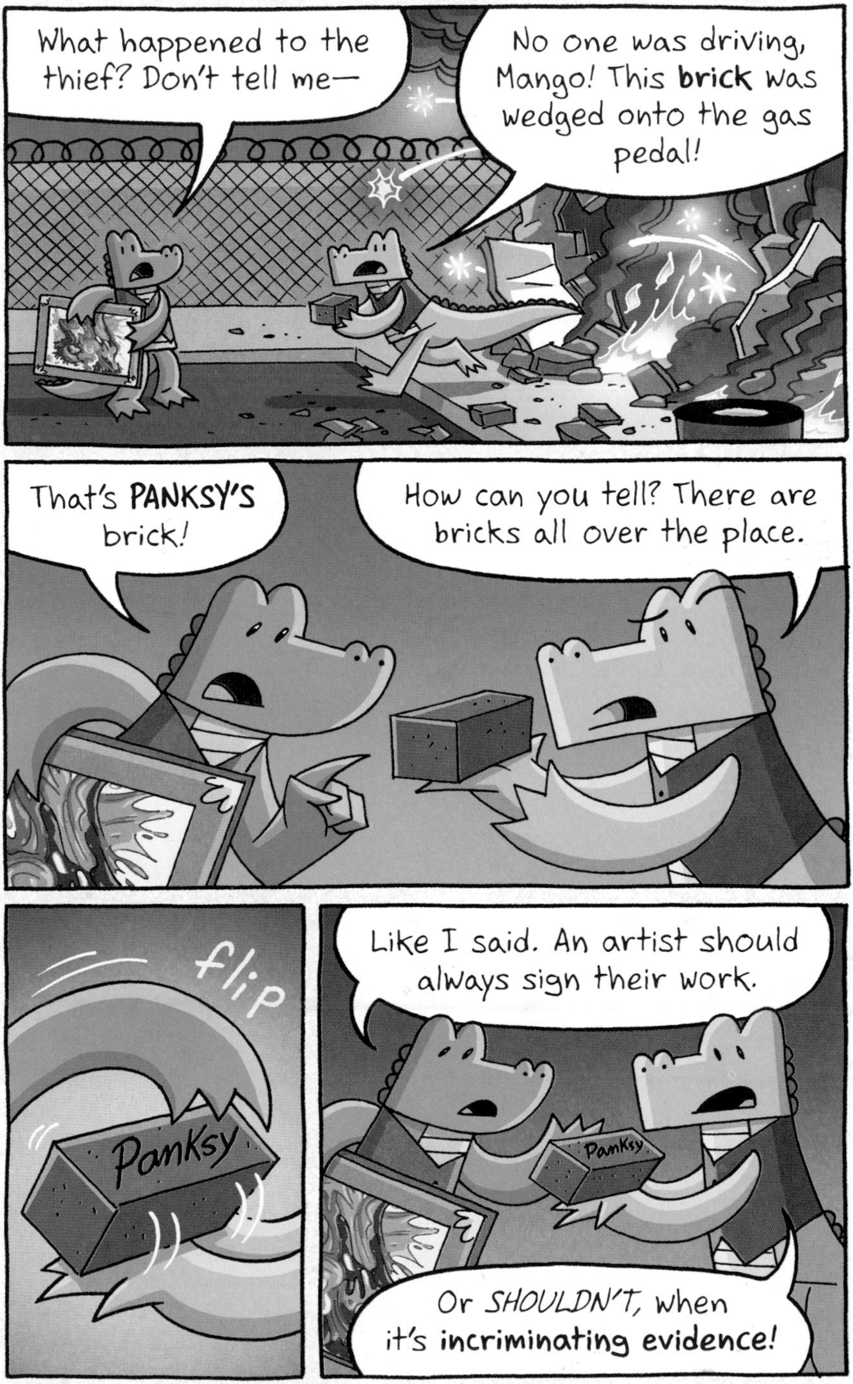
What happened to the thief? Don't tell me—
No one was driving, Mango! This **brick** was wedged onto the gas pedal!
That's **PANKSY'S** brick!
How can you tell? There are bricks all over the place.
flip
Panksy
Like I said. An artist should always sign their work.
Panksy
Or *SHOULDN'T*, when it's **incriminating evidence**!

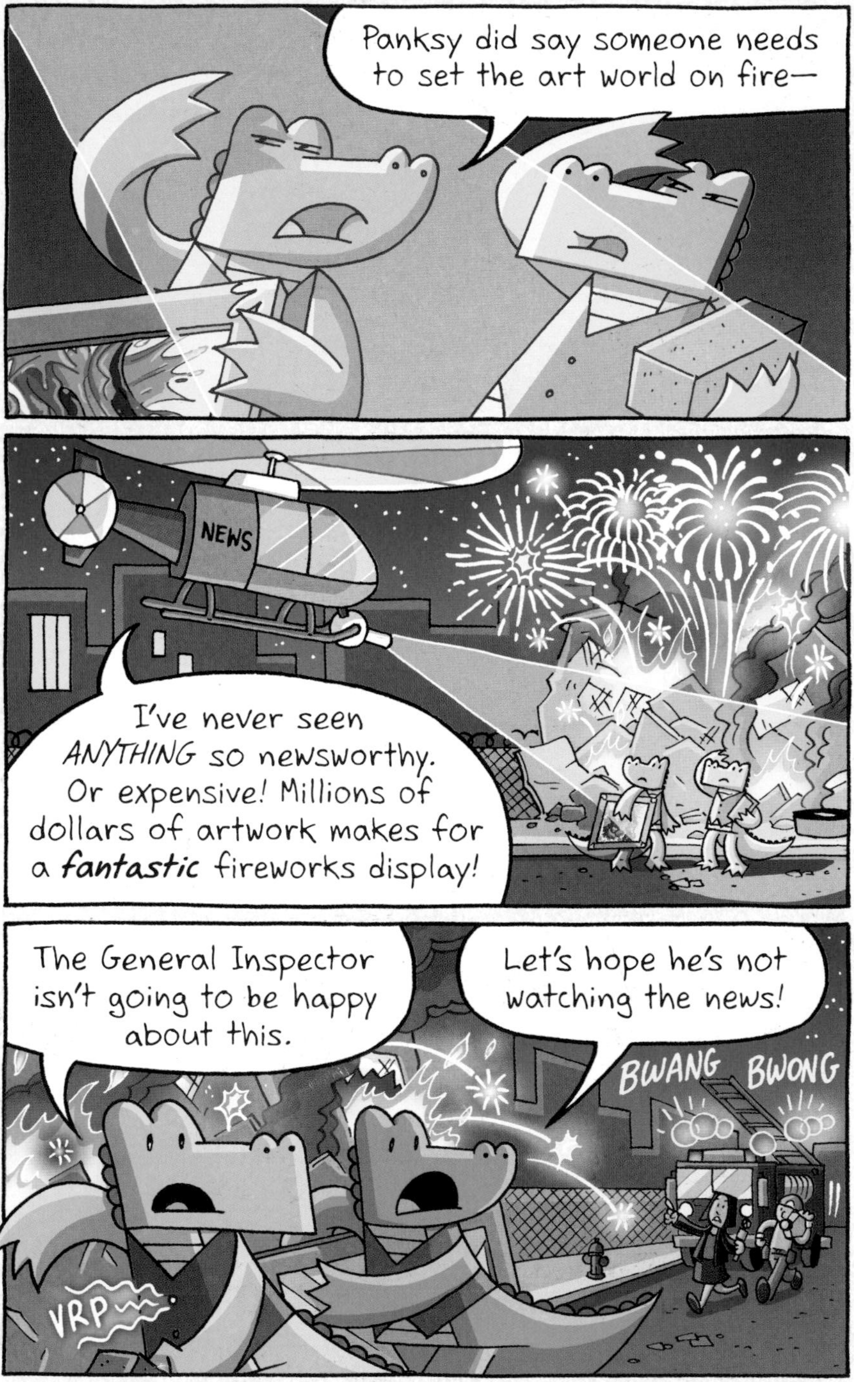
Panksy did say someone needs to set the art world on fire—
NEWS
I've never seen ANYTHING so newsworthy. Or expensive! Millions of dollars of artwork makes for a fantastic fireworks display!
The General Inspector isn't going to be happy about this.
Let's hope he's not watching the news!
BWANG
BWONG
VRP

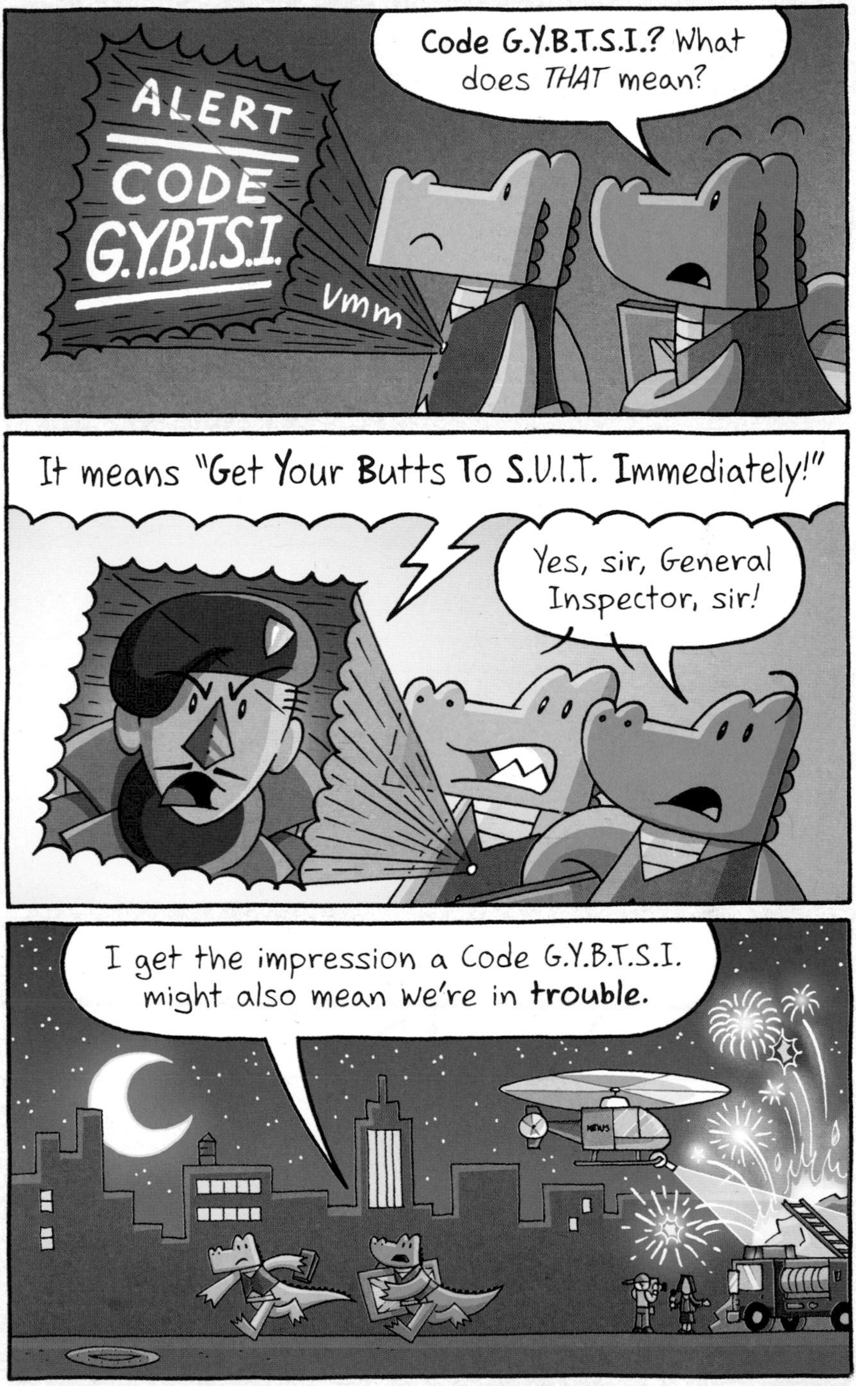
ALERT
CODE G.Y.B.T.S.I.
Vmm
Code G.Y.B.T.S.I.? What does THAT mean?
It means "Get Your Butts To S.U.I.T. Immediately!"
Yes, sir, General Inspector, sir!
I get the impression a Code G.Y.B.T.S.I. might also mean we're in trouble.

Chapter 14

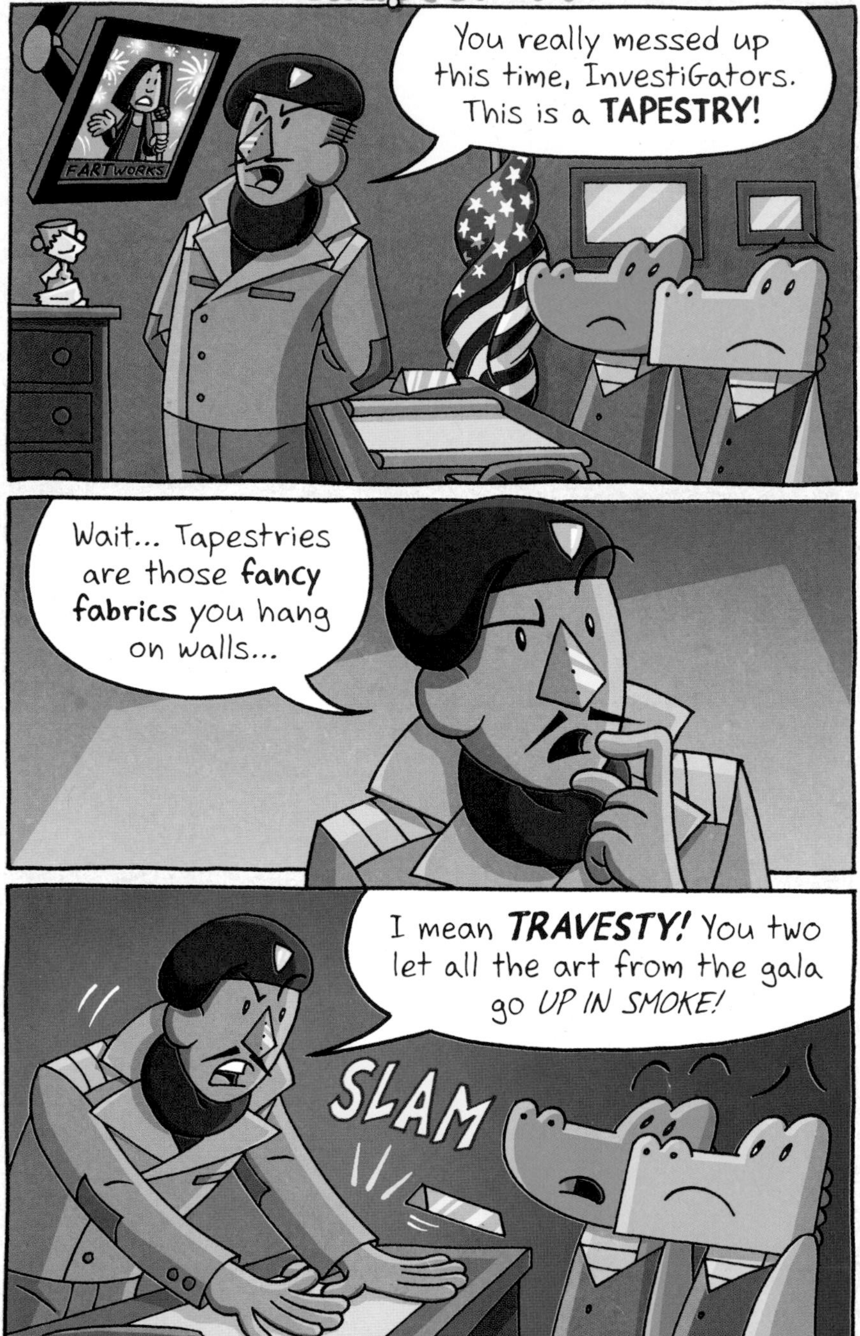

FARTWORKS
You really messed up this time, InvestiGators. This is a **TAPESTRY!**
Wait... Tapestries are those **fancy fabrics** you hang on walls...
I mean ***TRAVESTY!*** You two let all the art from the gala go *UP IN SMOKE!*
SLAM

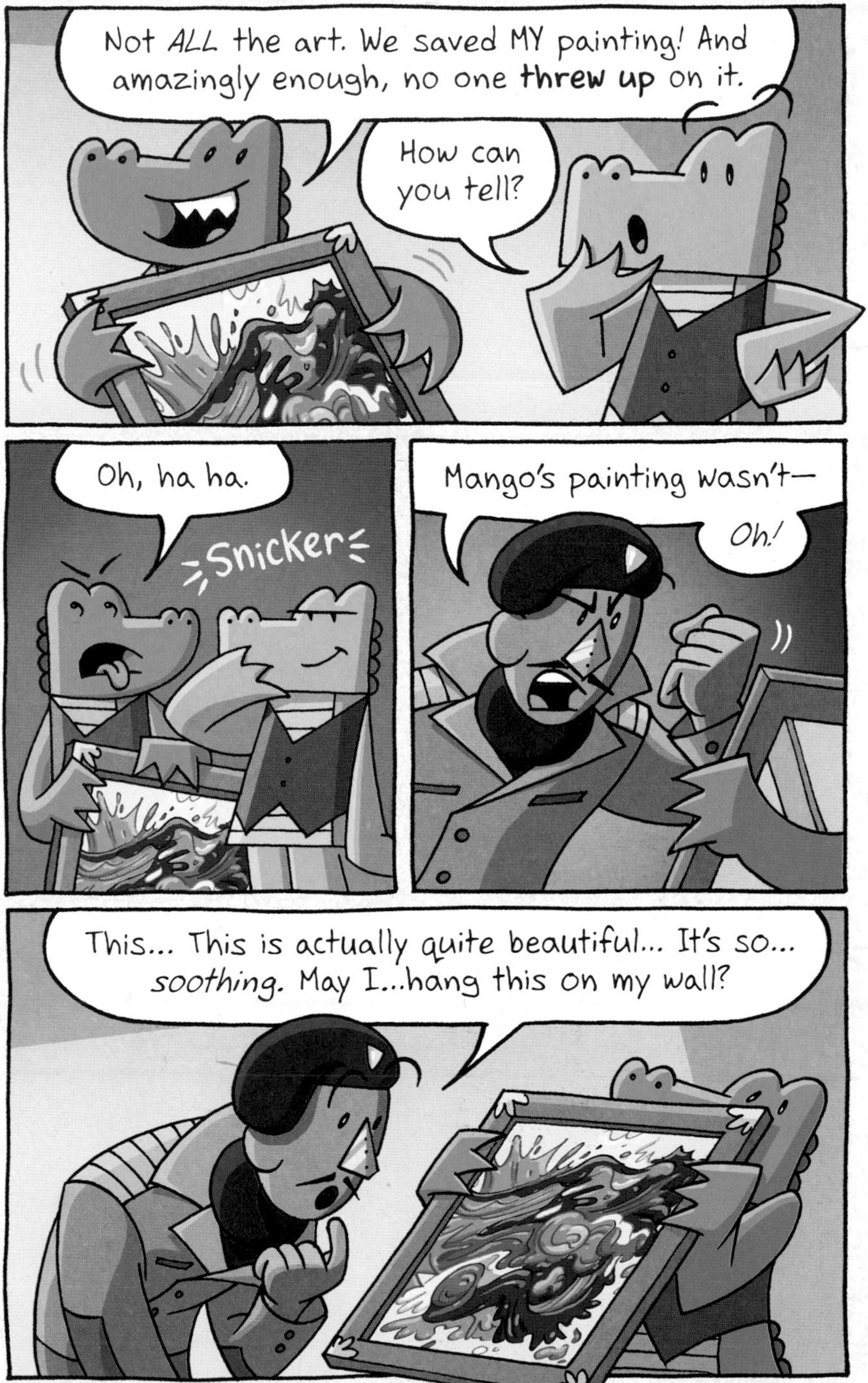
Not *ALL* the art. We saved MY painting! And amazingly enough, no one **threw up** on it.
How can you tell?
Oh, ha ha.
Snicker
Mango's painting wasn't—
Oh!
This... This is actually quite beautiful... It's so... *soothing*. May I...hang this on my wall?

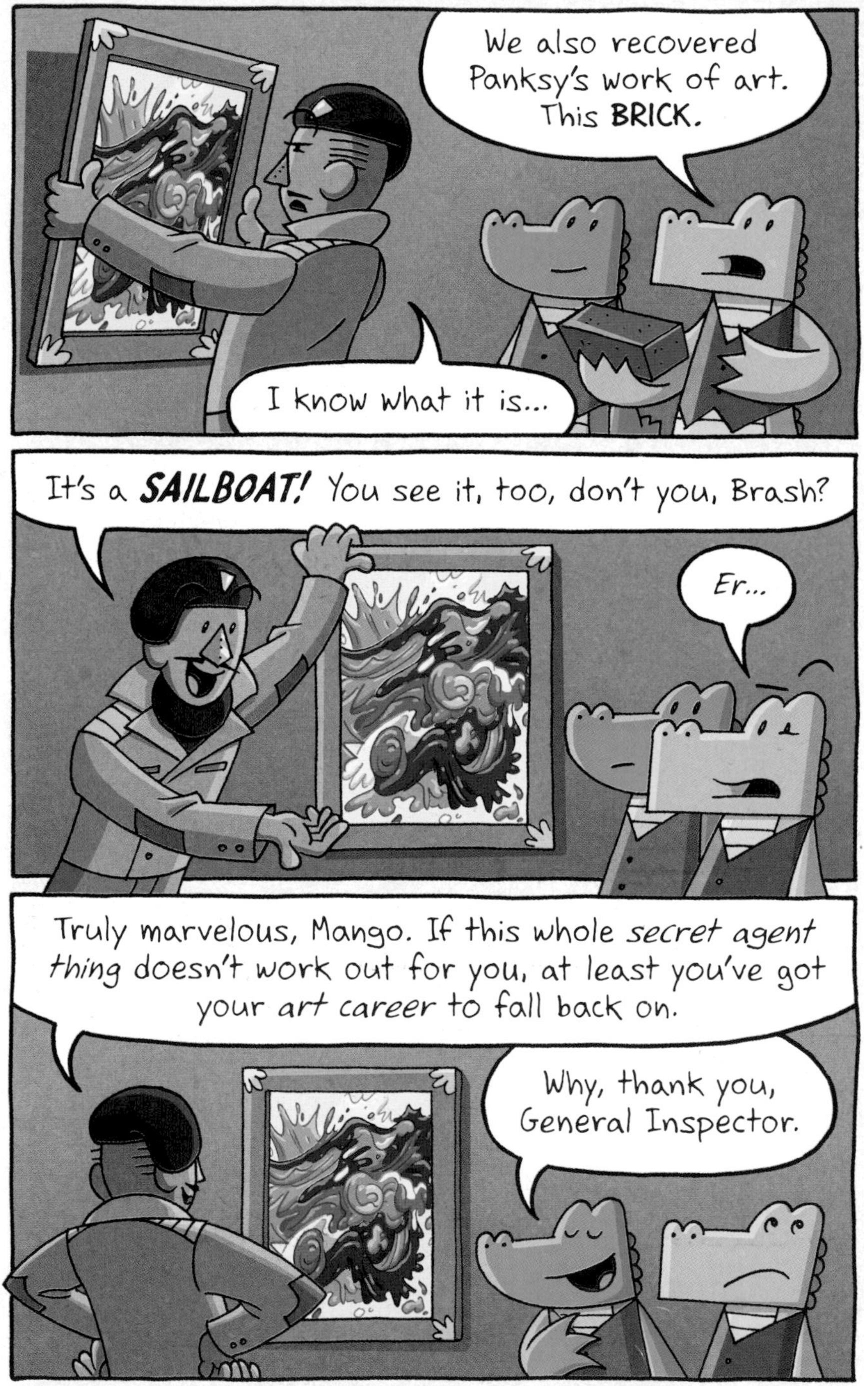
We also recovered Panksy's work of art. This **BRICK.**
I know what it is...
It's a ***SAILBOAT!*** You see it, too, don't you, Brash?
Er...
Truly marvelous, Mango. If this whole *secret agent thing* doesn't work out for you, at least you've got your *art career* to fall back on.
Why, thank you, General Inspector.

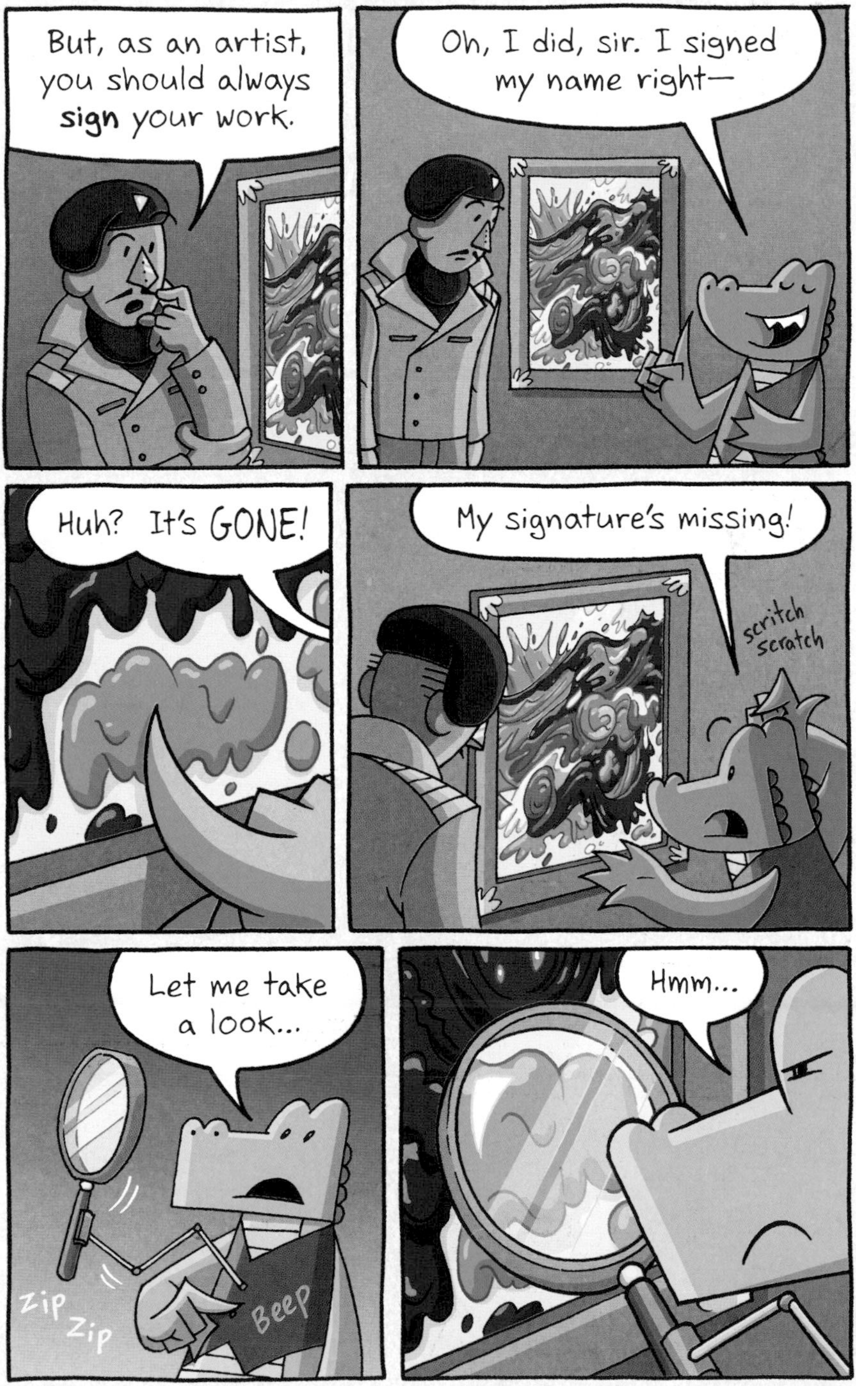
But, as an artist, you should always **sign** your work.
Oh, I did, sir. I signed my name right—
Huh? It's GONE!
My signature's missing!
scritch scratch
Let me take a look...
Zip Zip
Beep
Hmm...

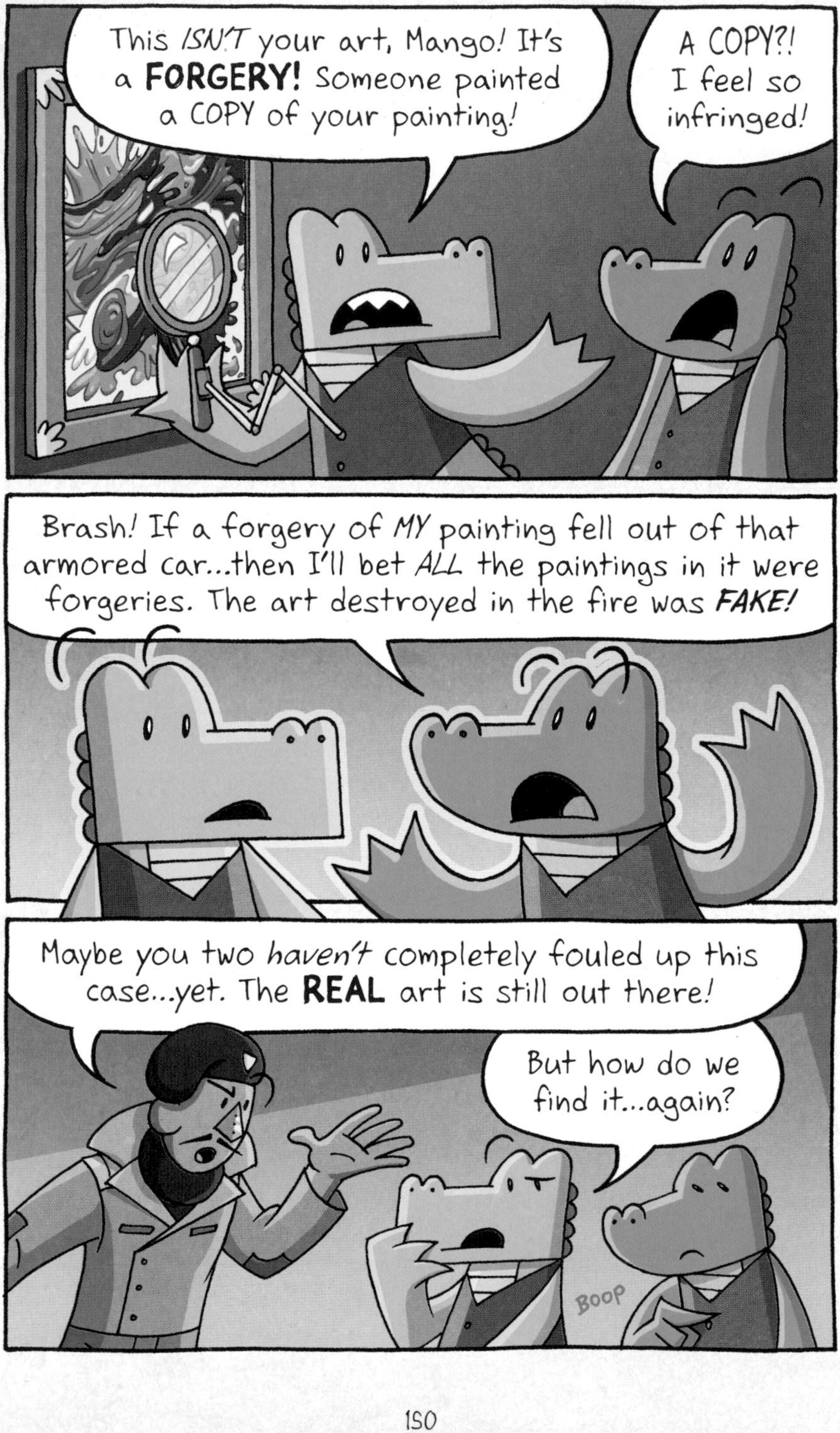
This *ISN'T* your art, Mango! It's a **FORGERY!** Someone painted a COPY of your painting!
A COPY?! I feel so infringed!
Brash! If a forgery of *MY* painting fell out of that armored car...then I'll bet *ALL* the paintings in it were forgeries. The art destroyed in the fire was ***FAKE!***
Maybe you two *haven't* completely fouled up this case...yet. The **REAL** art is still out there!
But how do we find it...again?
BOOP

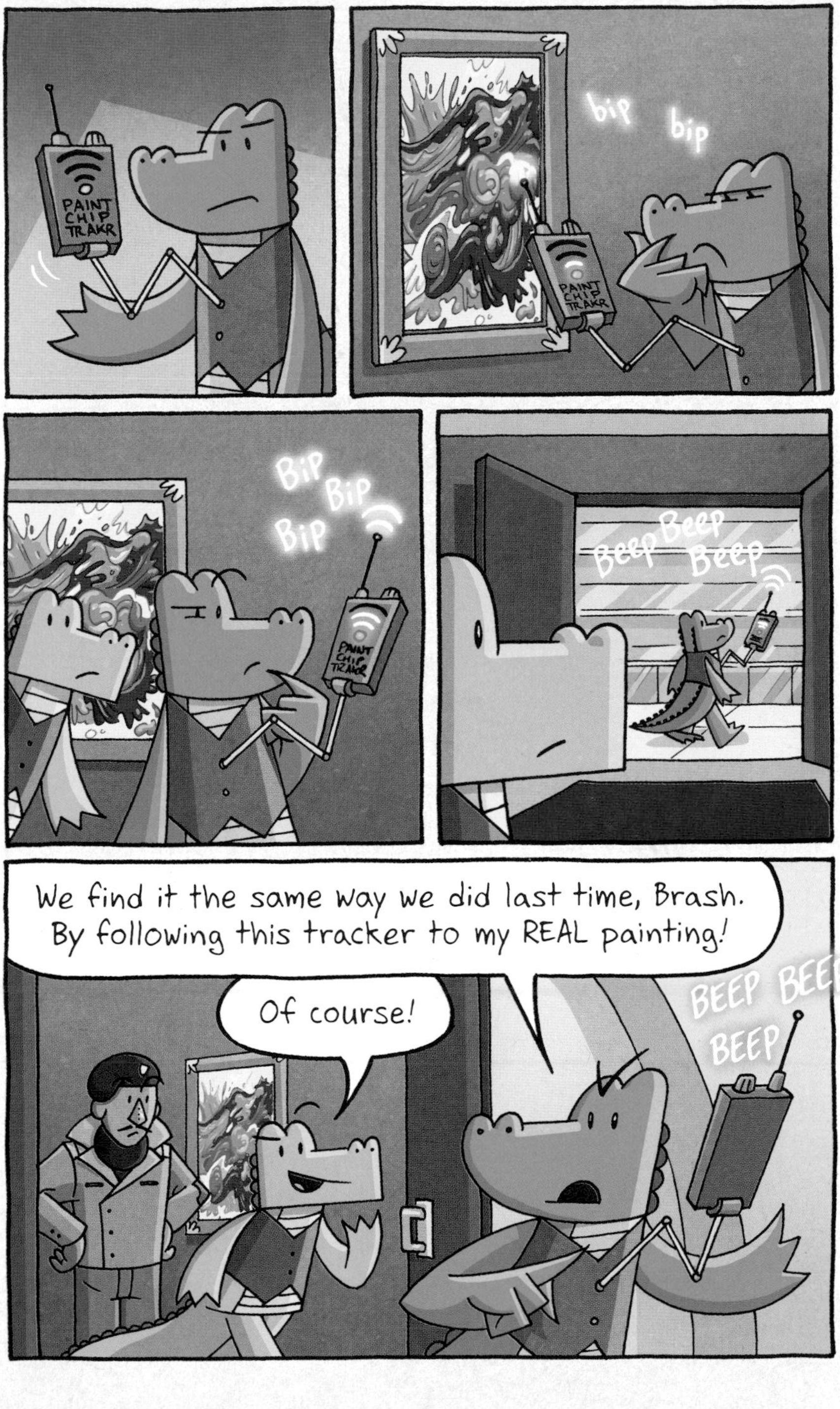
PAINT CHIP TRAKR
bip bip
PAINT CHIP TRAKR
Bip Bip Bip
PAINT CHIP TRAKR
Beep Beep Beep
We find it the same way we did last time, Brash. By following this tracker to my REAL painting!
Of course!
BEEP BEEP BEEP

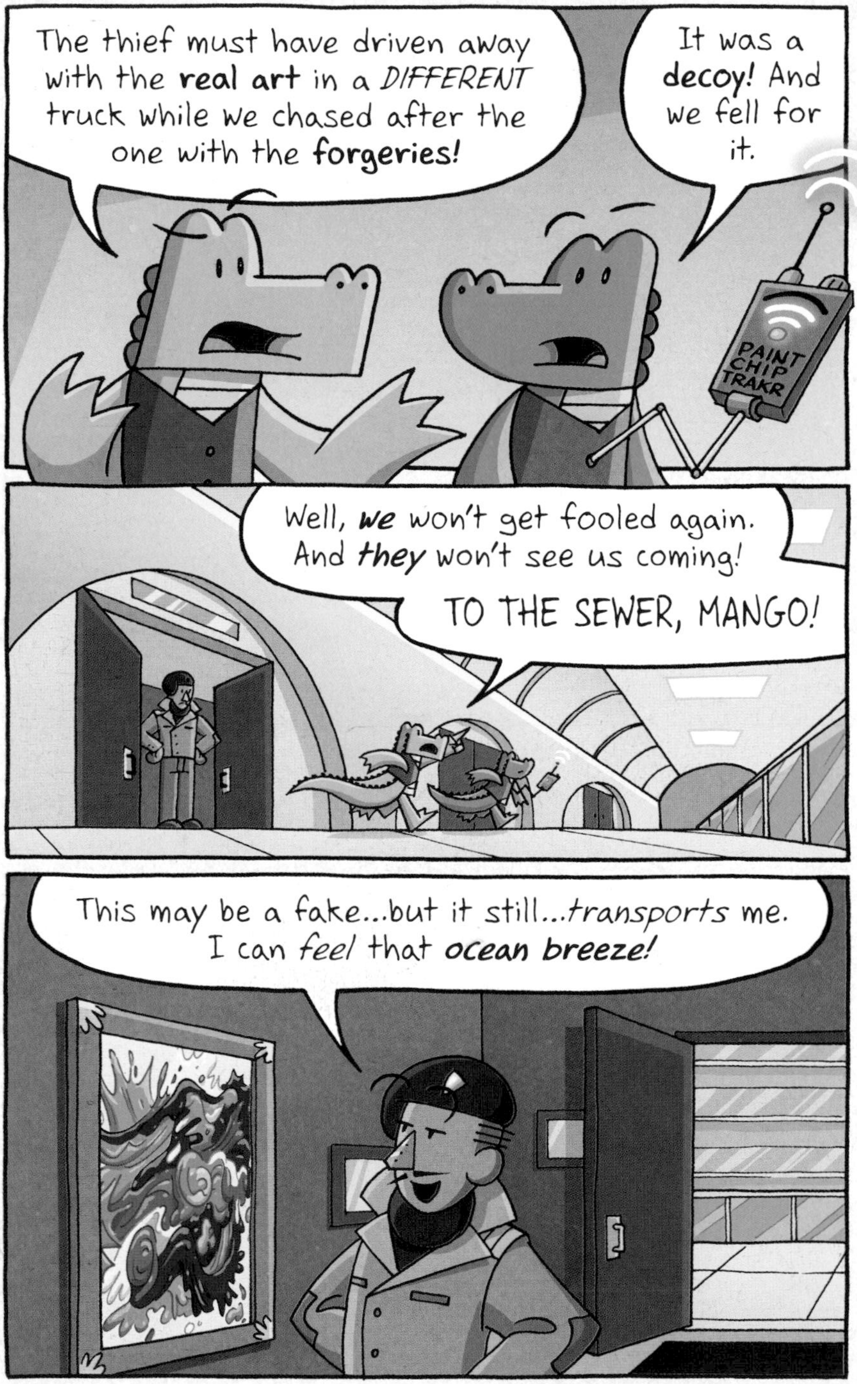
The thief must have driven away with the **real art** in a *DIFFERENT* truck while we chased after the one with the **forgeries**!
It was a **decoy**! And we fell for it.
PAINT CHIP TRAKR
Well, ***we*** won't get fooled again. And ***they*** won't see us coming!
TO THE SEWER, MANGO!
This may be a fake...but it still...*transports* me. I can *feel* that ***ocean breeze***!

Chapter 15

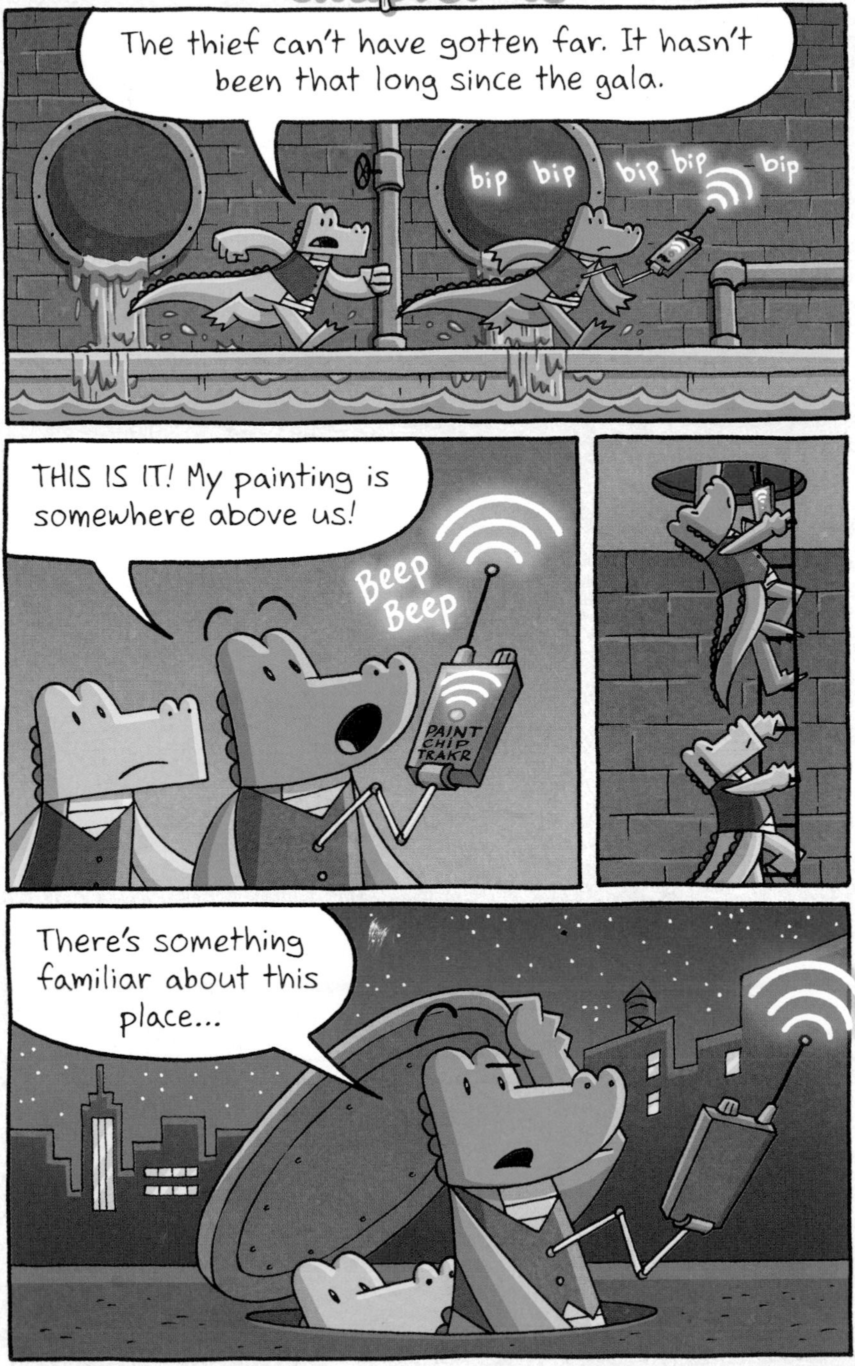
The thief can't have gotten far. It hasn't been that long since the gala.
bip bip bip bip bip
THIS IS IT! My painting is somewhere above us!
Beep Beep
PAINT CHIP TRAKR
There's something familiar about this place...

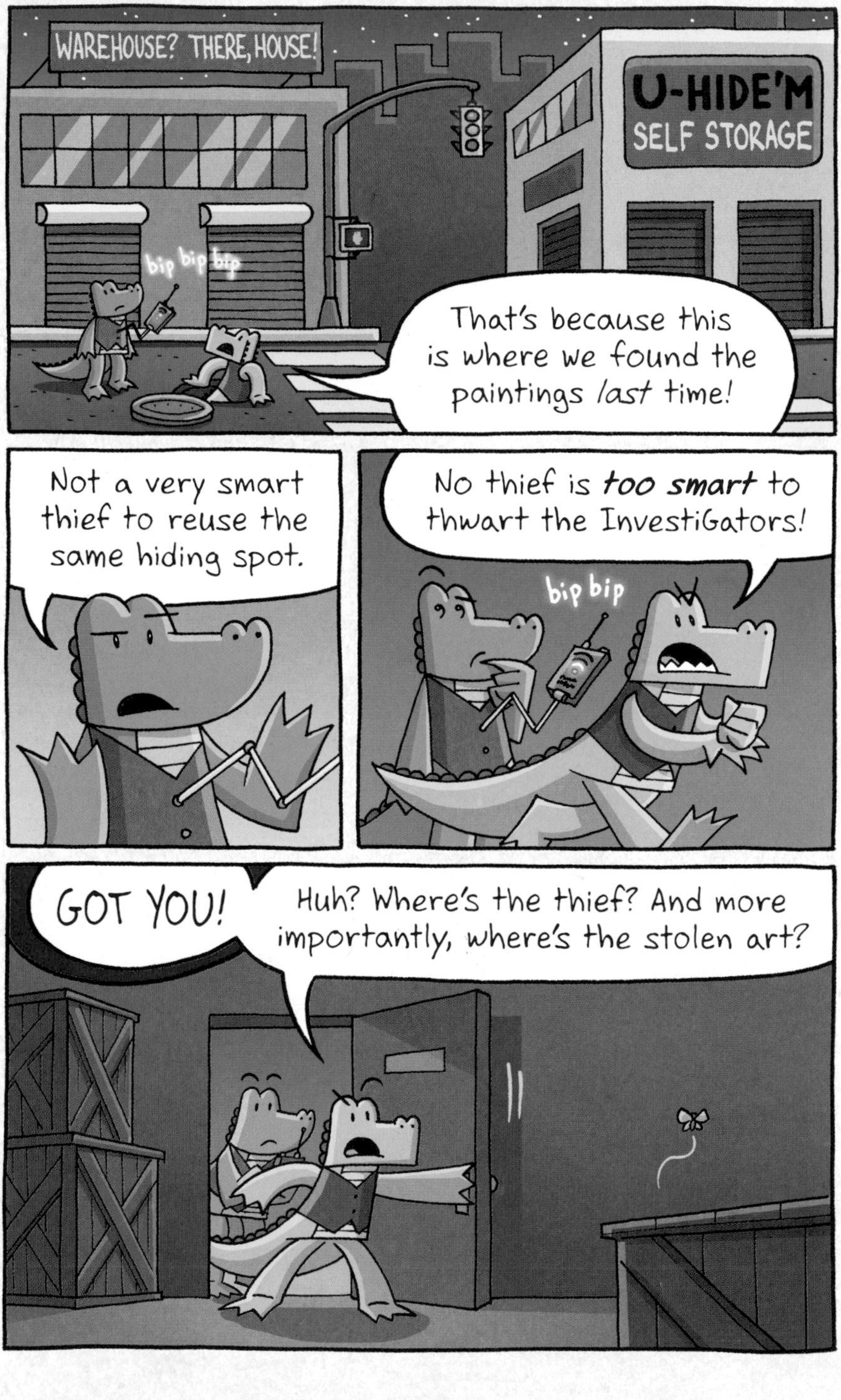
WAREHOUSE? THERE, HOUSE!
U-HIDE'M SELF STORAGE
bip bip bip
That's because this is where we found the paintings *last* time!
Not a very smart thief to reuse the same hiding spot.
No thief is ***too smart*** to thwart the InvestiGators!
bip bip
GOT YOU!
Huh? Where's the thief? And more importantly, where's the stolen art?

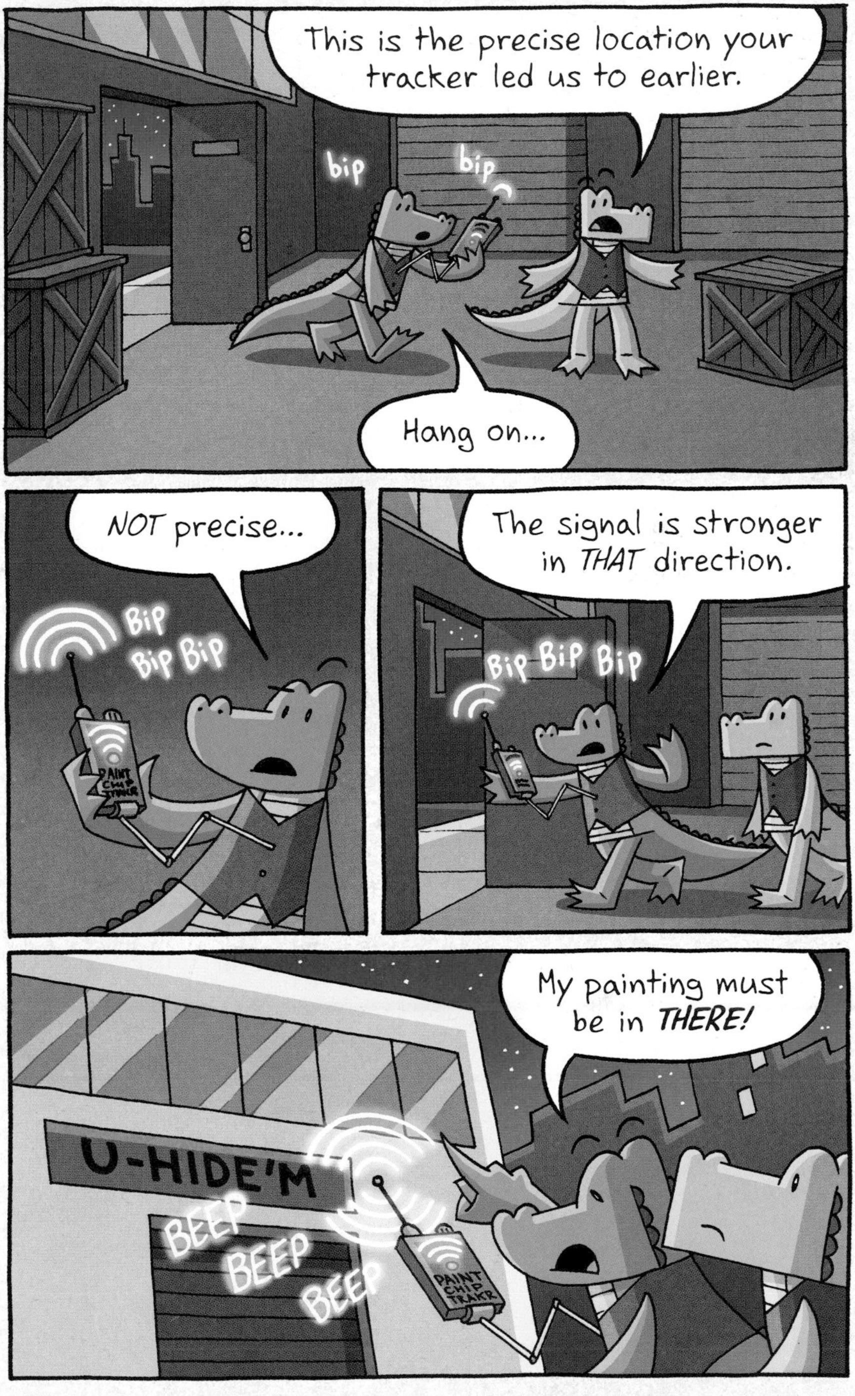
This is the precise location your tracker led us to earlier.
bip
bip
Hang on...
NOT precise...
Bip
Bip Bip
PAINT CHIP TRAKR
The signal is stronger in THAT direction.
Bip Bip Bip
My painting must be in THERE!
U-HIDE'M
BEEP
BEEP
BEEP
PAINT CHIP TRAKR

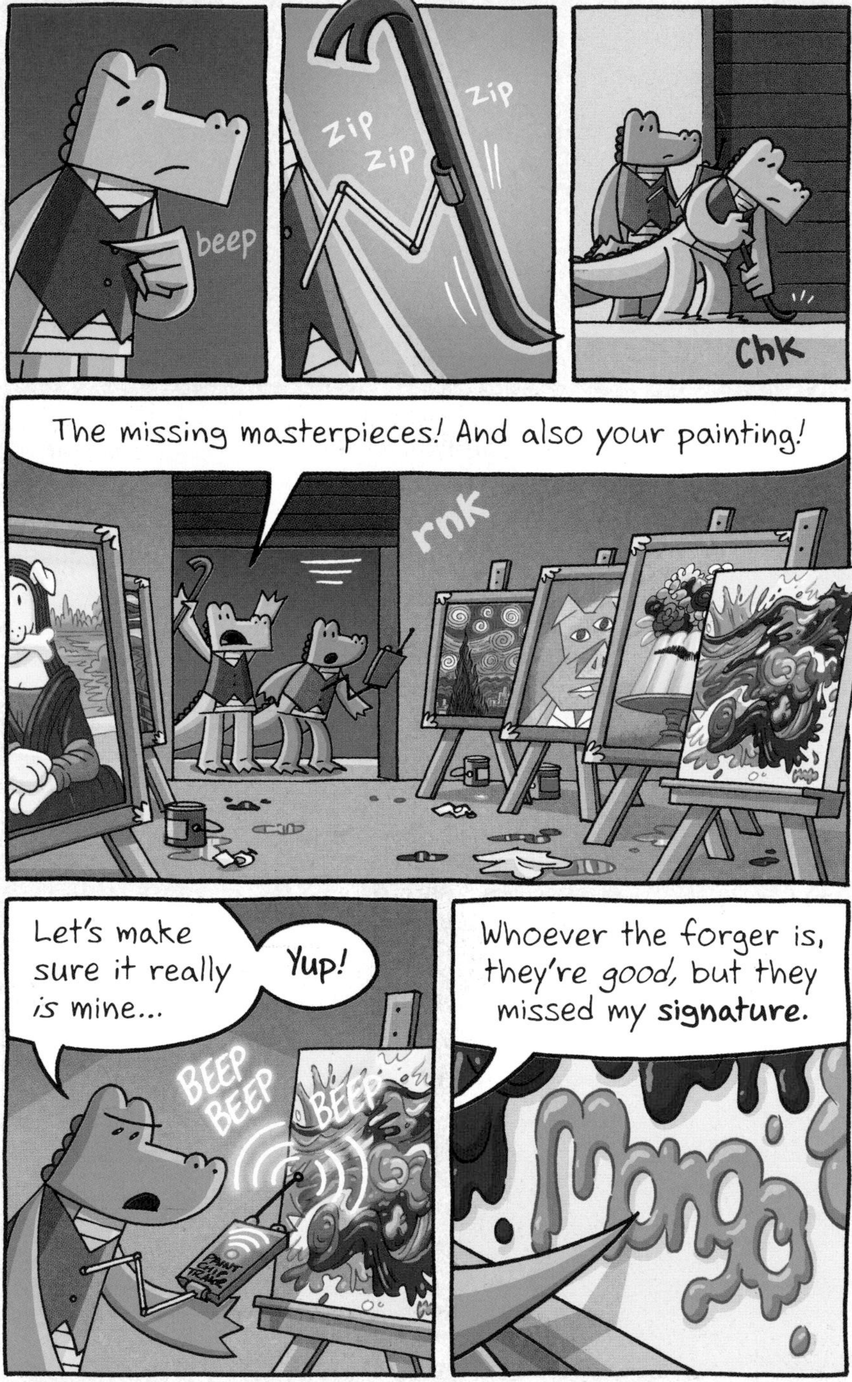
beep
zip
zip
zip
ChK
The missing masterpieces! And also your painting!
rnk
Let's make sure it really *is* mine...
Yup!
BEEP BEEP
BEEP
Whoever the forger is, they're *good*, but they missed my **signature.**
Monga

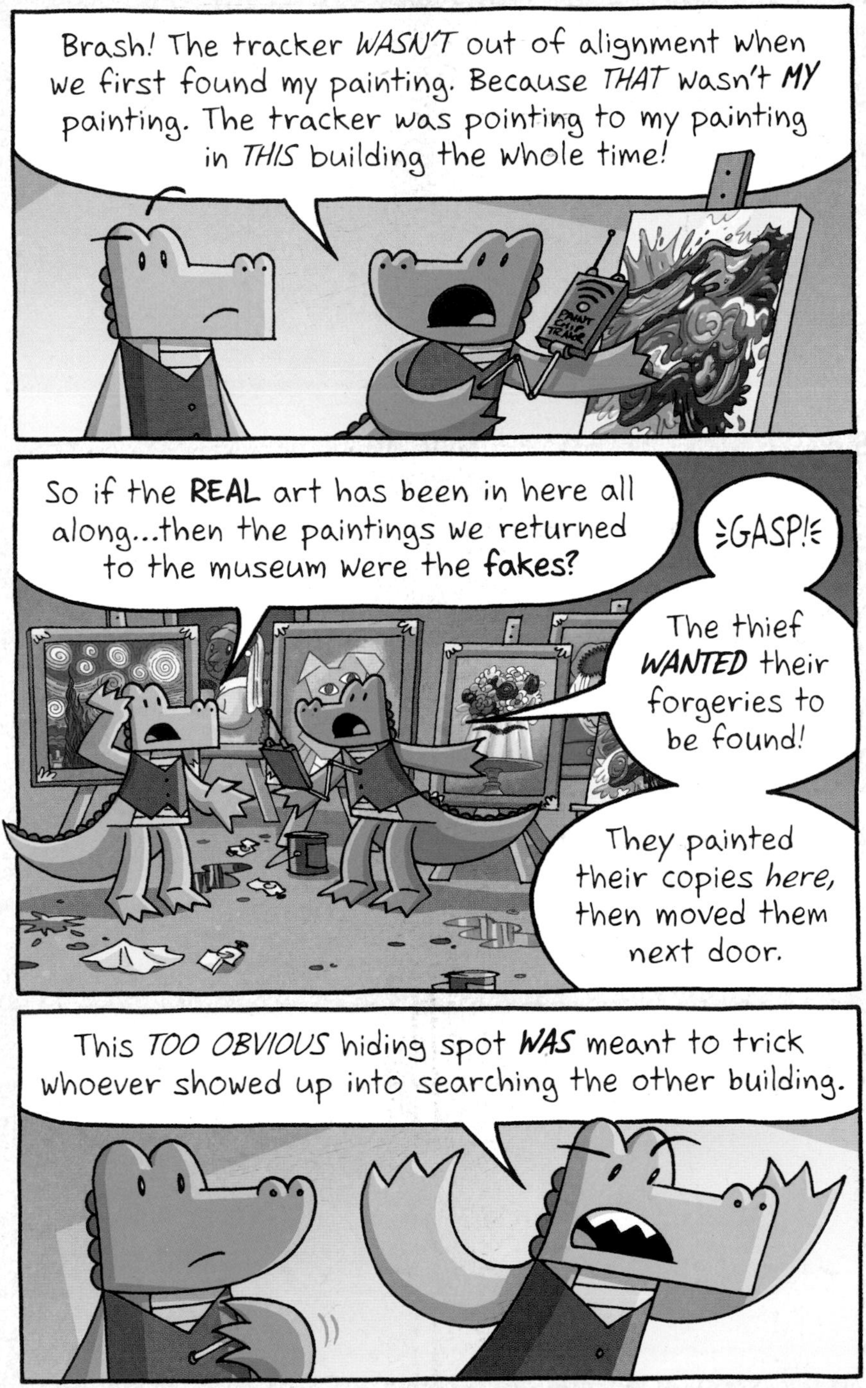
Brash! The tracker *WASN'T* out of alignment when we first found my painting. Because *THAT* wasn't **MY** painting. The tracker was pointing to my painting in *THIS* building the whole time!
PAINT CHIP TRACK
So if the **REAL** art has been in here all along...then the paintings we returned to the museum were the **fakes?**
GASP!
The thief ***WANTED*** their forgeries to be found!
They painted their copies *here,* then moved them next door.
This *TOO OBVIOUS* hiding spot ***WAS*** meant to trick whoever showed up into searching the other building.

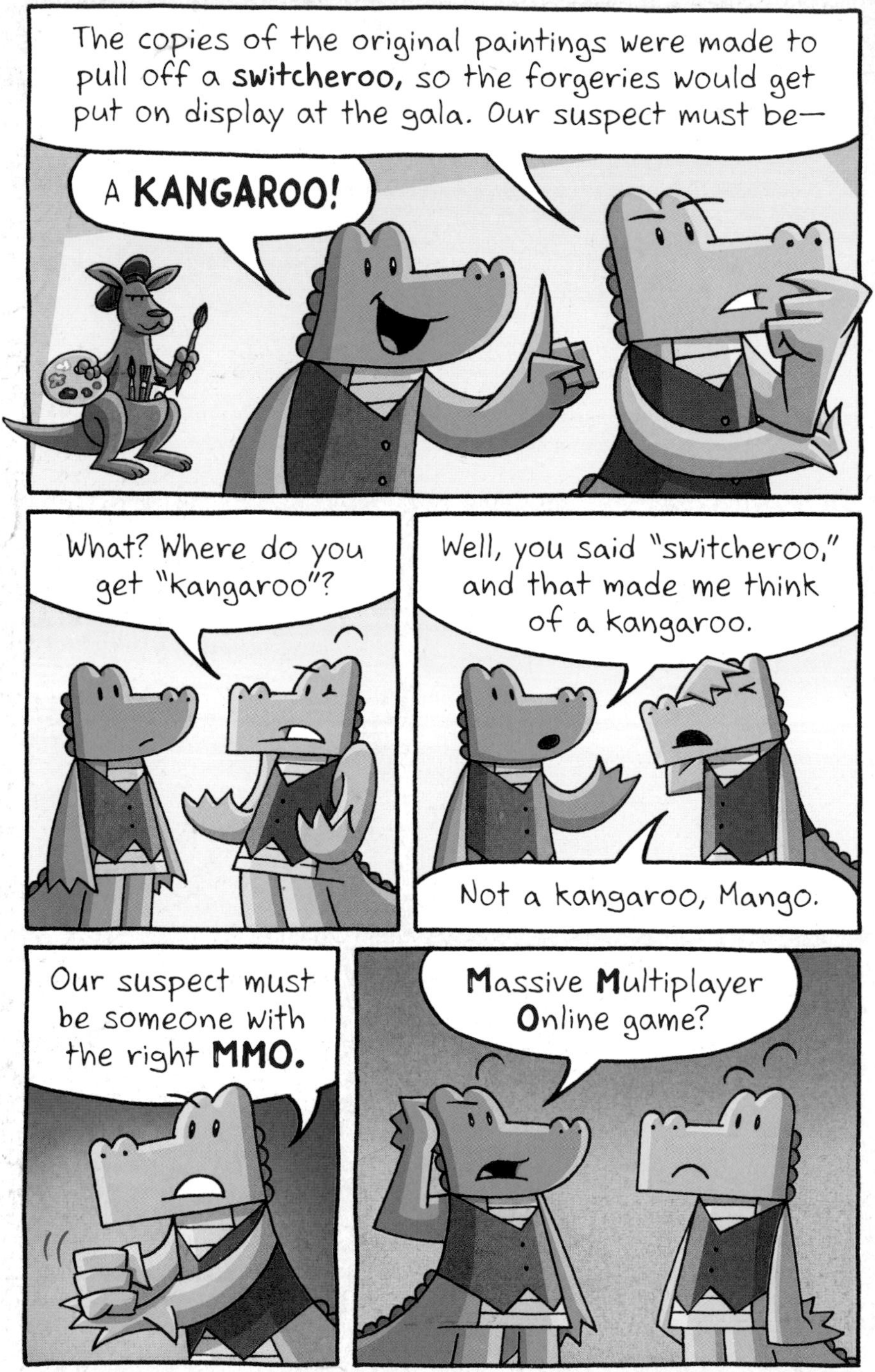
The copies of the original paintings were made to pull off a **switcheroo,** so the forgeries would get put on display at the gala. Our suspect must be—
A **KANGAROO!**
What? Where do you get "kangaroo"?
Well, you said "switcheroo," and that made me think of a kangaroo.
Not a kangaroo, Mango.
Our suspect must be someone with the right **MMO.**
Massive **M**ultiplayer **O**nline game?

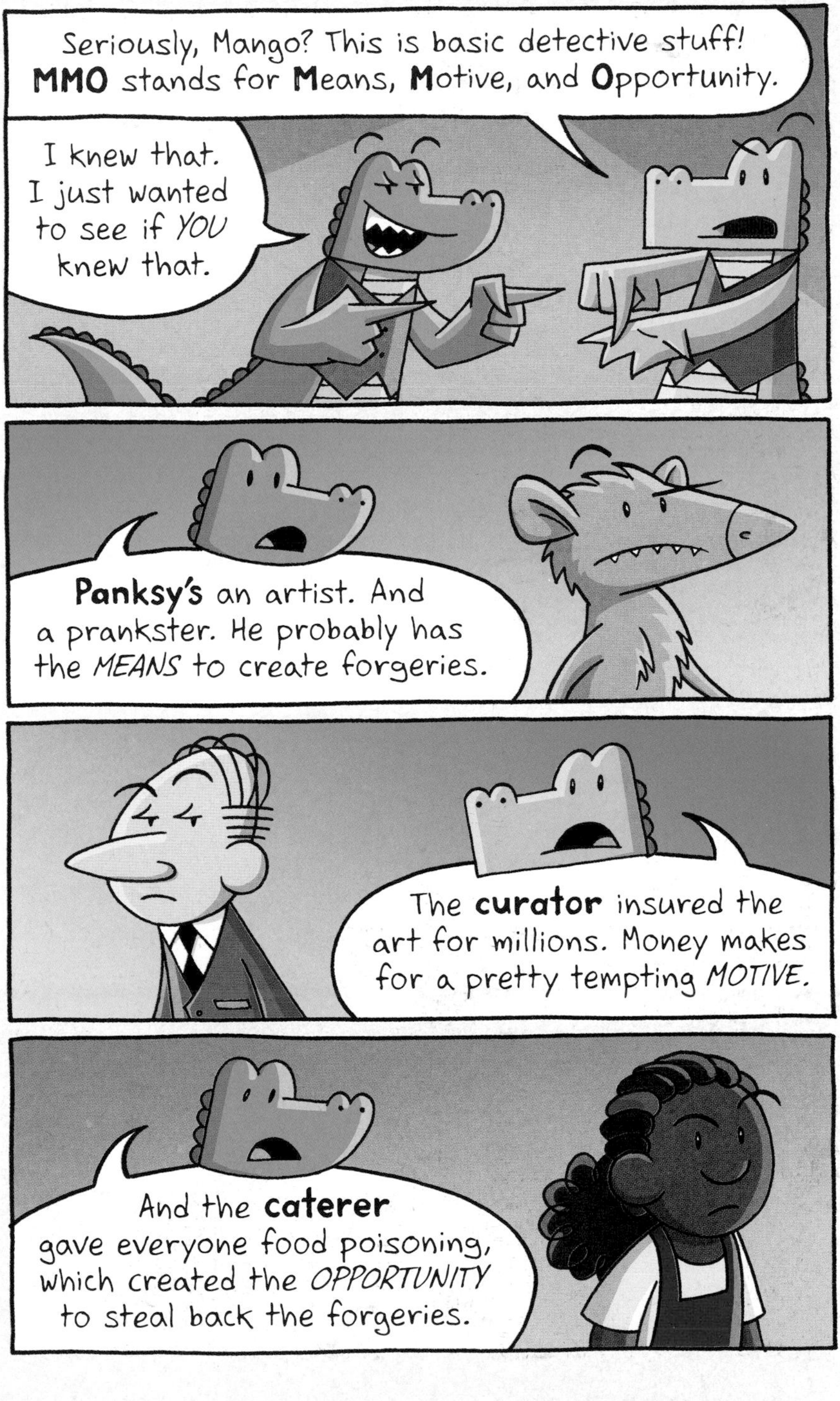

Seriously, Mango? This is basic detective stuff! MMO stands for Means, Motive, and Opportunity.
I knew that. I just wanted to see if YOU knew that.
Panksy's an artist. And a prankster. He probably has the MEANS to create forgeries.
The curator insured the art for millions. Money makes for a pretty tempting MOTIVE.
And the caterer gave everyone food poisoning, which created the OPPORTUNITY to steal back the forgeries.

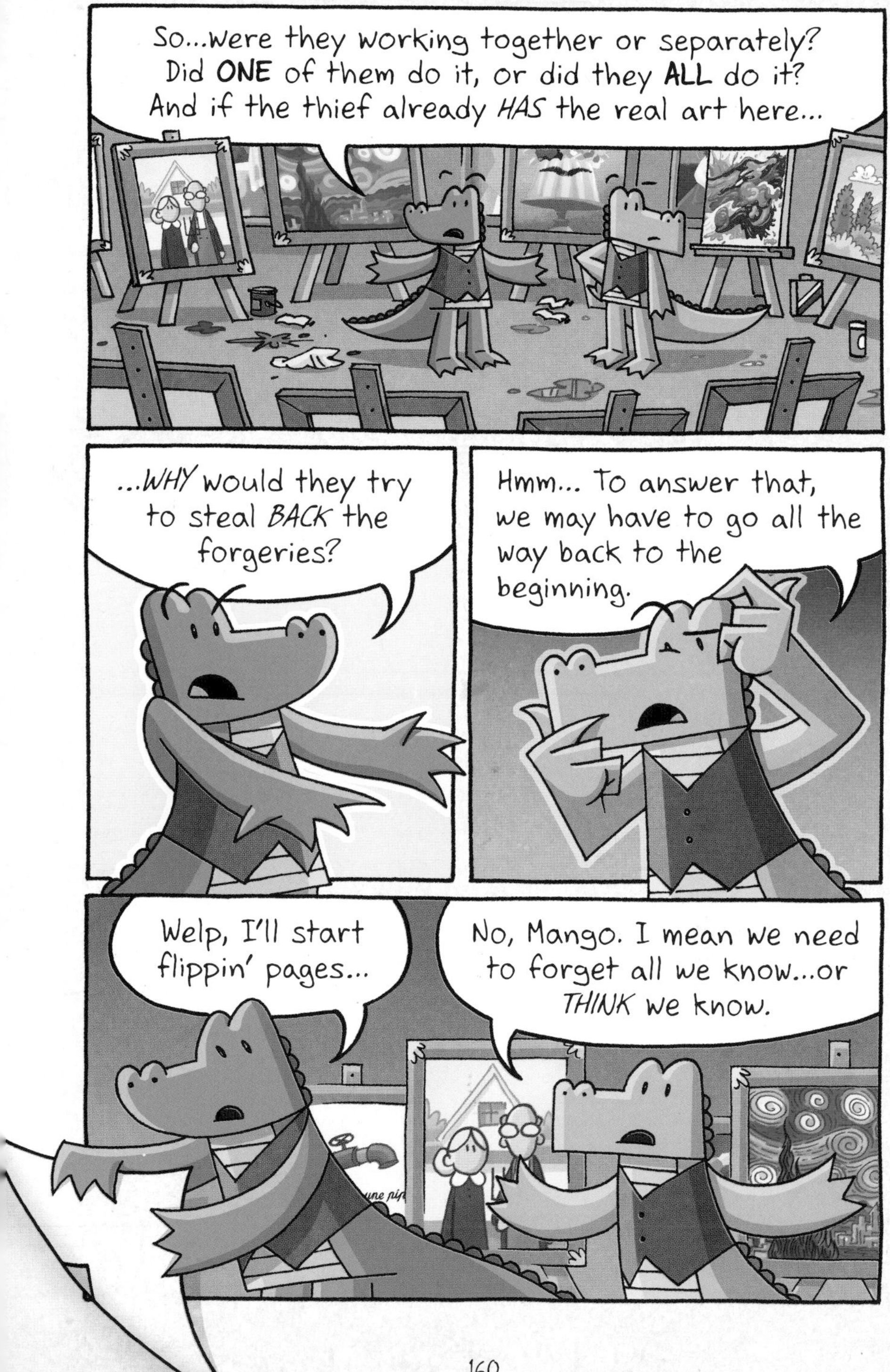
So...were they working together or separately? Did ONE of them do it, or did they ALL do it? And if the thief already HAS the real art here...
...WHY would they try to steal BACK the forgeries?
Hmm... To answer that, we may have to go all the way back to the beginning.
Welp, I'll start flippin' pages...
No, Mango. I mean we need to forget all we know...or THINK we know.

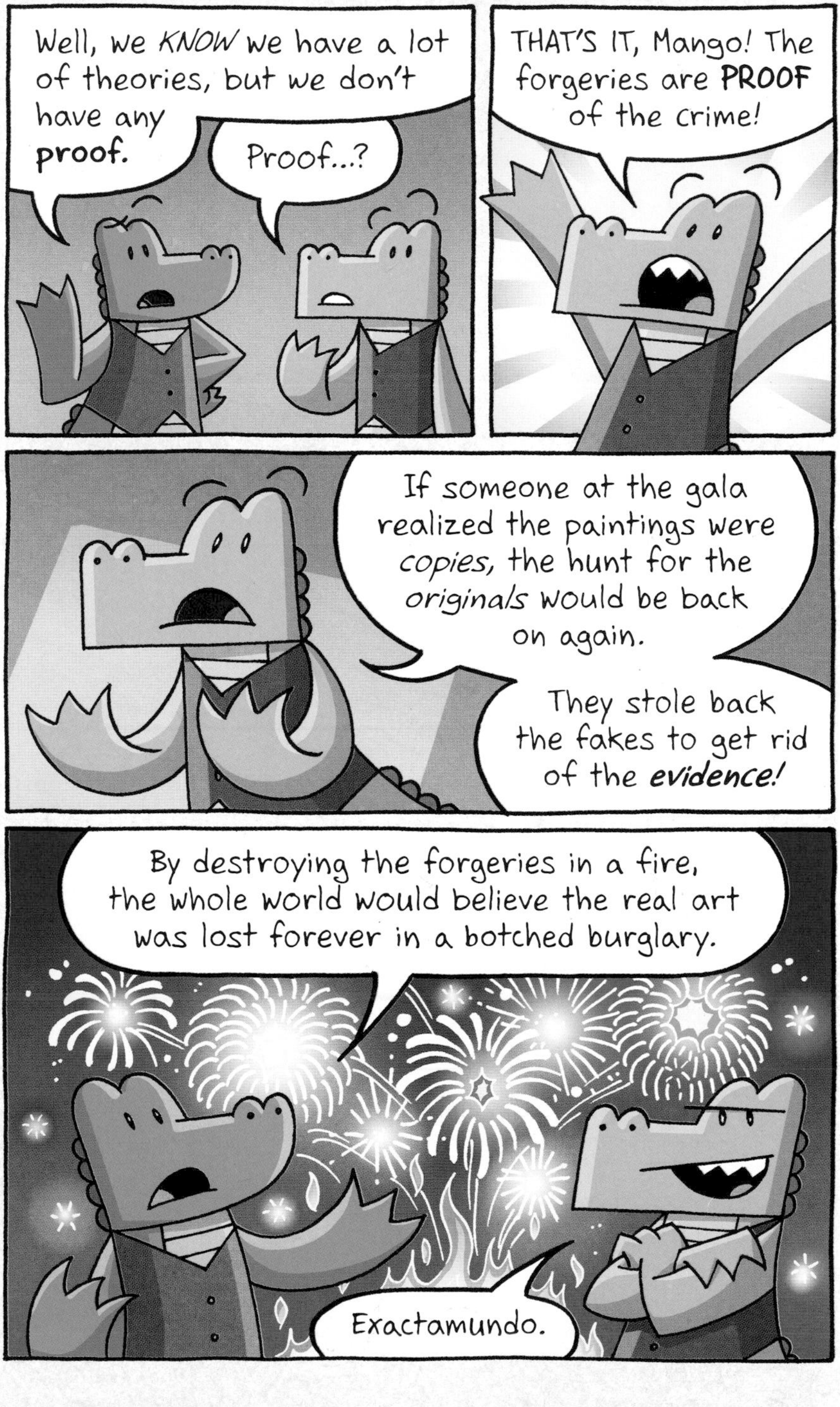
Well, we *KNOW* we have a lot of theories, but we don't have any **proof.**
Proof...?
THAT'S IT, Mango! The forgeries are **PROOF** of the crime!
If someone at the gala realized the paintings were *copies,* the hunt for the *originals* would be back on again.
They stole back the fakes to get rid of the ***evidence!***
By destroying the forgeries in a fire, the whole world would believe the real art was lost forever in a botched burglary.
Exactamundo.

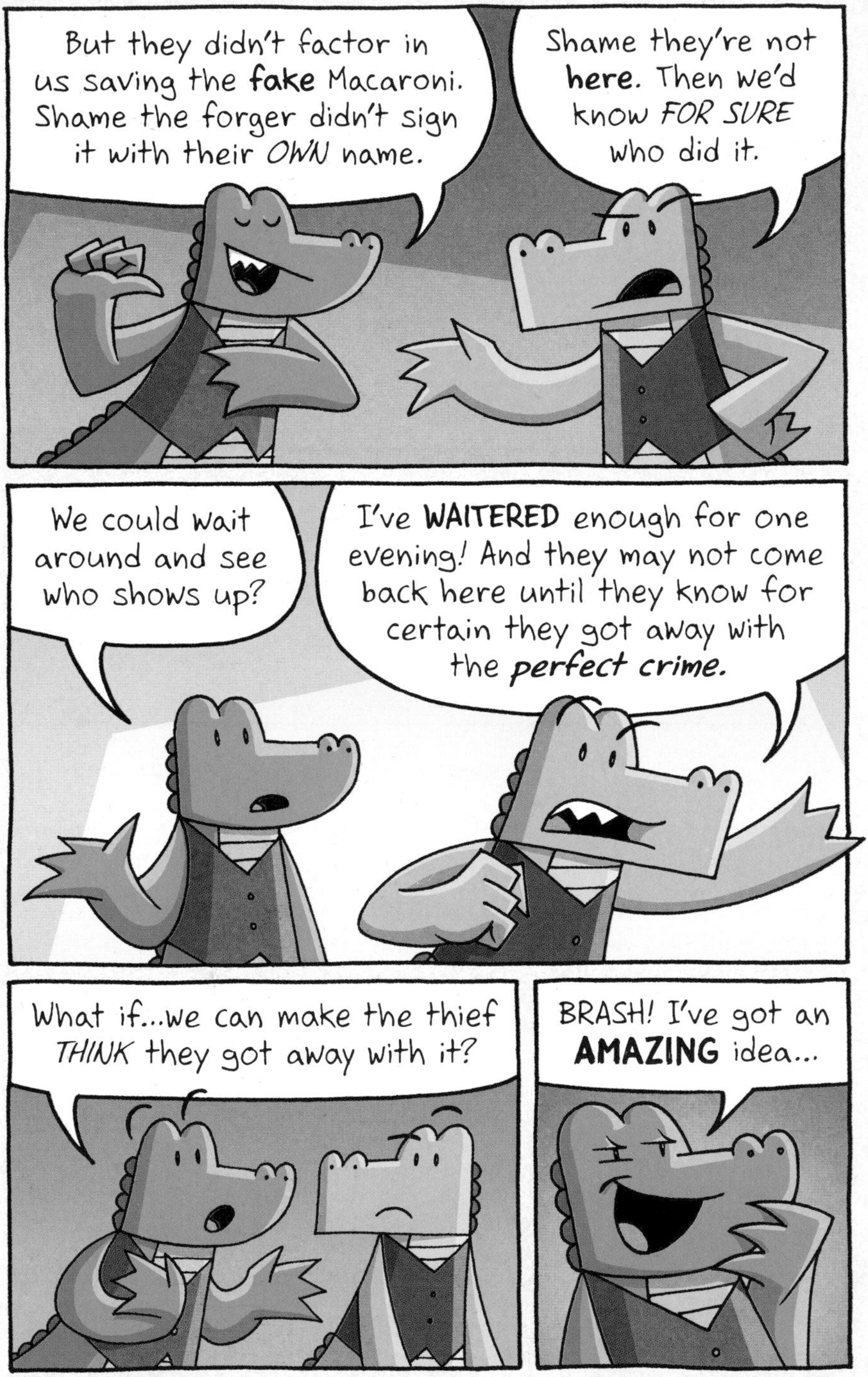

But they didn't factor in us saving the **fake** Macaroni. Shame the forger didn't sign it with their *OWN* name.
Shame they're not **here**. Then we'd know *FOR SURE* who did it.
We could wait around and see who shows up?
I've **WAITERED** enough for one evening! And they may not come back here until they know for certain they got away with the ***perfect crime.***
What if...we can make the thief *THINK* they got away with it?
BRASH! I've got an **AMAZING** idea...

Chapter 16

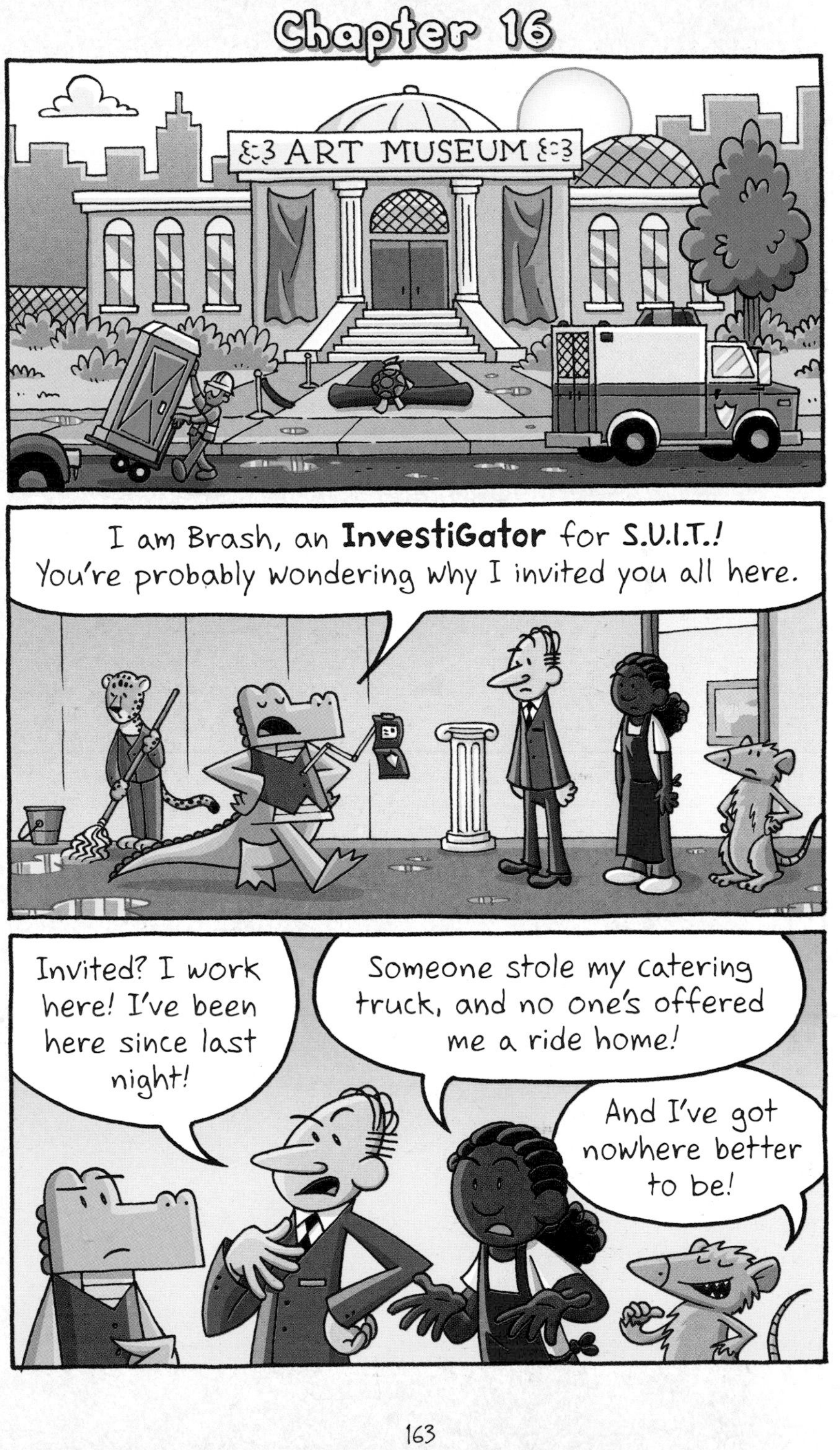

ART MUSEUM
I am Brash, an **InvestiGator** for **S.U.I.T.**! You're probably wondering why I invited you all here.
Invited? I work here! I've been here since last night!
Someone stole my catering truck, and no one's offered me a ride home!
And I've got nowhere better to be!

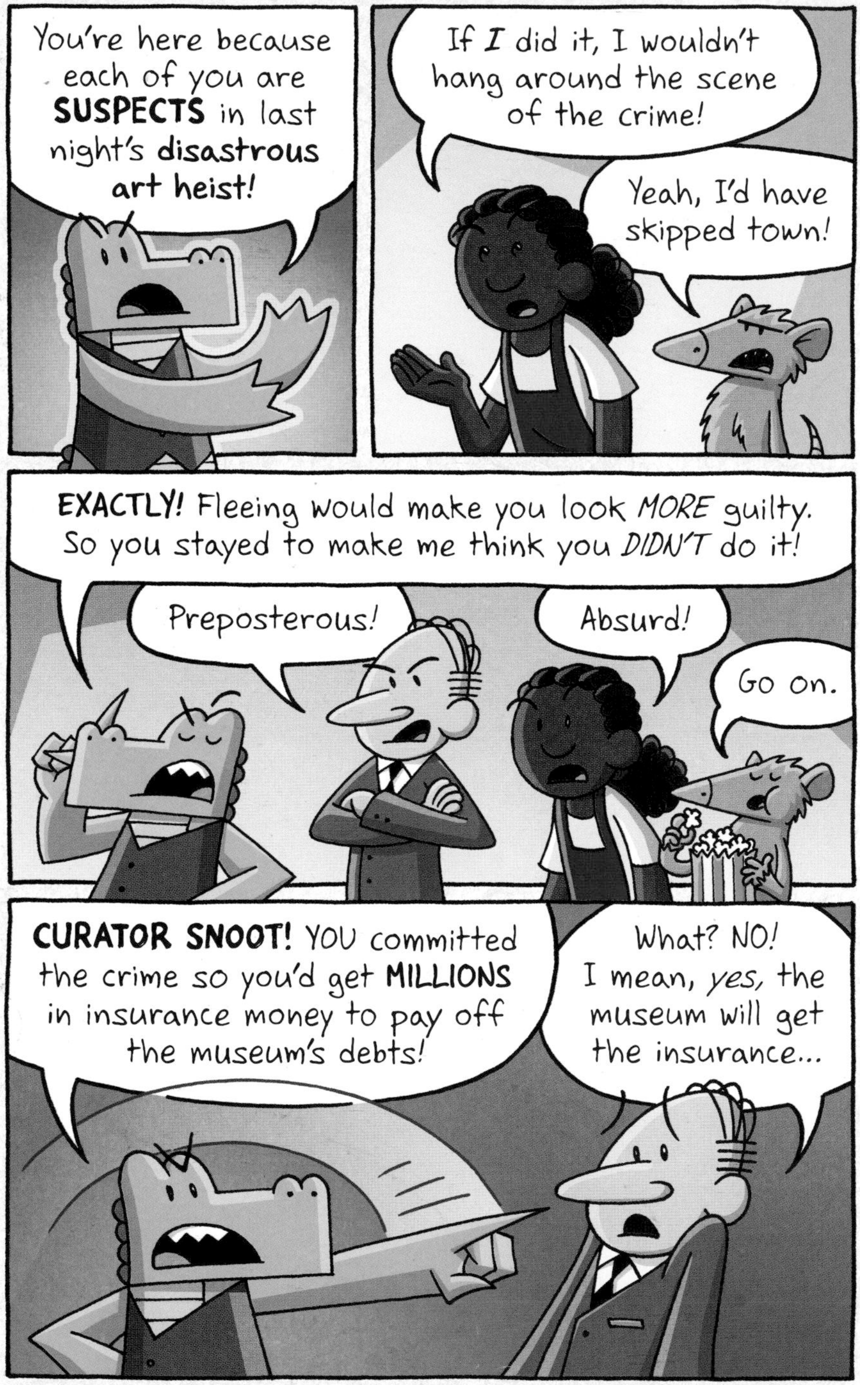
You're here because each of you are **SUSPECTS** in last night's **disastrous art heist!**
If *I* did it, I wouldn't hang around the scene of the crime!
Yeah, I'd have skipped town!
EXACTLY! Fleeing would make you look *MORE* guilty. So you stayed to make me think you *DIDN'T* do it!
Preposterous!
Absurd!
Go on.
CURATOR SNOOT! YOU committed the crime so you'd get **MILLIONS** in insurance money to pay off the museum's debts!
What? NO! I mean, *yes,* the museum will get the insurance...

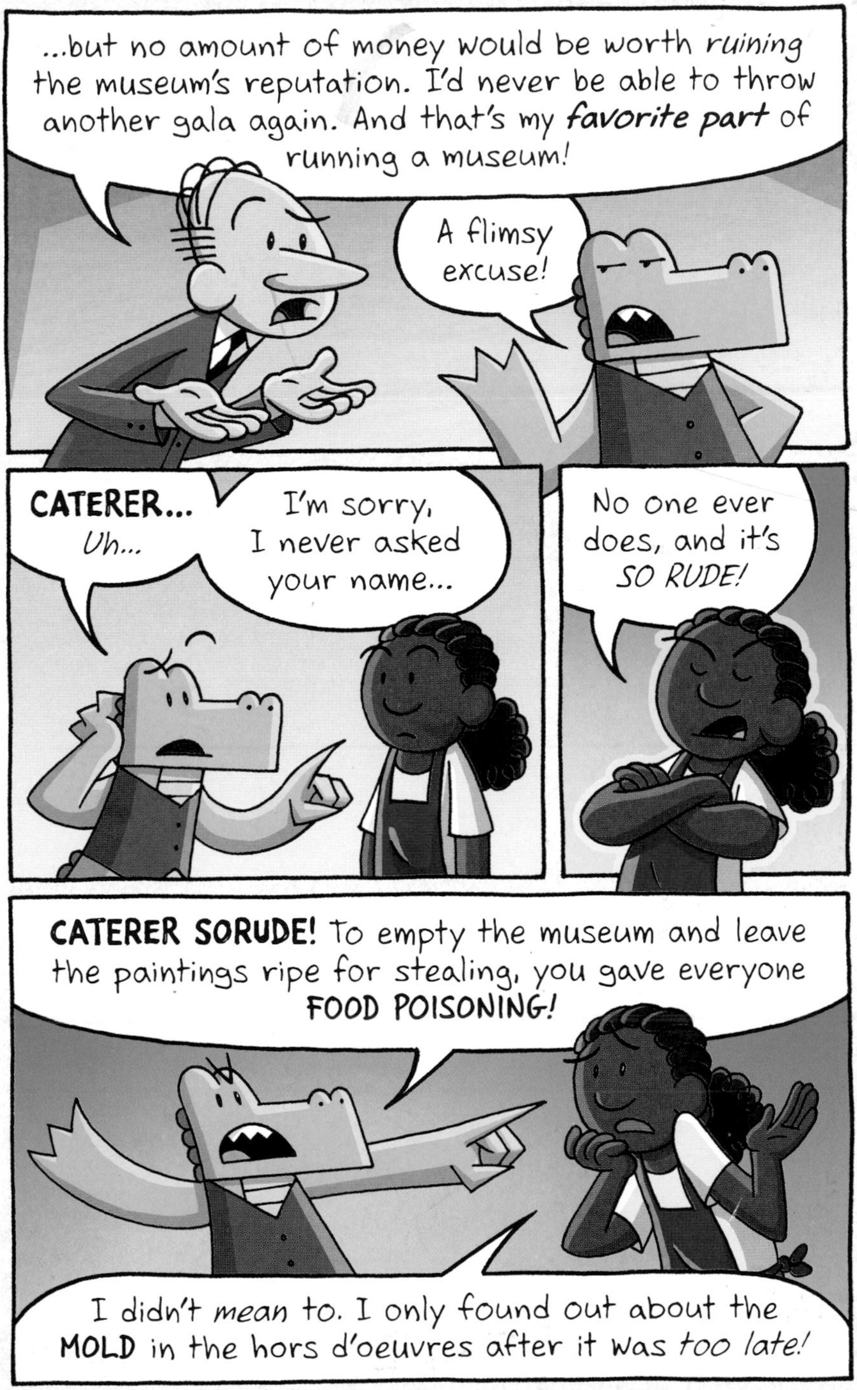
...but no amount of money would be worth *ruining* the museum's reputation. I'd never be able to throw another gala again. And that's my ***favorite part*** of running a museum!
A flimsy excuse!
CATERER... *Uh...*
I'm sorry, I never asked your name...
No one ever does, and it's *SO RUDE!*
CATERER SORUDE! To empty the museum and leave the paintings ripe for stealing, you gave everyone **FOOD POISONING!**
I didn't *mean* to. I only found out about the **MOLD** in the hors d'oeuvres after it was *too late!*

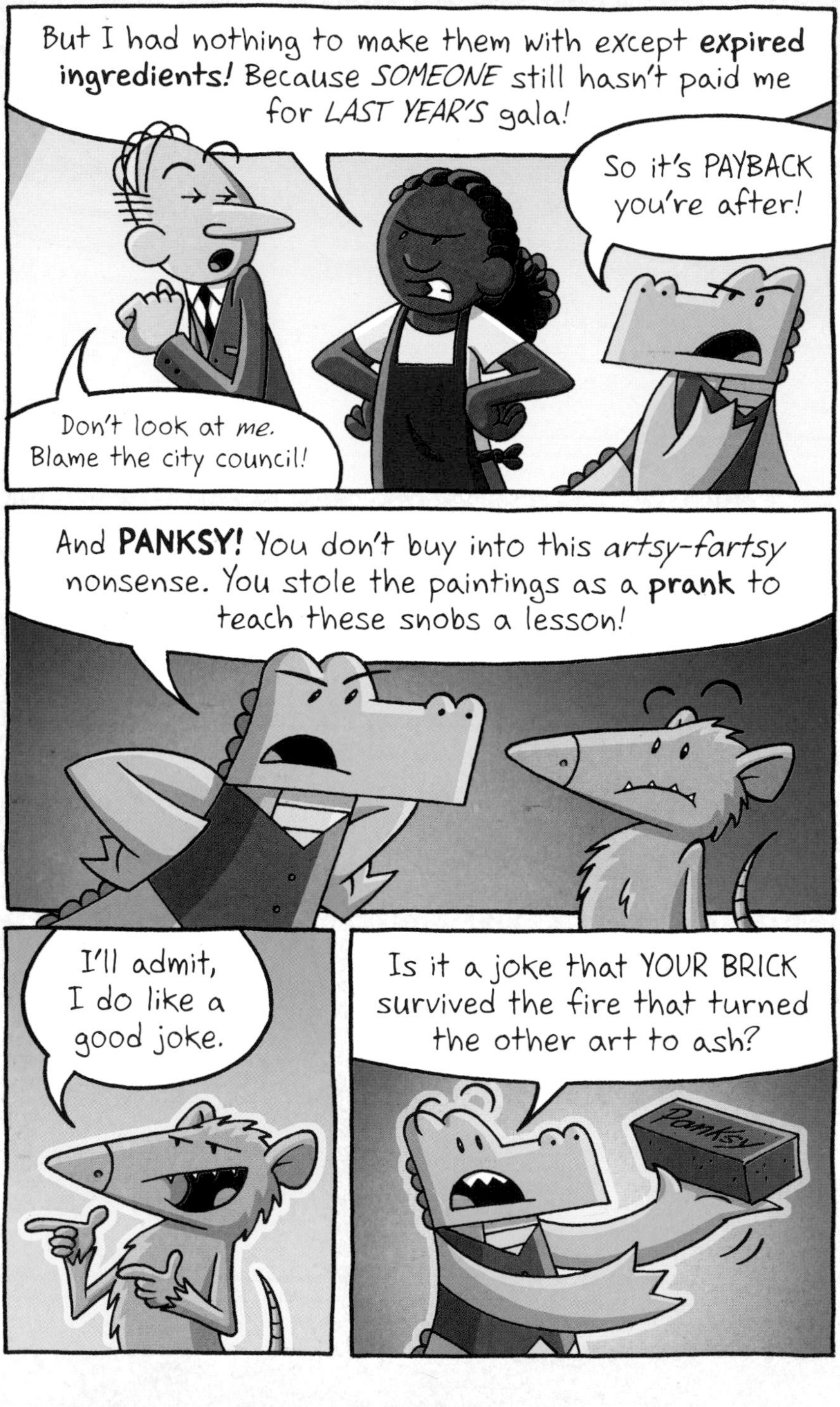

But I had nothing to make them with except **expired ingredients!** Because *SOMEONE* still hasn't paid me for *LAST YEAR'S* gala!
So it's PAYBACK you're after!
Don't look at *me.* Blame the city council!
And **PANKSY!** You don't buy into this *artsy-fartsy* nonsense. You stole the paintings as a **prank** to teach these snobs a lesson!
I'll admit, I do like a good joke.
Is it a joke that YOUR BRICK survived the fire that turned the other art to ash?
Panksy

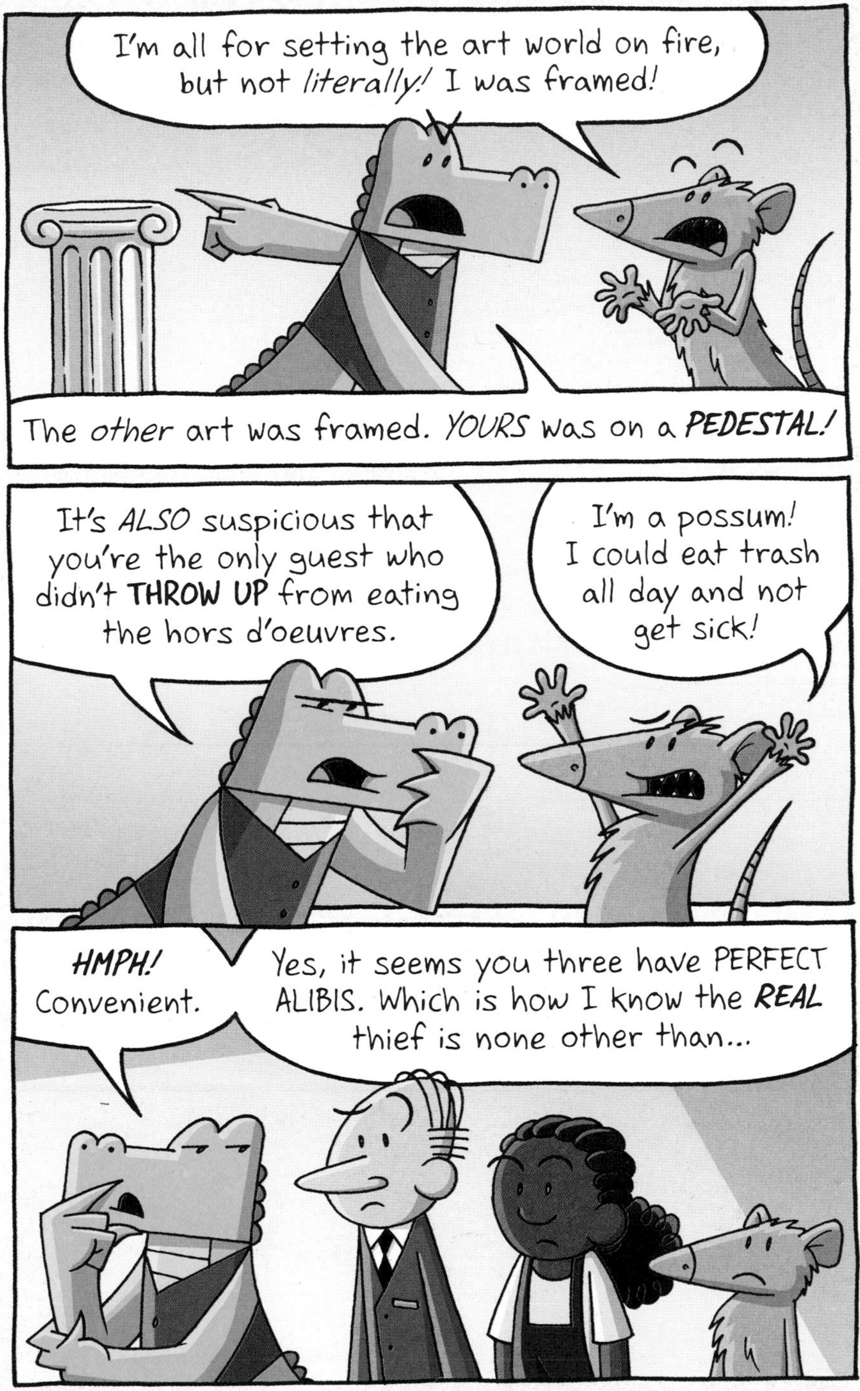
I'm all for setting the art world on fire, but not *literally!* I was framed!
The *other* art was framed. *YOURS* was on a ***PEDESTAL!***
It's *ALSO* suspicious that you're the only guest who didn't **THROW UP** from eating the hors d'oeuvres.
I'm a possum! I could eat trash all day and not get sick!
HMPH! Convenient.
Yes, it seems you three have PERFECT ALIBIS. Which is how I know the ***REAL*** thief is none other than...

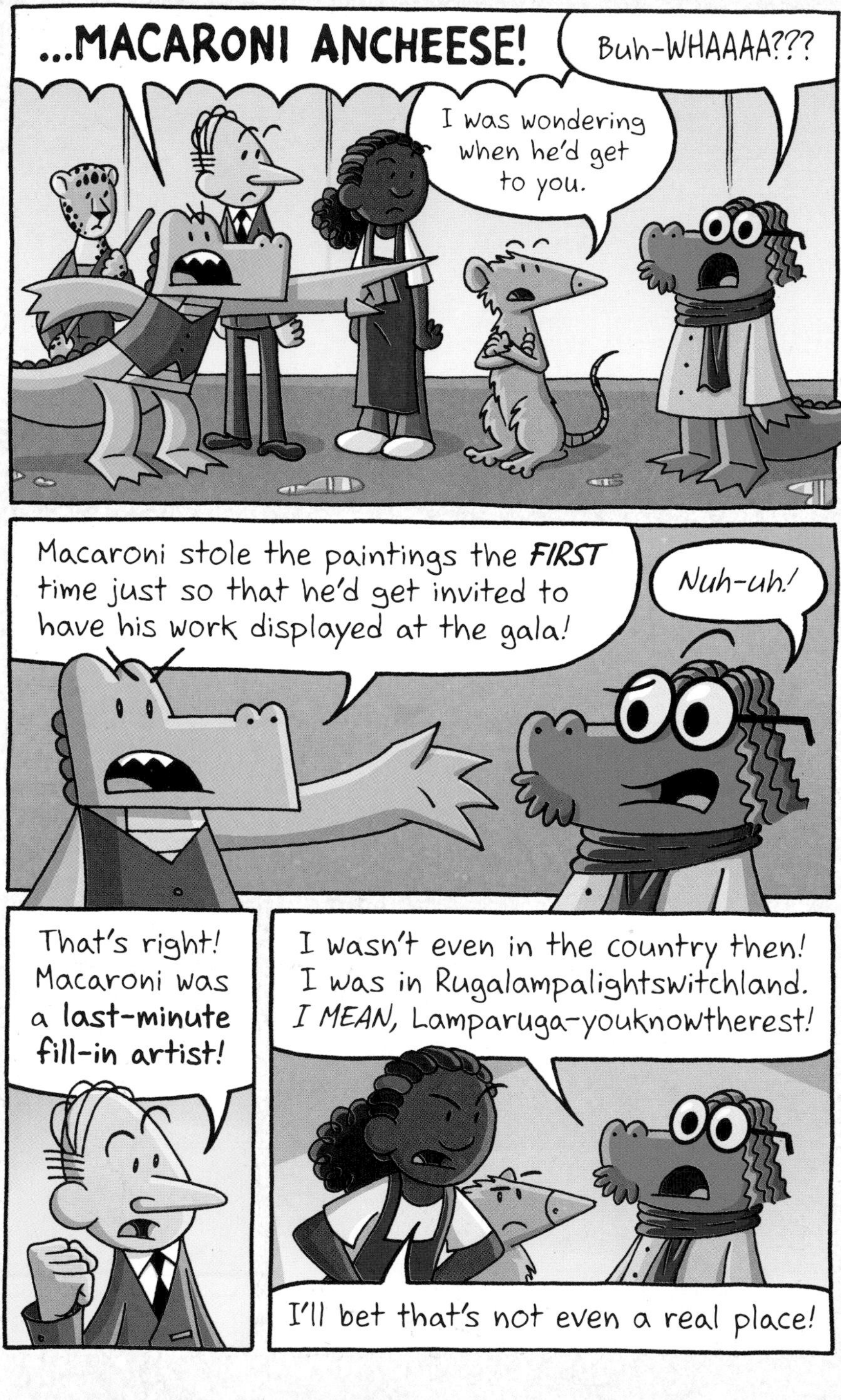
...MACARONI ANCHEESE!
Buh-WHAAAA???
I was wondering when he'd get to you.
Macaroni stole the paintings the FIRST time just so that he'd get invited to have his work displayed at the gala!
Nuh-uh!
That's right! Macaroni was a last-minute fill-in artist!
I wasn't even in the country then! I was in Rugalampalightswitchland. I MEAN, Lamparuga-youknowtherest!
I'll bet that's not even a real place!

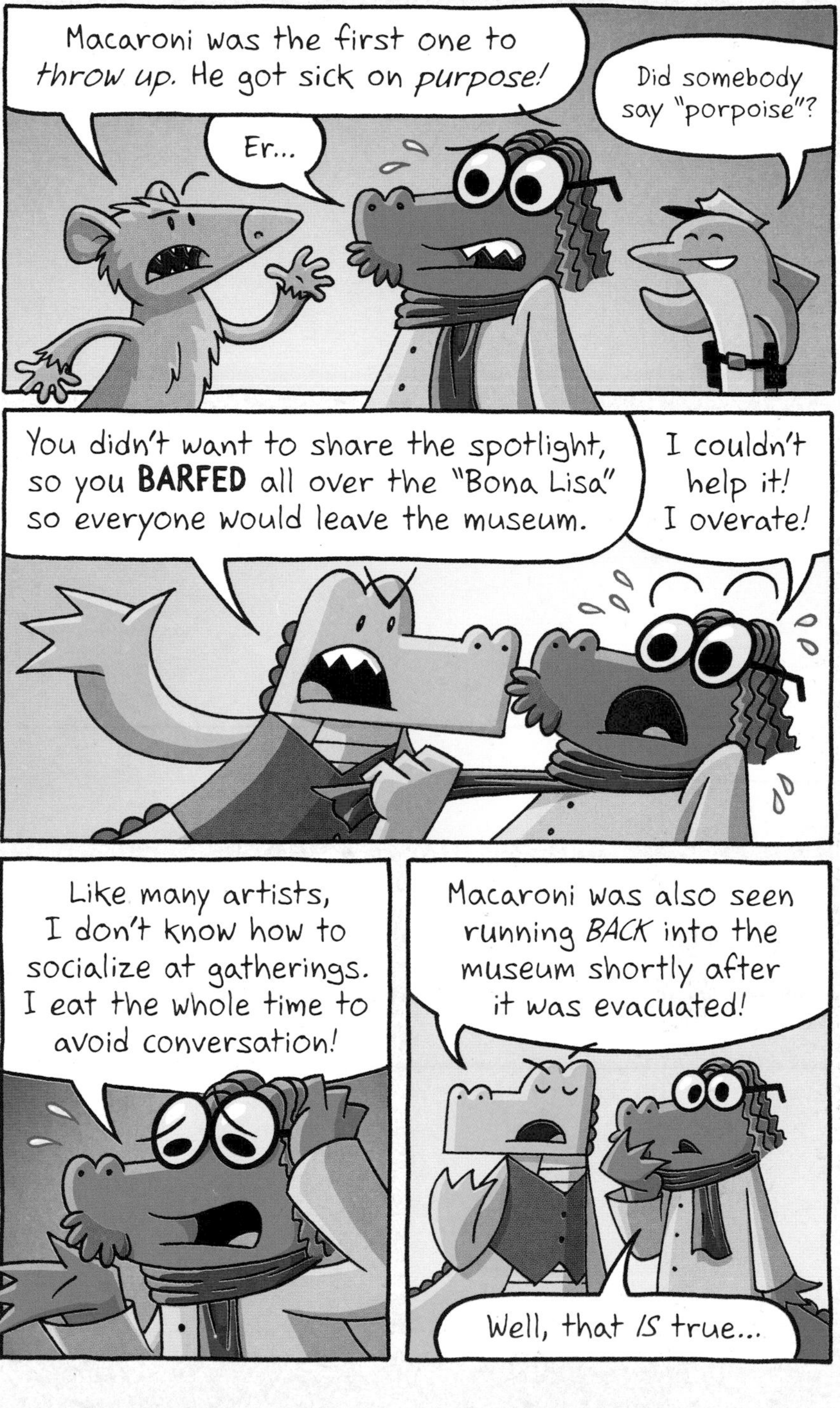
Macaroni was the first one to *throw up*. He got sick on *purpose*!
Er...
Did somebody say "porpoise"?
You didn't want to share the spotlight, so you **BARFED** all over the "Bona Lisa" so everyone would leave the museum.
I couldn't help it! I overate!
Like many artists, I don't know how to socialize at gatherings. I eat the whole time to avoid conversation!
Macaroni was also seen running *BACK* into the museum shortly after it was evacuated!
Well, that *IS* true...

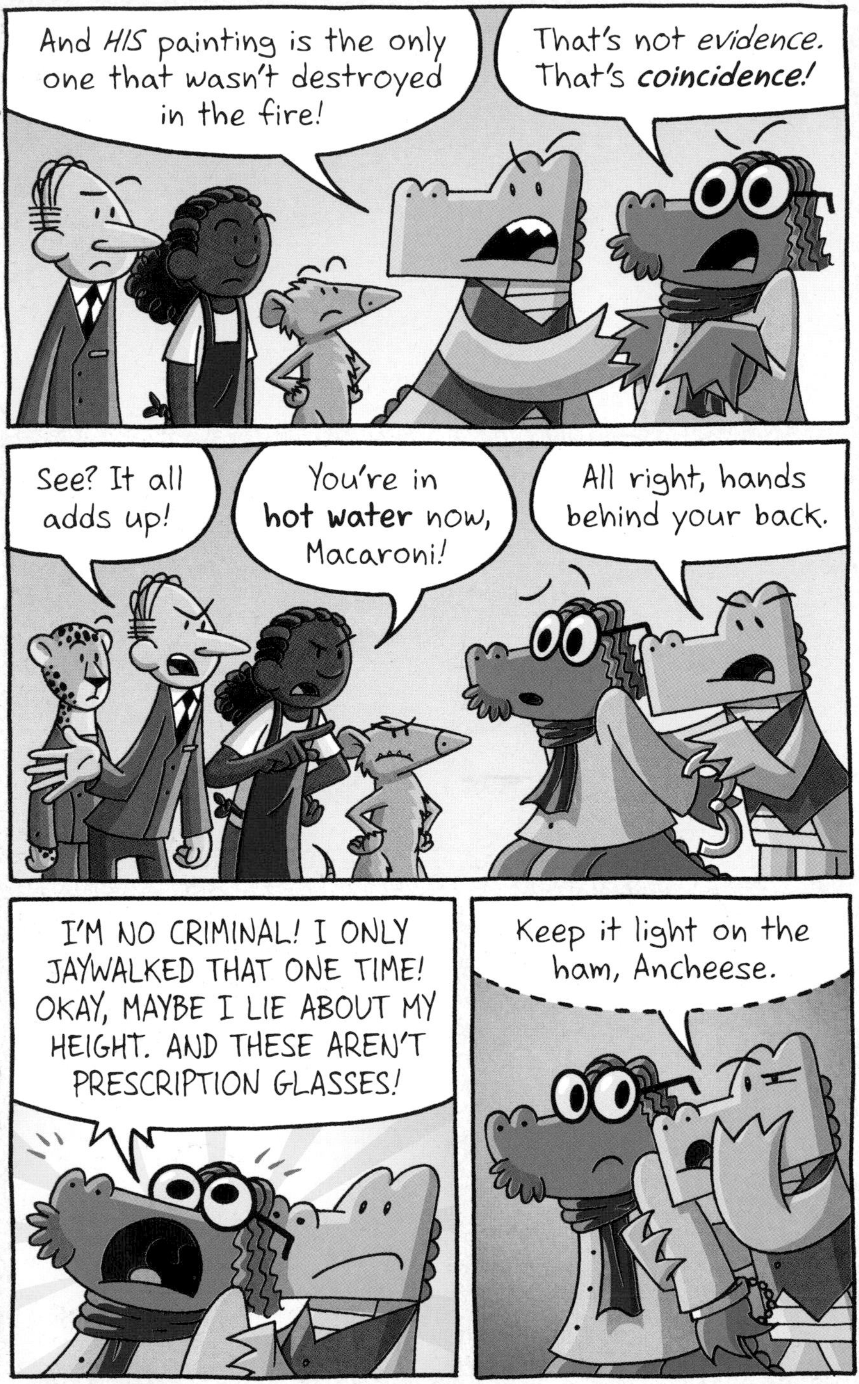
And HIS painting is the only one that wasn't destroyed in the fire!
That's not evidence. That's coincidence!
See? It all adds up!
You're in hot water now, Macaroni!
All right, hands behind your back.
I'M NO CRIMINAL! I ONLY JAYWALKED THAT ONE TIME! OKAY, MAYBE I LIE ABOUT MY HEIGHT. AND THESE AREN'T PRESCRIPTION GLASSES!
Keep it light on the ham, Ancheese.

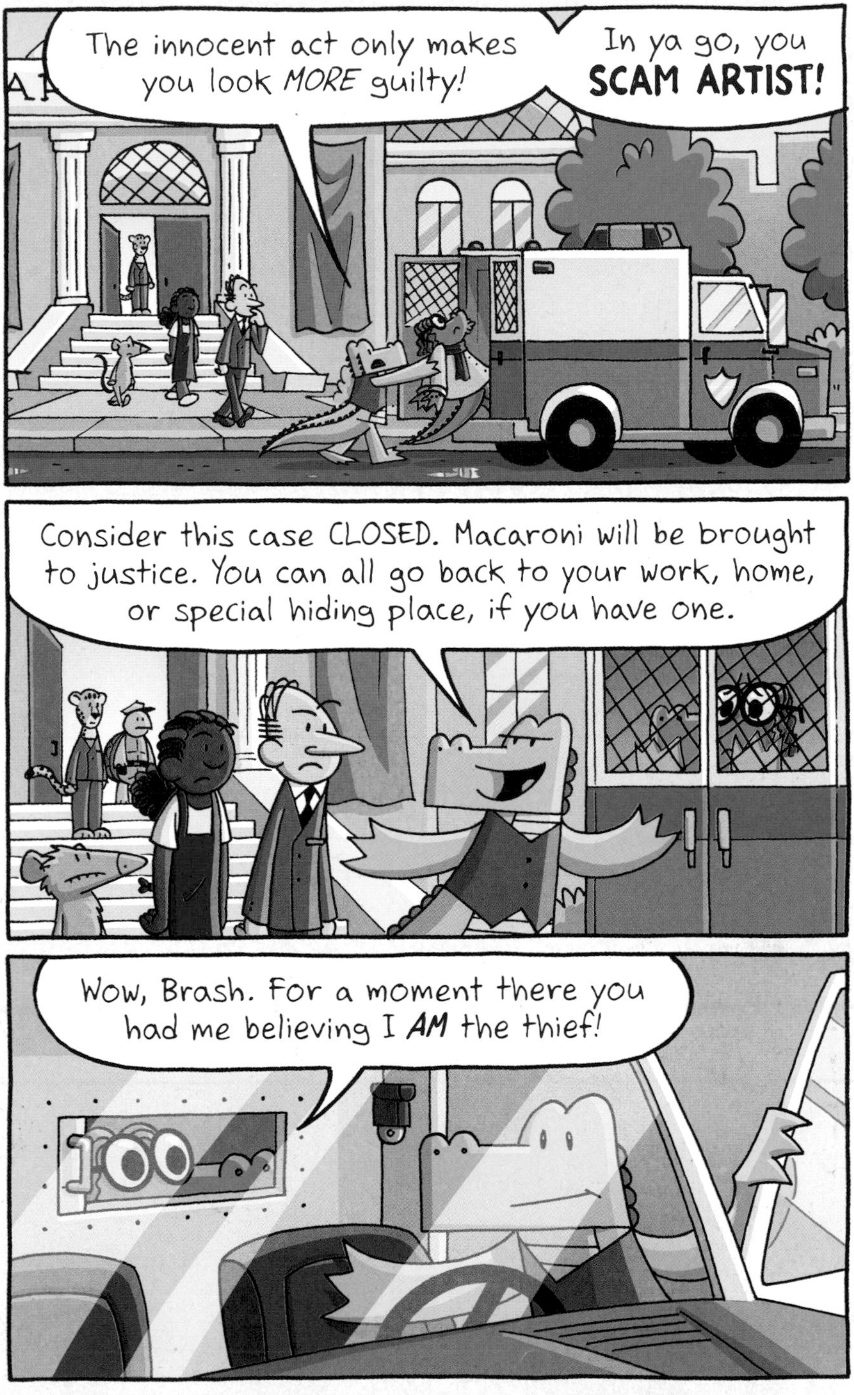
The innocent act only makes you look *MORE* guilty!
In ya go, you **SCAM ARTIST!**
Consider this case CLOSED. Macaroni will be brought to justice. You can all go back to your work, home, or special hiding place, if you have one.
Wow, Brash. For a moment there you had me believing I *AM* the thief!

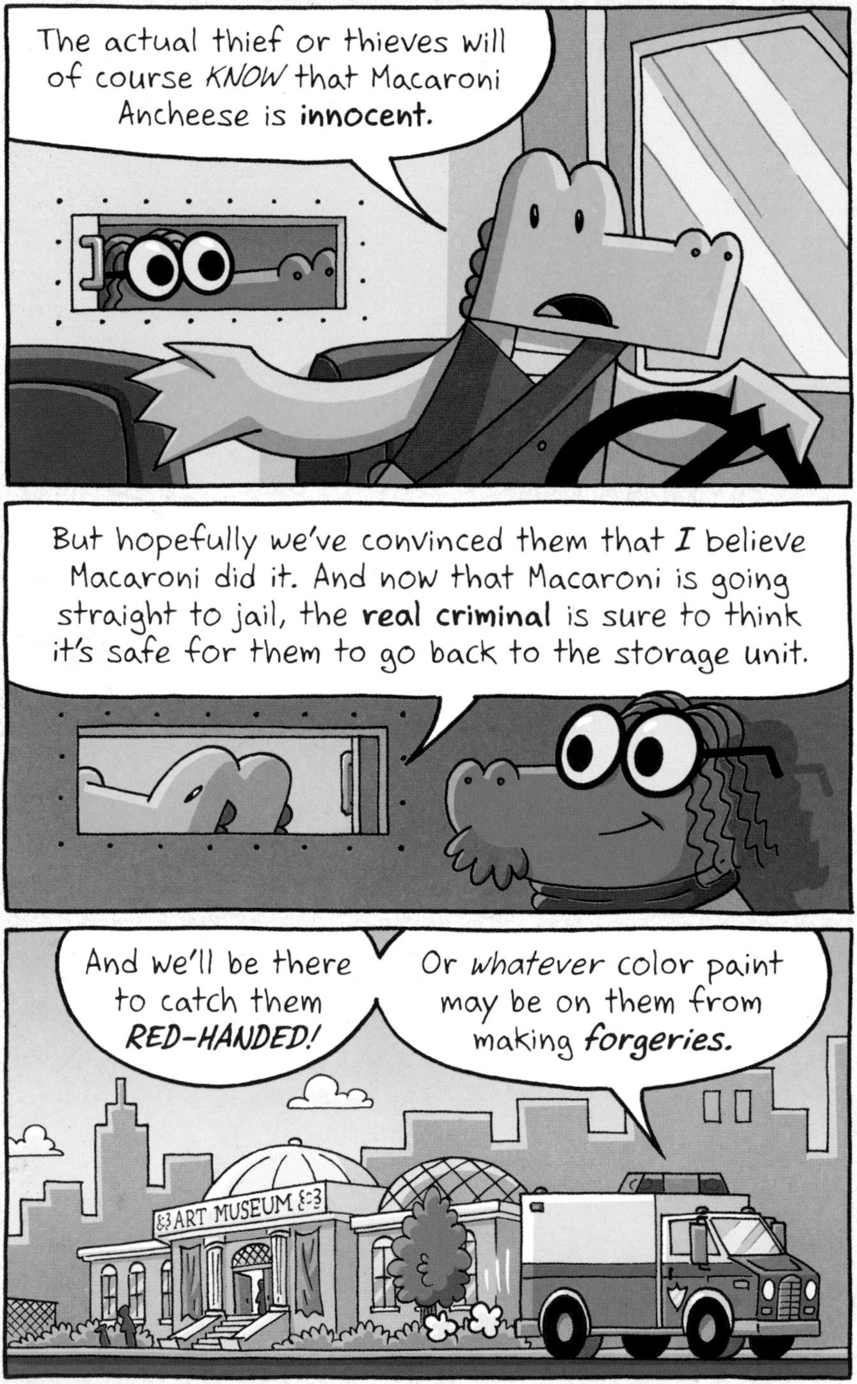
The actual thief or thieves will of course *KNOW* that Macaroni Ancheese is **innocent.**
But hopefully we've convinced them that *I* believe Macaroni did it. And now that Macaroni is going straight to jail, the **real criminal** is sure to think it's safe for them to go back to the storage unit.
And we'll be there to catch them *RED-HANDED!*
Or *whatever* color paint may be on them from making ***forgeries.***
ART MUSEUM

Chapter 17

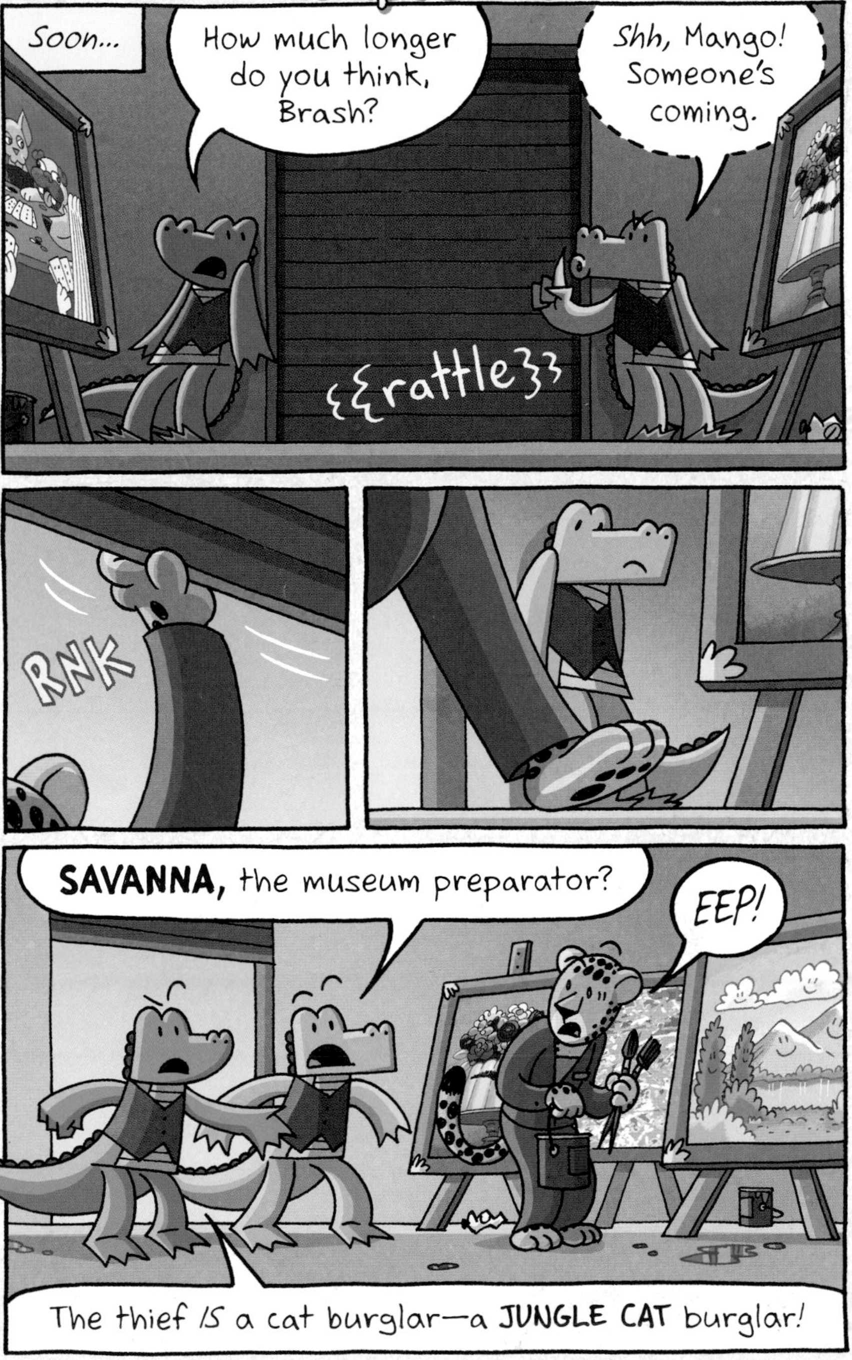
Soon...
How much longer do you think, Brash?
Shh, Mango! Someone's coming.
{{rattle}}
RNK
SAVANNA, the museum preparator?
EEP!
The thief IS a cat burglar—a JUNGLE CAT burglar!

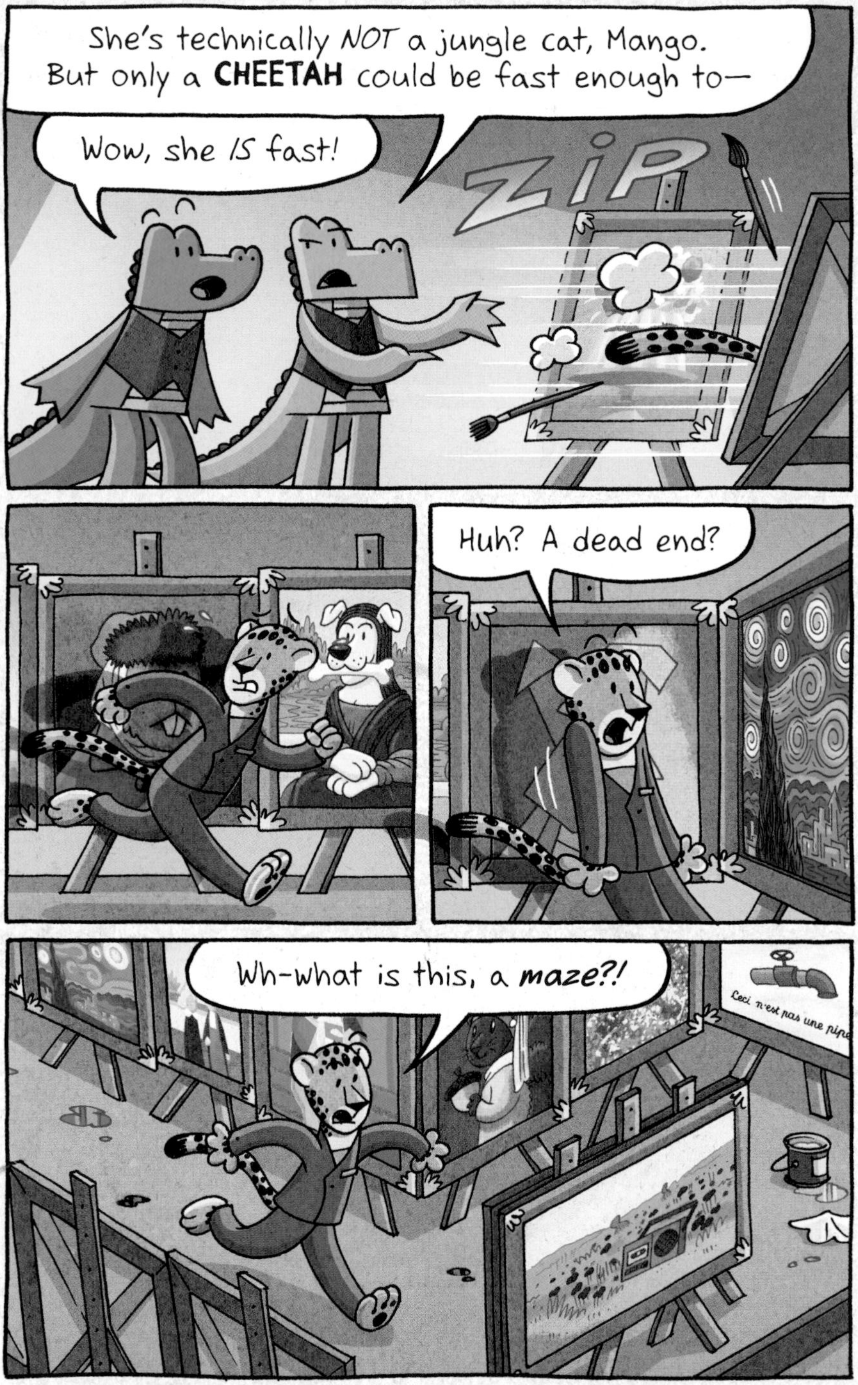
She's technically *NOT* a jungle cat, Mango. But only a **CHEETAH** could be fast enough to—
Wow, she *IS* fast!
ZIP
Huh? A dead end?
Wh-what is this, a ***maze?!***
Ceci n'est pas une pipe

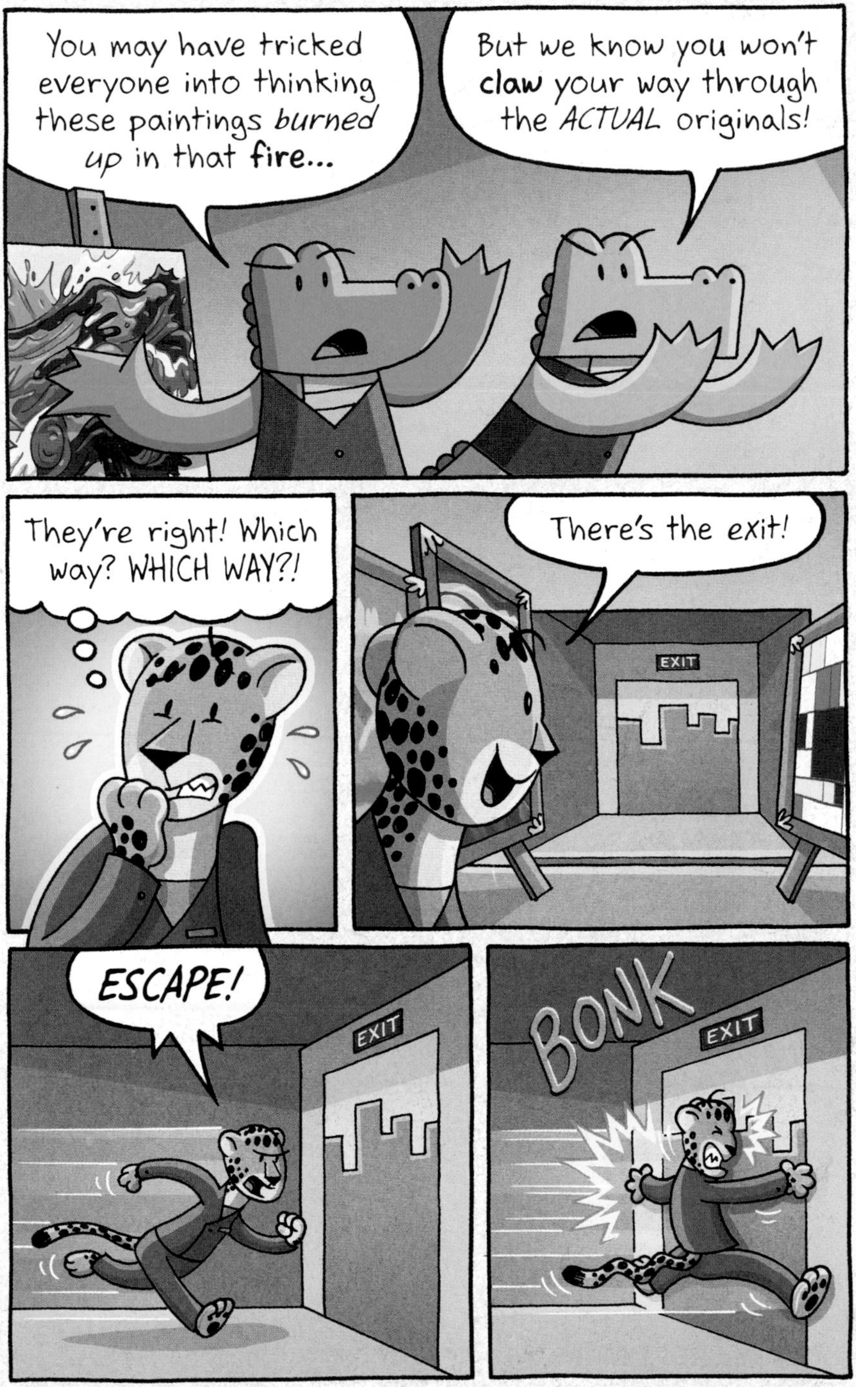
You may have tricked everyone into thinking these paintings *burned up* in that **fire...**
But we know you won't **claw** your way through the *ACTUAL* originals!
They're right! Which way? WHICH WAY?!
There's the exit!
EXIT
ESCAPE!
EXIT
BONK
EXIT

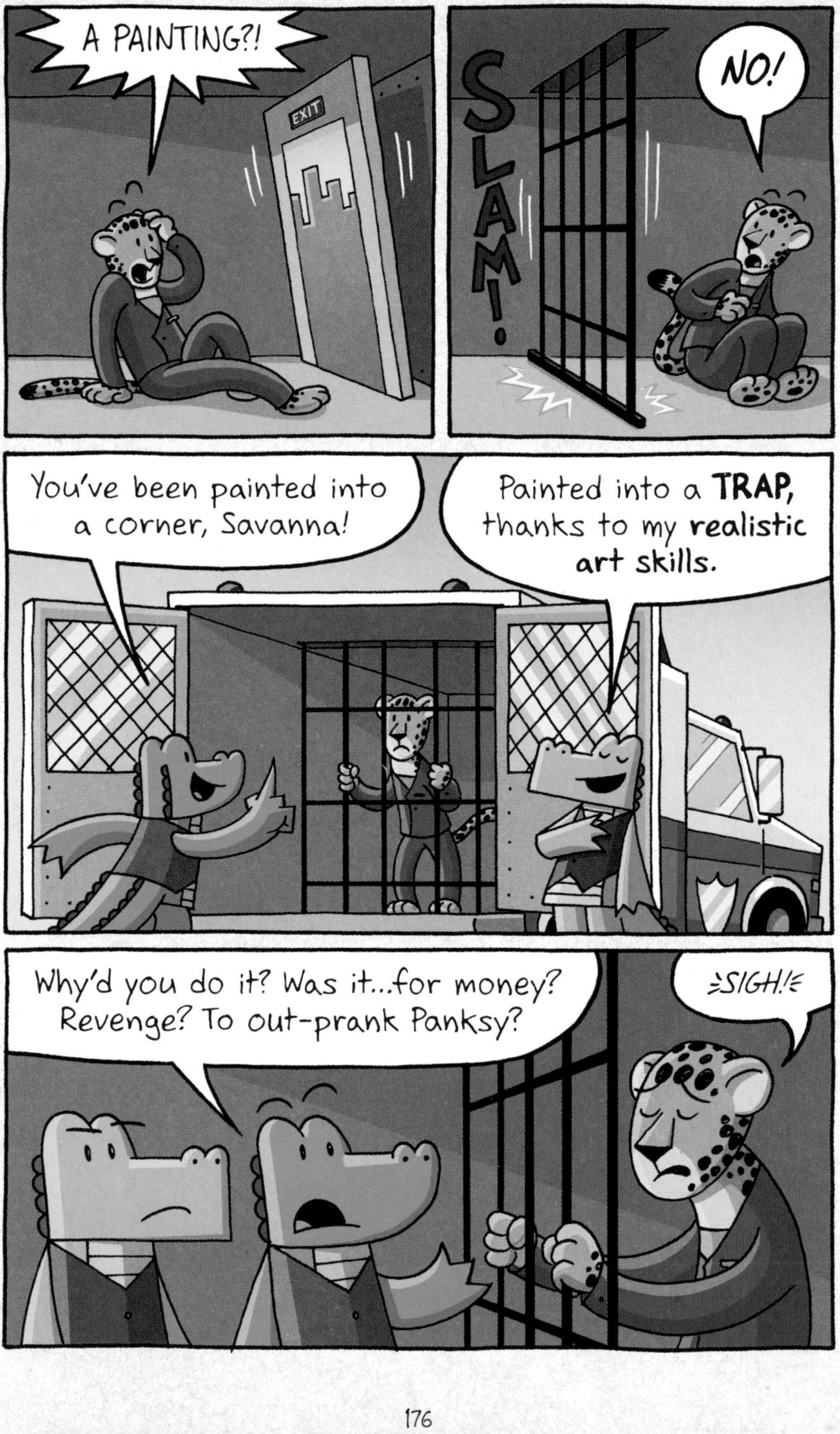
A PAINTING?!
EXIT
SLAM!
NO!
You've been painted into a corner, Savanna!
Painted into a **TRAP**, thanks to my **realistic art skills.**
Why'd you do it? Was it...for money? Revenge? To out-prank Panksy?
SIGH!

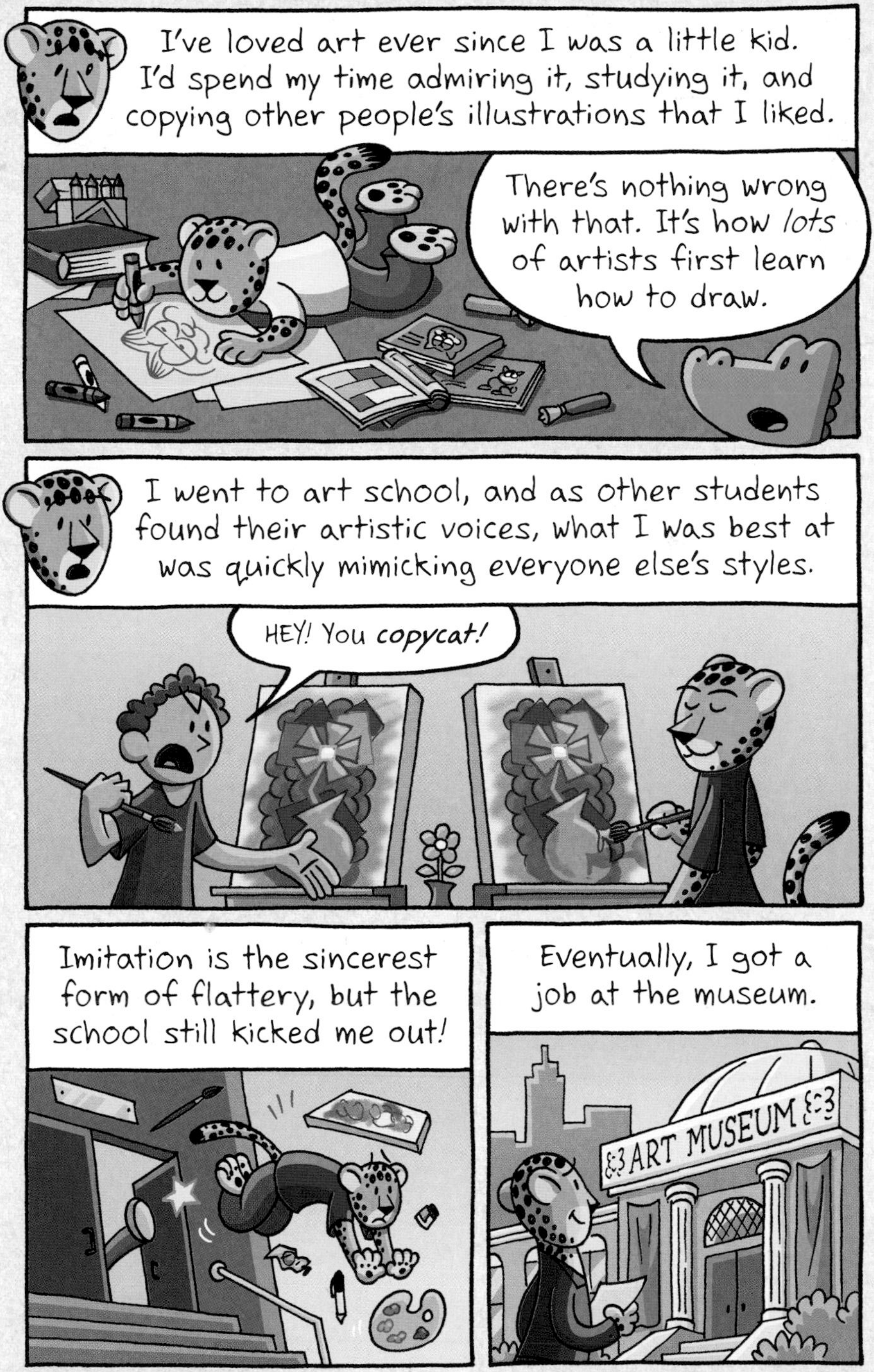
I've loved art ever since I was a little kid. I'd spend my time admiring it, studying it, and copying other people's illustrations that I liked.
There's nothing wrong with that. It's how *lots* of artists first learn how to draw.
I went to art school, and as other students found their artistic voices, what I was best at was quickly mimicking everyone else's styles.
HEY! You **copycat!**
Imitation is the sincerest form of flattery, but the school still kicked me out!
Eventually, I got a job at the museum.
ART MUSEUM

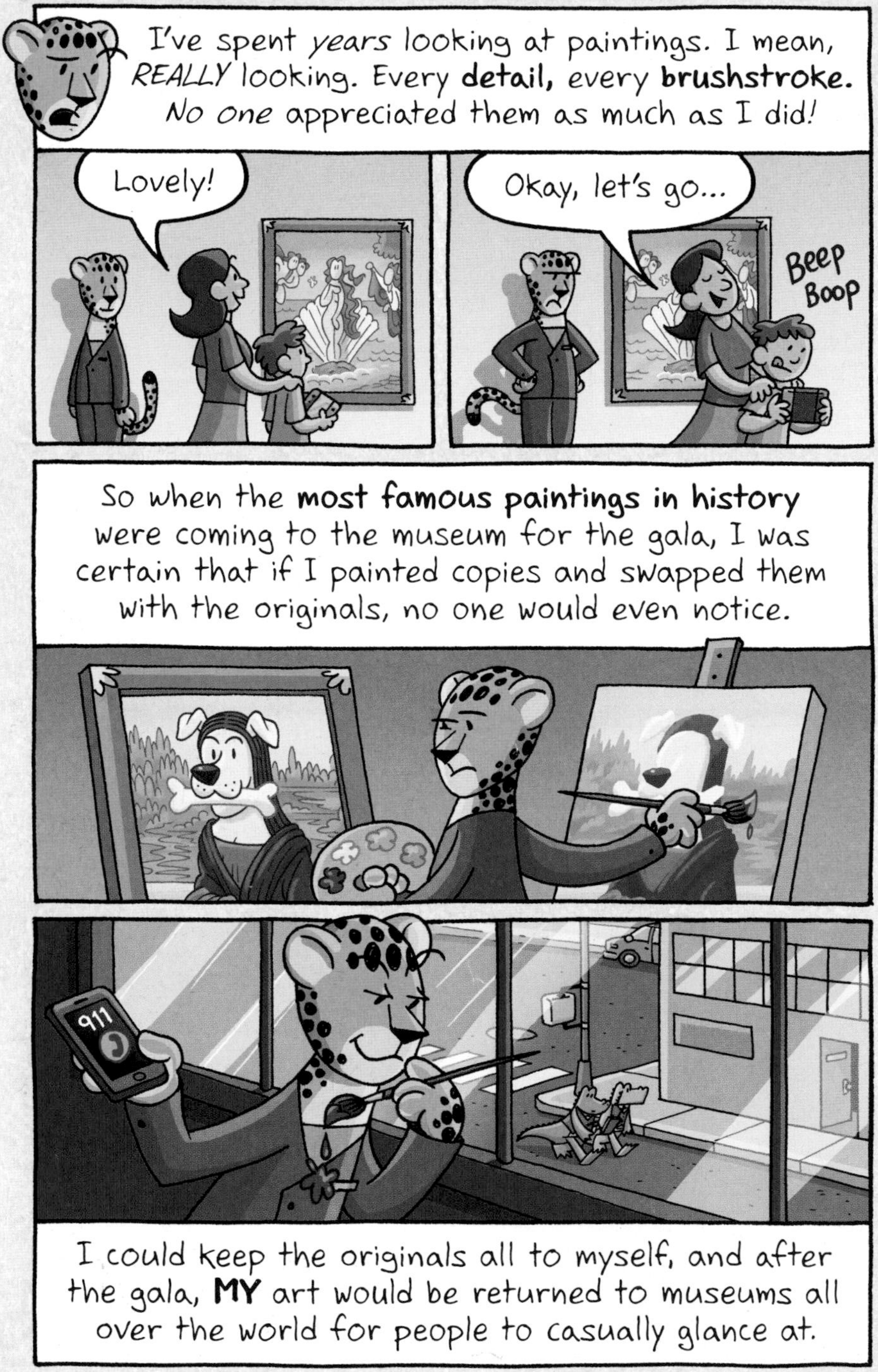
I've spent *years* looking at paintings. I mean, *REALLY* looking. Every **detail,** every **brushstroke.** *No one* appreciated them as much as I did!
Lovely!
Okay, let's go...
Beep Boop
So when the **most famous paintings in history** were coming to the museum for the gala, I was certain that if I painted copies and swapped them with the originals, no one would even notice.
911
I could keep the originals all to myself, and after the gala, **MY** art would be returned to museums all over the world for people to casually glance at.

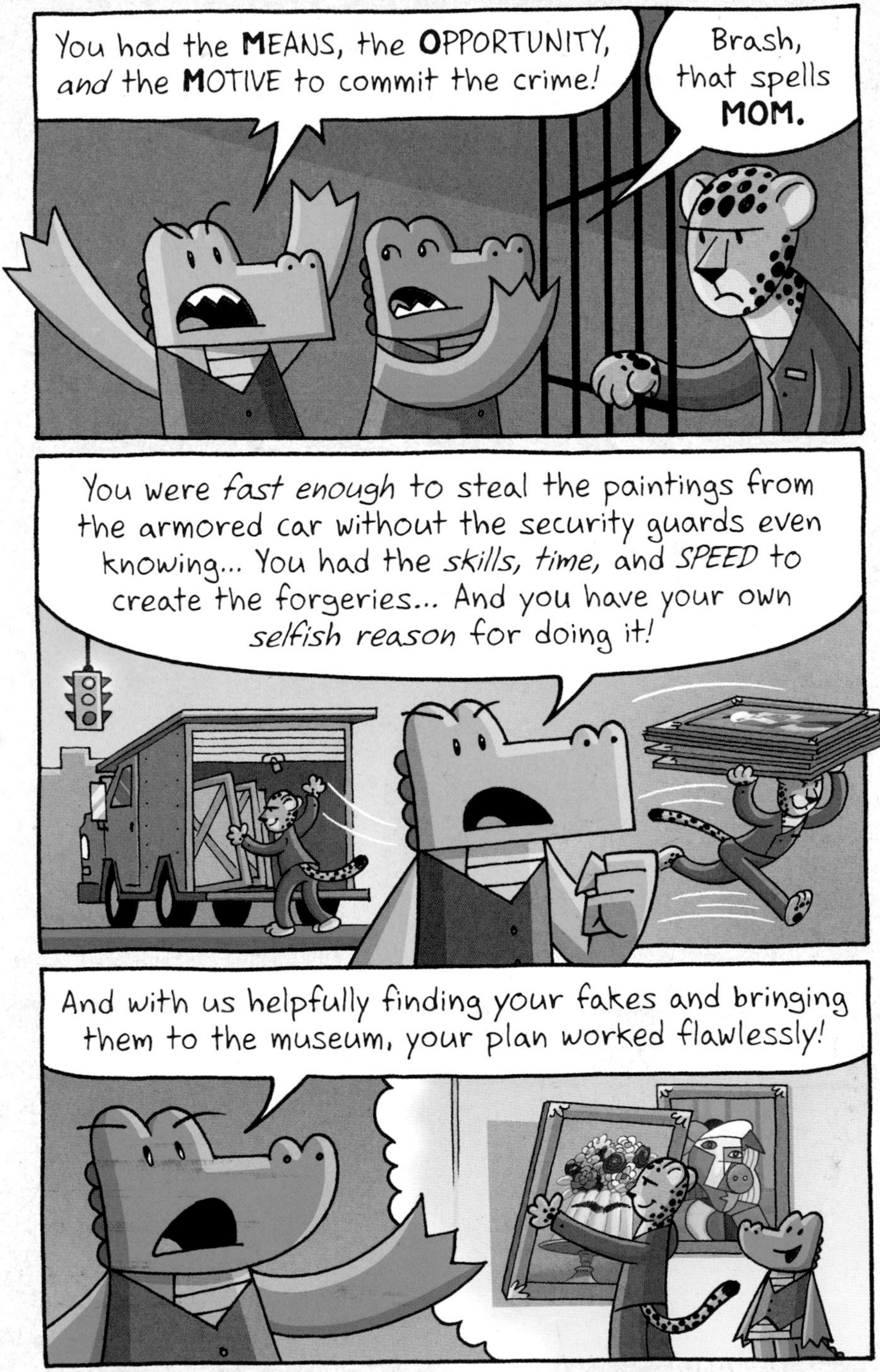
You had the MEANS, the OPPORTUNITY, and the MOTIVE to commit the crime!
Brash, that spells MOM.
You were fast enough to steal the paintings from the armored car without the security guards even knowing... You had the skills, time, and SPEED to create the forgeries... And you have your own selfish reason for doing it!
And with us helpfully finding your fakes and bringing them to the museum, your plan worked flawlessly!

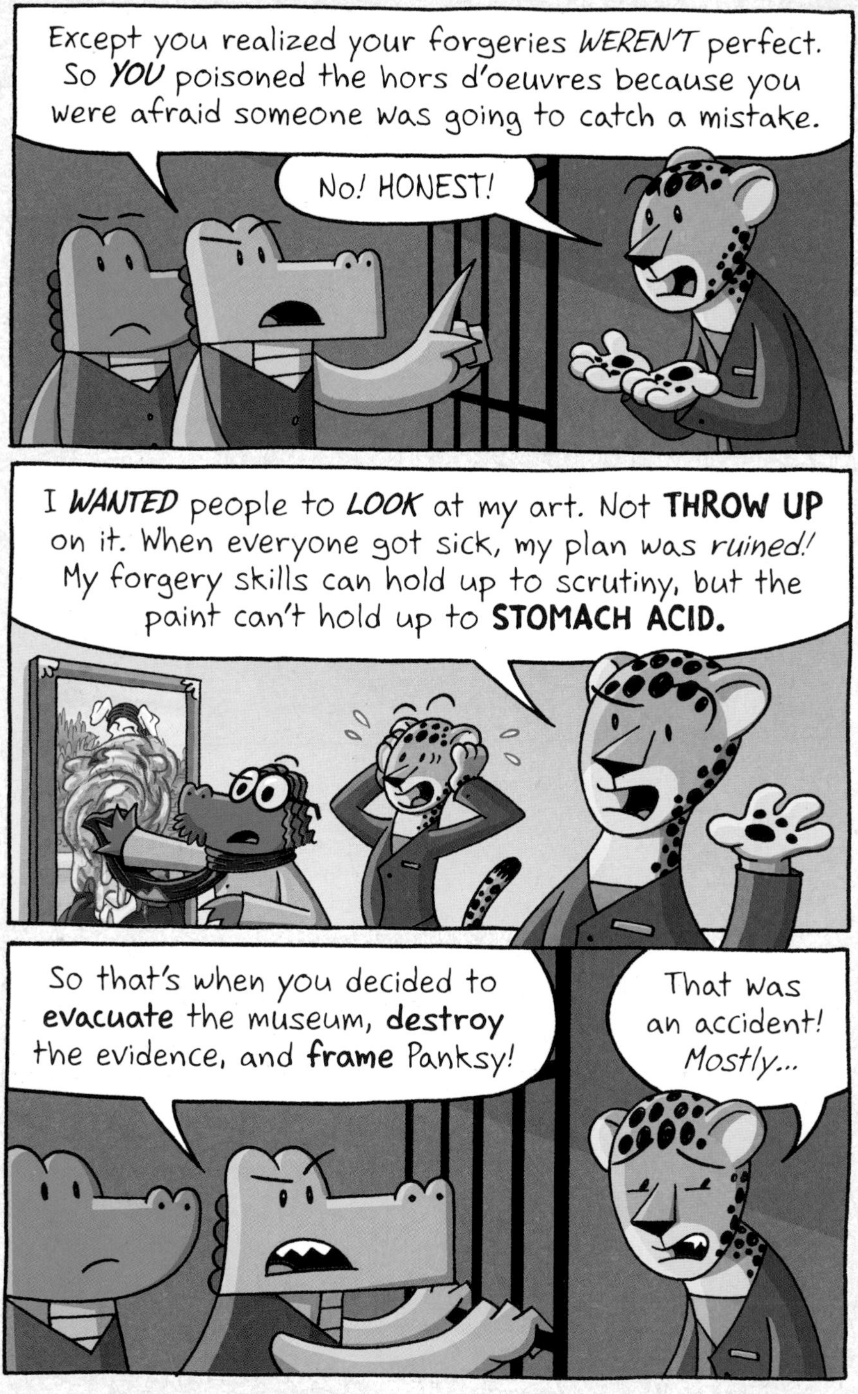
Except you realized your forgeries *WEREN'T* perfect. So *YOU* poisoned the hors d'oeuvres because you were afraid someone was going to catch a mistake.
No! HONEST!
I *WANTED* people to *LOOK* at my art. Not **THROW UP** on it. When everyone got sick, my plan was *ruined!* My forgery skills can hold up to scrutiny, but the paint can't hold up to **STOMACH ACID.**
So that's when you decided to **evacuate** the museum, **destroy** the evidence, and **frame** Panksy!
That was an accident! *Mostly...*

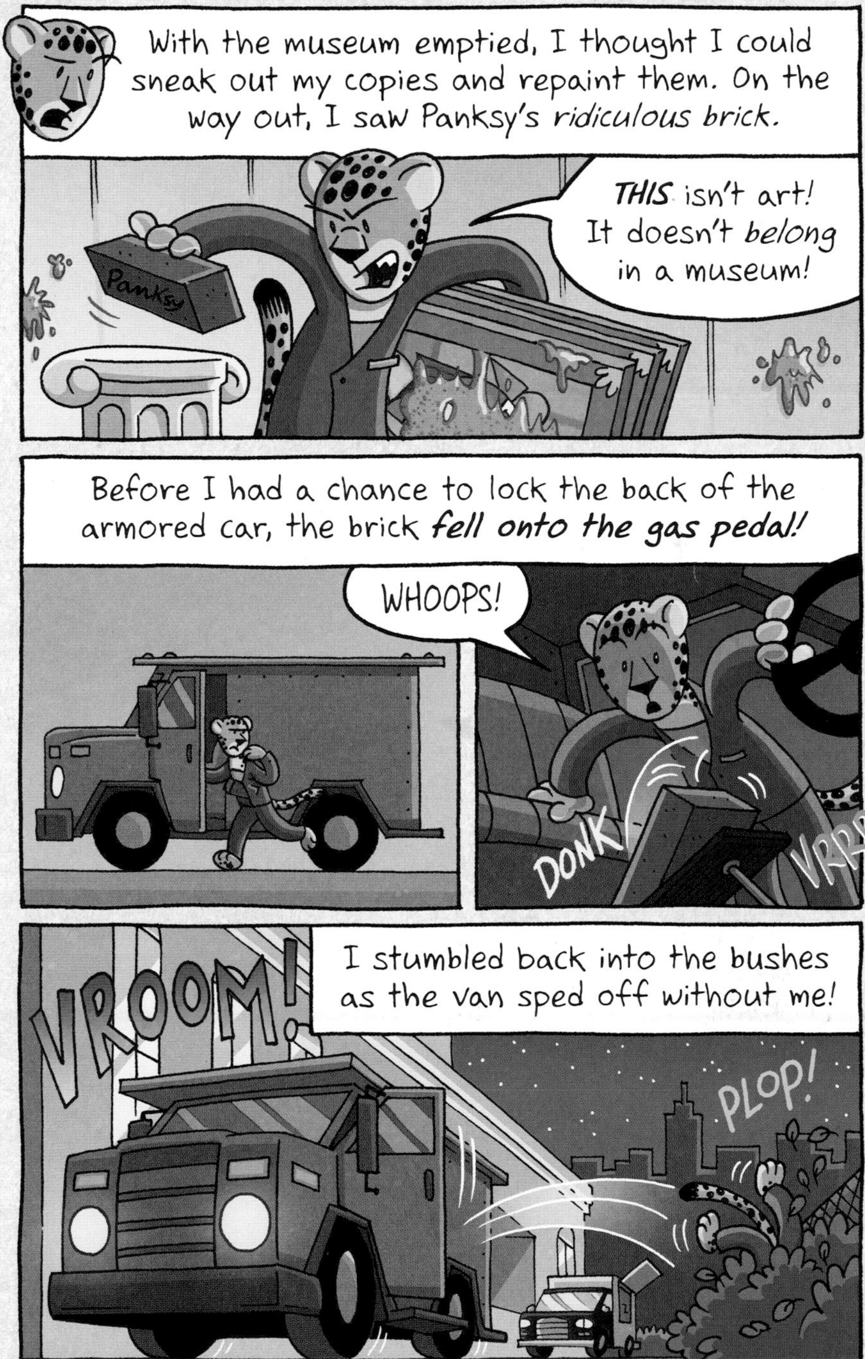
With the museum emptied, I thought I could sneak out my copies and repaint them. On the way out, I saw Panksy's *ridiculous brick.*
Panksy
THIS isn't art! It doesn't *belong* in a museum!
Before I had a chance to lock the back of the armored car, the brick ***fell onto the gas pedal!***
WHOOPS!
DONK
VRRR
VROOM!
I stumbled back into the bushes as the van sped off without me!
PLOP!

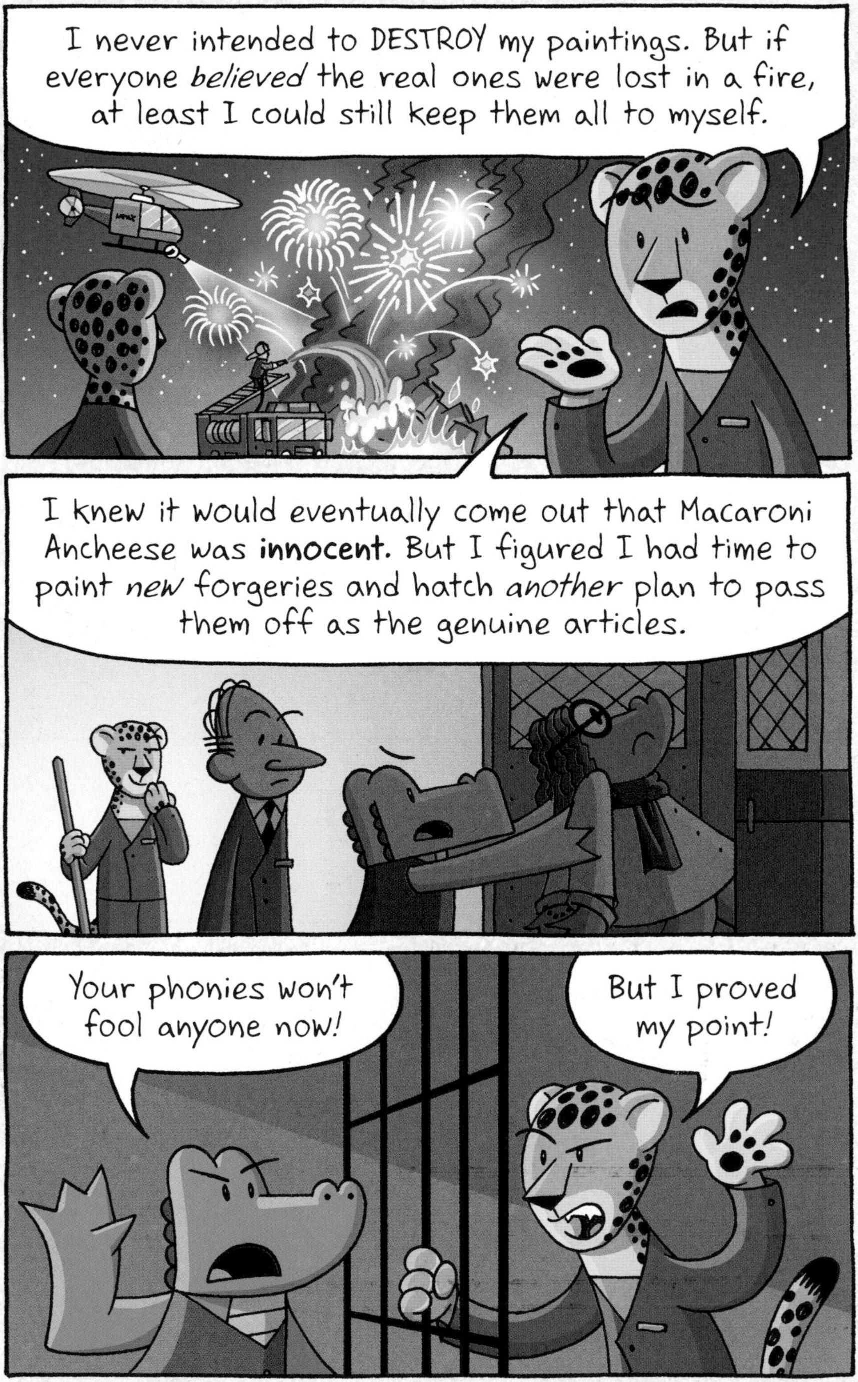
I never intended to DESTROY my paintings. But if everyone believed the real ones were lost in a fire, at least I could still keep them all to myself.
I knew it would eventually come out that Macaroni Ancheese was innocent. But I figured I had time to paint new forgeries and hatch another plan to pass them off as the genuine articles.
Your phonies won't fool anyone now!
But I proved my point!

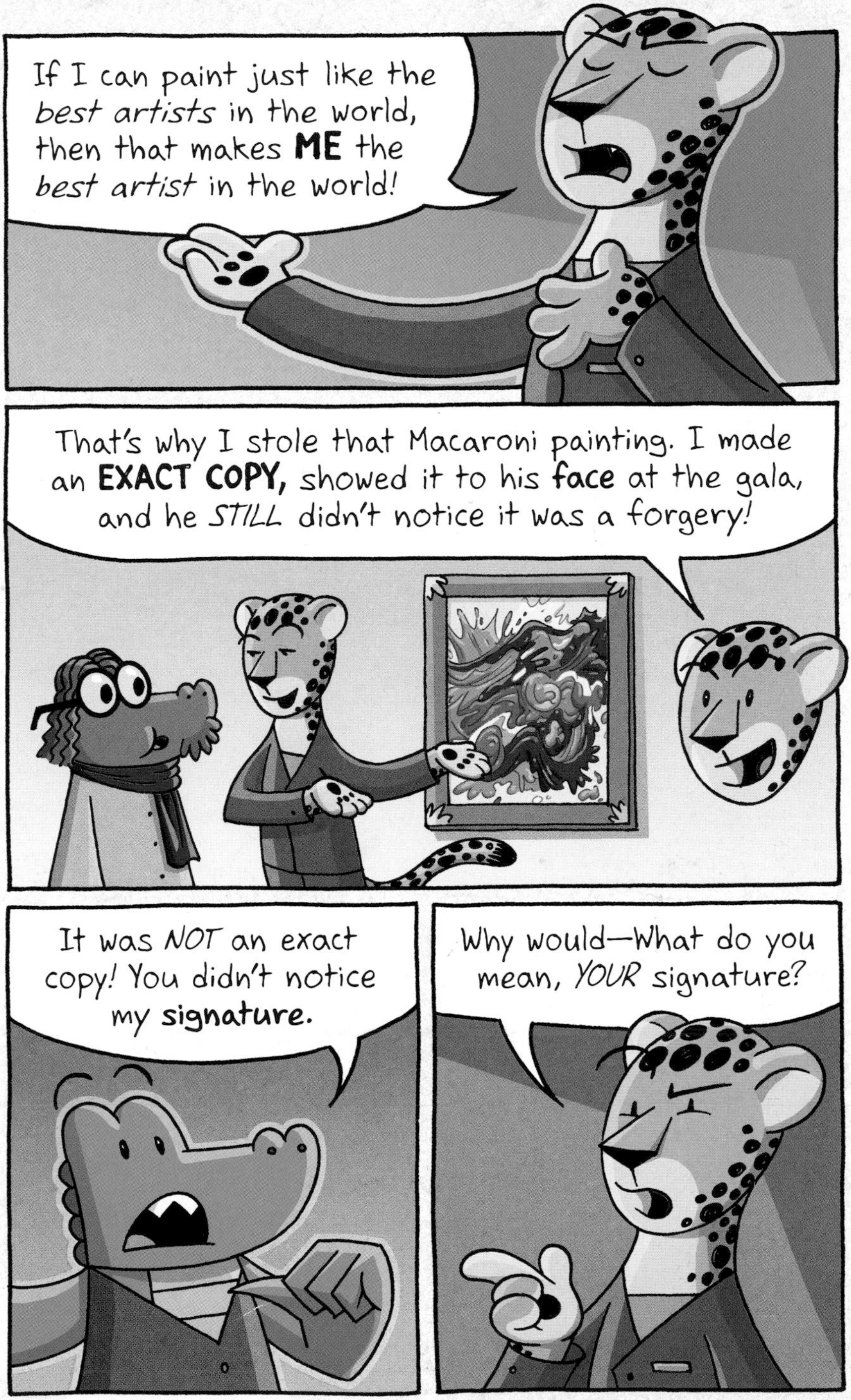
If I can paint just like the *best artists* in the world, then that makes **ME** the *best artist* in the world!
That's why I stole that Macaroni painting. I made an **EXACT COPY,** showed it to his **face** at the gala, and he *STILL* didn't notice it was a forgery!
It was *NOT* an exact copy! You didn't notice my **signature.**
Why would—What do you mean, *YOUR* signature?

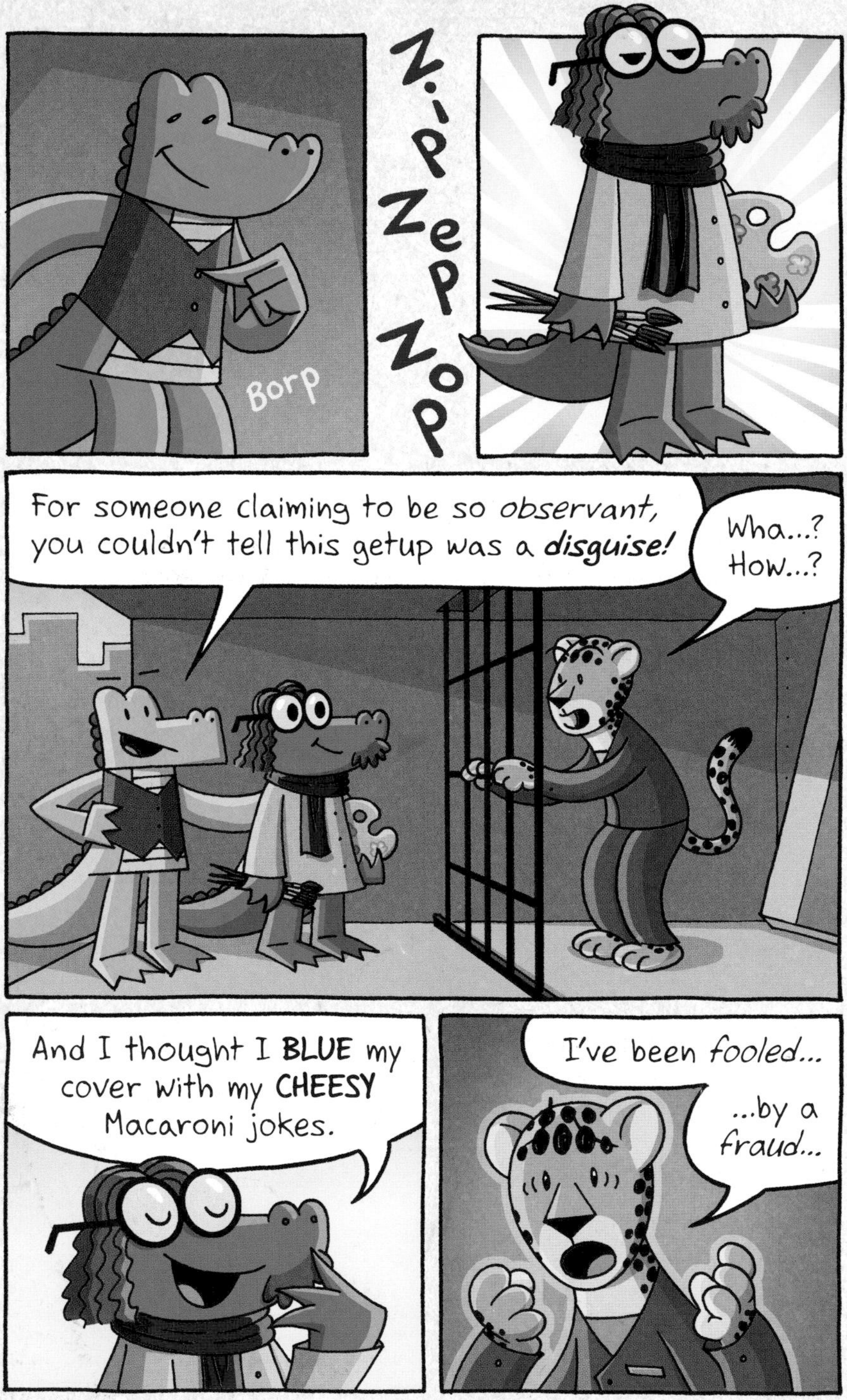
Borp
ZipZepZop
For someone claiming to be so *observant*, you couldn't tell this getup was a ***disguise!***
Wha...? How...?
And I thought I **BLUE** my cover with my **CHEESY** Macaroni jokes.
I've been *fooled...*
...by a *fraud...*

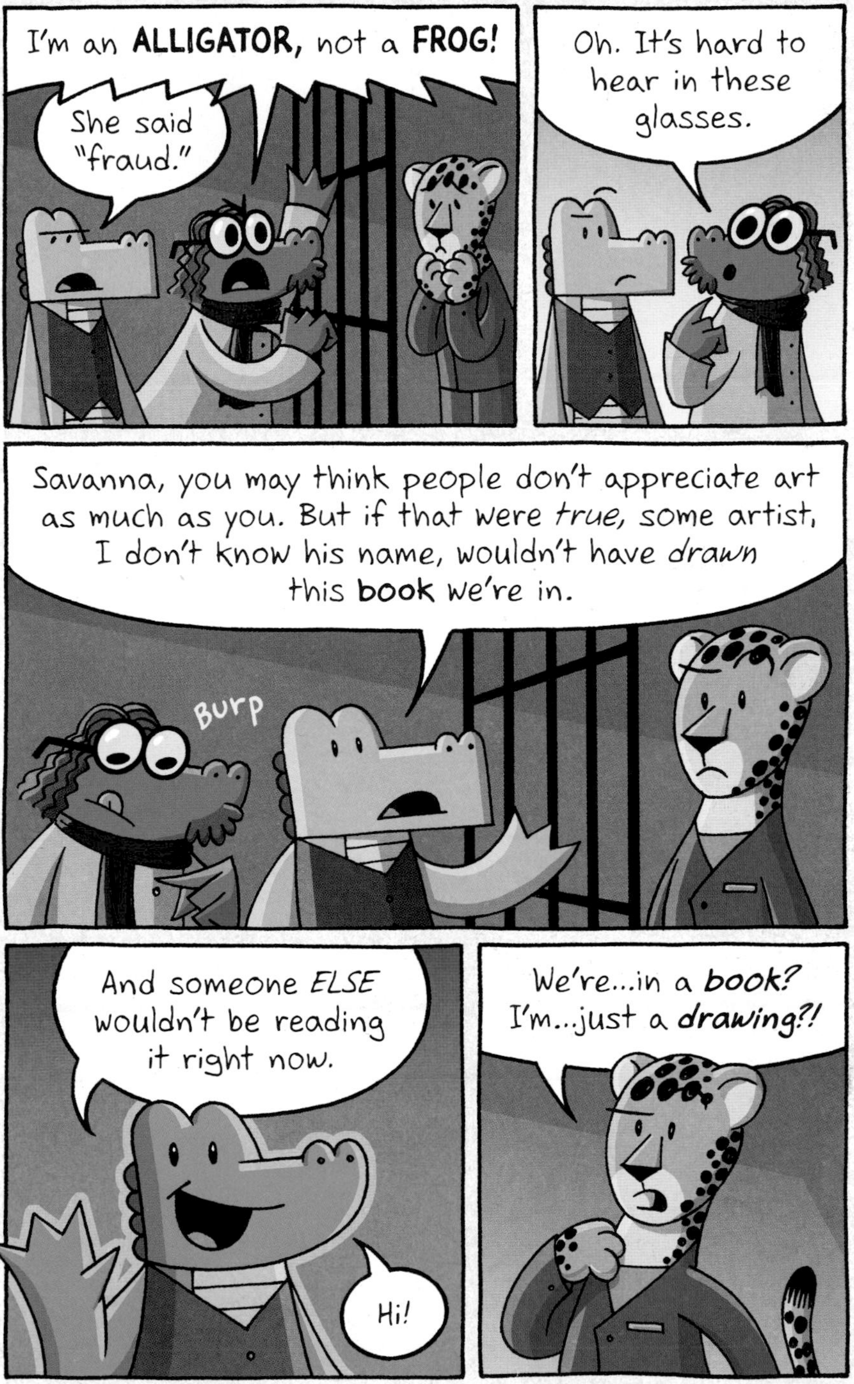
I'm an **ALLIGATOR,** not a **FROG!**
She said "fraud."
Oh. It's hard to hear in these glasses.
Savanna, you may think people don't appreciate art as much as you. But if that were *true,* some artist, I don't know his name, wouldn't have *drawn* this **book** we're in.
BURP
And someone *ELSE* wouldn't be reading it right now.
Hi!
We're...in a ***book?*** I'm...just a ***drawing?!***

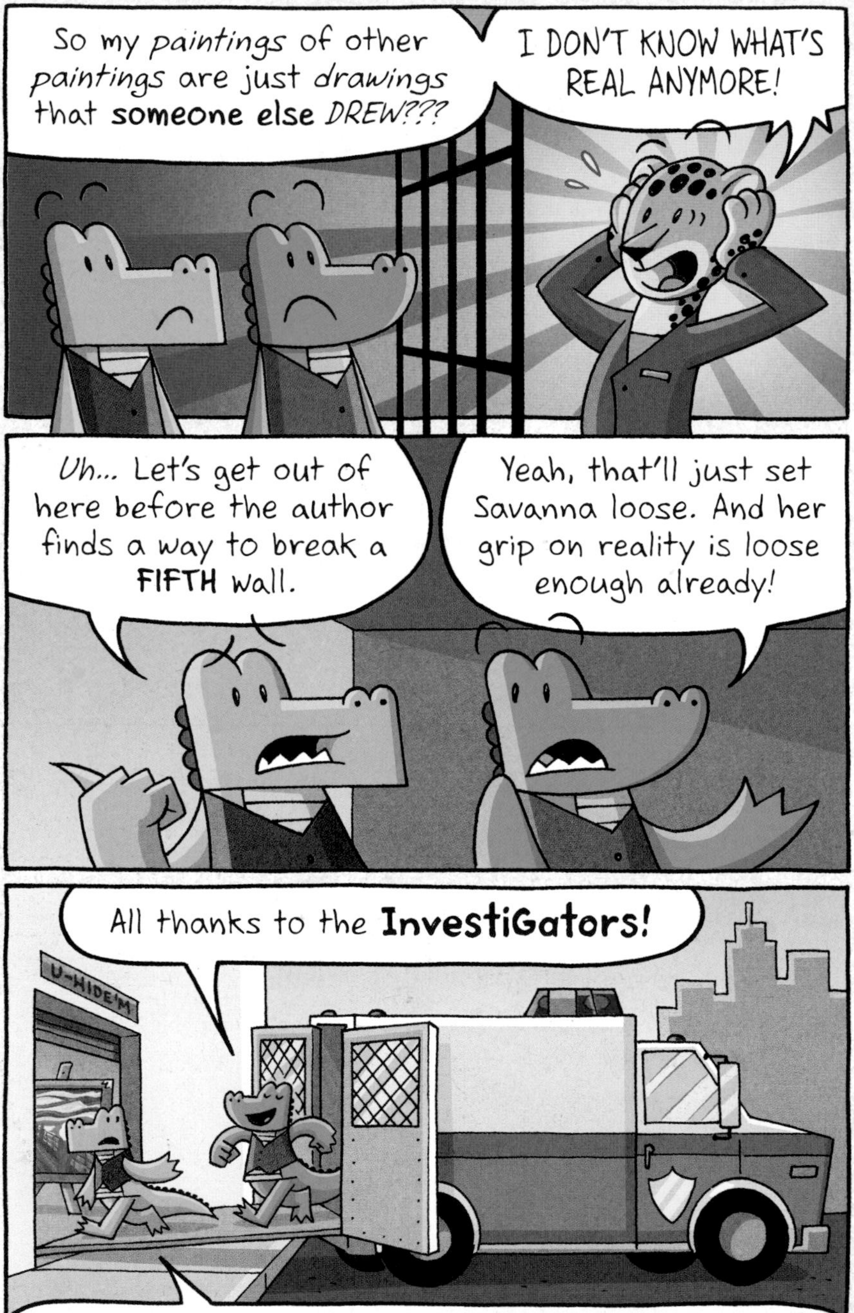
So my *paintings* of other *paintings* are just *drawings* that **someone else** *DREW???*
I DON'T KNOW WHAT'S REAL ANYMORE!
Uh... Let's get out of here before the author finds a way to break a **FIFTH** wall.
Yeah, that'll just set Savanna loose. And her grip on reality is loose enough already!
All thanks to the **InvestiGators!**
U-HIDE'M
I wouldn't pat myself on the back for *THAT,* Mango.

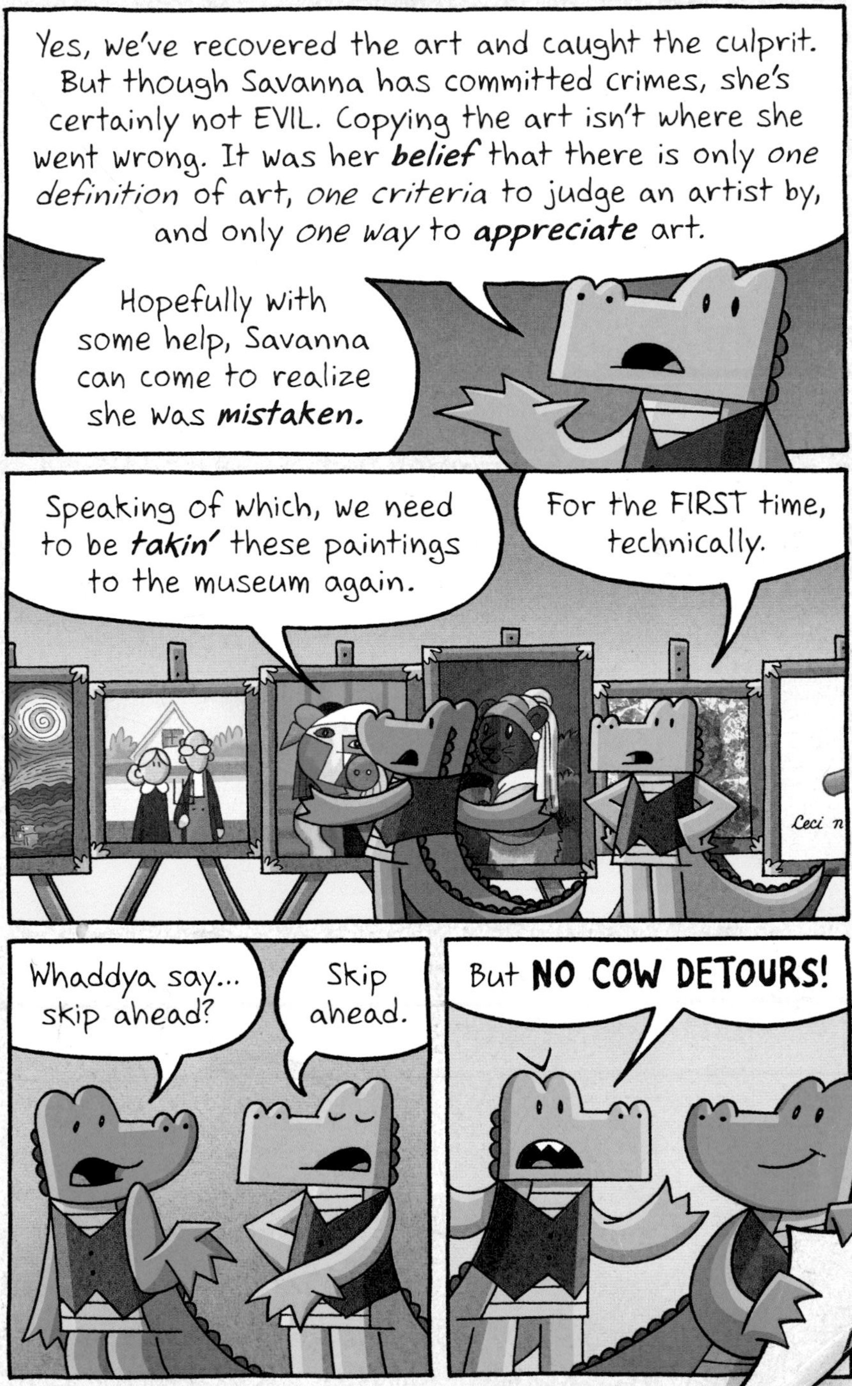
Yes, we've recovered the art and caught the culprit. But though Savanna has committed crimes, she's certainly not EVIL. Copying the art isn't where she went wrong. It was her ***belief*** that there is only *one definition* of art, *one criteria* to judge an artist by, and only *one way* to ***appreciate*** art.
Hopefully with some help, Savanna can come to realize she was ***mistaken.***
Speaking of which, we need to be ***takin'*** these paintings to the museum again.
For the FIRST time, technically.
Ceci n
Whaddya say... skip ahead?
Skip ahead.
But **NO COW DETOURS!**

Chapter 18

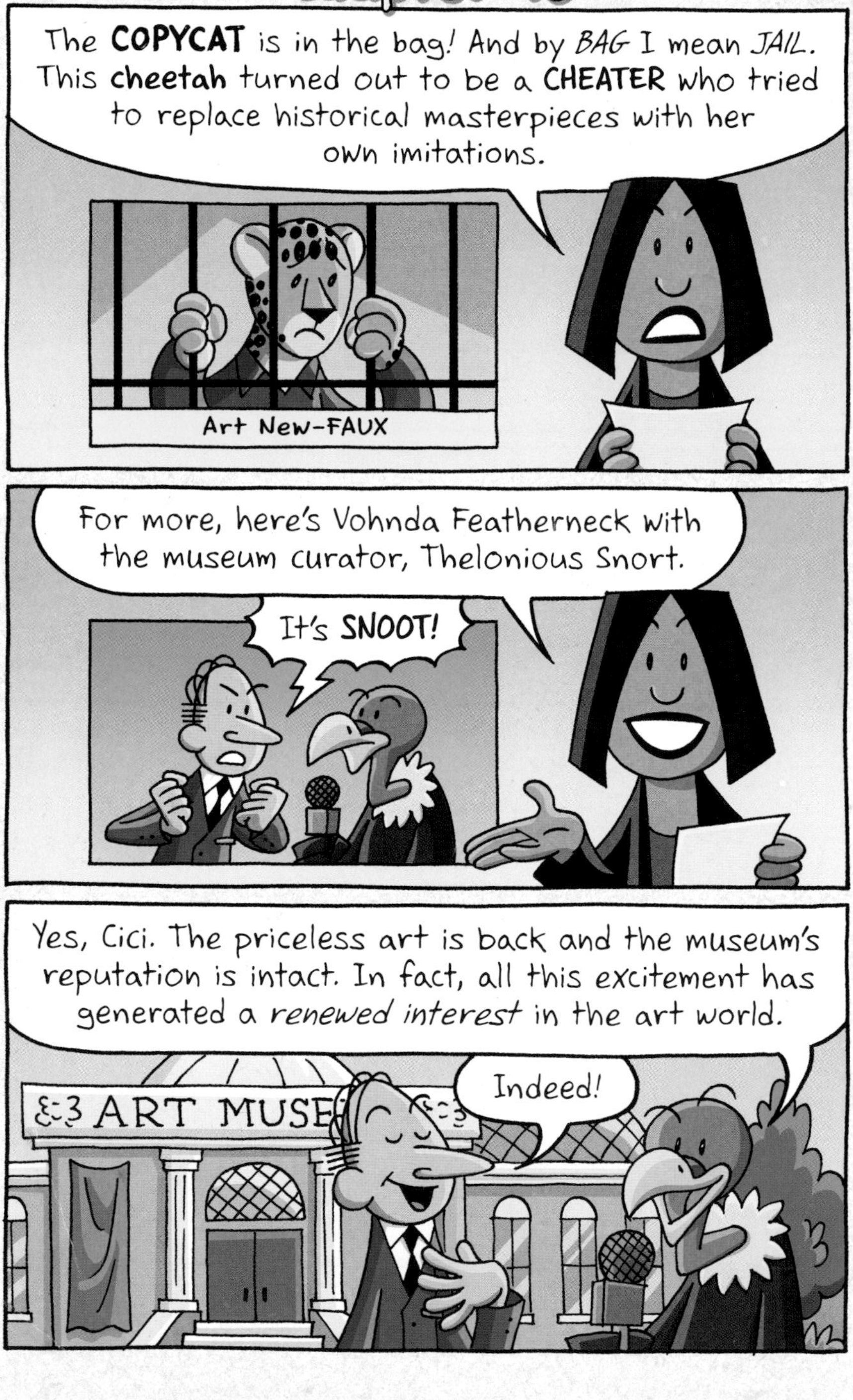
The **COPYCAT** is in the bag! And by *BAG* I mean *JAIL*. This **cheetah** turned out to be a **CHEATER** who tried to replace historical masterpieces with her own imitations.
Art New-FAUX
For more, here's Vohnda Featherneck with the museum curator, Thelonious Snort.
It's **SNOOT!**
Yes, Cici. The priceless art is back and the museum's reputation is intact. In fact, all this excitement has generated a *renewed interest* in the art world.
Indeed!
ART MUSE

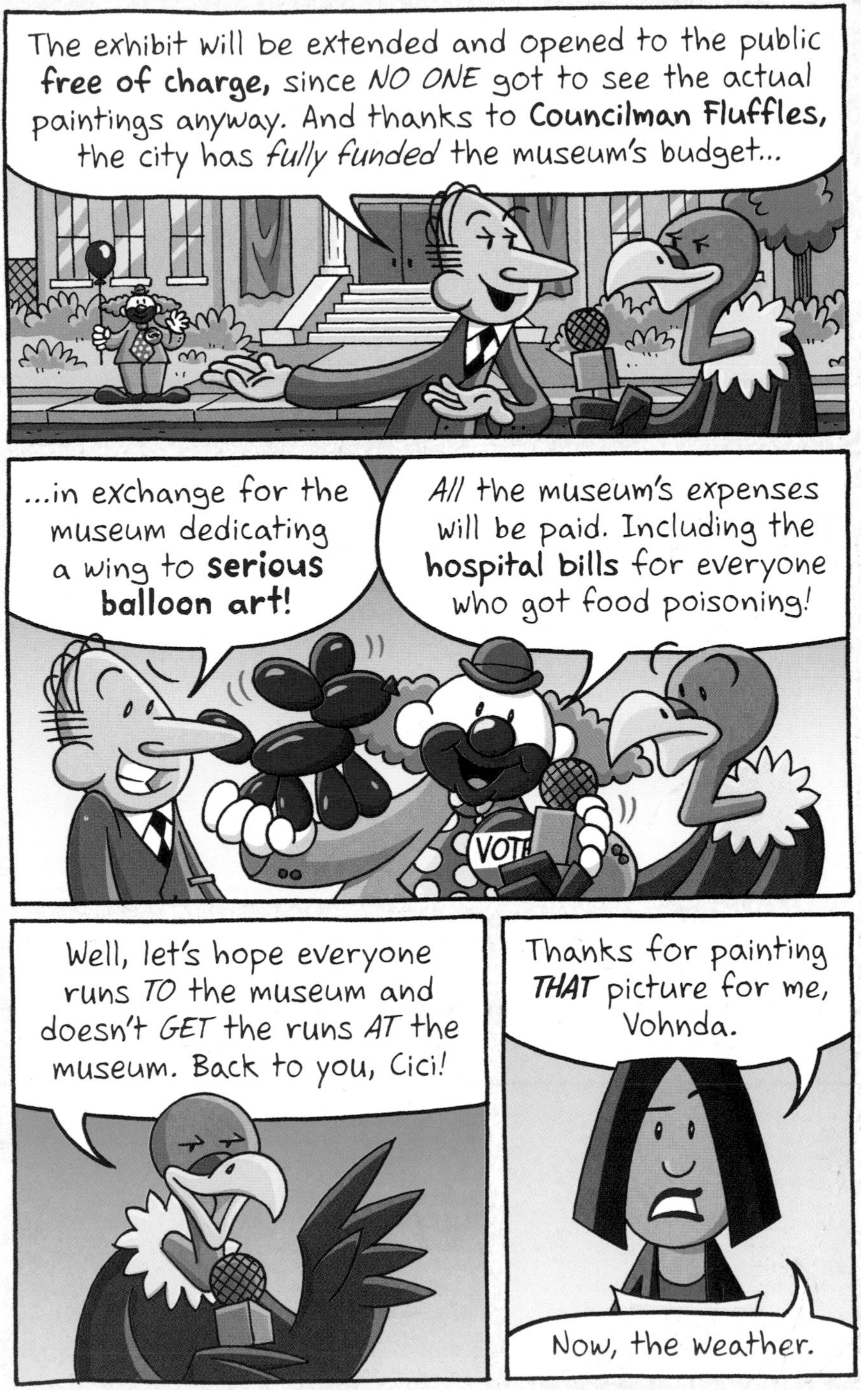

The exhibit will be extended and opened to the public **free of charge,** since *NO ONE* got to see the actual paintings anyway. And thanks to **Councilman Fluffles,** the city has *fully funded* the museum's budget...
...in exchange for the museum dedicating a wing to **serious balloon art!**
All the museum's expenses will be paid. Including the **hospital bills** for everyone who got food poisoning!
VOTE
Well, let's hope everyone runs *TO* the museum and doesn't *GET* the runs *AT* the museum. Back to you, Cici!
Thanks for painting ***THAT*** picture for me, Vohnda.
Now, the weather.

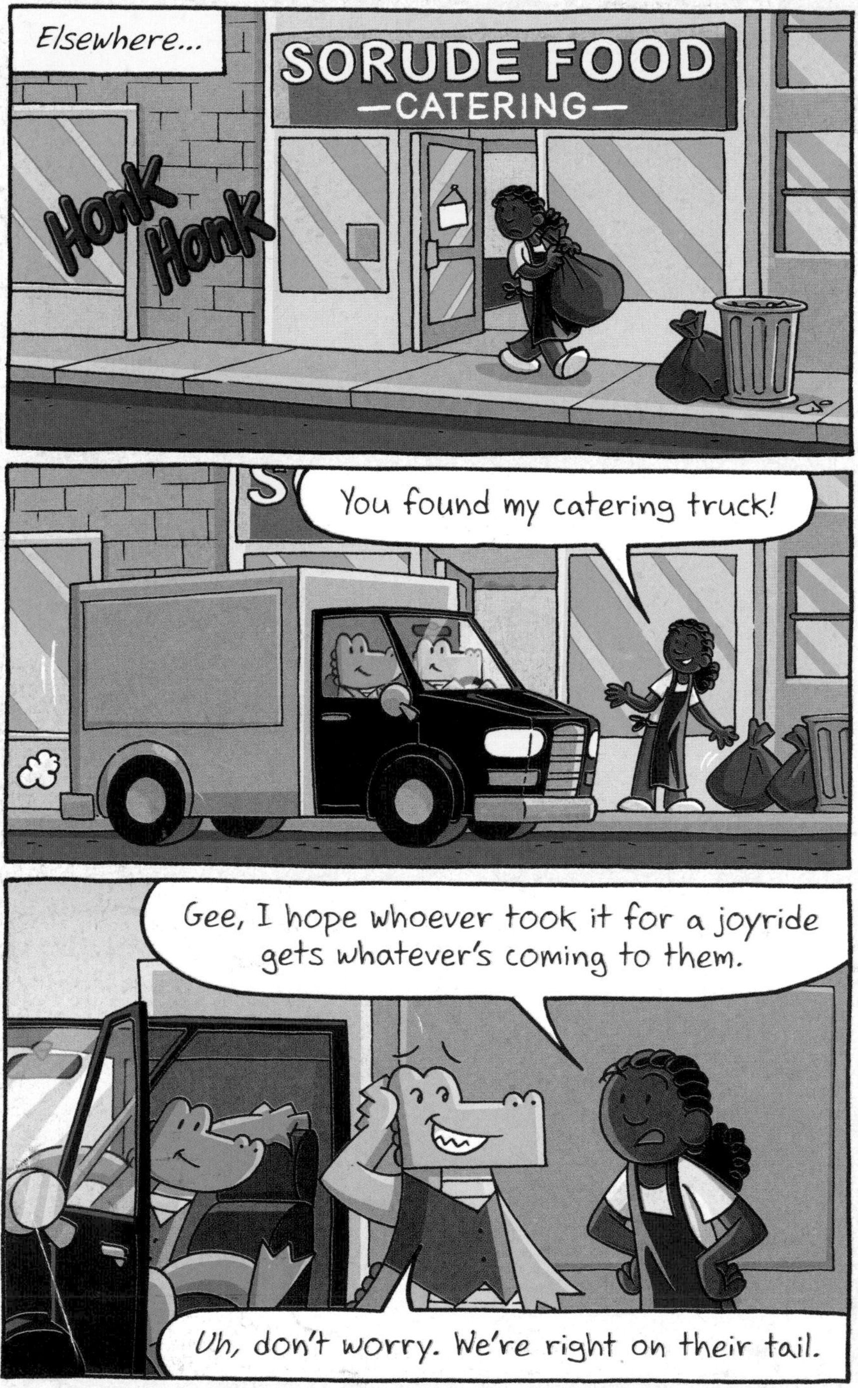
Elsewhere...
SORUDE FOOD
—CATERING—
HONK HONK
You found my catering truck!
Gee, I hope whoever took it for a joyride gets whatever's coming to them.
Uh, don't worry. We're right on their tail.

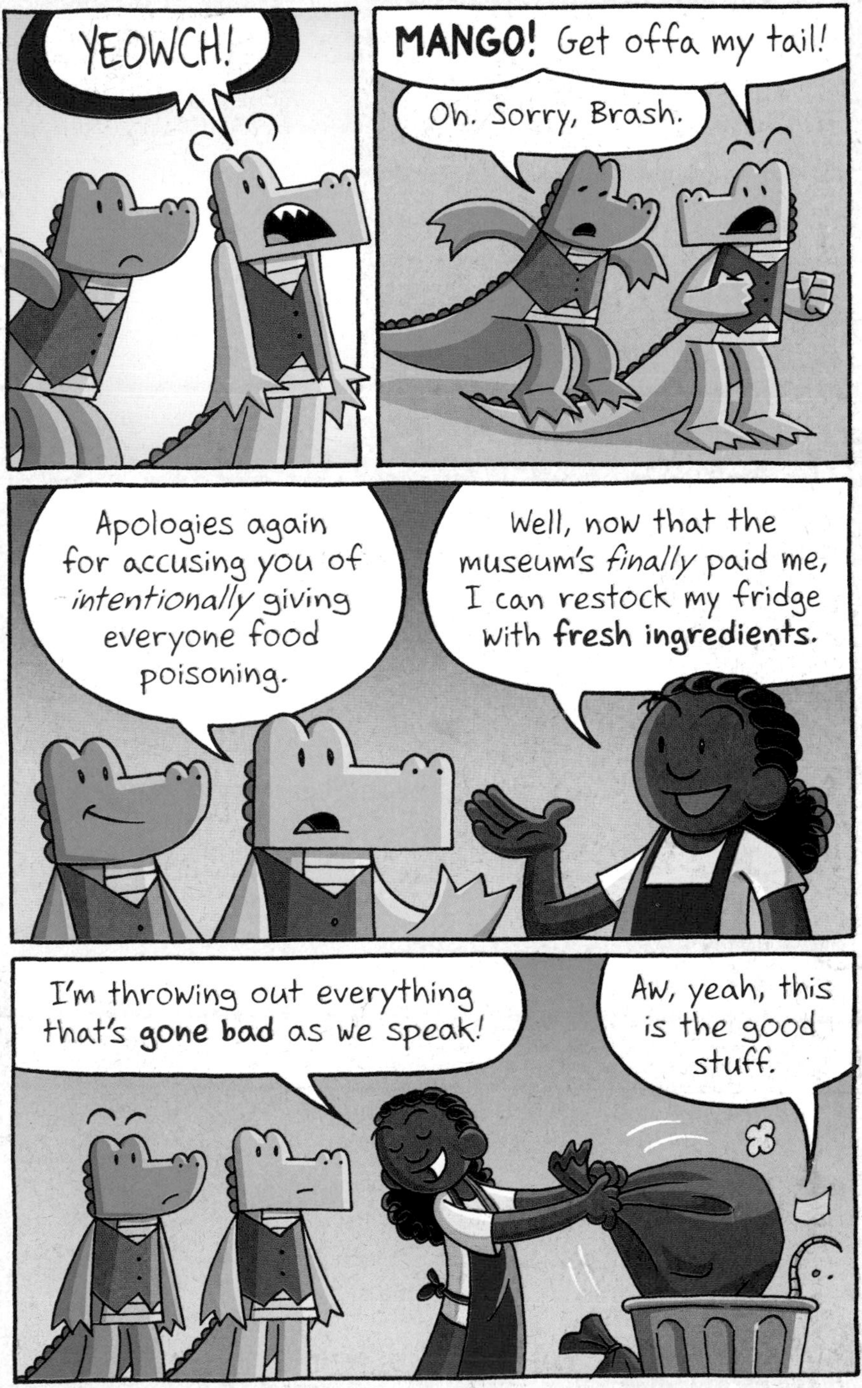
YEOWCH!
MANGO! Get offa my tail!
Oh. Sorry, Brash.
Apologies again for accusing you of *intentionally* giving everyone food poisoning.
Well, now that the museum's *finally* paid me, I can restock my fridge with **fresh ingredients.**
I'm throwing out everything that's **gone bad** as we speak!
Aw, yeah, this is the good stuff.

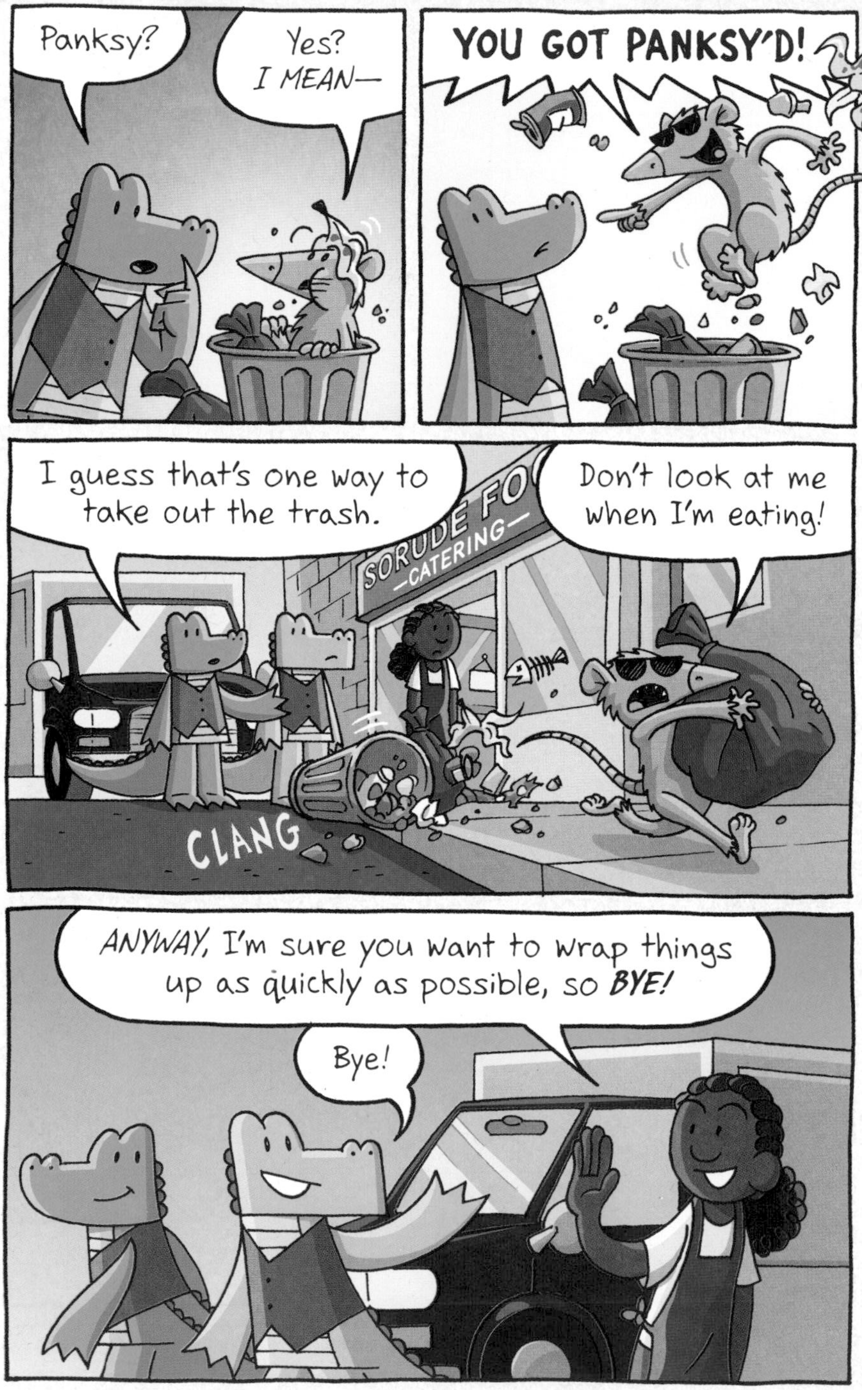
Panksy?
Yes? I MEAN—
YOU GOT PANKSY'D!
I guess that's one way to take out the trash.
SORUDE FO
—CATERING—
Don't look at me when I'm eating!
CLANG
ANYWAY, I'm sure you want to wrap things up as quickly as possible, so BYE!
Bye!

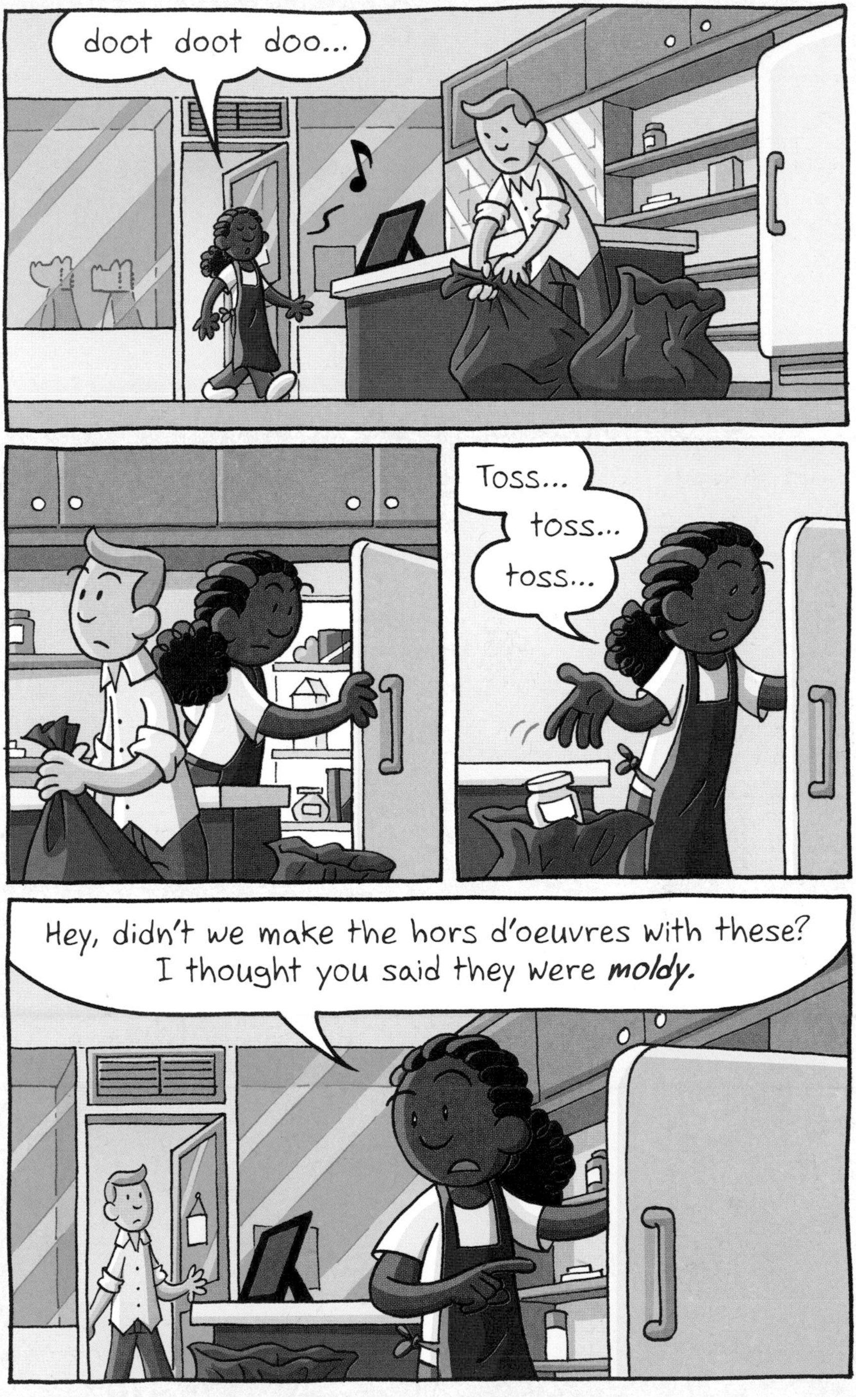
doot doot doo...
Toss... toss... toss...
Hey, didn't we make the hors d'oeuvres with these? I thought you said they were *moldy.*

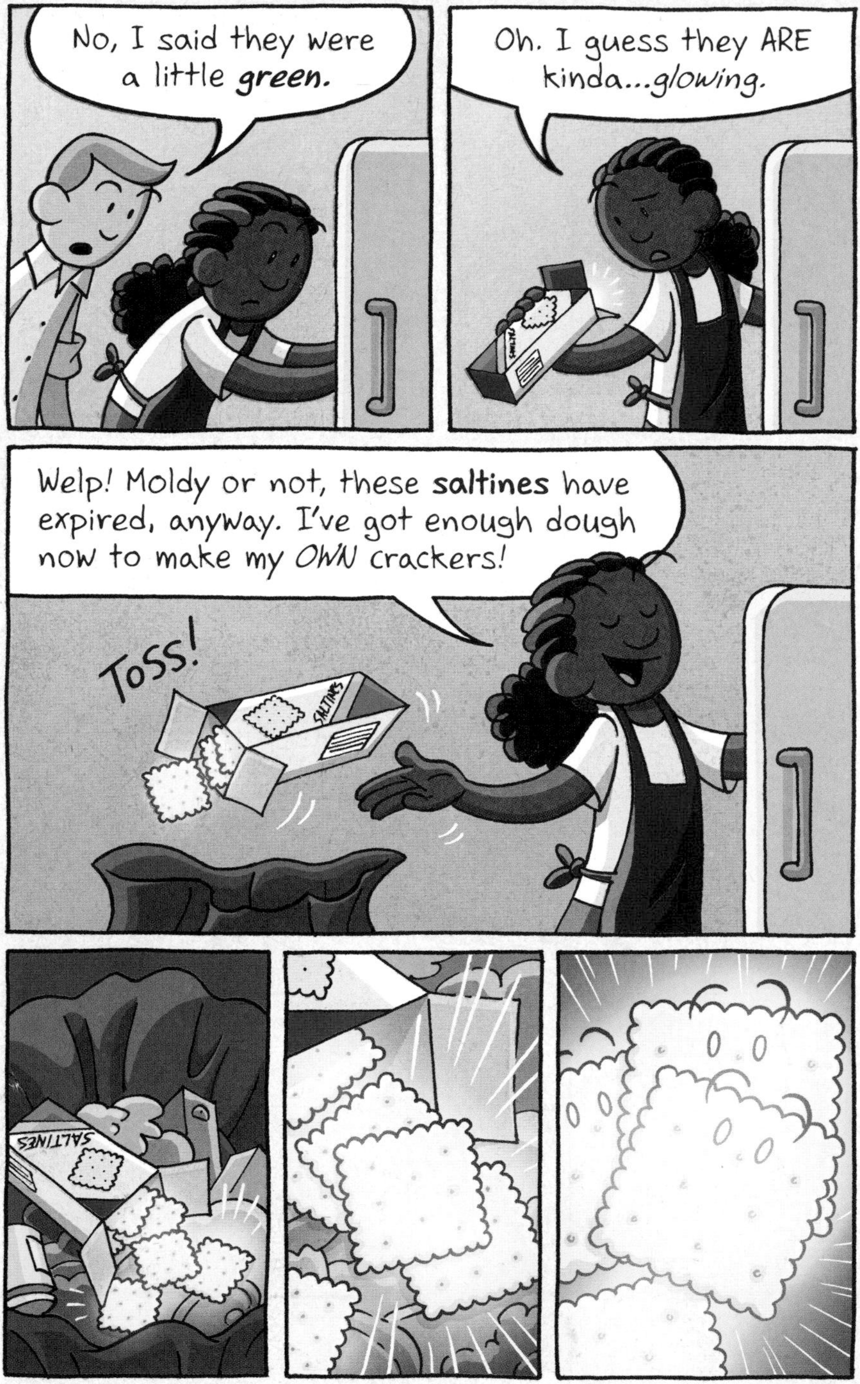
No, I said they were a little **green.**
Oh. I guess they ARE kinda...*glowing.*
SALTINES
Welp! Moldy or not, these **saltines** have expired, anyway. I've got enough dough now to make my *OWN* crackers!
TOSS!
SALTINES
SALTINES

Epilogue

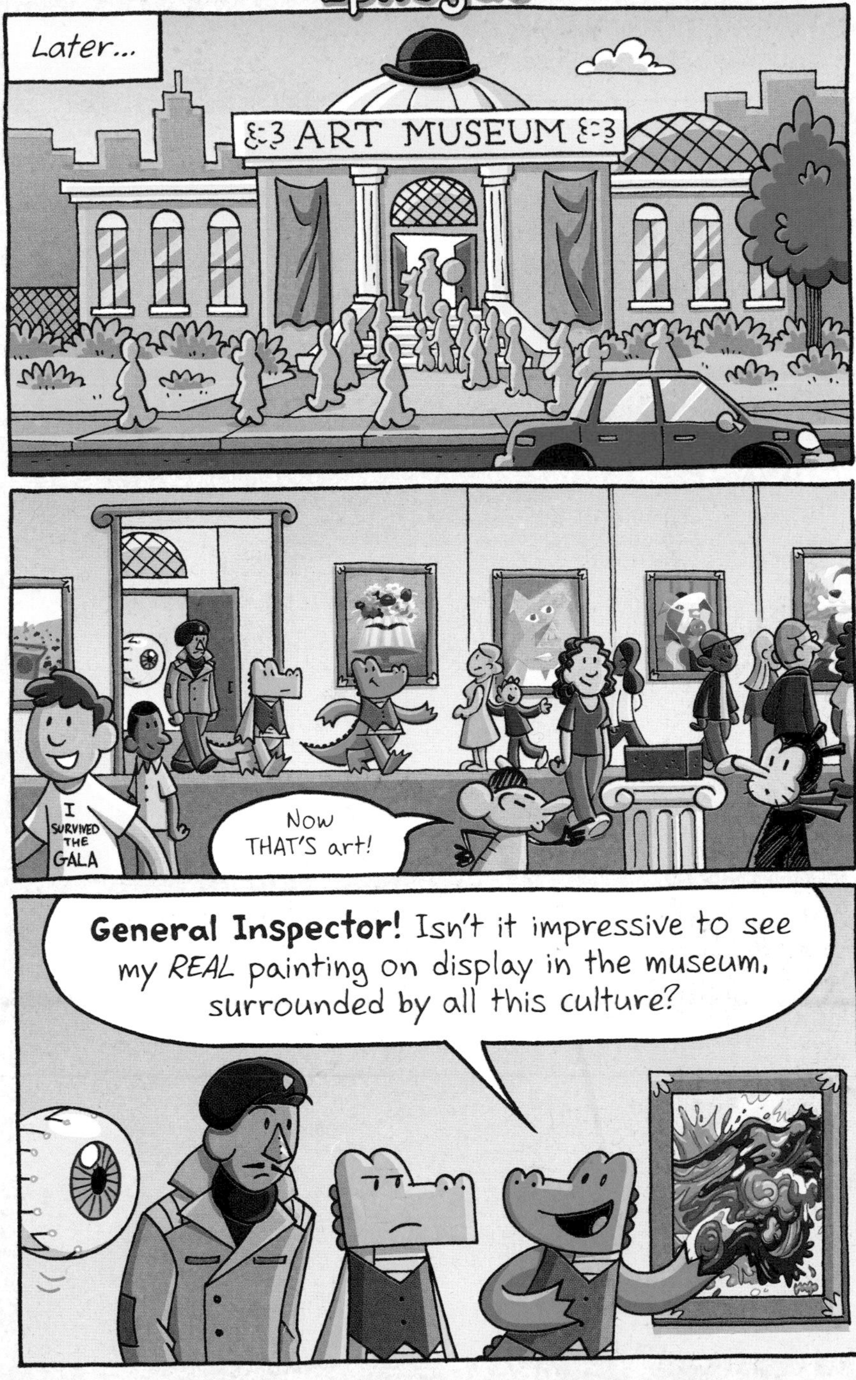

Later...
ART MUSEUM
I SURVIVED THE GALA
Now THAT'S art!
General Inspector! Isn't it impressive to see my *REAL* painting on display in the museum, surrounded by all this culture?

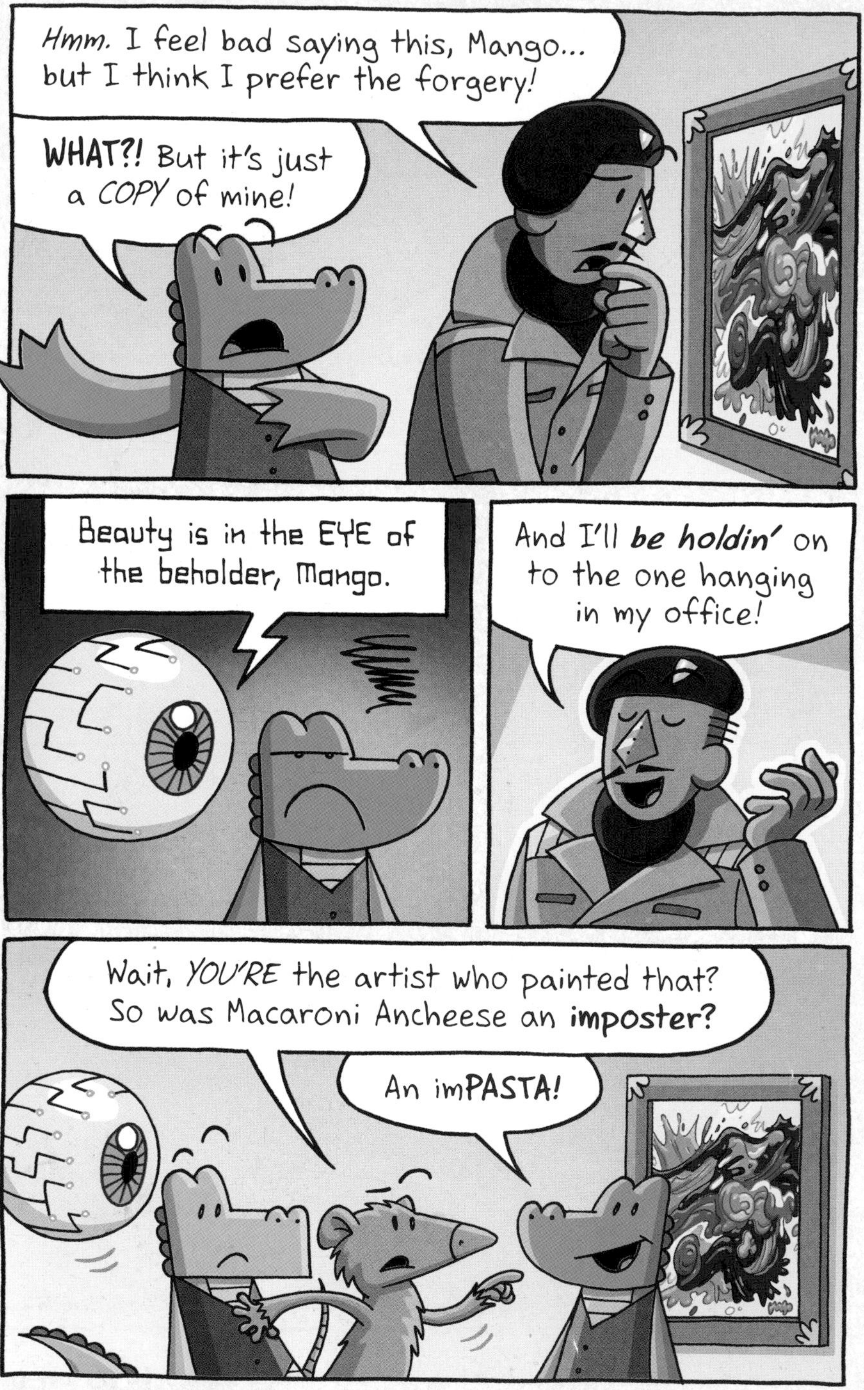
Hmm. I feel bad saying this, Mango... but I think I prefer the forgery!
WHAT?! But it's just a COPY of mine!
Beauty is in the EYE of the beholder, Mango.
And I'll be holdin' on to the one hanging in my office!
Wait, YOU'RE the artist who painted that? So was Macaroni Ancheese an imposter?
An imPASTA!

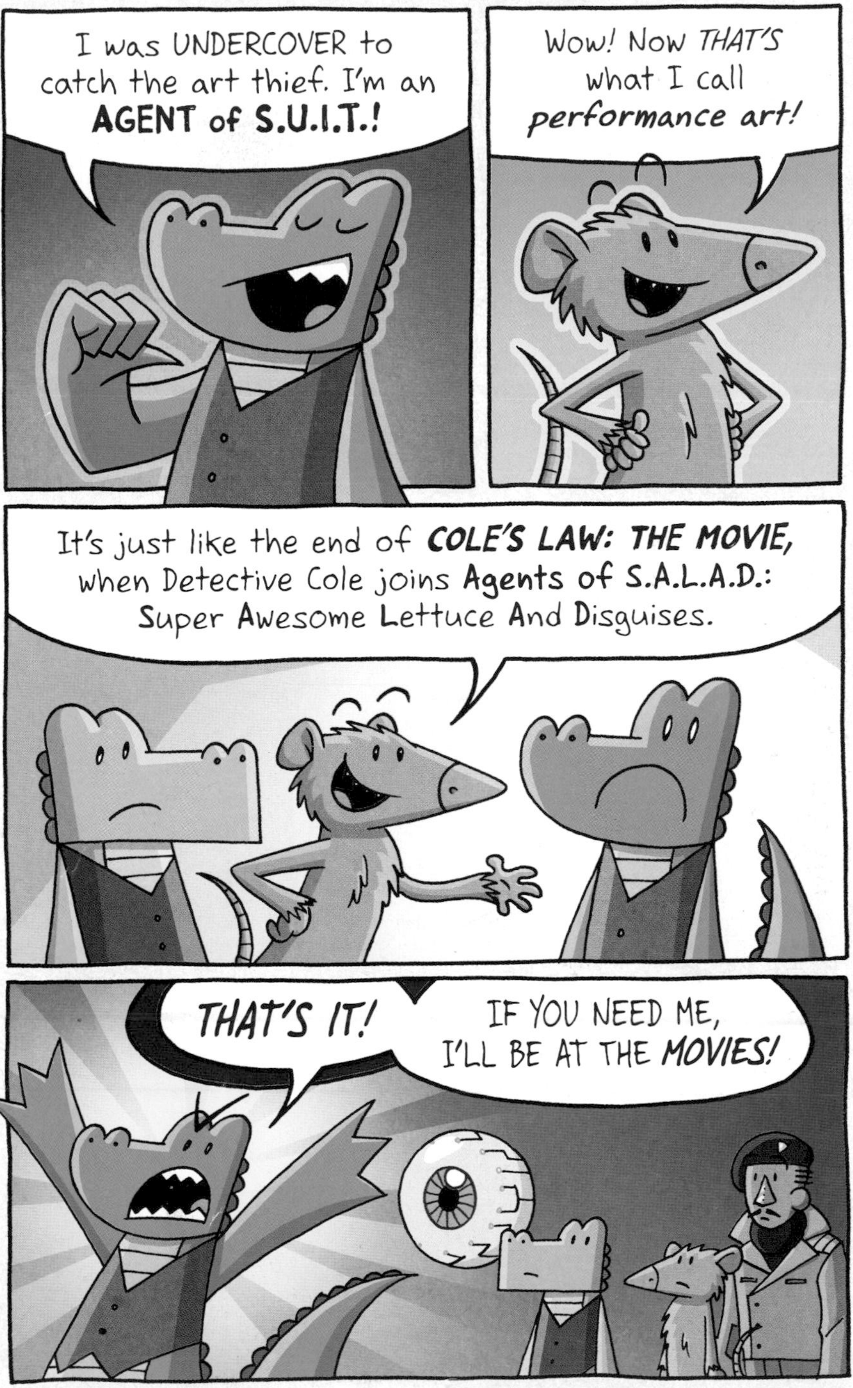
I was UNDERCOVER to catch the art thief. I'm an AGENT of S.U.I.T.!
Wow! Now THAT'S what I call performance art!
It's just like the end of COLE'S LAW: THE MOVIE, when Detective Cole joins Agents of S.A.L.A.D.: Super Awesome Lettuce And Disguises.
THAT'S IT!
IF YOU NEED ME, I'LL BE AT THE MOVIES!

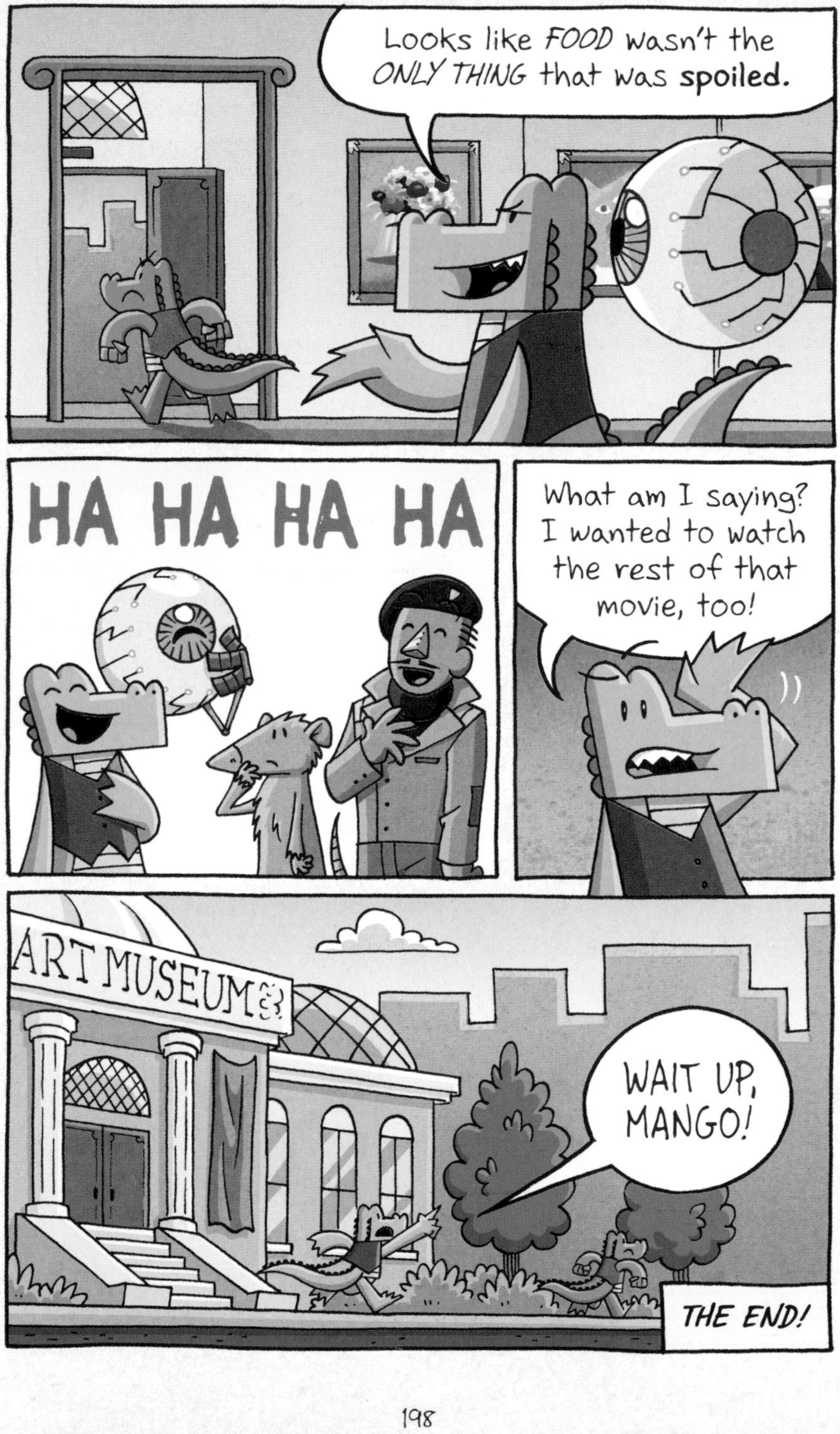
Looks like *FOOD* wasn't the *ONLY THING* that was **spoiled.**
HA HA HA HA
What am I saying? I wanted to watch the rest of that movie, too!
ART MUSEUM
WAIT UP, MANGO!
THE END!

INVESTIGATORS

How to draw the COPYCAT

And remember: Copying is how many artists first learn how to draw!

1. Start with an upside-down egg shape, with the narrower part by her chin. Leave plenty of room on the page below for her body.

2. Draw half-circles on each side for ears and a triangle for her nose.

3. Draw a shape similar to a bowling pin or a soda bottle for her body.

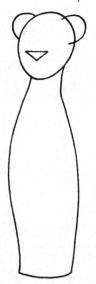

4. Add arms and legs, plus hands and feet. Erase any unneccesary lines.

5. Draw facial features like eyes and a mouth, and her jacket and blouse.

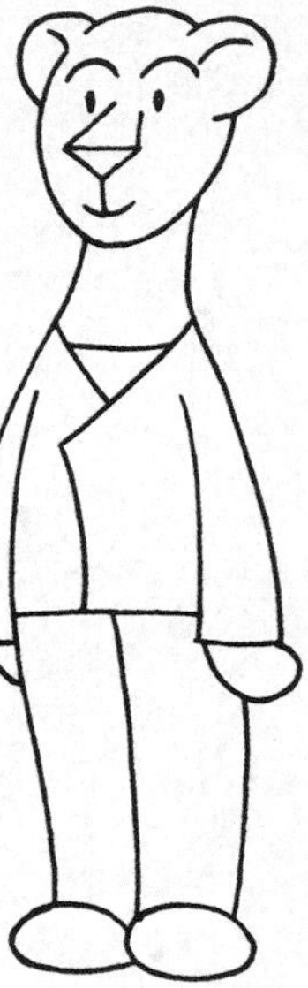

6. Give her fingers and toes, and clothing details. Don't forget her tail!

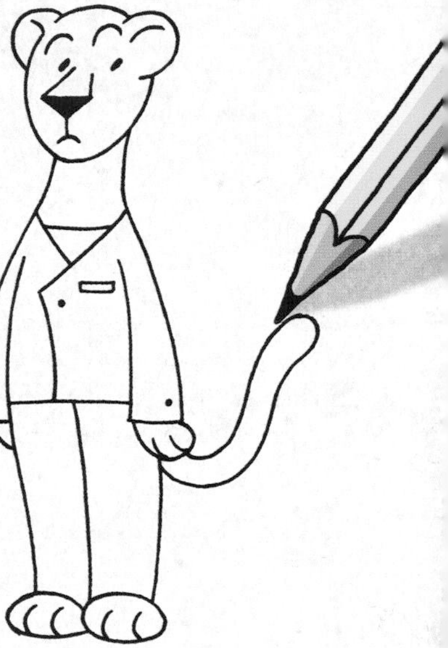

7. This cheetah's not complete without her spots! Add some color to make your drawings really come alive.

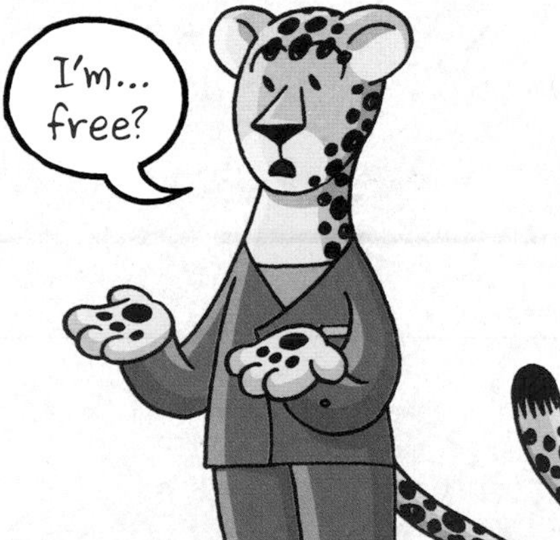
I'm... free?

8. Lastly, *ERASE HER BEFORE SHE ESCAPES!*

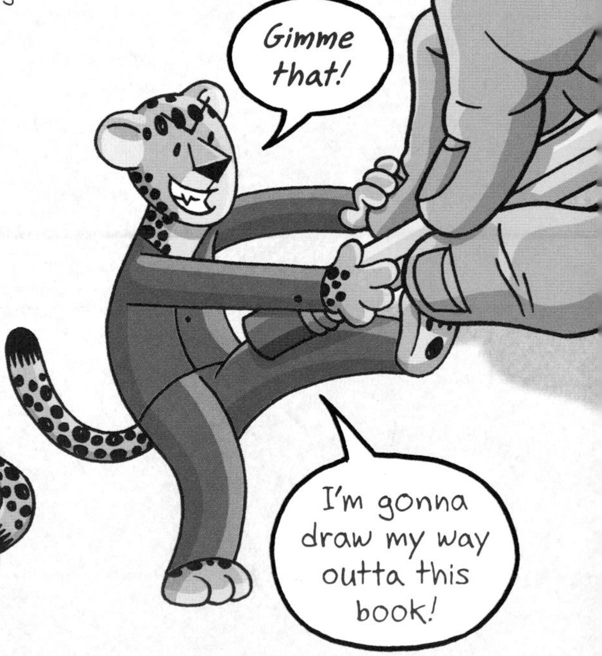
Gimme that!
I'm gonna draw my way outta this book!

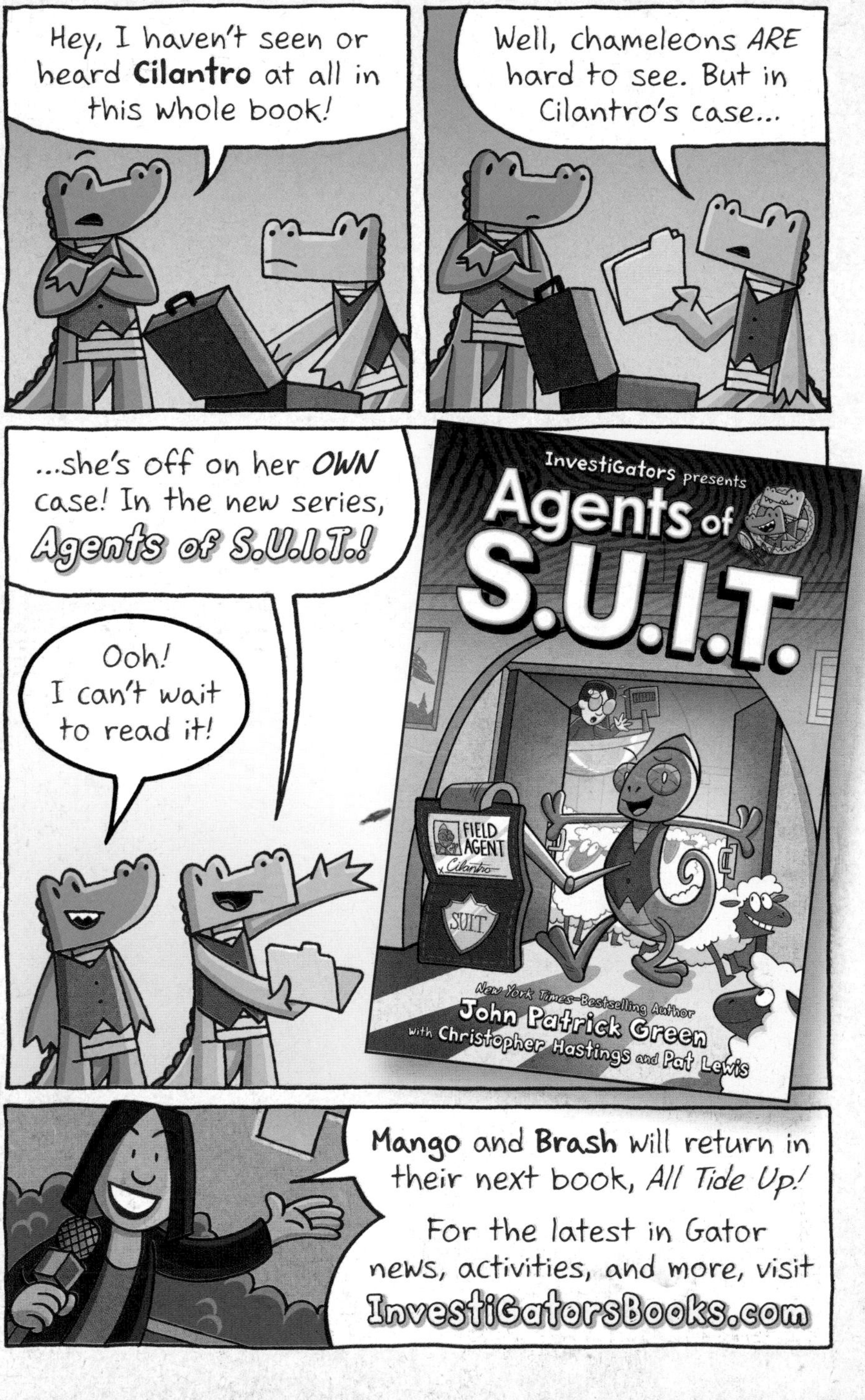
Hey, I haven't seen or heard **Cilantro** at all in this whole book!
Well, chameleons *ARE* hard to see. But in Cilantro's case...
...she's off on her *OWN* case! In the new series, Agents of S.U.I.T.!
Ooh! I can't wait to read it!
InvestiGators presents
Agents of S.U.I.T.
FIELD AGENT
Cilantro
SUIT
New York Times–Bestselling Author
John Patrick Green
with Christopher Hastings and Pat Lewis
Mango and **Brash** will return in their next book, *All Tide Up!*
For the latest in Gator news, activities, and more, visit
InvestiGatorsBooks.com

Special thanks to...

Wes Dzioba for his sensational colors.
My brilliant editors, Calista Brill and Dave Roman.
Everyone at First Second and Macmillan, especially Kiara Valdez, Molly Johansen, Kelsey Marrujo, Cynthia Lliguichuzhca, Melissa Zar, Johanna Allen, and Leigh Ann Higgins.
My steadfast agent, the amazing Jen Linnan.
All the movies, TV shows, songs, books, etc. I've ripped off—*I MEAN,* lovingly paid homage to.
And my family, of course, who—***HEY!*** There's a cheetah erasing my face!

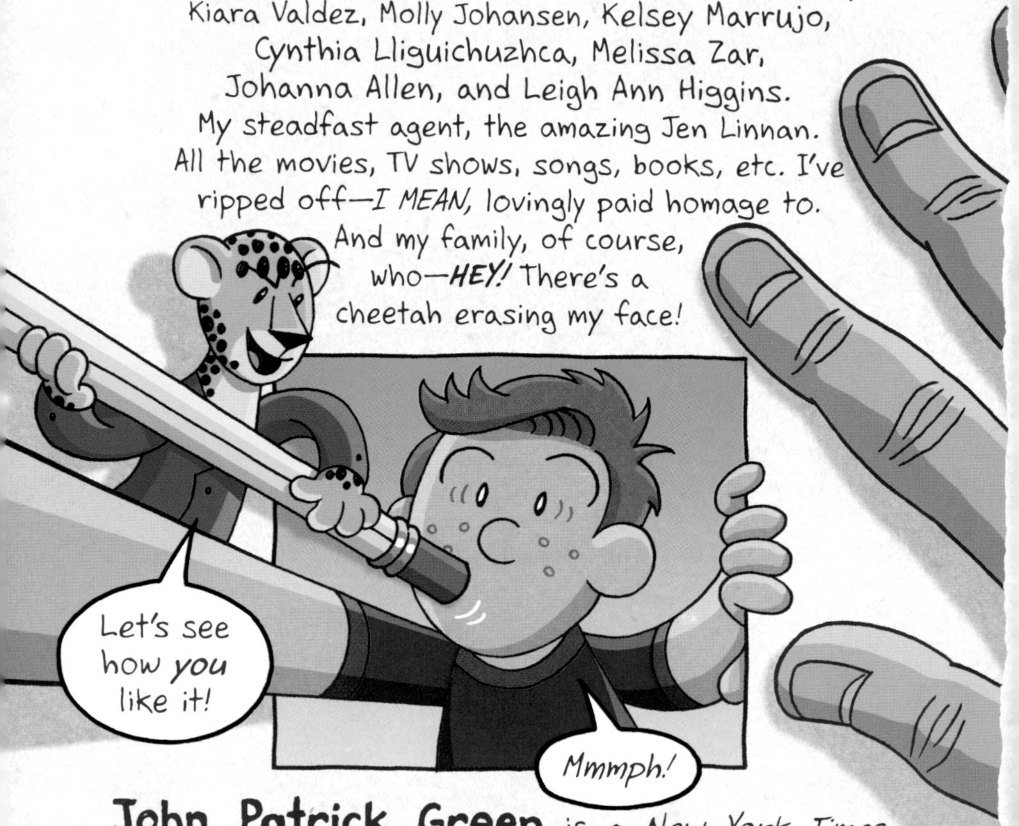
Let's see how *you* like it!
Mmmph!

John Patrick Green is a *New York Times*-bestselling author who makes books about animals with human jobs, such as *Hippopotamister*, the Kitten Construction Company series, and the InvestiGators series. John is definitely not just a bunch of animals wearing a human suit pretending to have a human job. He is also the artist and co-creator of the graphic novel series Teen Boat!, with writer Dave Roman. John lives in Brooklyn in an apartment that doesn't allow animals other than the ones living in his head.